# Branding Lily

Men of Cardosa Ranch

A Dark Romance

Gracin Saywer

OTHER BOOKS BY GRACIN SAWYER

*Branding Lily – Jacob and Lily's story*
*I'll Be What She Wants - Diesel and Samantha's story*
*Take Me Back - Carter and Callie's story*
*Whiskey Burn - Jax and Bryer's story*
*Burnt Skies - Bear and Hailey's story*
*Falling for London - Fox and Cadence's story*

Copyright ©2019, 2022, 2024, 2025 Gracin Sawyer
Branding Lily
Second Edition / Revised
Cover by Misty Polish
Edited by Cassaundra Wilcox

**ISBN:** 9798356241277

All rights reserved.
No part of this book may be reproduced or transmitted in any form or by any means, electronic or mechanical, including photocopying, recording, or by any information storage and retrieval system without the written permission of the author, except for the use of brief quotations in a review.
This book is a work of fiction. Names, characters, places, and incidents are either products of the author's imagination or are used fictitiously. Any resemblance to actual persons, living or dead, events, or locales is entirely coincidental.

## *Author's note:*

The reality that adults and children are taken every day and sold is an unfortunate truth. The threat is real. It is that very thing Jacob Cardosa has vowed to fight. His name, his riches, his power and sway... it all goes to saving them. He and his men, Diesel, Carter, Jax, Bear, and Fox, put their lives on the line to protect those they love. These books are their stories. Each told in an alternating POV and are complete with a happily ever after ending, while holding an overall series arc. Each book has a different level of darkness and sexual intensity. Thank you for reading.

# A Warning from Jacob Cardosa

I don't do warnings. But for you? I'll make an exception.

This story isn't soft. It isn't sweet. **It's dark, raw, and real.** If you need sugarcoating, walk away now. But if you stay, you better be ready.

✓ **Kidnapping & Captivity** – Lily was taken. Twice. The first time, she barely survived. The second time? I made damn sure no one touched her and lived.

✓ **Suicidal Thoughts & Attempt** – She thought she was being hunted again, so she tried to end it. But I don't let go of what's mine that easily.

✓ **Violence & Revenge** – I kill men who deserve it. Traffickers. Monsters. Men who take women and children and think they own them. There's blood, there's pain, and there's no regrets.

✓ **Torture & Hostage Situations** – I took a bullet for her. Got locked up. But it was nothing compared to what Lily endured.

✓ **Degradation & Forced Exposure (SA)**– They stripped her, touched her, tried to break her.

✓ **Possessiveness & Obsession** – I don't do casual. When I love, it's brutal. It's **over-the-top, all-consuming, and non-negotiable.** Lily belongs to me, and I'll kill anyone who says otherwise.

✓ **Explicit Sexual Content/Virgin** – I was her first, but she'll be mine always. No games, no limits—just us.

Lily gets her happy ending. I make sure of it. But if you think this is a **pretty love story,** you're in the wrong damn place.

A HUGE thank you to Cassie for your support. You cheered me on, stayed up with me on long nights, read and reread, and you were always available to listen to me rant and mumble about ALL THE WORDS. Because of you, Gracin was born.
Everyone needs a best friend like you.
I love you, woman!
This book is for you.

# Chapter 1

## *Lily*

Crouching down behind a tree in the dead of night, I held my breath. The rough, sappy bark of the pine tree scratched my palms as I braced myself against its tall support. Rope burns circled my wrists and smoldered like fire under the soft lighting of the waxing crescent moon. Snapping the restraints hadn't been easy, and my skin had paid the price.

The forest around me created shadows of people I knew weren't real but scared me just the same. I waited for the sounds of imminent footsteps chasing after me. The man I ran from wouldn't give up easily. He hadn't yet.

Thinking of what he would do to me had me inching up to the tree. My body tensed, and pain shot through me in waves. Tonight had to be the night. I wasn't sure I would live long enough to try again tomorrow. Slowly, I released the longest breath I had ever held in my twenty years. Even with the slim sliver of a moon, I could see well enough to watch my breath come out in white wafts.

The crunch of twigs breaking under the pressure of footsteps echoed around me. I was frozen in place, afraid to move, afraid to breathe. Lightheadedness took over, but I couldn't pass out. He'd find me, and then I wouldn't be able to fight back. Not that I could. Knox was stronger than I was. Always stronger. But I was no longer the fifteen-year-old girl he kidnapped. I was older. Smarter. Determined.

Another twig snapped, and I huddled closer to the tree, hoping to blend in with the trunk. My legs throbbed as I hunched down.

I desperately wanted to stretch but wasn't in the clear yet. After hours of half-running and half-jogging, I was worn out, yet I couldn't stop. He inevitably would come after me. This time if he found me, he would kill me. I was sure of it.

A horse brayed, breaking my resolve to stay hidden. The thought of being bound and dragged behind a horse had me sprinting across the mountain floor.

My legs threatened to give out. Each step sent sharp pains through my calves and knees. My lungs ached, making it harder to breathe. I didn't care. Everything hurt anyway, so my lungs could just suck it up. I'd be damned if they were the reason I got caught, not if my exhausted legs could carry me this far. My head pounded in protest, and pain split my side. Damn. It was as though my body was betraying me.

Behind me, I could hear the gaining sounds of the horse. Pushing through the pain, I begged my body to keep going, promising to rest soon.

The world around me spun as I succumbed to the dizziness, slowing my pace to a shuffle. I could hear more than one horse now. And voices. Men's voices. My heart sank as I realized Knox must have gotten help to find me. He often got drunk and told me his "gang" would help him if I ever escaped.

Running was useless. I dropped to the ground in defeat.

"Over here," a man hollered from somewhere in the shadows. His voice held a trace of alarm.

On my knees, I shook my head. "No." A small whimper escaped my parched lips. I had to get away. I couldn't let them take me. I wouldn't go back. Tears blurred my vision as I scrambled to get up but continued to fall back to the damp earth.

"No," I repeated over. I was running out of options. Frantically, I looked around the forest floor for my way out. There had to be something I could use as a weapon to end my life before Knox could get to me. At least if I were dead, I wouldn't have to endure the torture he had planned for me. It would be a slow, painful death under his touch. I shuddered.

Steeling myself against the possibility, I resolved to kill myself as the man drew closer. I refused to give Knox the satisfaction of ending my life. My hands dug through the fallen leaves and pine needles until my fingers grazed over something that might work. An old bone, probably from a deer, poked up from under the vegetation. Death was a last-minute decision, but it was the only option I had left.

Clutching the bone in my shaking hands, I realized it wasn't sharp enough to do the damage I hoped to create. I pushed away the undergrowth until I found a large rock. Placing the bone back on the ground, I thrust the stone down near the middle of the bone, shattering it in half, and creating the sharp points I needed. Trembling, I picked up the shard as the man on the horse appeared before me.

"Whoa," he told his horse as he jumped from the mare's back. Or maybe he talked to me, I didn't know, but it didn't matter. There was no way I would go back.

He held his hand out between us as if to stop me. He wore a cowboy hat low across his forehead, shadowing his face, making him appear menacing. With his hand still out, he crouched lower as he took slow, steady steps toward me.

"Get away," I cautioned, my voice breaking.

"Hey, it's okay," he vowed softly, but I wasn't buying the guise of safety. "Let me help you."

"I won't let you take me back." My voice wasn't as powerful as I wanted, but I meant every word. Taking the bone, I jammed it into my stomach and dug as deep as possible before the brittle shaft broke. I wasn't sure if I had gotten it deep enough, but there wasn't much more I could do now.

Excruciating pain exploded up through my body, and I cried out. Hot blood pooled out of the wound onto my shaking hands. Expecting pain and experiencing it became two very different things. Nothing had ever hurt this bad before. I fell all the way to the ground holding my stomach, the bone still embedded in my flesh.

Breathing hurt. Watching the man panic and run toward me hurt. I wanted to throw up but was sure that would hurt the worst.

"Shit!" The man grabbed the piece of broken bone I still held in my hand and tossed the splintered fragment away. "Shit, shit, shit."

Despite the pain, I smiled weakly at him, knowing I'd won. "I told you I won't go back."

His hands moved mine, but I didn't care anymore. I did it. Knox could go to hell.

"Diesel, get your ass over here!" The man untucked his flannel shirt and ripped off a strip, pressing the makeshift rag down on my wound, making the pain worse. But who cared? I only had a few more minutes to live. Besides, I'd been through worse.

He looked down at me, distress etched on his strong, ruggedly beautiful face. He was probably worried about what Knox would say when he brought me back dead.

"Why did you do that? Damn it, we need Doc." He looked up again. "Diesel! Shit, she's gonna die. What do we do?"

My breathing slowed, and the pain lessened to a bearable pulsating throb. I had to be going into shock. It was blissful. "Don't," I tried to speak, but forming words proved difficult. "Don't take me back." My weak voice cracked. I could no longer see the man past the tears and hated that I couldn't stop them from flowing.

*Please don't take me back to him*, I repeated in my mind. I didn't want to be buried near Knox's house. The thought had me wanting to laugh, but a tight cough was all that escaped. Knox wouldn't take the time to bury me. I would be discarded like the carcass of an animal, just like my mother.

"Honey, ain't no one taking you back to wherever you came from. We're taking you to the boss. He'll know what to do." His voice was gentle, but his words scared me. The boss. He had to be talking about Knox. I struggled to break free and run, but I couldn't. I didn't have enough strength to even lift my head.

"Shhh, don't move. It's okay. You're safe," he cooed, using one of his bloodied hands to stroke my head.

Safe? I'd never been safe. There was no reason to trust him. But I couldn't fight him. The forest disappeared as my eyes closed against my will.

"Holy shit, Jax, what happened?" Another man's voice sounded far away, but I knew he was close. Too close. It wasn't hard to mistake another set of hands as they pressed down on my stomach. "We need to get her out of here, fast."

Darkness consumed the world, and I felt weightless as they carried me away. Hot tears flowed down my cheeks as I wept. Why couldn't they just let me die here? His strong arms cradled me tightly against his chest as he mounted the horse. Even in his quick movements, he was careful, but I couldn't understand why. Knox wouldn't care how they handled me. Knox would've tossed me over the saddle and complained about how I would be getting blood all over.

Keeping me close, the man kicked the horse to move faster, but the jostling made everything hurt ten times worse. Why wasn't I dead already?

Then, like an answer to a prayer, peaceful unconsciousness took over, and I let myself slip into the deep void where I hoped death awaited me.

# Chapter 2

## *Jacob*

A rap of knuckles on my bedroom door jolted me awake.

"Boss!" Flapjack hollered.

Immediately, I was up and snatching the Glock I kept on the nightstand beside the bed. No time to grab a shirt, I slipped on a pair of jeans and boots before running down the stairs.

No one would dare yell for me like that, especially in the middle of the night, unless it was an emergency. My heart raced, anticipating the worst. I hadn't heard any gunshots, but the lack of firing didn't mean there wasn't any trouble.

In the distance, I could see Jax and Diesel's silhouettes riding hard toward the house. I gripped the handle of my Glock tighter and looked for any other signs of danger. Instinct took over in moments like this.

Flapjack ran up to meet me on the porch of the main house. "They have a girl. She's hurt pretty bad, I guess. They radioed on their way back."

What the hell was a girl doing roaming around my property? Shit, it would be odd for *anyone* to be on my ranch unless they had a death wish.

"Where's Doc?" I looked for the only man I'd let stitch me up if ever needed.

Flapjack nodded to the ranch house he shared with Doc and Bear. It was the smallest of the four buildings spread out to board my crew. "He's setting up in the kitchen, grumbling about how he's not a real doctor."

I chuckled. "He's the closest thing we've got." All humor vanished as Diesel reigned in his mount next to the house. Dust billowed as his horse skidded to a halt.

A willowy figure hung limp in his arms. Stuffing the gun in the back of my waistband, I sprinted over to help, reaching up for Diesel to hand her to me. He lowered her into my arms with ease before dismounting. Blood caked his shirt and jeans, but none looked like his. "You good?" I asked, giving him a once over and a nod.

Diesel grabbed his reigns and leaned over, bracing his hands on his knees. "Yeah, it's all hers."

The woman in my arms whimpered. The bright red blood on her shirt shined under the floodlights mounted near the barn. The sticky warm liquid pooled against my bare skin. Fuck.

Tightly drawing her against my chest, I rushed up the small porch and barged through the door where Doc waited. He looked at her and faltered, stumbling as he guided me to the kitchen.

Holding her in my arms, I had expected more weight, but she was like a feather. Dark hair hung wildly in tangles and mats as her head lulled back. Blood encrusted her hands. Her softly parted, full lips were more feminine than any woman had the right to have. Even in this disarray, a fire ignited inside of me from her beauty.

*Shit. Now was not the time*, I chided myself. I had no right to look at her hungrily, not when she was dying in my arms. What the hell was wrong with me?

Doc lifted her blood-soaked shirt enough to look and cringed. "Place her on the table." He may have been old enough to be my grandfather, but he still moved as sprightly as someone half his age. In usual fashion, he sported his long white hair in a single plait down his back. Only a few strands of dark brown streaked through in memory of the young man he used to be.

I wasn't used to people ordering me around, but I let his instructions slide under the circumstances. Lowering her to the table, my arms felt an unexpected longing to scoop her back up and hold her close. I stepped away, making room between the woman and myself.

"Is she gonna be okay?" Jax questioned, walking up behind me. His shirt was ripped and told a story I knew nothing about yet.

"Too soon to tell. What the hell happened?" Doc asked the same question I had.

Jax stepped closer to the table, looking at me before speaking. I nodded at him to go ahead and tell us.

"The alarm tripped, so Diesel and I saddled up and rode out to investigate. I found her about a mile from the property line. She was on the ground and had a piece of animal bone." Jax watched the woman for a moment. "I never saw anything like it before, boss. She looked so desperate. She stabbed herself with the bone before I could stop her."

I watched the woman. Her chest's slow but steady rise and fall reassured me she hadn't yet died. Her breasts amply filled out the hideous flannel shirt that belonged to a man, not the kind of shirt a woman like her should be wearing. A ping of jealousy hit me, thinking of her wearing some man's clothing.

What the hell? She was dying, and all I could think of was how some other man already had a claim on her. I didn't even know her! I unquestionably needed to get my thoughts under control.

Doc winced and braced himself against the table, shaking his head. "Damn it. She looks so much like her."

I didn't have to ask who. His daughter and granddaughter had been taken a few years ago before he started working for me. That was how he became a part of my family. I'd never met them, but I could imagine how hard this would be for him.

He stood up straighter and sucked in a long breath. "Well, damn, I wouldn't let her die if it was her. Help me, would ya?" Doc peeled her shirt away, and I did my best to look away from the old, tattered bra barely holding her generous mounds.

With the shirt gone, I could see a bloody wound the size of a quarter near the middle of her abdomen. I flinched at the brittle piece of bone sticking out from the center. What in the world happened to this woman to make her do this? Bitterness crept up through my skin and boiled under t the surface. It was the same anger I felt whenever I saw any woman in anguish.

Memories flooded me, igniting the fury, but I remained calm for the men around me.

I learned a long time ago to mask my feelings outwardly. I didn't become the head of this empire by showing my emotions. Cattle ranching was merely a ruse, not for profit. The ranch helped with a cover story for the local authorities. They knew who I was and what I did but left me alone. I learned how to cover any trail, leaving nothing behind for them to prove anything.

Doc breathed out a sigh of relief, bracing himself against the table. "It doesn't look too deep, but I'll need help."

I nodded. "Jax, you and Diesel are still on guard, so get cleaned up and get back out there. Flapjack, go with them. She might not be alone, and I don't want any other surprise visitors." I had no doubts my men would listen and do as they were told. My word was law. I couldn't take my gaze from the woman. "And I'll stay and help."

"Her pulse is weak but steady." Doc furrowed his brow. "She needs a real doctor, not some cartel cowboy."

"Bullshit. You're a real doctor. Stop wasting time and help her." I didn't leave room for an argument, and Doc knew it.

Doc, whose real name was Roger, was a medic in the war and had more training, especially in trauma, than any doctor in the nearest small town.

Nevada was still wide-open spaces with room to move, grow, and bury a body or two. It also meant other towns were hours away. The closest one to the ranch was still more than sixty minutes away. Solitude was great for a man like me, but it came at a high price with a lack of medical care. Not that I would send any of my men to a doctor. The cops would come snooping around and asking questions—again.

Doc didn't argue with me and pulled out his medical tools. Tonight wasn't the first time he'd used them, and it wouldn't be the last. Doc gripped a pair of pliers, clamping onto the bone.

The woman moaned while remaining unconscious as he yanked the fragment out. Bright red blood spilled out like a

9

faucet. It wasn't too surprising, as I'd seen my fair share of knife wounds. Flinging the bone to the floor, Doc grabbed a fistful of ripped-up sheets, pressing them to her wound before focusing on me. "I'm gonna need a rod and a hot fire."

My stomach turned. "You can't be serious. You're not gonna burn her. She's barely alive as it is. It would kill her."

Doc hung his head. "She's already paler than when she arrived. I don't know how much blood she's lost, but it's enough. If I don't cauterize the wound, she *will* die. She'll bleed out."

Damn it. I gripped the back of my neck and scowled.

His eyes locked on mine. "Jacob, I don't want to do this anymore than you. If there was another way, I'd do it."

I stepped away from the table and strode outside. A few guys waited on the porch, standing guard. Good men. "I need a rod, like rebar or something. Get the cleanest one you can find and start a fire there." I pointed off the steps, knowing we would need the hot coals close for this to work right. I sure as hell didn't want to see it done more than once.

I'd seen many men get cauterized. Hell, wounds happen all the time, especially in our line of work. But not on a woman. The thought twisted my stomach again.

Darting back into the house, I found Doc pressing down on her stomach, trying to staunch the bleeding. Blood soaked through the cloth in his hand. She may not have stabbed deep with the bone, but it was deep enough. I rubbed my hand on my worn jeans. "Did she hit any organs?"

Doc shook his head. "I don't think so, but I need to make sure all the bone is out before we do this. I'm gonna move this and do it quickly, then you need to reapply pressure."

Grabbing a new cluster of rags, I prepared myself to help. Blood didn't bother me. Nothing could be more gruesome than some of Gunner's wounds over the years. But this wasn't Gunner.

Doc tossed the scrap of cloth to the side and used his fingers to dig inside her flesh, feeling for any remaining fragments. His shaky hands moved around quickly, but he'd doctored too many wounds in his life for me to start worrying now. He knew what he was doing.

"It's clean, and I don't feel anything punctured inside. Ready?" Doc moved his fingers out, and I pressed my hands over her wound.

I had no idea who this woman was, but I wasn't ready to let her die.

Nash came in with a foot-long iron rod. "It's all I could find, boss." He pointed over his shoulder to the door. "And Bear has a fire going."

I nodded at him in approval. Nash handed the rod to Doc before leaving, knowing that unless I needed him, to stay out of the way. He was learning fast, wanting to climb the ladder, but he could only ascend as quickly as I let him, and something was off just enough for me to keep him right where he was.

"Jacob, I need you to do it." Doc's voice shook.

I twisted to face him, but my hands stayed firmly in place. "What?" I knew Doc didn't just tell me *I* would have to burn the woman.

He held out the rod to me unsteadily. "I'm sorry, I know how hard this will be for you, but I'm not as good as I once was. If this were one of the guys, I wouldn't think twice, but I just can't shake the fact that she looks so much like my granddaughter."

"Shit." Reaching with one hand, I grabbed the cold metal. "Hold this rag down. I'll be right back."

Doc took over for me, pressing down on the wound. For what good it did, I had no idea. Blood still seeped through the cloth.

Marching outside, Nash moved out of my way, and Bear stood up beside the fire. The defeated angel tattooed on his left arm danced under the flickering flames. He had a powerfully broad frame, giving him his name, but I knew he was more growl than bite. Although, his bite could be quite vicious. He was also incredibly dedicated.

Crouching down, I shoved the rod into the fire, letting the end come to life in a fiery red glow.

"Want some gloves, boss?" Nash held out his pair of leather work gloves.

Bear's muscular form dwarfed Nash's lean physique, making Nash look more like a teenager than a man. His curly reddish-blond hair stuck out in thick tufts under his Stetson.

"No," I barked. If she burns, I burn. I was a man, and by hell, I would not wear gloves. The pain I was about to put her through ripped me apart, and I refused to soften my end of the situation.

With the tip of the rod glowing red, I yelled for Doc. "I'm ready. You ready?"

"Just get in here. I don't think she can lose any more blood."

Looking up at Bear and Nash, I gave them a hard stare. "I need you to go in there and help hold her down in case she wakes up. You know the drill. We've done it before."

"Not on no woman we ain't," Bear challenged. This would be hard on any of us. We weren't in the business of hurting women. Quite the opposite, actually. At least we had some good virtues.

"Woman, man, it all works the same," I vowed with a resolve more for myself than my men.

But neither of them argued with me. They both nodded and headed into the house. I followed close behind them, taking a deep breath before reaching the table.

Doc pulled the cloth away, exposing her wound. Clearly, she was still losing blood. "You need to go straight in and out. Don't leave the rod in for more than two seconds. Otherwise, you'll damage healthy tissue."

I'd watched Doc do this many times, but I held the iron this time. I nodded to no one but felt I needed to let them know I was ready. "Damn it, I'm sorry," I apologized as I held the rod over her stomach and braced myself. I shoved it into her flesh and counted to two before pulling it out. The sizzling sound of blood on the hot iron faded into the background.

Her eyes opened as she screamed. Her pain-ridden shrieks would haunt me forever. She tried to thrash around, but

Bear and Nash held her solidly in their grasps. In seconds, she fell back into unconsciousness. Her silence competed with my heartbeat as it pounded in my ears.

The smell of burned flesh permeated the air, but her wound was already sealing, and the blood had stopped flowing.

She could rest for a while with any luck and let her body heal from the trauma. She had been through more tonight than most people would endure in a lifetime. I nodded at Bear and Nash, letting them know they were done, and gave Bear the rod before he left.

"You did good, Boss." Doc praised me, but I didn't feel worthy.

Instead of answering him, I grabbed a wooden chair, dragging it next to the table to sit beside the woman. I didn't want to leave her. She was like a magnet I was drawn to.

Sweat trickled down my bare chest. Her blood smeared on my skin. Shit. What if we missed other wounds?

Standing back up, I untied the makeshift rope belt around her waist and unbuttoned the manly carpenter pants she wore. Why in the hell did she wear such clothing? The jeans were at least ten sizes too big and did nothing for her womanly figure.

Sliding the pants off exposed more wounds, some new and others old. But they were not self-inflicted. Someone had done this to her. The bruising discolored her legs to match her purplish-blue ribs. I pulled her arms out to see burn marks, probably from a rope around her wrists. The anger I had before couldn't compare to what I felt now.

Gently, I touched her face. An old bruise surrounded a minor cut under her eye. With the sun creeping up over the mountains, the room began to fill with light, making it easier to see the beautiful woman in front of me.

Doc came back with a basin of warm water and clean rags. "I thought you could use these, boss."

"Who in the hell would do this to a woman?" I stared at him, daggers shot from my eyes, but the old man knew my wrath wasn't pointed at him.

"There are a lot of sick people in this world, Jacob. You know that."

As if I needed to remember. I tried to forget. I took the basin from him. "Go get some sleep. I'll take care of her. And tell the men to stay out. They are not to come in while she's here. I'll move her as soon as she's stable enough."

Doc nodded, and like the others, there was no argument. I placed the basin of water on the table next to her. Carefully, I wiped away the sticky blood and dried dirt from her delicate body. Every inch of her was vulnerable to me. However, I didn't see anything but someone who needed me. My protective nature roared like a beast, and I was in full primitive defense mode.

I didn't know who she was, but I knew she would be mine right then. And I protected what was mine.

# CHAPTER 3

## *LILY*

The pain was intense, worse than anything I'd endured before, radiating a slow burn from my abdomen to my chest. It hurt so bad I wasn't sure I hadn't died and gone to hell. I tried to sit up, but the movement seared across my torso, immobilizing me. Shit, now I'm beyond pissed that I'm not dead.

I hadn't heard Knox's voice, but he had to be behind the evil I experienced. A hot poker branding my flesh was a new kind of punishment. And the damn monster didn't even have the audacity to do it himself. I will never forget how it felt as the tip buried into my stomach.

I hated them all. Their hands touching my body revolted me. My flesh crawled, and bile rose to my throat. Even though Knox had threatened to touch me sexually, he'd never actually done it. He saved that for my mother. But since her death, keeping him from doing those things had been more challenging. His eyes would roam over me in lustful waves, and his fingers would try to graze my breasts before he beat me, always telling me I was worth more if he didn't touch me. Whatever that meant.

Although, I was grateful because I wasn't sure I could have endured the price of freedom if fulfilling his sexual appetite was the cost.

But now, it seemed as though he would let these men have their way with me. I was practically naked in front of them, and one of them had already washed me down with a rag. It didn't matter how gentle he was or how he slowly wiped over the tender spots. Fear glued my eyes shut. I didn't want to see the man about to take the only thing that belonged to me.

My stomach rolled, and I fought the need to vomit as bile rose, burning my throat. I tensed as fingertips grazed the rope burn on my wrist. So far, the man hadn't ventured to touch my breasts or lower between my legs, but I braced myself against the thought.

"It's okay, honey. I won't let anything happen to you. You're safe." His voice was deep and soothing. My soul responded, wanting to hear him speak again, but I pushed out the thought. I must be delirious.

It took more strength than I had, but I finally managed to mutter words in the back of my mouth. "Just let me die." Damn, it hurt to talk. Even the air hurt my throat. "Don't touch me."

He pulled away. "Who are you? Who did this to you?"

I flinched.

He walked away, his footsteps heavy on the floor, but all too soon, he returned. I squeezed my eyes shut harder, trying to block out whatever he was about to do, wondering if I had any strength left to fight back.

A soft layer of warmth enveloped me, and I jerked. My eyes disobeyed my commands to stay shut as they fluttered open. I had to blink a few times to adjust to the light. It was no longer nighttime, and I panicked. I focused on the kitchen, noting the white porcelain sink over dark wooden cabinets and dingy cream-colored walls. The smell of coffee wafted from the pot sitting on the counter. How long had I been out? What did they do to me while I was unconscious? Hell, I didn't want to know. Maybe that was better.

"It's okay. You're safe." He kept saying that like it was real, except I knew better. But he kept soothing me until his voice lulled me into a scary calm.

His large frame stood over me, shirtless and covered in blood. His chest was muscular, as well as his shoulders and arms. But strong scared me. I would be no match for his strength.

Staring down at me, his eyes startled me. They were a brilliant amber that looked clear like glass. His hard-set stare made me feel vulnerable. I didn't have to know him to know what anger looked like.

A chiseled jawline had him looking as if he were carved of stone. His hair was golden brown and kept short but long enough to lie against his head. He's the exact opposite of Knox, a short, pot-bellied, unkempt man. Ideally, this man was everything that I believed a real man should look like.

Not that it mattered. I didn't care what he looked like.

He adjusted the blanket, pulling it up to my chin, leaving my body covered. All I could do was stare at him. Why was he doing this? Is he dragging out the suspense of my punishment?

"I'm Jacob Cardosa. You're on my ranch, and you're safe now."

I stiffened. "Cardosa?" I knew that name. I'd heard it many times. Knox always told me about his boss and how he would kill me if I tried to run.

Oh shit. I ran right into the lion's den.

# Chapter 4

## *Jacob*

How she stiffened at the mention of my name caught me off guard. She had heard of me. But then again, most people in these parts had, so it shouldn't have bothered me. I braced myself against the onslaught of guilt my past brought and tried to look calm. Hell, I didn't want her afraid of me.

She stared at me with wide cerulean blue eyes. They were so brilliantly bright that I swore I could see through her soul. They mesmerized me, and I couldn't look away. "What's your name?"

She eyed me cautiously but said nothing.

"Okay, how about… where did you come from?" I tried again.

Her gaze darted from me to the door.

This was going to be more complicated than I thought. It didn't matter how many women I helped; this part was never easy. Just because this particular woman came to me instead of the other way around didn't mean she knew she was safe.

"What are you going to do to me?" Her voice was soft and silky. Only a slight tremble echoed through her words.

There were many things I'd like to do with her, and even *to* her, but this wasn't the time. Hell, I didn't even know her name. The way my body responded to her was foreign and surprising. But it was more than that. Something about her spoke to me. The physical attraction was fucking over the top. No denying that, even in her disarrayed state, her presence captivated my mind. But, right now, all I wanted was to help her. "I'm going to move you to the main house so the men can have their beds back."

"I don't understand."

I smiled. "Well, they're sleeping outside right now because I told them they couldn't be in here while you were here. You caused quite the commotion last night."

"And they listened to you?" She asked, her tone full of doubt.

"Everyone listens to me."

She flinched but recovered with a set stare of her own. I was silently proud of her for not crying and whining, as I assumed most women would do if they were in her position. I've seen a few not in as bad of shape as her that cried uncontrollably. Damn, it baffled me how no other woman had ever affected me like this one.

"Are you going to kill me?"

I half-choked on air and half-chuckled. It was a good question. I've killed many people, but they all deserved it. "It looks like you tried to do that yourself."

"I'll do it again too, but next time I won't fail."

I cringed, and my heart thumped wildly at her affirmation. I wanted to wrap my arms around her and hold her close until she knew she was safe. "Why?"

She guffawed. "Are you serious? You know why."

Now I was baffled. I leaned back in the seat and folded my arms. "Why don't you tell me what I'm supposed to know." How in the hell should I know why she wanted to kill herself?

She rolled her head so she couldn't see me. "Does he know I'm here yet?"

"Listen, honey, I'm not sure who you're talking about. But the only ones who know you're here are my men and me." If the man she asked about ever showed up, he wouldn't get close enough to see her. He'd be dead. It was a promise, but I wouldn't tell her that. I had a feeling talking about this man any more would add to her fear. But it wasn't the end of this conversation. I will find out more later. "How are you feeling? Ready for a bed and not a table?"

Her lips trembled when I stood, but not a tear fell from her eyes. "Whose bed?"

I chuckled. I couldn't help it. She was in the safest place in the world, but she had no idea. One day I would make sure the man who did this to her would pay. "Your own bed, honey. No sharing." I would kill any man who even tried to share a bed with her. That would be my place one day. No one else.

Shit. I couldn't believe how fast my mind laid a claim on her. My mouth went dry thinking of how one day my body would too. Fuck, I needed a drink. Or two.

I looked down, mesmerized by this little bit of a woman. My mom always told me my heart would tell me when I met the right lady. It would come without warning, and it would be fast, but there would be no denying it.

Hell. She was right. I wasn't so sure about my heart, but the rest of me was already branding myself to this woman.

"I'm gonna pick you up and carry you." She deserved the warning. I didn't want to scare her anymore.

She nodded but didn't say anything.

Carefully, I slipped my hands under her knees and shoulders. She winced as I picked her up. "Are you okay?"

"Yeah. I just hurt. It's fine."

It was most definitely not *fine*. I held her tight to my chest, loving the feeling of her skin against mine. I hadn't ever left her side to change clothes or put on a shirt, and right now, I was glad. The contact with her was almost too much to bear as I held her in one arm and pulled the blanket over her. She didn't need to worry about being seen in her bra and panties around my men.

Damn it. Her petite frame fit perfectly, curled up in my arms. As wrong as it was, it was so right.

# Chapter 5

## *Lily*

Holy shit. Jacob Cardosa was holding me. Knox's boss. The man who would kill me if he knew who I was.

Jacob's gentleness was welcoming, although my nerves didn't know how to take it. After years of fight or flight, I didn't know how to relax. Not that I could or should. But my heart leaped as my skin made contact with him.

Even though he was covered in my blood, he smelled clean and fresh. If I could, I would have taken a deep breath and held it in to savor the scent.

Outside, the air was warm. September in Nevada was usually temperate. His solid hold kept me from jostling around too much, but I still winced with each step he took.

"Hey, boss, how's she doing?" I recognized the voice from last night. He was the man who found me.

I cringed and tucked my head into Jacob's shoulder, afraid of seeing the other men. Seeking comfort or shelter from another human being was odd for me, but it was so natural with him.

"Jax, tell the men she's out of the house. You can go back in now." Jacob's voice ground out orders like melted butter. He didn't even seem to mind me curling up closer to him.

"I'll let 'em know."

Wow. I had expected Jax to question Jacob, but he didn't. Jacob told him what to do. He clearly held all the respect. And that scared me more. What would he do to me when he found out who I am?

I shivered. Unsure if it was from nerves or a fever. Maybe both?

21

Once inside the house, I unburied my face to look around. It was clean and tidy. The walls were a golden green with a brick fireplace nestled into the far back wall of the living area. Encased bookshelves filled with various pieces and art framed both sides of the wooden mantel. Dark wooden beams ran across the ceiling giving deep pockets for recessed lighting. It was not a home I expected someone like Jacob to live in.

My childhood house had high vaulted ceilings with pristine white marble and porcelain everywhere. It was like living in a china shop. But here, I was immediately drawn into a comfortable warmth. Even though it was Jacob Cardosa's, I felt welcomed.

The past five years had been a living hell in a cabin as small as Jacob's sitting area with generated electricity and barely any running water. It was basically a one-room fort. Knox had kidnapped my mother and me to use as a bargaining chip with my father, but I doubted my dad even knew we were gone. I wanted to scoff at the misuse of assets Knox thought he had taken. Garcia Ramirez was not a man to negotiate with anyone, not even for his family's safe return.

I expected Jacob to set me on the couch, but he kept walking. Instinctively, I tensed. He said my own bed, but I hadn't believed him.

"Don't worry, we're almost there." He walked up the stairs and down the hall. Pushing open a door, he carried me to a bed covered in a soft blue blanket. The room was bare except for the bed, nightstands, and a dresser. "This room is across from mine, so if you need anything, I'll be right here."

Compared to the table, the bed was like resting on a marshmallow. My head sank into the pillow like a cloud. He pulled the covers down and picked me up one more time to place me under them, taking the other blanket and tossing it in the corner of the room.

The sheets were as warm and soft as butter. Every inch of my body hurt, but I relaxed into the foam top of the mattress. It was like heaven. I'd almost forgotten what a soft bed felt like. The old, tattered mattress my mom and I shared had barely held together the last few years. My eyes filled with tears thinking of my mom. I thought we would both escape, but it was just me in this queen-sized bed.

Jacob sat on the edge of the bed and moved my hair off my face. His touch sent bursts of heat through my skin. But his eyes and their intense gaze pinned me to the mattress. "I'm gonna have Doc come look at your stomach, then see about Flapjack getting you some food."

"No." My heart raced at the thought of someone else seeing me. "Please." I gripped the covers like a lifeline. I didn't care if I died of infection. Dying was the whole point. I didn't want to be a showcase for everyone to look at.

"Hey, I told you, you're safe here." Jacob gently took my hand in his.

"Just you." I couldn't believe I said that. I should want Jacob Cardosa, of all people, as far away from me as possible. Once Knox tells him who I am, it will be the end of the safety he keeps telling me about.

His eyes narrowed as he knit his brows together. "Honey, I promise I will be right here. He won't be alone with you."

My fingers froze to the blanket, thinking of more people seeing me. What if they knew who I was?

Jacob got up, leaving me alone in the room. I tried to sit up, but the pain in my stomach sent my head reeling. Acid rose to my throat, but I choked it back down, afraid to vomit on the bed. How did I not succeed in killing myself? It should have worked. Damn men. I'd be dead in the woods if they hadn't found me. And Knox wouldn't be able to have me.

It didn't take long before Jacob came back, walking through the door slowly. "Doc is with me, okay."

Was he asking permission?

My muscles tightened painfully as he came closer, an older man with white hair close behind him. A man I knew. My heart skipped a beat.

The other man's sweet face lit up with a smile. "Hey now, it's good to see those beautiful blue eyes awake. You had us all scared last night."

He ambled to the bed, and I worried he didn't recognize me.

"So, Jacob here tells me you couldn't wait to see me." He took another step closer, inching his way to my bed. "I'm Doc. It's nice to meet you."

Everything inside me plummeted as my grandfather confirmed he didn't remember me. After all this time, I guess I shouldn't be surprised he moved on. He probably assumed I was dead. I should have been. Before I could call out to him and tell him who I was, Jacob touched the top of the blanket. "I'm gonna pull this back for him to look at your wound, okay, honey?" The way he kept calling me honey caressed my broken soul.

With the blanket gone, my entire upper body was exposed to both men.

I was mesmerized by my grandfather's deep wrinkles and concerned look as he studied my stomach. He looked much older than I remembered, but it was possible I was wrong, and this wasn't him. Jacob said his name was Doc, and the man I remembered was Roger. Five years was a long time, and it was likely both of us had changed too much.

He barely touched where I stabbed myself, and pain erupted throughout my body. I couldn't stop myself from crying and begging him to stop. It hurt so bad I thought I would pass out again.

Doc frowned. "It might be getting infected. We'll have to watch it. I have some leftover antibiotics from Gunner's last fight with a gun. I'll go grab them just to be safe."

"Please don't touch me again," I begged through tears.

"We aren't, honey. It's okay." Jacob pulled the blanket back up over me.

"I don't want to hurt anymore," I whispered to myself, but I knew he heard me. I didn't care. I was exhausted and tired of the pain.

His jaw flexed, and his shoulders visibly tightened. Instantly, I realize I shouldn't have said anything. Pissing him off was not something I wanted to do.

He didn't say anything but gave me one last look before leaving with Doc, and the room was once again empty. I honestly didn't know how I was going to live through this.

# Chapter 6

## *Jacob*

Once outside her room, I stopped Doc. "How bad is it?" I had to know. Her last words had me reeling.

"I've seen worse." He gazed at her closed door. "I have to say, this is much harder than I thought it would be. She looks so much like my Lily that I nearly rushed and hugged her." He straightened and met my stare. "Don't worry. I won't let anything happen to her."

It wasn't the answer I wanted. Blowing out a breath, I ran a hand over my mouth. "I'm sorry. It's got to be hard. But are you sure it's not her?"

He shook his head. "No. But I can't see how it could be. She's been gone for over five years now. There's no way she'd end up this close to home."

I clamped a hand on his shoulder. "You'd be surprised. Many women are taken across the border, but some end up in the house down the street. I know it's been a long time, but don't lose hope." It was my famous speech I gave to everyone who has lost a loved one. I rubbed a hand down my face. "I'm gonna go get cleaned up. Have one of the guys come up and stand outside her door in case she needs something, but *no one* is to go in her room." My words lingered with a threat, daring anyone to cross me.

Doc assured me he would find something for her pain and left to search through his medicine bag.

Just beside her door, I paused. I wasn't sure of the draw this woman had over me. Maybe it was only the lack of sleep and adrenaline causing me to feel attached.

And memories. Not of her, but of my mother. My father would beat her too. One night it went too far, and my mother didn't make it. My old man made me help bury her. At seven, it was difficult to process the emotions as I tossed dirt on my mother's once beautiful face.

The rage inside me couldn't be contained, and I broke. I raised the shovel and whacked my old man across the back of the head. It was the first time I had ever killed. My aunt took over my care, keeping the family business running until I was old enough to take over.

I had vowed then never to hurt a woman like my father. And by damn, if I ever saw another man hitting a woman, he would pay. And many had.

But this was worse. This woman wasn't just being hit. She was tortured into thinking she had to kill herself as the only way out. I had no idea the extent of how deep her wounds went or how long they had been going on. I knew nothing about her.

I left her door alone and went to my room. My bed was still unmade from when I jumped out last night.

It was a large room with a door to the bathroom. Windows filled the far wall giving me a perfect view out the front of the house, over the smaller places where my men lived and a barn. And trees. Lots of trees.

I placed my Glock back on the nightstand and sat on the bed.

Stretching, I laid back and stared at the ceiling. The woman had stiffened when I introduced myself, so she had to know who I was. But who was she?

I rubbed my hands down my face. The harsh stubble scratched at my palms, reminding me how much I needed to clean up.

Grabbing clean clothes, I headed to the bathroom and stood in front of the large mirror that went the length of the wall. Her dried blood on my chest and stomach was a reminder of the night.

I will never forget how the rod felt as I shoved it into her stomach to stop the bleeding. I shuddered.

I had to shake it off. I did it to save her, not torture her. I'd rather place the hot poker in my eye than hurt her again.

Stepping into the shower, I braced myself against the wall and let the hot water run down my back. The water mixed with the blood, trailed down the drain in red swirls.

This woman, whoever she was, had already intertwined herself with my future. I may not know much about her, but I knew I would die protecting her.

# Chapter 7

## *Lily*

I listened as the sound of water sprayed the wall. It had to be Jacob. But the thought of him standing naked in the shower made my stomach flutter. It had been a long time since I'd had a crush. But now, I wasn't a young teenager. I was a young woman. Could I even use the word crush anymore? Too many years had been taken from me, and I was confused.

After being held against Jacob's chest in his strong arms, I had a taste of security, no matter how fleeting, and craved it. I shouldn't think that way of the man who would kill me once he found out I ran from Knox, but my body reacted on its own, careless of the consequences.

With him out of my room, I pushed through the blinding pain and sat up, but I had to hold my head to stop the room from spinning. I needed to move. I needed to know I could run and, this time, either succeed in hiding or, at the very least, kill myself. But with each movement I tried, the pain rendered my body immovable.

The room got dark, and I closed my eyes against the waves of an unconscious void beckoning me to surrender. I wanted to scream and cry, but it wouldn't do any good.

The dizziness got stronger, and I tried to lie back down but fell from the bed. I couldn't control the yelp of pain as I hit the floor. The wood was cold, hard, and unforgiving on my wound as I lay on my stomach.

Instantly, the door opened, and a man came in. "Boss!" Great, he hollered for the one man I both wanted and needed yet shouldn't be around.

The man, who I presumed to be a guard for my door, limiting my escape, rushed to me. He reached out to help me but was pulled back by large hands.

"I said no one was to enter her room." Jacob was there, grabbing the man by the collar of his shirt and pushing him out the door, slamming it shut.

I winced. Seeing a part of his anger scared me more for my future. Not that being kicked out of a room was all that bad, but what would happen to the man later?

Jacob's hair was still wet, but he was fully dressed in jeans and a button-down shirt, complete with boots. Crouching down, he scooped me up and cradled me to his chest. He smelled of fresh soap and aftershave.

It was sad that I was exactly where I wanted to be but scared that I was too close at the same time.

Instead of setting me on the bed, he sat with me, holding me tightly on his lap. His heart hammered in my ear as I leaned my head against his chest. "What happened? Are you okay? Did he hurt you?"

Why was he so concerned about me?

I shook my head. "I fell. He just came to help."

The wound in my stomach pulsated, sending throbbing pains throughout my abdomen. I winced and bit my tongue to keep from crying. If I did, he would move me, and I wasn't ready for him to let go yet.

He relaxed a little bit and leaned his chin down on my head. "I don't know why, but I lost it when I saw him next to you. I told you, you're safe here, and I meant it."

Why did this man have to have such an effect on me? The concern he showed me seemed so genuine that I almost believed him.

He got up and placed me back on the bed, returning the covers over my nearly naked body. It was strange wearing only my bra and panties. Red crept up my face, warming my cheeks. I glanced away from Jacob, but his thumb gently touched under my chin and turned me back to him. "Don't hide from me. I won't hurt you. I promise."

I sucked in my lips, pursing them together, afraid of my mouth saying something it shouldn't.

"What's your name?"

I gulped. He would find out sooner or later. But maybe later would buy me enough time to escape. "Rachael." Using my mother's name might not have been the smartest, but it was all I could give him.

He stared at me, his eyes narrowing on me. "My gut says you're lying."

I gasped and held my breath, watching him with wide eyes, wondering how he knew. Maybe he already knew who I was, and that was a test?

His face softened. "One day, you'll tell me everything. Including your name." He stood and left the room.

Shit. What was I going to do? Every nerve flared to life, anticipating what would happen next. He knew. He had to know. I gulped. If he knew, why hasn't he killed me yet? And where in the hell was Knox? Surely, he would want to watch his precious asset be murdered by a notorious cartel cowboy.

# Chapter 8

## *Jacob*

The woman lied to me right to my face. I saved her life, and she still didn't trust me. The way she said Rachael was too slow, as if she had to think about a name. She didn't deny the lie when I confronted her, either.

Downstairs, I found Flapjack in the kitchen preparing dinner. "Hey, boss. How's the girl doing?"

"Doc said he's seen worse." I marched to the coffee pot and poured a cup. It had been a long night and day, and it didn't look like it would ease up anytime soon. "I need you to make something for her to eat, like soup or something. I don't want anything harsh on her stomach."

"Of course, boss. I already started some earlier, just in case."

Flapjack was one of the better cooks on the ranch and took his job seriously. I haven't had a complaint since he started. Going to a fancy culinary school across the ocean helped him gain his position as my main chef.

But, you couldn't run from a cowboy nickname when working on a ranch. Flapjack was named after the amazing eggnog pancakes he made when interviewing for the job. Of course, he'd been a low man on the totem pole, doing odd jobs for the business for years before going to school. That was how he paid for two years abroad.

Doc came in and held up a leather bag. "I got some stuff. You want to head up with me?"

Hell yes, I was going up with him. Rachael, or whoever she was, would not be alone with anyone but me.

I downed the last swallow of coffee and took a glass Flapjack handed me full of water. "For the girl."

I appreciated the gesture. "Thanks. Bring her dinner up when it's done. Leave it outside her door."

Leading the way, I took the steps two at a time, apparently anxious to see her again. Doc followed close behind me. "She tried telling me her name was Rachael, but I don't believe her."

Doc's steps faltered on the stairs, and he tripped up them, catching himself with the railing. "And you don't believe her?" A hint of surprise resonated in his voice.

"Nah, that's not her name. She didn't admit it but didn't deny it when I told her she was lying." We made it upstairs when I turned to face Doc. "She's hiding something, but I don't know why. There isn't a man here who wouldn't protect her. She's scared, though." I carved a hand through my hair. "When I find the piece of shit who did this to her, he will pay."

"Jacob, I know you've seen more in your life than most people in this world. Hell, you were born into this life. You can't escape it. If I were that man, I'd be hiding from you."

"There isn't anywhere in this world he can hide." I looked at her door. "I don't know, Doc. Something pulls me to her. Maybe I just want to have someone to protect again."

Doc clamped a hand down on my shoulder. "I hope you get that, but don't get your hopes up. She came here pretty broken. A man may not be what she wants right now."

That was almost like a challenge. "Or maybe a man is what she needs."

Doc glanced at her door. "Jacob, Rachael was my daughter's name. Do you think maybe she's hiding behind her mother's name? Do you think it could be Lily?"

My gut twisted. "Doc, I can't give you false hope. I didn't know either of them, but I do know if that woman in there is your granddaughter, then you're right, she's been through hell, and we need to be there for her."

"Her eyes, they're the same. But she didn't recognize me." He let out a long breath. "I'm just an old man who wants too much."

I chuckled. "Nothing wrong with wanting things, old man." Hell, I had a new want of my own. I only hoped Doc wasn't setting his hopes too high. I'd hate to see him heartbroken.

The idea that this woman could be Doc's granddaughter had me questioning my feelings towards her. Lily Ramirez was Garcia Ramirez's daughter, presenting a new problem. We weren't exactly friends. He and I regarded each other professionally, but I left him alone as long as he left the human trafficking alone. I didn't have time for the drug cartel. My hands were full with so many jobs that I now had to turn too many away.

It was no secret I took over my father's legacy and turned it into a rescue mission. My fortune used to be made by my father selling women into the sex trade. Now I took money to save those taken from their families and most times sold into the same trade my father had a hand in. I hated that part of my past. Anyone low enough to kidnap kids and women to fulfill their greedy sick desires deserved to die.

My missions took me all over the world, following leads for those who paid me to find their loved ones. Most times, I was successful, but I had to come home empty-handed a few times. Those times were hard. Not just for the families but for me. I didn't want to fail. I wanted to save them all. But it wasn't possible.

Now I had a woman who had found me, and I couldn't help but wonder who she really was. And how in the hell did she end up on my property? I wasn't home often, so I was glad I was between jobs to help her. I'd hate for her to have tried killing herself and succeeding because we were gone somewhere across the world. The image of finding her dead in the woods sent my stomach rolling.

I knocked lightly on her door before opening it. She looked so peaceful sleeping on the bed. I hated to wake her. She stirred, and her eyes fluttered open, locking her gaze on me.

Yup. I was as good as lost in those eyes.

# Chapter 9

## *Lily*

Sleep beckoned me, and I wanted nothing more than to fall into a deep, dreamless sleep, but I hadn't had the freedom to do that in years. Always on alert, waiting for the moment when Knox would decide it was time to do something to me.

A light knock on the door startled me. I watched Jacob walk into the room, filling it with his presence. "It's Doc and me again. No one else."

Why did he act like he cared? Why did he play these games with me? Mentally, this was harder than just taking a hit.

Coming to the bed, he set a glass down on the nightstand. "I'm gonna help you sit up to take some pills, okay?"

I shook my head and pursed my lips together. I didn't want to be drugged up. I needed to be mentally aware.

"It's just some antibiotics and painkillers. You need them." Jacob sat beside me and slowly lifted me. Taking the glass from the nightstand, he held it to my lips, and I took a swallow.

It was cool and felt amazing on my parched throat, but it burned all the way down. It had been since yesterday that I had anything to drink, and my body wanted to reject it. I coughed with the second sip but continued to drink.

Jacob held the glass for me, careful not to let the water spill. "That's it. Drink all you want."

I pulled back, afraid of drinking more. He set the water down and held his hand out for Doc, who put a couple pills on his palm.

"Here, take these, and then you can try to sleep." He placed the pills between my quivering lips and grabbed the glass to help me wash them down.

Doc smiled at me, a faint but familiar gleam flashed in his eyes, and it was almost like he recognized me. My heart raced, ready to find out. He winked. "My job here is done. I'll see you later, pretty lady." He acknowledged Jacob before leaving us alone. Obviously, he wasn't who I thought he was.

Carefully, Jacob lowered me back to the pillow. Even with help, it was strenuous, and the throbbing catapulted with the movement. I focused on Jacob's face. His features were the only thing that made it through the blinding pain. I winced, and a hiss escaped as I tried to move to get more comfortable. "Why are you being so nice to me?"

Jacob reached out to trail a finger down the side of my cheek. The feather-light touch had my insides bursting into flames. I should be backing away, not moving closer to his touch.

"Knowing kindness is so foreign to you it makes my blood boil." He moved his hand away from my face. "Not all men are bad."

"But…" Did I dare say what I thought?

He tensed. "But what?"

Looking up at his handsome face, I melted. Maybe he was telling the truth, and I would be safe? Maybe he wouldn't recognize my name? But what if he did?

Screw it. I'm a dead woman either way once Knox shows up.

Closing my eyes, I gave him a secret I was scared to part with. "Lily. My name is Lily." I braced myself, waiting for his wrath, but it never came.

His face lit up with a wide smile. "Now that, I believe. Lily fits you."

Holy shit. He had no idea who I was. Unless this is a game too, I may have just bought myself some time.

# Chapter 10

## *Jacob*

Lily's head rested against my shoulder. Her eyes closed, and I could feel her body relax next to mine. It was innocent, but her closeness stirred my body to react with a deep craving for more.

Lily. I repeated her name in my mind. How easily it flowed from my lips. It was like I was meant to speak it. I knew I needed to tell Doc, but she asked me not to go until she fell asleep, and I couldn't tell her no. Even after her eyes closed, I found it hard to leave.

I leaned back against the headboard, afraid to move and wake her. There were many things that I needed to do, but the world would have to wait until I was ready. More correctly, until *she* was ready. Even revealing who she was to Doc would have to wait. For the first time in a long time, I was going to be selfish. I knew it might cost me in the end, but damn it, if it bought me any time with her, it would be worth it. No matter the price.

The blanket slid as she moved, revealing her naked shoulder with only a threadbare, thin strap to her bra. She was going to need some clothes. I had her other clothes burned.

Rosa, my housekeeper and Gunner's wife, should be able to help. I'll have to send her to town tomorrow morning. I also needed to get a message to Detective Rodriguez to let him know I had Lily. She had been reported missing by Doc and her father, and as much as I hated letting that man know, we needed to put her files to rest. It might even help me find the man responsible for her kidnapping and abuse. There had to have been a suspect or a lead. I couldn't see how this would have been an ice-cold case.

Having an inside source at the police station wasn't cheap but always needed. Not that Detective Rodriguez cared. He got a fat paycheck from me, and when the time came, he got to take credit for certain situations, courtesy of my men and me. Staying under the radar was the only way I could continue my job, but everyone knew who was really behind it all.

There wasn't a drug cartel who didn't know the Cardosa name. My father had a legacy before me that still lingered like an old ghost story meant to scare women and children.

Outside her door, Flapjack's frame filled the doorway. He was deadly silent, one of his many talents. Sneaking up on people had its worth in a business like ours. Hell, I didn't even hear him climbing the stairs. The kid had a future.

The tray he carried held a steaming bowl of soup for Lily. It smelled good enough to make my stomach grumble.

Lily's eyes opened as my stomach finished its symphony. Instantly, her body tensed, and she gripped the covers with white knuckles.

Flapjack didn't dare enter the room, setting the tray down next to her door, and then left without so much as a loud exhale.

"Who was that?" Lily's groggy voice sounded alarmed.

"Our chef. He brought your dinner." Slowly, I leaned away and slid my arm out from under her.

"Where are you going?" She watched me with her wide beautiful eyes. Eyes that would never again have to see the abuse she'd endured so far.

I smiled. "I'm not going far." And I meant it. I was there until I knew she was okay.

I picked up the dinner tray and noticed a small, scribbled note on top of a covered plate.

*Boss, thought you could use something too.*

Two glasses and a carafe of water finished the tray. Carefully, I returned to her bed and set the tray on the nightstand so I could help her sit up.

"Smells good," she said, peering over at the food.

"Flapjack takes his job seriously. You probably have the best soup in Nevada right now." I winked and flashed her a smile.

She winced as I picked her up and helped her into a sitting position. I hated knowing I had hurt her worse to make her better. My hands tingled with the memory of the hot iron.

The blanket fell, unable to cover her upright body. She was so beautiful, bruises and all. I would show her the opposite of evil and let her see how a real man treated a woman. And one day, I'd taste all of her and show her how her body would fit with mine. The thought of exploring every inch of her had my dick growing and pulsating against my tight jeans.

Shit. I was a sick person. Thinking about her like that would only bring us both pain. She deserved better than that. I needed to stay away from those thoughts and find safe ground. "I'll be right back." I had to leave so she couldn't see my reaction to her. It's not her fault she's so damn gorgeous.

I found myself in my room, pulling dresser drawers open, searching for a T-shirt. Soft cotton folded at the back of the drawer peeked out from behind lounge pants I never wore. Sleeping with clothes was too restricting.

I brought the shirt to her and told her to hold her arms up as I slipped the fresh clothing over her. In a way, I was pleased it was my shirt she was wearing and not some other man's.

*Safe ground.* I really needed safe ground.

"How are you feeling?" Yeah, that was safe.

"Better, I think. It hurts, but it's not as tender." She looked away from me, red creeping up her neck and face. "I'm sorry. I shouldn't be here."

Taking my place next to her on the bed, I tipped her chin to see her eyes. "You never have to be sorry for being here. I'm glad you're here." I picked up the bowl of soup and held the spoon to her lips. "You'll feel better once you eat."

"Mmm, that's really good." The way she closed her eyes and relished every sip did nothing to keep me on safe ground. Hell. How was eating soup so attractive?

Halfway through the bowl, she raised her hand. "I can't. No more."

It worried me that she had such a small appetite, but to be fair, I didn't know much about what she went through. "So, do you want to tell me who did this to you?"

Her face went ashen white, and I knew I wouldn't get any answers today. Whatever this monster did to her, she was scared shitless. Whatever he did, he would be getting returned tenfold.

"I'm sorry." She trembled, pushing herself back into the headboard as if afraid of me.

Her response killed me. She was so afraid of anger that she couldn't tell where it was intended. "You have nothing to be sorry about. You've done nothing wrong."

If having me this close made it worse on her, then I didn't need to be in here. No matter how badly I wanted to be with her, it was selfish on my part. I tried to stand, but she grabbed my hand, pulling me back down. "Please don't leave me."

It was then that I knew my heart attached itself to this woman. How could I refuse a request like that?

# Chapter 11

## *Lily*

My heart hammered in my chest as I grabbed his hand. It was a bold move, but I was confused and needed him to stay still while I figured it out.

I swore he was angry. All the signs were there, tense muscles, blood boiling in his eyes, clenched jaw. But he was gentle, not rough with me at all.

Telling me I had nothing to be sorry for felt foreign and strange, and I didn't believe him. Deep down, I always tried to understand how every beating Knox gave me was my fault, but it never entirely made sense. Saying sorry was as crucial as breathing.

Just touching Jacob, his demeanor changed back to the tender man I was beginning to know. Maybe I could keep him from learning who I really was? The way my body reacted to his closeness, I sincerely hoped he wouldn't have to kill me. I'd rather he douse the fire he was creating inside of me.

Maybe it was the guise of safety that captivated me, not the man. But then again, I wasn't falling for the façade either. He couldn't ever really offer me complete asylum.

That was a sobering thought, and I dropped his hand. I was deranged to even think a man like Jacob Cardosa could save me. He was a murderer, not a saint. I'd been relatively secluded all my life with my father, not knowing who Jacob was, but after Knox kidnapped me, he told me about all the people Jacob had killed.

It seemed I ran from one monster to another. But my body didn't understand and burned for him to touch me just one more time.

All the pain in the world couldn't stop the pulsating throb between my legs. I'd never experienced that sort of pleasurable yet suspenseful need before. It was scary that he had that much of an effect on me.

But if just sitting next to me or holding my hand could do that, I wondered what else he could do.

The mix of painkillers and the warm soup had my eyes drooping. I was too tired to fight with my mind. My body could enjoy what he had to offer, and I wasn't going to stop it. It might be the only bit of bliss I get in this life—however long I live.

"I think I'd sleep better if you were here." Honestly, I didn't want to sleep, but I was losing that battle too. But if he was with me, then he wasn't talking to Knox.

Slowly, I slithered back under the covers, unassisted. A huge gold medal for me for that task. Then, taking a more significant risk, I held the covers up, offering him room next to me.

This might be the worst idea I've ever had. I had just escaped to keep from ending up in bed with a man.

Keeping his clothes on, for which I was equally disappointed and relieved, he climbed into the bed. He reclined on his side, propping his head up with his arm. "Who are you, Lily? I want to know you."

I wanted to know him too, but there wasn't anything I could tell him that would make me live until tomorrow. Knox's threats still hung heavily in my mind. He used Jacob's name like an outlaw with his gun, brandishing it whenever he felt threatened by me.

And here was Jacob, in the same bed as me, promising protection to a woman he could never pledge it to.

"Let's start with the easy questions. What's your favorite color?"

I laughed but grabbed my side. It hurt too bad to do that. "Seriously?"

"Yeah, my new favorite color is blue. The exact color of your eyes." He brushed the hair away from my face, lingering with a feather-light touch on my cheek.

I couldn't breathe. If I did, it would ignite the little flame into a raging bonfire. "I'm sure you say that to all the women."

He chuckled. "What women? My housekeeper is a cranky old woman who happens to be married to one of my men. It isn't like they are waiting in line at my front door. Guys like me don't get the lady in the end." He moved his hand back to his side. "You're the only one here."

"What happens when you don't get the lady?" My heart slowed, waiting for some crazy response like he killed them or something.

"In my line of work, I'd never met someone who made me feel like I couldn't live without them. In the end, what I do is just too dangerous, and I've never thought about putting a woman through that before."

Before? Before what? Before me?

This was crazy.

"Green. My favorite color is green."

He leaned back but held his arm out for me to rest on his shoulder. I gladly accepted and relished the comfort he offered. "Why is green your favorite?"

Staring at the ceiling, I tried to describe what the color green meant to me. "It didn't use to be green, but it changed a few years ago. It's like spring. The green returns after a harsh winter, giving me hope to see it. Like, if the grass could survive, so could I."

"Lily," the deep timbre of his hoarse whisper sent heat waves down my body. "You're safe here. I promise."

"Don't say that. He'll find me, and then you won't have a choice." I didn't have to admit who *he* was.

"That's where you're wrong, honey. It will be *him* who doesn't have a choice. Just trust me, and I'll take care of him. If you let me, I'll take care of you."

If only that were true. "I can't."

He leaned his head onto mine. "Just get some sleep. We'll talk later."

Talking to Jacob was like dodging bullets, but it wouldn't be long before the right question hit me where I had to answer.

The sun was setting for the first real night away from Knox. It was hard to believe it had only been twenty-four hours since running away. And I'd found sanctuary with the one man sworn to kill me.

# Chapter 12

## *Jacob*

It was pure torture to lie next to Lily with her head on my shoulder. I wanted to reach out and caress every inch of her. Slowly, she was opening up to me. But she protected the man who hurt her. I needed to find out who he was so I could take care of him. She shouldn't be afraid of saying his name.

It was after midnight, and the grandfather clock downstairs ticked loudly throughout the house, but I couldn't sleep. Lily rested peacefully, so I slipped out of bed and headed to my room. I couldn't wait until tomorrow. I needed to get started on Lily's paperwork now.

Picking up my cell phone, I called Detective Rodriguez. I didn't pay him to sleep.

"What the hell do you want?" His tired voice grumbled into the phone.

"I need you to pull a missing person report on someone for me. It's for Lily Ramirez." He was used to me giving him nearly dead-end leads but did what I needed.

"Hell, Jacob, can't you ever give me something easy? Her case is locked up tight. Garcia paid to seal it shut."

"Just do what I pay you to do." I slid the screen to end the call and tossed the phone on the bed. Why in the hell would Garcia pay to close his wife and daughter's missing person cases? It didn't make any sense. That fact had me reeling. Why didn't he want anyone to look into who took them?

A slight knock on my door startled me. Flapjack entered. "Sorry, boss, but the boys said they found a trail. They thought you'd want to ride out with them to see where it led."

"Is it hers?"

He nodded. "They think so."

Finally, a lead. Lily didn't just manifest from thin air. After Lily had fallen asleep, I sent Jax and Diesel to look for clues as to where she came from. Diesel was a better hunter than most of his men. For human or animal, it didn't matter, so it didn't surprise me that he found her trail.

"Get my horse. I'll be right there." After pulling my boots on, I grabbed my shoulder holster and strapped it on, pushing my gun down into the sheath. Snatching my Stetson before heading out, I stopped briefly to ensure Lily was still asleep.

I didn't want to leave her, but she was safer in my house than anywhere in the world.

Doc found me as soon as I stepped off the front porch. "What the hell is going on, boss?"

I walked to Lady, my already saddled horse. Her marbled grullo coloring blended in with the midnight shadows like camouflage. I reached up and ran my hands down her strong neck. "I'm heading out with the boys. I need you to go up and sit outside her door. Make sure she stays safe."

"Don't worry about her."

Swinging up into the saddle was one of those feelings of freedom. Being a cowboy wasn't just a cover. It was a way of life. Moments like this, I could feel the roots in my soul spark. It was an instinctive nature that I couldn't deny.

Jax and Diesel were already saddled and waiting for me. "Let's ride." Turning Lady, I spurred her sides to run.

We reached the edge of the woods and slowed the horses. It would be harder to maneuver through all the trees. Diesel led the way to the spot where they found Lily. "This is it."

"Whoa," I crooned Lady to a stop and jumped down.

Half a broken bone lay near a puddle of dried blood. It was hard to imagine Lily there, stabbing herself.

"It took a while, but I finally tracked her coming from that way," Diesel said, pointing away from the scene. "She was limping most of the way from what I can tell."

I climbed back into the saddle. "Let's see where she came from."

Following the trail wasn't as easy with her weaving between the trees. But the longer we followed the path, the more confused I became. I thought she would have come from off the property, but we kept climbing the mountain higher and higher.

Diesel held his hand up, and his horse stopped. Jax and I immediately did the same. Getting off our horses, we stepped lightly on the forest floor. I peered into the darkness, searching for whatever Diesel saw.

Up ahead was a small cabin. Her trail came from there. Heat raged inside me as I realized she had been this close, right under my nose, on my own fucking property this whole time, and I hadn't known.

Using hand gestures that we'd used on many raids; I told them I was going first. I didn't care who was there. As pissed as I was, they wouldn't stand a chance. Hell, they wouldn't get close enough to shoot me with this fury bursting out of me. That son of a bitch had better hope he wasn't there, but then again, if he wasn't, my hunt would terrify him until I cornered him to the ends of the earth.

I grabbed my Glock and cocked the hammer. Kill first, clean up later. The only motto to live by in my job.

Each step closer to the eerily silent cabin sent my heart into a sickly excited anticipation. I didn't kill for the fun of killing, but tonight I would make an exception.

The door opened easily, and the retched smell that rolled out made my stomach churn. It was sweat mixed with blood and vomit.

It was a one-room hut, poorly maintained. Whoever was here with Lily was gone now. I flipped the light switch, and a generator growled outside before the light flickered overhead.

An old, tattered bed with shreds of a blanket used as a cover sat in the far corner. Chunks of rope were still tied to the bedposts. Situated near the end of the bed was a filthy clawfoot tub with no curtain or privacy of any means, not that any human would want to touch the grimy surface.

Beer bottles, broken, full, old, and empty, lay around the small space. Deep indents in the couch cushion told of it holding numerous bodies. It was ripped and shredded, caked in soiled waste.

What the hell.

Bile rose to my throat, and behind me, Jax gagged.

Was this seriously where Lily came from? I can't imagine her here, tied to the bed, forced to shower while someone watched. What other horrible things did she have to live through?

Flashes of my mother streaked through my mind, and I closed my eyes to catch them. Her hands had been tied too. Things my father forced her to do, even with me watching, stabbed at my heart.

It was the very reason I became who I was.

Opening my eyes, images of my mother were gone, replaced by visions of Lily. I didn't care how long I'd known her. She was obviously sent to me for a reason, and I would cherish her. If for no other reason than she deserved it.

Jax darted out of the house, retching off the porch. I met Diesel out with the horses. "I can't imagine anyone living in that place, boss. That's worse than any of the others we've seen."

I ground my teeth. "She didn't live here. She simply existed."

How in the world did I not know this was on my property? Every inch of the four thousand, eight hundred acres would be searched and documented starting tomorrow. I would not be unaware again.

I promised Lily I would protect her, but I lied. She was here the whole time, and I didn't even know. Time was now critical. I couldn't wait for Rodriguez to get back to me with news on Lily's report. It was hard to believe one of my men knew about this place yet failed to tell me. It was even harder to think it could be one of my men.

I vowed right then that if someone betrayed me, they had better be ready to die slowly. Betrayal would be dealt with in my father's way.

# Chapter 13

## *Lily*

Every sound in the empty house had me alert. Waking to find Jacob gone was disappointing. It was crazy that I'd want to be around him so much after one night and day. There was probably a physiological explanation, but I didn't want to hear it.

As bad as he was for me, I equally wanted him to be my knight in shining armor. Armor that consisted of boots and chaps.

Doc sat outside my door, guarding me. Always a prisoner. The sun was up now and shining through the bedroom windows. I wouldn't get the rays until the afternoon, but they still warmed me despite losing the warmth of Jacob's body.

The smells from the kitchen had my stomach begging for a small taste. I wasn't sure if I could ask for food or not. Doc had given me another dose of antibiotics but then promptly left my room. No offer of food was mentioned.

But I was so hungry.

I didn't eat a lot, usually only what Knox brought home and made me cook. A lot of rabbits that I made into jerky. My mother taught me how to make food sufficiently with what we had. I would dream about eating hamburgers and milkshakes.

She made me promise never to stop trying to escape. I wished she had lived long enough to be here with me now. We would probably laugh about how much Doc looked like my grandpa. She would lay awake at night with me and talk to me about the future after we escaped. We planned my wedding, and we would name future grandkids. She was always optimistic about escaping and living our life.

But laying in this bed, not feeling a spring dig into my back, I wondered what other things we dreamed about that she wouldn't be there to experience with me. I wasn't exactly free, but I was closer to keeping my promise. I also couldn't help but wonder what she would have thought about Jacob.

Thinking of my mother, I no longer felt hungry. Grief had a way of taking all that away.

But I did have a new need. One I hadn't thought about because I was obviously dehydrated. I worked my way to a sitting position, relieved not to hurt as bad while moving. I quietly cleared my throat.

Doc immediately opened the door but remained outside. "You okay?"

"Um, well, I kinda need," I stuttered. Asking to relieve myself was so embarrassing.

"Whatever you need, it's yours. Don't deny me the pleasure of helping such a pretty little thing. Besides, if Jacob found out I didn't do whatever asked, he'd have *my* head."

What if I asked to be let go? To be free. I doubted Jacob would be happy Doc did that for me. "I just need a place, to you know… I must have drunk too much water."

His face lit up in understanding. "Oh, sure, darlin'. It's just down the hall a little ways."

Down the hall. Great. Now I had to get there.

Throwing the blankets off, I twisted slowly, so my legs dangled from the bed. My feet hit the wooden floor, and I gradually pushed my weight onto them to stand. My stomach burned in pain, but it was tolerable. I could at least move, but it wouldn't last long. I would be worn out by the time I reached the door.

I used the bed to support me while I shuffled to the footboard.

Downstairs, the front door closed, and Doc released a sigh of relief. "You stay right there, don't move." He left his post as heavy footsteps ascended the staircase. A slight mumble was audible, but nothing more.

I couldn't wait for him to come back. I needed to go. Reaching out, I grasped the top of the dresser and worked to move away from the bed.

Big strong arms scooped me up, and I almost protested until I saw Jacob's face. He was back. "What are you doing?"

A slight blush crept up my face, but I held my head high. "I was walking to the bathroom."

He chuckled. "That was not walking."

Still dressed in just his shirt and my undergarments, I snuggled closer to him. He carried me out of the room and down the hall. I only caught a glimpse into his room, but it was just how I'd imagined. Strong accents with wood and a four-poster bed. It was extremely masculine.

Holding me in one arm, which amazed me, he opened the door and carefully set me on the counter. "I won't be in here if you don't want, but if you need help, just say something. It's a natural thing, so nothing to be embarrassed about."

Except for the fact that he's had privacy his whole life and never had an audience. And it didn't help that I wanted him to see me naked. Although looking down at my legs, I changed my mind. I was so discolored and ugly. No one should ever have to look at me like I wanted him to. "I got it. Just help me off the counter."

He lifted the lid to the toilet before picking me up and gently setting me on the floor, slowly letting me regain my balance. "I'll be right outside the door."

The door closed, and I lowered myself to sit, feeling more worn out and in pain than I was a few minutes ago.

Now that I was done, I didn't think I could stand back up. I really didn't want Jacob to see me stuck here with my panties down around my ankles, but I didn't have a lot of choices.

"Jacob," I started but didn't even have to finish because the door opened, and he stood there with alarm etched on his face.

I dipped my head, unable to look at him and not blush. "I can't stand up."

He squatted down, slipped my panties off, and tossed them in the trashcan. I gasped and started to reach for them when he picked me up. "I need those," I squealed.

"Trust me, you won't need them." The deep timbre of his promise consumed me.

I didn't care about the panties. I was glad they were gone. A hot wet feeling spread between my legs, but instead of being alarmed, it made me want to be closer to him. A lot closer. Pain or no pain, I wanted to see how he could fix this yearning. Like instinct, my body told me he was the only one who could quench this new thirst.

I was utterly screwed.

He carried me back to the bed and covered me with the blankets. His eyes had a strange haze as he stood over me, but it wasn't the look of anger. It was different. It was sultry. My heart raced.

"I'll be right back."

Maybe I had read him wrong after all. Besides, we just met. It wasn't like he would have the same feelings and need for me.

# Chapter 14

## *Jacob*

Holy hell. I didn't think I had that kind of restraint. I could smell the desire coming off Lily like perfume. My dick was so hard it throbbed, begging to be released.

I couldn't get to the bathroom fast enough. After splashing cold water on my face, I looked into the mirror.

I wanted her so bad it hurt. The need she created in me was unlike anything I'd ever felt. No short-time fling with a woman has ever made me feel like this.

She was so innocent, sweet, and incredibly sexy in my t-shirt and no panties. If I kept thinking like that, it would take an icy shower to calm me down. But damn, I wanted to bury my cock inside her and claim her as mine.

Rosa better hurry back from town with clothes to cover that woman up.

From my room, a muffled jingle from the cell phone I tossed to the bed last night helped pull me from my thoughts.

Three long strides, and I was answering the call from Detective Rodriguez.

"Don't get mad, Jacob, but there isn't much for me to go on."

After seeing what I saw last night, that wasn't a good enough excuse. I demanded answers. "Bullshit. You've found more on less."

"Listen, I have one lead, but it doesn't make sense. Hell, I don't know. Maybe it's nothing."

I was losing my patience. "If you have something, tell me. Stop wasting my time and do what I told you to do."

"Calm down, Jacob. I'm not the enemy."

Rodriguez knew his place in my world, but he was foolishly overstepping. "Like hell, I'll calm down. You don't get to tell me what the fuck to do."

"Alright, look, I found a report for Rachael Ramirez, but not for Lily."

I clenched the phone as I prepared to hear what he had to say.

He continued, "Garcia reported his wife missing but not his daughter, and as for any report from Doc, I can't find one."

Shit. My brain couldn't work fast enough to draw the lines together.

"Jacob, there's more."

"Rodriguez, stop dragging this out. You know I don't *need* you." It wasn't an empty threat. He could be replaced.

He must have taken the clue because he began spilling everything he knew about Rachael. "Jacob, I found a death certificate for Lily."

More betrayal. More questions. When I figured this out, there wasn't a single person I wasn't going to investigate. Loyalty was everything, and by hell, I would not have secrets held from me. "What?" I managed to grind the one word out between clenched teeth.

"Don't kill me. I'm just doing my job. But Garcia's name is on the death certificate. It was signed five years ago when Rachael went missing."

Was he serious?

I slid the screen, ending the conversation. What in the hell was I going to tell Doc now? I'd like to know what Garcia got into that forced him to sign his daughter's death certificate, completely erasing her from the system. No one had even thought to look for her in five years because everyone thought she was dead.

"Sir," Rosa called to me from the doorway, her arms loaded with bags. Her black hair streaked with gray was frizzy and wildly untamed around her shoulders. "I have what you asked me to get."

"Thank you, Rosa," I said, walking to her. "I'll take them. Get things ready for a shower. I'm sure she'll like to get cleaned up. And tell Flapjack I need some saran wrap and tape from the first aid kit in the kitchen."

The old woman nodded at me and handed the bags out for me to grab. She was more obedient than most but usually had an attitude to go with it. Thankfully, she didn't say anything because I wasn't in the mood.

Lily was sitting up in bed and watched me curiously as I came in. Those gorgeous blue eyes held me captive.

I held the bags up, breaking the trance before I needed more cold water. "I guessed your size. I hope you like them."

"My size?" She blushed. "I don't think I even know my size anymore."

"Well, I guess we'll both be surprised then." I placed the bags on the bed and began pulling out the garments. I had to hand it to Rosa; everything she picked out was perfect for Lily.

"You bought me clothes?" She gingerly touched the hem of a shirt lying on the bed.

"I'm partial to you staying in my shirt, but I don't want the other guys to see you that way." Hell, I was partial to seeing her with nothing, but sooner or later, she would need to leave the bedroom.

Her blush warmed my insides. "I have Rosa getting the shower ready for you. You will feel better after getting cleaned up."

Flapjack was at the door as if on cue, and Lily grabbed the covers, holding them to her chin. I knew he wouldn't look at her, or he'd end up missing his eyeballs, but she was still scared. And she had every right to be. I wasn't sure what she had endured, but after seeing that cabin, I could assume many things.

"Here, boss. Rosa said you needed these." He held out the saran wrap and tape.

"Thank you." I looked at Lily. "This is Flapjack. He's our cook. Flapjack, this is Lily."

"Nice to meet you, mam." He stayed at the door, heading the warning for no one to enter her room, not unless I let them.

"Hi." Her voice was hushed, but she relaxed the grip on the blanket, lowering it slightly. It was a start.

"I'll be in the kitchen if you need me."

"We need to stand you up so I can put this over your wound. I don't want it getting too wet." I held my hand out, and she took it without hesitating. With her standing, she was only as tall as the top of my collarbone. Such a little thing.

I peeled the plastic wrap back and ripped off a piece. Kneeling down so I could efficiently cover her wound, I remembered how I'd thrown her panties in the trash.

She lifted the shirt, holding it up for me. Her hands trembled.

My hands wanted to reach behind her and pull her to me. I was at the perfect level to taste her sweetness. Soft curls beckoned me to search for the treasure hidden between them. I loved that she wasn't bare. Why women wanted to wax off that part of them was beyond me. I much preferred a natural woman, because that's what it was to me, a woman. A bare pussy looked like it hadn't matured yet and was not ready for a man like me.

Holy hell.

How I kept my hands steady was a miracle. Lifting the wrap over her wound, I taped it to her skin. I was honestly impressed by how it looked. I never would have guessed it was less than forty-eight hours since I'd burned her.

"I'll carry you there, and then Rosa will help you." I didn't want to tell her I couldn't because we'd be finding a new way to use the tub.

She nodded. "Thank you."

Scooping her into my arms was becoming so natural. She wrapped her arms around my neck and snuggled closer. There was no way I could let her go now.

In the bathroom, a deep garden tub sat in the corner, but the shower was separate. It was a walk-in with river rock walls. Rosa set the water temperature, and steam rolled over the ceiling. The joining door to my bedroom had been shut and locked, making me chuckle to myself.

"Set the poor girl down. You don't have to manhandle everyone." Rosa tsked and held her arms out for Lily.

I lowered Lily to the floor and let Rosa take her arm to steady her.

Rosa shooed me off. "Now, you just get out of here. She doesn't need a man like you watching her shower."

I backed out of the bathroom, and the door shut. Somehow, I felt like my mother had just chided me, but it only made me chuckle. Lily may not need me to watch her, but I sure as hell wanted to.

Downstairs I decided to get some work done and went to my study. It wasn't long after I took over the business that I made all the changes, including this room. I wanted nothing to do with the space that reminded me of my father. Everything in it was handpicked by me, right down to the cherry wood paneling.

A large mahogany desk sat center stage in front of the large fireplace I had installed with the remodel. The wall opposite the windows was lined with shelves and books. Most of them were old and worn, some barely able to hold their pages. It seemed I had a soft spot for damaged things in all areas of my life. Women included.

Sitting at the desk, I tried not to think about Lily upstairs, naked, wet... Oh, for fuck's sake. I needed to get a grip on this.

I grabbed the accounting book and tried to focus on the numbers. I knew I didn't need to, I paid people to do them for me, but I liked to be in control of everything and went over them anyway. I wasn't worried about money. Hell, I had more than I'd ever need in my life, but I also liked knowing where it all went. And I wanted to make sure I was getting the money owed to me on time as well.

My services weren't cheap.

A loud crash upstairs had me running through the study and up the stairs quicker than I'd ever moved before. The bathroom door was open, with the shower still running. I didn't care about anything other than Lily's safety. Naked or not, I wasn't leaving until I knew she was okay.

Finding Lily picking herself up off the ground had my emotions flying off the handle in all different directions.

I rushed over to her and picked her up.

"I'm sorry, I just fell."

"Lily!" Rosa called as she reentered the bathroom, looking at Lily naked in my arms. "I'm sorry, I just went to change her sheets, so they'd be fresh when she got out. I was only gone a few minutes."

"So you leave her alone? Rosa, she could have hurt herself again. Just get out of here. You're no longer needed tonight." My voice rose higher and deeper than I had wanted, but my heart was still hammering at seeing Lily on the ground, alone and soaking wet.

Lily stiffened. "It wasn't her fault. I'm sorry I fell."

Rosa obviously knew not to argue with me right then because she turned with a scowl meant for me and left.

"I told you, Lily, you don't ever have to be sorry with me." I stood there, holding her in the bathroom, with nothing to hide her beauty from me. "You are so beautiful."

Her sad smile broke my heart. "I'm nothing."

"Don't ever say that again because you are quickly becoming everything to me." It was a true statement. But everything about her has been fast. Even her arrival had been a spur of the moment. I hadn't been able to relax since.

Her hair was dripping water onto the floor, and she smelled so sweet. The stuff Rosa picked up was definitely feminine, helping Lily smell like her name's sake.

Her breast's soft, supple mounds begged to be cupped and caressed until the peaks stood erect. Lifting her close enough, I dared to taste the forbidden fruit and took a nipple into my mouth.

She gasped, but before I let her go, she began to moan. The sound escaping her lips was like a drug, and I needed more.

Capturing the bud between my teeth, I flicked my tongue over its softness, making it rigid with need. I wanted to feel all of her, but tonight wasn't the night. I wanted to draw it out and make it last forever.

Letting her go, I lowered her to look into her eyes clouded with desire. I didn't think she could look any sexier as she did right then.

It didn't take me long to carry her to her room. The need to make her mine burned like a branding iron through my soul.

Setting her on the bed, I waited for her to push me away or tell me to leave, but instead, her hand reached up, grazing my face. I kissed her palm while lowering her onto her back.

I braced myself with one hand while I used my other hand to trail my fingers down her neck, to her collarbone, slightly over the curve of a breast. Her lips parted as I stopped, and I seized them with mine.

It was slow and easy, but her mouth moved with mine, touch for touch. I didn't want to scare her and rush into the deep kiss I was yearning for. Hell, I didn't even know what she's been through. This might be the worst thing I could do with her.

I pulled back, afraid of making this worse for her. This wasn't right, no matter how badly I wanted it.

"I'm sorry," she said again. Another apology.

I backed up. Not trusting myself to be close to her, but all I could see was her, lying naked in front of me.

"I've never kissed anyone before. I probably did it all wrong."

Was that truly what she thought was wrong? I kneeled down on the floor next to her. "Damn it, no. The kiss was perfect. I just don't want to do something that you'll regret. You deserve better."

"So you're not mad that I don't know how to be with a man?"

I nearly choked. I also said a prayer of thanks to the big man upstairs. "Honey, I promise, knowing that has me feeling many things, but mad is not one of them."

"I just thought you'd probably want someone who knew what they were doing. That's why you stopped."

Oh shit, she had to stop talking like that. Her innocence made my cock throb more, wanting her. Unclaimed territory. She would be mine in all ways. "It wasn't why I stopped, that's for sure. One day, I'll show you how a real man loves his woman."

She blushed, and her eyes filled with desire again. "Could you at least kiss me again?"

"If I kiss you, I won't stop until you're satisfied." The idea of seeing her reach ecstasy by my hands had my dick aching with a new need, but it would have to wait. Tonight was for her.

She nodded and reached for me. I don't think I'll ever be able to deny this woman anything. Screw it. If I had a chance to be with her like this, I would enjoy every moment.

My lips crashed down on hers, deeper and harder this time. My hand quickly found her breast and kneaded it softly, swirling my thumb over her nipple.

The moans grew louder as my hand carefully went over her stomach and lingered at the curls between her legs. I leaned back as her eyes flew open. She started to protest but stared up at me while biting her bottom lip to stop herself. Complete trust showed from the deep blue pools in her eyes. Fuck, she was so damn innocent. She had no idea what she was doing to me.

Slowly, I slipped my finger down through her slit, gliding over her little nub. I captured her mouth with mine again and slid my hand lower. She was so wet.

Slipping just one finger inside her, I was met with the most beautiful sounds erupting from her throat. Her moist heat consumed me, and she tightened against my finger as I moved slowly within her.

"Jacob, I can't. It feels like I'm going to explode."

I smiled and watched her face. Pleasure held her on the edge. "Honey, I want you to explode. My finger won't stop until you do."

She raised her hips slightly, grinding toward my hand. "Please. I don't know what to do. Please fix it."

"Fix what, honey?" I wanted to hear her voice, as sultry as fuck. I needed her to tell me.

"I don't know. I just know you can fix it. Please. Please, Jacob." Her head began to thrash back and forth, and her breathing picked up.

She was so damn beautiful. And I would be her first. First kiss, first orgasm, and soon her first man.

"I'm trying, honey. Just trust me. Let it go."

She looked at me wide-eyed again. "While your finger is still *there*?"

I let out a deep groan of my own. "Especially while my finger is inside you."

"Oh, Jacob. I might just die."

"You won't die. I won't let you." I kissed her again and thrust my finger deeper, wanting to use more but not wanting to panic her. She was already worried about dying on one finger, wait until I used my mouth, or when I filled her with my cock.

Her hands reached up and pulled me down to her lips, winding her fingers through my hair, and then fumbled hesitantly until she grasped my shirt collar.

Inside, she was tightening, getting ready to reach a new level of ecstasy. A flood of warmth flew around my finger, and her body shuddered. Her moan held my name on her lips as she came.

Watching her, I needed a release. I was close to coming just doing what I did to her. Reaching down, I unzipped my jeans and grabbed my dick. Hell, it hadn't ever been so hard before.

Her face flushed with satisfaction but was quickly replaced by doubt as she watched me. She nibbled at the edge of her bottom lip and watched my hand move over my dick. "Can I do something to help you?"

I didn't deserve her. "When you are ready, you can help all you want, but tonight you already did everything I could ask for." And she did. My hand was still dripping with her wetness as it slid over my manhood while I pumped one more time before exploding.

She watched me with wide eyes as I spilled out. "Oh crap. Are you okay? I'm so sorry."

My body shuddered. I was breathless but smiled for her, leaning in to kiss her forehead. "I'm better than okay."

"I just don't know about this stuff. It's the one area my mom never talked to me about. I'm so stupid."

My hand was still wrapped around my dick, still sensitive and pulsating. "Honey, you are far from stupid. I'd be lying if I told you that your inexperience with men didn't please me. Hell, I get to be the one who shows you."

I didn't think the red on her face would ever go away. One day, we'd make love, and there would be no blushing after. I'll show her that everything we do together is natural and beautiful, not embarrassing. I couldn't wait to show her more. "I'll go get something to clean you up."

Walking back to the bathroom for a wet rag, I leaned against the counter and tried to catch my breath. Damn. If just doing that could cause me to cum, I couldn't wait to do more.

I couldn't be happier, but that worried me. I wasn't a fearful person, but I'd never had someone to lose before.

# Chapter 15

## *Lily*

Holy shit. *Holy shit!*
What just happened? I had let Jacob Cardosa touch me. And not just touch me but put his finger *inside* of me. My body exploded into a million pieces just thinking about it.

I had no idea anything could feel so incredible.

Lying on the bed, I could only relive the moment of pure bliss. I was too worn out to even think of moving.

Jacob returned, his jeans still unzipped, but everything was tucked away from sight. Too bad. It was kind of mesmerizing to watch him. Seeing him spill out had been a surprise. I definitely didn't expect that. But seeing that part of him was the most intimate thing I'd ever done, aside from his finger.

After sharing such an intense moment together, I wasn't sure what I wanted to do. I knew I should leave before he found out who I was, but maybe he wouldn't find out. I was going to stick to that. I never had to tell him that one small secret, and he'll never have to kill me. I could make this work. I could hide here from Knox.

"I'll clean you up so you can rest." Jacob sat on the edge of the bed and gently wiped between my legs with the rag. Just that had my body reacting to his touch. It was easy to feel that I was extra sensitive too.

He really needed to stop.

I watched him, mesmerized by how careful he was with me. His hands seemed like anything other than a murderer.

"Jacob, can I ask you a question?"

He stopped washing me and pondered my inquiry. "You can ask anything you want. Just remember, you might not always like the answer."

That was fair. He may not like the question either, so there was that. "Do you really kill people?"

His jaw clenched. "When it's needed."

Tears filled my eyes. It would be needed if I told him I was Garcia's daughter and the one Knox kidnapped.

"Lily, I would never hurt you."

That was a lie. He'd already sworn some stupid oath with Knox. How could I be so stupid to think I could play pretend? I couldn't stay here.

Anger turned to rage, thinking of how I let Jacob anywhere close to me when it would never be real. It was like a game of cat and mouse, and I was the mouse. He was only toying with me, leading me along, and making me feel safe. But really, he was the predator.

He stood and zipped his jeans. "I have to go find Doc. I'll be back later tonight." Leaning over, he planted a light kiss on my forehead.

"I think I'll be fine alone tonight."

I didn't need a guard. I didn't need to be supervised. And I didn't need Jacob Cardosa.

His brow furrowed, but he never said anything. He just nodded and left the room.

Carefully, I sat up. My hair wasn't quite dry from the shower, but I needed to find clothes. Rosa must have put them away when she came to change the sheets.

Turning to leave the bed, I braced myself for the burning pain in my stomach. Those muscles would probably always hate me. Then again, it was still a fresh injury.

I ripped off the plastic and tape. The area around the now scabbed wound itched, but it wasn't red. The antibiotics must be working for me.

Each step was easier than the last, and finally, I made my way to the dresser. The first drawer I pulled was full of panties and bras, still with the tags.

It had been years since I owned a new set of garments. My mother helped me alter hers for me, sometimes going without so I would have them. Seeing a drawer full made my eyes water. We lived through so much together. What would she say to me right now, knowing where I was and what I just did?

I pulled out a black matching set. The white ones seemed too clean for someone like me. I could only imagine having to wash white clothing.

I sat on the end of the bed and pulled the panties on before the bra, snapping it closed behind me. Jacob must be remarkably knowledgeable with women to guess a size this well. My other bra didn't come close to this comfort or fit.

But now, where were the rest of the clothes? Spotting the closet door, I slowly made my way there. Inside, there was a mass of hanging clothes. Pants, shirts, dresses. I'd have to thank Rosa for picking them out, but I wasn't sure how or if I should take them when I left.

I picked out a green long sleeve shirt with slits in the sleeves. Completely unfunctional but was pretty. I slipped it over my head with minimal pain in my movements. A small victory for me.

It was so soft and light. Nothing like the flannels I was used to wearing.

Grabbing a pair of jeans, I frowned at them. They were so small. No way would I fit in those. But Jacob had been right on everything else, so I decided to try them on. I had to sit on the bed again, unable to bend over that far.

The jeans moved up my legs easily. Standing back up, I slid them the rest of the way over my butt. They rested low on my waist, which was nice because it didn't interfere with my wound.

Wow. I couldn't believe they fit. They were snug, but not in an uncomfortable way.

It was a slow effort, but I finally made my way to the bathroom and found a brush in a drawer. It was much nicer than the one my mom and I used the last few years. Then again, everything away from Knox has been nicer.

Now, if I could just make it down the stairs. Maybe I could find the kitchen. My stomach rumbled, agreeing with my idea. I was starving.

Holding onto the railing like a lifeline, I took the steps one at a time, pausing shortly to keep from wearing out too fast. I didn't want to fall again like in the shower.

It took forever, but I made it downstairs.

It was very open but so much bigger than what I had become used to. The table was long enough to seat at least twelve people. It had been just me, my mom, and sometimes Knox for so long that I couldn't imagine having that many people to feed.

On the days Knox was gone working for Jacob was more challenging because he never left enough food for us, so we had to ration it.

My stomach grumbled again. I needed to stop thinking about food and find some.

It wasn't hard to find the kitchen as there was only a counter separating that room from the one I was in. It was huge. I couldn't believe the size of the refrigerator. We had a tiny one beside the bed, close enough to get to with our ropes. Knox would tie us up to the bed when he left, with just enough slack to use the makeshift toilet and close enough to the fireplace to put wood on, but not close enough to burn our ropes. My mother tried that once, and that was enough.

But we were never close enough to reach each other's ropes to untie each other. Knox was crafty. He was smart. Always one step ahead of us.

Subconsciously, I touched my wrist, where I'd probably have permanent scarring from the ropes I had to rub against the wooden bed frame to get away. It took a while before they were frayed enough to fall off, and it hurt like hell. But it was worth it. I'd do it again too.

Flapjack startled me as he came around the corner. "Lily, are you okay? Does Jacob know you're down here? I can go get him." His golden eyes softened with a smile.

67

"No," I said, a little too fast. "I'm just hungry. I was going to look for something to eat. Is that okay?"

His face lit up. "Now that I can help you with. My specialty is feeding hungry people. Come on." He walked to the kitchen and gestured to a stool on this side of the counter. "You can sit there. I'll fix you something."

It was a little high, but I could do it. With a little effort and wincing, then I was finally sitting. Getting off later might be another story, though.

Flapjack went right to work, pulling things out of the fridge that I could only imagine what they were. He placed a glass jug full of milk on the counter and paused, giving me a raised eyebrow. "Before I empty this fridge, is there anything you *can't* have?"

"Can't have?" I didn't know. "Is there something I'm not supposed to eat?"

He chuckled. "No, I mean, gluten, dairy, things like that. Anything you're allergic to? The soup I gave you yesterday didn't have those things just to be safe."

I didn't even know what those things were. "Um, I don't know. I don't remember being allergic to anything."

He never looked at me like I was stupid but just continued to pull things out and set them on the counter. "Okay, can you have things like bread or milk?"

"I think so. My mom made a lot of bread, so that should be fine. I haven't had a lot of milk lately, but I think I'm good with it."

He leaned against the counter in the middle of the kitchen and slowly watched me. "Lily, maybe it would be easier for you to tell me what you've eaten. I can help you from there."

I had no idea finding food would entail this. I might just starve before he gave me a piece of bread. "Rabbit, lots of rabbit. And deer occasionally. We had a small garden with potatoes and carrots. And when we had flour, we made biscuits, which is bread to me." I twitched my mouth to the side, thinking of what else I ate. I was confused. I hated that life before Knox kidnapping me seemed so distant and foreign like it wasn't even my life. I couldn't remember things like what foods I could eat. My eyes lit up at a memory. "And berries. I've had some berries once with my mom." And then, like that, the memory turned dark, and I closed my eyes against the evil.

My mom had gotten her and me out a few years ago. We stopped to rest after a whole day and night of walking. There were berries that we picked for breakfast before Knox found us. We were so close to being free.

"Lily, I'm gonna make you the best pancakes you've ever eaten, and I have some sweet homemade berry syrup to pour over them. You're gonna love it."

I smiled. I could almost call him an ally, but in the end, he still worked for Jacob. I couldn't trust any of them. "Thank you."

It wasn't long before he set a steaming pile of pancakes in front of me with a triumphant smile. He handed me a syrup jar and told me to pour as much as I'd like on the cakes.

On the first bite, I was hesitant, but the sweet melody of flavors had me drooling. Food should not taste this good. What would happen if you had to ration it? You wouldn't want to. You'd want to keep eating it!

He set a tall glass of milk down by my plate. "Wash it down with this."

It was ice cold and really did hit the spot. Wow. My stomach ached as I demanded it fit all the food given to me, not wanting to waste any of it.

"This was amazing. Thank you so much." I meant it. It was the best meal ever.

"If you like it so much, I'll make sure you have some brought up tomorrow morning for breakfast."

I couldn't imagine getting more. This was more food than I'd eaten all week. "Thank you so much." He really was sweet. And wherever he learned to make food taste like that must have been fancy. How fun it would be to learn to do that.

"Well, as fun as that was, I have to get back to work. Feeding all these guys isn't easy." He chuckled and began chopping some strange vegetable.

I said goodbye and carefully got off the stool. I was so full it almost hurt. I was still slow, but at least I wasn't worn out yet. And with each step, I felt stronger.

I decided to stroll through the house and look around. Jacob's voice came from the back of the house, and I froze. He sounded angry.

Carefully, I tiptoed to the room where he talked to one of his men. I held my breath, hoping it wasn't Knox.

"Where's Doc? I said I wanted to speak with him, not you." Jacob was calm as he reprimanded his guy.

"He's gone, boss. He went to that cabin you found last night. Said he had to see something for himself. I don't know, Jacob, he just left."

At least I knew that voice wasn't Knox. But the mention of a cabin Jacob found last night had me frozen to the floor. I couldn't move, couldn't breathe, couldn't speak.

What were the odds he found *my* cabin? Well, Knox's cabin.

I had to leave. I had to get out of there. But it was too late. Jacob was there, staring at me. "Lily, how long have you been here? Are you okay?"

I tried to swallow, so I could speak, but nothing worked.

Jacob placed his hands on my arms. "Honey, it's okay. I know you heard I found the cabin. It was empty. You're okay. It's safe here, remember?"

No, it was the opposite of safe. Knox wasn't there, so that meant he was here. But where? I was a dead woman either way.

I shook my head and pulled myself from his grasp. "I have to go."

The front door seemed so far away, but Jacob didn't stop me. He didn't hold me back. In fact, when Flapjack tried to keep me from leaving, Jacob told him to let me go.

I didn't understand why he just let me leave. Hot tears streamed down my face, and I wiped them with my hand. I just kept marching away from the house, away from Jacob.

He saw the cabin.

He knew.

And yet, he still treated me with kindness. More tears blurred my vision. I hurt, not just in my stomach but in my heart as well. If he knew, why did he do what he did to me earlier?

I must be a sick joke to him.

# Chapter 16

## *Jacob*

I watched Lily from far back. To hell, if I was just going to let her walk out there alone, unprotected. She was mine, and I wouldn't lose her now.

Besides, the sick man who hurt her was still out there somewhere. She wasn't thinking clearly. But she wasn't a prisoner held captive. I had to let her see that. Letting her go was the only way.

She needs to know that I'm here to protect her, to love her, to fight for her. My mind spun at the thought of love. I'd heard of people falling in love almost instantly, knowing a person was meant to be theirs forever after meeting them, but I never believed in all that until now.

It wasn't just because I saved her, either. I couldn't explain it, but there was something there that wound every part of my soul to hers.

I stayed far enough back that she still hadn't realized I was there. Then again, no one would know I was there unless I wanted them to. I wasn't as good as Flapjack, but I wasn't without skills. I'd been on many raids and not once was I noticed until I was ready.

This wasn't what I had planned tonight, but it didn't matter. Lily had things to work out, and I wouldn't stand in the way of her healing.

I'd seen some pretty bad things, and the way women handled them were all different. I wouldn't be the one to tell any of them how to deal with what they've been through.

I chuckled, thinking how my old man must be rolling in his grave knowing I turned his lifelong business of sex trafficking into a backward mercenary business, saving women sold by sex traffickers. My men and I joked about being cartel cowboys, but really, we were so much more.

The light was growing dim in the woods as the sun sank lower in the sky. We only had about an hour or two before it would be completely dark. But I'd be out here all night for her.

Lily stopped walking and dropped to the ground. I ran to her, scared for the worst.

Her shoulders shook as she sobbed, her eyes were swollen, and tears continued to flow in torrents. She looked up at me, defeated. "I can't do this anymore."

"Honey, I'm right here."

Her weeping was soul-wrenching. What could I do to help her? The only thing I was good at was killing, and I had already promised to kill the man who hurt her, but she wouldn't even tell me who that was.

"I can't." She shook her head. "I can't do this. It doesn't matter. He'll kill me, or you will. Either way, I'm dead."

Her words were like a knife to my stomach. "What the hell are you talking about?"

"It's useless." She hiccoughed, and her frame shook as she struggled to breathe.

I grabbed her shoulders, and she flinched. Shit. I didn't want to make this worse on her, but maybe it was the only way to get her to tell me what happened and who did it. "Lily, look at me."

She tried to look up but dropped her eyes.

"I said, look at me." It was more forceful than I'd talked to her before, but she did what I said. "You need to tell me everything. I need to know who will kill you because I promise I won't let them. I'll kill them first."

The tears came harder, and I was surprised she had any left. "Jacob, I'm sorry. Please don't kill me."

I shook her shoulders. "Lily, I'm not gonna kill you. Now tell me who abused you."

She sniffed and wiped at her face. "Knox."

It was one word, but not one I recognized. "Okay, good girl. Do you know his last name? What he looks like? Anything for me to go off of?"

She shook her head. "He works for you."

What the fuck? My skin burned as the words seethed from her like venom. "What?"

She sucked in a sharp intake of air. "He said he worked for you. He said," she paused, and tears fell again. "He said you would kill me for him if I escaped."

Fucking son of a bitch!

Some asshole was using my name to hold captive and abuse women. And not just any woman, my woman. Anger like I'd never felt before raged inside of me.

"Lily." I tried to speak calmly for her, even though the deep hatred for that man rang through. "Lily, I promise I will never kill you. It would kill *me* to hurt you."

"Really?" She squeaked.

"There is nothing I could say more truthful than that. I *will* protect you."

She flung herself around my neck and knocked us both over. My arms wrapped around her, and I stood up, holding her. "My Lily. I'm so sorry, honey. Whatever he said to you, whatever he did to you, I'm sorry. I promise I won't hurt you."

"Jacob, I'm sorry. I thought you'd kill me," she mumbled into my neck.

I lifted her, so I had an arm under her legs to carry her back to the house.

Once she was settled, I'd be going after Doc. He had some explaining to do. I wanted his story, and I wasn't going to take no for an answer. I was going to find Knox, and I was going to kill him.

# Chapter 17

## *Lily*

Being in Jacob's arms felt so right. He amazed me with his stamina. Carrying me for so long couldn't be easy, but he never complained.

My eyes burned, and my body ached. I'd done too much, too fast, and I wanted nothing more than to be back in his house in my bed. I had walked a lot farther than I thought. It was dark now, and I still didn't see the open yard with the houses yet.

It was confusing to find out Jacob had no idea who Knox was. All the empty threats binding me to that cabin and to Knox for all those years enraged me.

Jacob broke the silence first. "Can you tell me more about you? I want to know everything. I want to know you."

I leaned my head against his shoulder. "There isn't much. I was born here in Nevada, and until I was fifteen, I lived with my mom and dad. I doubt my father even cares that I went missing, so I'm pretty much on my own. I had a grandfather who actually looks a lot like Doc." I smiled despite the weary heaviness of my soul. "I wanted it to be him, but I think that's because I wanted a connection to my mom. He was her dad. But he didn't recognize me, so it couldn't be him."

"Lily, I am not sure I'd give up on finding your grandfather just yet. I'm not the person to give false hope, but I can guarantee you will see him again." He stopped walking, holding me in the middle of the forest, peering down into my eyes. "I can't believe you've been there for five years, and I never knew about you. I swear, had I known, I would have saved you years ago." His voice was deep and resonated through his chest. But it no longer scared me. It did the opposite and calmed my nerves.

I believed him. But there was no way he would have known. Knox had two men that helped conceal the cabin, keeping me a secret. And it wasn't easy to find, hidden high in the thick woods.

But so many things didn't add up. My head hurt, trying to untangle it alone. "Jacob, if you don't know who Knox is, why did he say he worked for you? Why did he threaten us with you? He obviously knew who you were. We were even on your property."

As he started walking again, he released a slight growl that vibrated against my cheek. "Honey, I promise I will find out all those questions. Don't think I'm not kicking myself in the ass for not knowing about you."

I leaned out to look at him through the moonlight. "I believe you. I do. But what about the other guys?"

He searched my face intently. "What other guys?"

"Two other guys always came to check on things, especially when Knox was gone. They helped him keep us there. But I don't know their names. They used different ones around us each time." He picked up his pace. "I can walk. You don't have to carry me."

"Actually, I do. I have to know for myself you're safe, and right now, having you in my arms is the only reason I'm staying as calm as I am."

I loosened my hold around his neck. "I'm sorry, Jacob. I didn't mean to upset you."

He held me tighter. "*You* did not upset me. I obviously have a weak spot with the men, and I will fix it."

The way he said fix it worried me. I didn't want him to get hurt. I knew what Knox could do, and one on one with Jacob, Knox wouldn't stand a chance. But what if all three of them ganged up on Jacob? "You're going to kill them."

He nodded. "I won't hide who I am from you. You already know I've killed people."

"But what if they find you first? We don't even know who they are." I couldn't lose him. I chided myself. He wasn't mine to lose.

"You don't worry about it. There is no way someone like that will find me first."

And yet, I doubted it. Knox held my mother and me captive on Jacob's property for five years. He obviously knew Jacob well enough to have the upper hand.

"I know this is a sensitive question, but what happened to your mother?"

Up ahead, I could see the faint lights of the houses and knew our time alone was almost over. His question hit nerves that twanged inside me, but I was happy because I got to talk about the one person in my life who loved me. "She was everything to me. She taught me as much as she could with what we had. She kept me as safe as she could, even in the hardest situations, taking most of the beatings and all the other stuff. I would have to turn away because I couldn't watch that. Not that she wanted me to." I hesitated. Some memories were worse than others.

"Sometimes, the other two guys would join in and come after me, but her screams would fill the cabin, and they would beat her for making so much noise. But they left me alone." My eyes welled up with fresh tears. I didn't think I'd have any left from earlier. But there would always be a reserve for when I thought about my mom. "About six months ago, she didn't wake up after they beat her. Knox took her and tossed her somewhere in the woods. I don't even know where." My body jerked as the memory permeated my tears.

Jacob stopped again, just short of the barn. "Lily," he said, looking into my eyes. "I'll find her. She'll have a proper resting place."

I sniffed and tucked myself back into the crook of his neck. Being so open and vulnerable really had a way of wearing a person out, and I'd done more than my share of that tonight.

"Boss!" Flapjack jogged over to us. "I was worried about her."

I noticed his statement wasn't directed to me, leaving me from the center of attention, but letting me know he was concerned. His thoughtfulness was appreciated.

"Go get Jax and Diesel. Tell 'em we're going hunting."

I stiffened. He couldn't leave me yet.

Flapjack nodded. "Riding, driving, or flying?"

"Riding." Where I was hunting, a truck wouldn't work.

"You got it, boss."

Inside, the house was warm. I hadn't realized how chilly the evening had been until then. Jacob took me upstairs to my room and sat me on the bed, taking my hand in his. "I won't be gone long."

I held onto him tightly and tugged. Using his strength against him, I pulled harder, leaning back on the bed until he was over me, one arm on each side of my head.

"Lily," he started. His husky whisper flowed between us like syrup. His lips crashed down on mine. The scent of the woods mingled with his fresh aftershave, creating a wonderful, lightheaded experience.

His lips were soft at first, teaching me the dance. Then as I picked it up, he pressed harder, deeper. His tongue slipped past my lips, which surprised me, but I complied, opening my mouth for him. It was such a sensual feeling, having his tongue caressing mine. It created a need in me to do the same, and I didn't stop myself from bravely seeking his.

I may have been inexperienced, but my body seemed to react to his naturally, telling me what to do. And it must be right because he gave a deep-throated moan that sang to my soul.

"Is everything okay?" I asked between kisses, just to be sure.

"Everything is perfect. You are perfect." Jacob lowered himself so he was on his elbow, half on his side and half on me, careful of my stomach. His free hand grasped the back of my head and held me close. His kiss was dangerously on the side of making me feel like ripping my clothes off.

Someday, I hoped to make him feel the same way. I will devour and use everything he teaches me until I create the same raging fire in him.

All too soon, he lifted himself and pulled me back to sitting. "I won't have our first time be a quickie. It will last all night long, and I'll savor every inch of you the way a woman should be loved."

I squeaked, wanting to protest. My body burned, needing him to fix it like last time. How could I possibly just lay there all night like that?

"I'll be back, but I made you some promises, and leaving right now is me keeping them." Jacob leaned over and kissed my forehead before leaving me to burn alone on the bed.

# Chapter 18

## Jacob

Having Lily pull me in for a kiss surprised me, but I wasn't going to waste a single taste of her lips. Especially when she offered them so freely.

But the things she told me tonight raged through me. And she deserved better than a branding claim for her first time. Angry sex had its place, but not tonight. Especially when my anger wasn't directed at her.

In my room, I grabbed both holsters, belting one around my waist, and clicked the other over my shoulders, stuffing each one with pistols from the safe in the corner of my room. My favorite rifle felt right in my hands. A Tactical Remington 700 AAC with my preferred muzzle break had enough power and precision to easily hit my target within an inch at a hundred yards. It had taken down many targets over the years and held my complete trust, knowing it wouldn't hesitate when I squeezed the trigger.

I made sure the buttstock ammo band was full and pulled a box of cartridges out to fill in the empty spaces on my holsters for the Glocks. I was going with the intent to kill, and I refused to go underprepared.

Outside, Jax sat in his saddle, leading Lady to the house for me. He wore his own battle-worthy weapons. We each had our favorites to hunt with, and in this business, I wouldn't try telling another man what to shoot with. Each of us carried our own sins and guns.

Sliding into the saddle, I slipped my rifle into the scabbard. Lily's bedroom light was on, and she stood in the window, her silhouette reminding me why I was in the saddle and not upstairs, making her mine.

"Where's Diesel?" I clicked my heels into Lady's side and turned from the house.

"He's waiting for us at the tree line."

Spurring into a run, we met Diesel and took off, weaving through the trees. I knew the way and wasn't slowing down.

At the cabin, I jumped off Lady and marched my way to the door.

"What are we looking for, boss?" Diesel was right behind me while Jax watched our backs. We'd hunted for years together and trusted each other implicitly.

"This man has been here for five years, and we didn't know. Lily said two other men helped him."

"You thinking we have a snake problem?"

I walked around the filth and scooted things over with my boot. I was no longer surprised by how or where I found clues.

Diesel started in the corner by the couch. "Well, I've never hunted our own before, but if there's a traitor, I have no remorse."

"I have none either." That's one thing about Diesel, he would be loyal until death. I could trust him with my deepest secrets. There was a reason he was my right-hand man.

I had to get my mind in the game. There was more than enough here to tell me something. I just had to see it.

The bed where Lily spent five years bound to it by ropes fueled the need to find this bastard.

Taking inventory of what was around me, I started noticing the tracks Knox left for me to find. I grinned. His time on this earth was limited.

The malted liquor bottles scattered around the room were all the same brand. Dark amber glass with a white label.

"Hey, Diesel, you like malt?"

"Nah, I'm a whiskey man myself." He stopped to pick up an empty bottle, and a wicked grin spread across his face. "But I know an old man who does."

Damn it, my suspicions had to be right.

"Boss, we've got company," Jax said at the door. "Horses are already hiding in the trees, so we'll have better cover in here."

I grabbed the handle of my Glock and pulled it from the holster. All three of us backed up to the wall, close to the door. I used my fingers to ask if Jax saw one, two, or more visitors.

Jax held up two fingers.

It shouldn't, but the thought of them coming to us excited me.

Outside, voices of men I knew filtered into the cabin. "Shit, if Jacob finds out, there won't be anywhere to hide. Knox really screwed us over."

"Just shut up and make sure there's nothing here to tie us to him."

They really were making this too easy for me.

Gun ready, I confidently walked around the door to greet them. "Well, you're right. Knox really did screw you over."

They reached for their guns, but Diesel and Jax had my back and trained the ends of their barrels on them. Jax sneered. "I wouldn't do that. You should know better than to draw against the boss."

I replaced my gun and walked toward them, taking their weapons from their belts and stuffing them in mine. "Nash, I'm surprised to see you as a traitor, but Smokey, I'm really not shocked at all." His love of the malt liquor gave me a head's up, or I might have been stunned.

Smokey worked for my father back when he was a young gun. When I took over, he pledged that life was behind him and would change to stay with us.

I scratched at my chin. Rough stubble reminded me of the long days I'd had since Lily came. Then my thoughts went to her and these men standing before me. They betrayed me and hurt her.

Drawing my arm back, I thrust my fist into Smokey's face. He wobbled backward and covered his eye and cheek.

I gestured to him. "You can shoot the bastard. He's been around too long and won't talk. He's gonna die anyway, and he knows it."

Jax wasted no time squeezing the trigger, his aim straight and true, leaving no possibility of life.

"Oh shit!" Nash backed up. His eyes wide as Smokey fell to the ground.

I chuckled. I liked seeing his discomfort. "This one, though, hasn't been with us long enough to know how things work." He wouldn't be given a second chance, and I knew both Diesel and Jax knew that, but I needed to play with Nash a bit to get information.

"Jacob, I'm sorry." He took another step back, watching Diesel and Jax.

"And yet, you don't even bother to look at me while apologizing?"

His stare flickered to me. "Boss, please. I'll tell you anything."

Diesel sneered behind me. "Fucking snake. I hate snakes."

In one stride, I grabbed him by the collar, pulling him to me. "You're damn right you're gonna tell me everything, you pathetic son of a bitch."

I dragged him inside the cabin and threw him on the bed. Taking the rope that had been left tied to the posts, I wrapped them around his wrists and pulled them tight. My rage roared thinking of him doing this to Lily.

I snarled. I had no compassion for men like this. It didn't matter that he worked for me. If anything else, that made it entirely worse for him. "Everything you did to Lily and her mom will be done to you. You don't deserve anything less."

"Oh, hell no, please don't. Boss, just let me talk," Nash said, struggling with the binding around his wrists. His panic said so much, too much. He didn't need words to convey his fear.

Diesel kicked Nash's feet. "So, what? A piece of shit like you can dish it out to an innocent woman, but you can't take it? Damn, boss, this snake is a fucking coward."

Jax found a jug of gasoline outside and brought it in. It could be a good scare tactic, but I was thinking of a slower death. Although, in the end, it might just work.

"Strip him," I said, lifting a leg while Diesel grabbed the other. He bucked and kicked out but was no match for both of us. The scrawny son of a bitch might be able to pin down a woman but was a pussy with real men.

Jax grabbed the waist of Nash's jeans and yanked, ripping them off the man, then grabbed his shirt, shredding it as well until there was nothing left but skin. Diesel and I took the remaining rope and tied his legs to the bed, so he laid naked on his back, unable to move.

I grabbed the small stool and pulled it up to sit on. I could do this all night and wanted him to know I was in no hurry, even though I was. I wanted this to be over so I could return home to Lily. "Where's Knox?"

Nash's nostrils flared. "Fuck you! You're gonna kill me anyway, so why should I tell you?"

Jax chuckled. "Hell, he doesn't know how long this can be dragged out. This'll be fun."

"Hey, boss, it looks like this snake hasn't been circumcised. How 'bout we do that for him?"

"Not a bad idea. I haven't done that before, but it can't be that hard." I pulled out my knife and popped the blade. "You can hold his dick with the fire poker while I cut."

"Oh shit. No. Shit. Jacob, don't." Nash couldn't talk fast enough. He bucked and tried to get free, but I just smiled at him.

Jax grabbed the iron poker and stabbed Nash through the tip of his foreskin. Nash's screams sailed down the mountain, but I had no mercy. I could picture Lily tied to this same bed, scared and abused. Her mother had been beside her, trying to protect her while these guys forced themselves on her.

Nash's eyes rolled back, and his shrieking died. Passing out wouldn't save him. I could wait until he came to. It didn't take long before his eyes opened, and tears poured out of him. He shouted at us to stop, begging us. He was breathless, and if Jax moved slightly, he would yell out again. In between breaths, he finally started talking. "Knox goes to Tahoe... in-between days... to talk with Garcia. Please, stop!"

Tahoe. Garcia.

Holy shit. I knew who Knox was.

The knife in my hand dug into my palm as I tightened my grip. Everything made sense. How he was on my ranch, how he stayed hidden, why he did this just so I'd find out. Fuck.

"Finish him." I no longer wanted to torture him. I had what I needed out of him.

"Gladly," Doc's voice filled the cabin, and I spun around to see him just before he squeezed the trigger on his Glock.

Nash's body jerked, but Doc didn't miss.

"What the hell, Doc." Diesel growled.

Doc stared at Nash, his gun still smoking.

Something was off. "What in the hell is going on, Doc?" He had a lot to explain.

Doc lowered his gun. I'd never seen the old man as furious as he was, standing there, seething in rage. "They killed her. Rachael. My daughter."

Oh, shit.

# Chapter 19

## *Lily*

The morning came and went, but still no Jacob. I paced the upstairs hall, from one window to the next, waiting for some sign that he was okay. I wasn't sure if he understood the kind of man he was going after.

Noon came, and Flapjack found me staring out the hall window, searching the horizon for Jacob.

"I bet you've never had a Monte Cristo." His voice startled me. I hadn't heard him come up the stairs.

"I don't even know what that is." But if he made it, it was bound to be amazing.

"Come on, Jacob will kill *me* if you don't eat." He gestured toward the stairs, and I hesitantly left the window.

"Do you think he's okay?" I took a step down. At least it hardly hurt to move today, so descending the stairs was much faster than before.

Flapjack laughed. "Jacob? Oh, he's fine, no doubt. But the guys he went after? They are definitely dead or on their way."

"How can you be so sure? Those men are merciless."

We reached the bottom of the stairs, and Flapjack touched my shoulder to stop me. "Lily, let me tell you, just to ease your worry, that Jacob is scarier than all those men put together."

A lump in my throat formed, making it hard to swallow. "Should I be scared?"

I couldn't imagine being afraid of him again. The way he kissed me... touched me. The way he talked to me. It was the first time I realized I was beginning to feel safe with him.

Flapjack chuckled. "Lily, if something happened to you, I'd be scared because you are the one person he's decided to protect with his life. But you, no, you will never have to be scared of him."

I smiled softly. Flapjack was turning into such a good friend. I couldn't imagine having this talk with anyone else. Except for my mother. "What's your real name, Flapjack?"

"Carter." He ducked his head like a small boy. "No one calls me that, though."

"Well, Carter, I'm glad I met you."

He smiled. "You sure are something. I can see why the boss has taken a liking to you." He nodded to the kitchen. "Now, let's get you some food. I like feeding you, it's always a new surprise, and I love seeing your reactions."

It was my turn to laugh. "I bet I could outcook you with a rabbit. We'll have to try it one day. Then we can see who's surprised."

"You're on, Lily." He held his hand out for me to seal the challenge. I took it, and a bit of excitement rushed through me at the thought of doing something fun.

It could be a chance to show Jacob I could do more than just needing to be saved. "If I win, will you show me how to cook more than a rabbit?" The idea of learning to cook amazing food really intrigued me.

"You know, I'd love some help in the kitchen with someone who actually cares about food. Deal."

A deep growl resonated behind me, and Flapjack dropped my hand. "Jacob."

Jacob was back? I turned to see him standing at the doorway, watching between Flapjack and myself closely. "Jacob!" My heart fluttered at seeing him. I didn't understand why it did that with him and no one else, but I hoped it never stopped.

He held a rifle and wore enough pistols to look like a mercenary. I didn't see any blood, but he was dirty. The Stetson he wore cast a shadow over his eyes, darkening the intense gaze he held us in.

Between my legs began to ache. Like a magnet, they pulled me to him. I wanted to touch him, kiss him... make sure he was okay.

"What's going on?" he asked Flapjack.

"We just made a pact to see who could outcook who with a rabbit. I swear, boss, nothing else."

Jacob looked at me, his gaze softening. A small smile lifted the corner of his mouth. "Rabbit?"

I laughed. "Yeah, rabbit."

He took a step into the house and set his rifle down. Unbuckling the holster around his waist, he took it off and set it with his rifle, leaving the black one around his shoulders on. I could see why Carter was scared of him, but he did the opposite to me. I hadn't ever felt as protected as I did at that moment. Fear was replaced with security.

And Jacob Cardosa was the man who did that for me. I would forever be grateful.

"I was worried about you," I admitted, wanting to reach out and touch him, but I wasn't sure I should. I had kissed him last night, but what if he was upset about it? I was still learning things and might have overstepped my place.

Jacob closed the distance between us in one step, and his lips crashed down on mine. I couldn't explain how much I needed his kiss, but it was like dousing the already burning fire inside me with gasoline. I guess I hadn't overstepped because this kiss was a remembrance of what happened between us.

He leaned back and rested his forehead on me. "You never have to worry about me, honey."

I was breathless, unable to answer after the kiss. My knees were weak, and I didn't want to hold myself up.

All too soon, he stepped back but grabbed my hand. "We need to talk."

I nodded and let him lead me to his study. The last time I was close to that room, I thought he would kill me, and I ran away. But not today. No more running. No more being afraid.

"I need to tell you what happened last night."

I shook my head. I didn't want to know. Couldn't he just kill them and let me move on? He pulled a tall chair with wooden legs out for me, and I gladly sat down. It was close to his desk, and he half sat on it, still holding my hand. It was like he wasn't ready to stop touching me, either. And I loved it.

"I found the two men who helped Knox."

I tensed. No, I wasn't ready to hear this.

Jacob left the desk and kneeled before me. "Lily, it's okay. They can't hurt you anymore."

"They're dead?" I quivered.

His strong jaw clenched. "Yes."

I stuttered. "What about Knox?"

He looked up at me and touched the side of my face with his other hand. "Lily, I know who he is, but I swear he has never worked for me."

I fought back the emotions threatening to make me cry. I wouldn't cry. I was learning to be a strong woman. Strong like Jacob. If I was strong enough, he might let me stay with him. I nodded instead.

"There's more." He looked at the office door. "Doc, you wanna come in here." It wasn't a question. I was learning quickly that nothing Jacob said was optional.

Doc came in slowly, then took his hat off, showing his long white hair. He fumbled with the brim and stared at me. His eyes were glassed over.

"What's going on?" I asked Jacob.

He grabbed my other hand and squeezed. "Lily, I promised we'd find your mom."

"Oh no, Jacob, please don't. I can't." I shook my head, and the tears I held back welled in my eyes.

"Doc found her."

I knew she was dead, I saw her, but the thought of her body mutilated by elements and animals, just being discarded in the woods, had my stomach rolling.

"Lily," Doc started, still fidgeting with his hat. I stared at him through blurry eyes. "She was my daughter."

"What?" I looked at Jacob. "How did you know?"

His mouth twisted as he contemplated his words. "Twenty years ago, your mom fell in love with a man, but he was killed. It wasn't long after she got mixed up with Garcia and had you. She was only allowed to visit her father once a year, not leaving much time for an old man to bond with his granddaughter. But," Jacob hung his head, "damn this hard. They stopped coming to see him a few years ago because they were kidnapped. He came here looking for help in finding them." He looked back up at me. "Lily, I know you're Garcia's daughter."

I gasped. I didn't want him to know who I used to be. That wasn't who I was now. Knox took a lot of things from me, and my former life was one of them.

He kept going, not waiting for me to respond, not that I could. "I'm not sure what happened between Knox and your father, but Garcia reported you dead. It was his signature on the report." Jacob choked up but cleared his throat. "I'm still unclear about how you ended up with Knox or why you were never sold or moved from this property, but I'll find out. I promise you, there won't be any secrets."

I sniffed and looked at Doc. "So, you *are* my grandfather?"

His tears fell freely now. "Lily, I'm so sorry."

I stood up, reaching out for him. He embraced me tightly and cried into my shoulder. "I tried to find you guys. I really did."

"I know. It's okay." There was nothing to stop the floodgates from opening now. Tears soaked my face. I felt his grief mixed with mine. Years of wanting someone to save us, and he spent years trying to rescue us, it was a desperate link, but we both had one thing in common. My mom.

Doc pulled back first and wiped at his face, trying to man back up. It must be hard for an old cowboy to show so much emotion. "When Jacob told me you tried using your mom's name, Rachael. I think I knew then who you were, but I had to find her first. I couldn't just let her rot alone in the woods."

I smiled weakly. "I'm glad you found her."

Jacob pulled me so my back was up against his muscular chest, his hands on my shoulders, giving me comfort. "That's what took so long. We buried her, honey. I'll take you there one day so you can see for yourself."

"Thank you." I twisted to look up at Jacob. "No secrets, right?"

"No secrets." He gently squeezed my shoulders, reaffirming his side of the promise.

"I might know a little bit about why I was kidnapped."

Jacob tensed. "Lily, you need to tell me."

"Well, I don't know the details behind it, you'd have to ask my dad, but I think he was behind Knox taking me. My dad did something bad and needed to get rid of me. I don't know why he made a deal with Knox, except my dad wasn't supposed to know where we were. Knox said we were hidden from the world on this mountain, and no one would ever think to look here. Now I know why." It was sad how easy talking about being kidnapped and abused was, but talking about anything else seemed so foreign.

"Shit." Jacob looked at Doc, who just nodded in confirmation of the silent conversation they held. "It all makes sense now."

Jacob sat down and pulled me to his lap. "Honey, Garcia reported you as dead. There's a death certificate and everything. I think there is more behind your kidnapping."

"I'm sorry, I'm confused." Why would my dad have me taken and then report me as dead?

Doc flopped his hat back on his head. "No wonder we can't find Knox. Garcia's hiding him. But when he finds out Rachael is dead and their daughter is alive, Knox might have to run."

My heart raced. What did this mean for me? "Does this mean you're going to send me back to my dad?" I didn't want to go back. Yes, he was family, but he sold me to Knox for five years. He was as good as dead as far as a father goes. Only in my past was he allowed to live.

Jacob stiffened. "Hell no. You're mine, remember. You and me. I'm not handing you over to anyone." He paused briefly. "Unless you want to go."

"No, I want to stay here. I'm just trying to understand everything."

"Well," Doc started, "whatever Garcia did to have to make a deal bad enough to sell my daughter and granddaughter, we should find out. It would be a good start to weave the rest of this story together."

I stood up, not wanting to leave Jacob's comfort but needing to move. Pacing seemed like the best option. "But that means you'll have to let Garcia know about me. What if he just takes me?" I decided to use my father's name, letting him go as my father. It was freeing and empowering to be able to make such a change.

Jacob stood too but didn't make me stop moving. "Honey, I told you, I'll protect you with my life. He won't take you."

Doc cleared his throat. "*We* won't let him take you. I already lost my daughter. I won't lose my granddaughter again."

I nodded, uncertain. "But Jacob, I don't think you understand. Garcia is powerful. He could come here and just take me."

Jacob laughed, and Doc let out a chuckle. Jacob's hand found mine and gave it a gentle squeeze. "Honey, for as powerful as you think Garcia is, I am even more so. Trust me, he won't take you." He looked so calm and relaxed. I wished I could be the same way. "I don't know how he kept you hidden from me so long, right here under my nose, but I promise I'll right the wrong. I'll fix this."

I stepped closer to him and wrapped my arms around his neck. "Now I can hide *with* you."

His arms encircled me, his warmth penetrating through my clothes. "No hiding, Lily. I will never hide you."

# Chapter 20

## *Jacob*

It was hard for me to know it was because of my security and who I was that helped hide her. I would spend the rest of my life making it up to her.

Flapjack was able to get her to smile and even laugh at dinner, giving me hope. All I could do was watch her, mesmerized by her sweet laugh. I didn't care how it happened or who helped her get there, but I would do anything to hear that again and again.

Doc stayed in the main house to eat with us. They had lots to talk about, and I was lucky enough to hear a few memories they shared when Lily was a small child. I found myself a bit more attached to each one. Lily wasn't just some woman who came to me by chance. It was fate. I could hear my mother telling me to hang on to her and love her like she deserved.

After supper, we sat around the table, still talking while Flapjack cleaned up. "What's the next thing we need to do, boss?" Doc wiped his mouth with the linen napkin and placed it on the table.

"I'm gonna make a few phone calls tomorrow, one of them to Garcia, and we'll go from there. I'm not sure he'll cooperate, but I need to find out if he's hiding Knox." I'd have to extend an offer to have him meet with us. A *'keep your friends close and enemies closer'* deal was the only way to keep ahead of Garcia. "He might even help us kill Knox after he finds out his wife is dead."

Doc grumbled. "I suspect he might. Although, I'm not sure anyone wants to kill him more than me."

I found Lily's hand under the table and pulled it to my lap, giving her a gentle squeeze. "I do."

Doc looked between Lily and me. "Jacob, as my boss, I shouldn't say this, but as her grandfather, I sure as hell hope you know what you're doing. Don't break her heart. She's been through hell. This might not even be the right time to start something."

I chuckled. "Doc, I have no plans to hurt her."

"With that said," Doc stood and kissed Lily on the forehead, "I'm heading to bed. Hunting takes it out of a man, and I'm not as young as I once was."

Lily smiled. "Good night, grandfather."

Doc shook his head and chuckled as he walked out the door. "Grandfather. I never thought I'd hear that again."

Having Lily's hand on my leg seared me with intense heat, making me hard with a need only she could fulfill.

I leaned her way, cupping my hand at the back of her head, threading my fingers through her long soft hair. "Lily," I started, but she held a finger up, touching my lips.

"Tell me upstairs."

The blood in my veins pulsed to the hard beats of my heart. She stood up, still holding my hand, pulling me to her. "Jacob, whatever it is, show me, *teach* me, don't tell me."

Aw, hell. I don't think she knew what effect she had on me and saying that made my dick ready to show her everything. I scooped her up and carried her upstairs without breaking eye contact. My room or hers? Hell, they each had a bed. It didn't matter.

My room was closer by a foot. *That* mattered.

Laying her on my bed and seeing her hair spill over my pillow was the most sensual image. I wanted to go slow and savor every moment with her, sending her over the edge, watching as she writhed in delight.

"I'll go slow, I promise," I whispered in her ear as I nibbled down to her neck, wanting to touch and taste every inch of her.

She tilted her head to give me more access, elongating her neck and revealing her collarbone just enough to tease me from the top of her shirt.

Grasping at the shirt, I pulled it over her head, needing to see her. The black bra had my heart skipping beats. I knew how amazing her breasts were and couldn't wait to taste them again. The clasp was easy to undo with one hand, and I slid it off, tossing it away from the bed.

"Can I take *your* shirt off?" She ran her hands up and down my covered chest.

"You don't have to ask me, honey."

Her hands trembled as she unbuttoned my shirt, going lower until her fingers brushed the waist of my jeans. Just her touch about sent me over. I couldn't let that happen. I pulled back and finished taking my shirt off.

I quickly found my place over her, crashing down on her lips. Her breasts touched my chest, and I closed the space, careful of her wound and not pressing too hard, loving how she felt under me. She arched, needing something, but I knew she wouldn't know what until I gave it to her. I wouldn't rush this for her, though. After tonight, she would forever be mine, and no one would take her from me. They would die trying.

Claiming her would be like nothing else I'd ever experienced. I deepened the kiss, needing to blend us together.

I ran my hand down her neck to her breast and caressed it lightly, then harder. She moaned as I rubbed her nipple. I left her mouth to cover the tight nub with my lips, then held it between my teeth and licked it with short tastes.

Pressing my hardened manhood against her thigh, I groaned. I needed her, but first, I had to make sure she was ready.

Grasping at her jeans, I unbuttoned them and pulled the zipper down. I had to leave her to tug them off, revealing the matching black panties. For fuck's sake. It was like she was trying to kill me.

I snapped the tiny black string and ripped them off. I'd buy her more. A lot more. Because I wasn't about to take the time to pull them off.

She gasped, but her desire-filled eyes just watched me. Her level of trust in me did nothing to cool the raging inferno inside me. How I had earned that was beyond me, but I was damn pleased about it.

From the foot of the bed, I spread her legs enough to climb between them. I began kissing her legs, moving higher until I reached her thighs.

Just like last time, my fingers found her wet. She whimpered in pleasure as my finger brushed her small nub. Slipping a finger inside her, she arched to meet me. I pulled out, only to be met with a plea to help her.

"I promise to help you, honey. I'm just getting started. I told you, I won't let our first time be quick." My dick pulsed in my jeans, protesting my desire to take it slow.

"Jacob." That was all she said, yet I understood. There would be a moment when all I would be able to say was her name.

This time I slipped two fingers into her. She stiffened around me, gasping and arching. She was so tight I was worried I'd hurt her. Her body would have to make room for me.

Leaning forward, I removed my fingers to lick her opening. She was the perfect mix of sweet and salty. Once she realized what I was doing, she tried to stop me, clenching her legs, but I reached up and grasped a breast, kneading it as I slipped my tongue inside her. The warmth I found sent me reeling. She relaxed, and her legs widened, letting me lick her.

Her moans didn't stop as my tongue darted in and out. I covered her with my mouth and sucked gently. There was no way I could ever get enough of her.

Leaving her nipple hard and erect, I found her wet opening and glided three fingers inside again. She was so fucking tight. The way her body reacted to my tongue and fingers had me ready to spill out in my jeans.

She thrashed on the bed, her head moving side to side. "Jacob."

Screw it. I couldn't go any slower. She was mine. I removed my jeans, watching her reaction as my hard cock stood tall and ready to claim her.

I knelt on the bed, one knee between her legs. She reached down and hesitantly touched my dick.

"Is this okay?" She asked as pre-cum dripped from the tip. She used her finger to swirl it around in an agonizing stroke. My dick pulsed and throbbed under her feather-light touch. I ached for more.

"Grab it." I covered my hand over hers and wrapped her fingers around my length. "Fuck, yes." I began moving her hand. "Just like this."

She moaned in enjoyment, but not deeper than me. Holy shit. Her hands were like silk, gliding over my dick in an intense motion.

My fingers found her opening again while she stroked me. I pushed three back inside, as deep as I could. Each stroke she gave me, I matched.

I was close to losing myself all over her. But I refused not to brand her as mine. I pulled away and opened the nightstand drawer for a condom. I sure as hell wasn't pulling out, but neither of us was ready for kids.

Her eyes widened as I pulled the condom down my full length. "I... I don't know how *that* will fit inside me." She nodded at my newly decorated cock.

"You will fit me like a glove, honey. The first time will hurt, but then it will be amazing and easy. I promised you I'd go slow, remember."

"Jacob, I trust you." She held her arms out for me, and I complied, lowering myself atop her.

I pushed her legs open with my knees and let my dick barely touch her, letting her know I was there.

"I'm scared." Her body shook.

"Honey, I won't do anything you don't want. I told you the first time can hurt, and you're so tight. If you aren't ready, just let me know, and I'll stop." My voice caught in a groan as she ran her hands down my chest and stomach before lightly running a finger up my dick.

"I didn't mean I was scared of *that*. I'm not scared of anything you could do to me. I'm scared I won't be good enough for you."

Oh, fuck. My lips crashed down on hers. I couldn't wait any longer. "Lily, you are perfect for me. Now let me in."

She opened her legs wider. I trailed my fingers back down to her slip through her folds to help her relax before entering her. Her moans were the sexiest sound I'd ever heard and as effective as if she held me in her hand and stroked, making me thrust harder. Her wetness called to my cock pressed against her thigh.

Removing my fingers, I centered myself over her and barely pushed, slowly entering her. Inch by inch, my dick slipped into the tightest cocoon of heat. The last inch had the thin barrier I had to push through, making her mine.

I kissed her as I broke through, and her muffled cry melted against my lips. As much as I wanted to move, I stayed still, letting her body adjust to my size.

She was truly mine now.

I trailed light kisses down her cheeks, taking her tears away. "I'm sorry I hurt you."

"It's hard to explain. It hurts, but it feels so good." Her voice was husky and filled with ecstasy.

I continued to kiss her. "Just this time, the next time won't be like that. It will just be good."

I started to move, and her tight walls clenched around me. A moan met each thrust. I plunged harder and deeper, faster. Her eyes filled with rapture as I moved inside her.

"Lily." It was all I could say as I felt her wetness spread around me and her body quake. She arched to meet me one last time, and I spilled out, pushing myself into her as deeply as I could.

My body shook, and my strength was gone. Holy hell. We stayed like that, with me pulsating inside her while she found the ability to breathe.

Slowly, I pulled out and slipped the condom off, making sure to keep everything contained. "I'll get you cleaned up."

Tossing the condom in the trash, I grabbed a warm wet rag and found her still flushed on the bed. "Jacob, are you okay? Did I do it right?"

I wiped her clean and tossed the rag across the room. I needed to lay with my woman. Naked, our fully satisfied, sweat-laden bodies pressed together, still needing to be as close as we could get.

I couldn't get over it. She fit me, every inch, and became my woman. I was more than okay. Fuck cloud nine. I was on cloud one hundred.

"You were perfect." I kissed the top of her head as she curled up next to me. "Lily, I don't think I could ever do that enough with you."

She giggled. "Thank you."

"No. Thank you. Thank you for being mine." I finally had something of my own to protect.

# Chapter 21

## *Lily*

Sleeping in Jacob's arms, I felt peace like never before. Finally, I was safe. I had no doubts that he would protect me from Knox.

Carefully, I slipped out from under his arms and the cocoon of warmth his body offered. As I padded across the floor to the bathroom, I noticed that I was slightly sore where Jacob had entered me last night, but my stomach hardly had any pain. I smiled. I would take this pain any time to experience that again.

Tossing a look over my shoulder, the bed looked as wild as I felt, but the naked man lying on it was the image of perfection. Everything he did last night was incredible.

I stopped in front of the bathroom mirror and saw a woman I hadn't seen before. I looked happy. Aside from the old bruises, I looked healthier than I remember being. Even the tiny wound on my stomach was shrinking and healing.

It seemed like forever that I tried to kill myself. And now, I was glad I failed.

I closed my eyes and drifted off to last night. Jacob was so patient. And now, he claimed me as his. My stomach fluttered excitedly.

Feather-light touches to the small of my back had me smiling, and I opened my eyes to see the man who was quickly becoming the holder of my heart behind me. His fingers trailed up to move my hair aside, and he kissed my shoulder, working his way up my neck.

"Good morning, beautiful," he said, his voice husky and deep.

"Good morning," I replied. A slight quiver escaped my lips as he kissed up to my ear and nibbled.

How did a kiss feel so good?

"Waking up without my woman is not how I intended to start today." He continued to kiss me, wrapping an arm around me while his other hand found my breast. "There are other ways to wake up, and I'm gonna show you."

All I could do was moan in pleasure as he fondled my nipple. He could do anything he wanted as long as he never stopped touching me. I could feel his manhood growing harder, pressing up against me.

"Lily," he whispered.

I leaned into him. We weren't close enough. I needed more.

"Boss!" Outside the bedroom door, Doc's voice rang through the hall.

Jacob snapped up, instantly alert. "Stay here," he locked the bathroom door connected to the hall and slipped into the bedroom, grabbing his gun.

He carefully cracked the door open. "What the hell is going on?"

"Keep Lily in there. We have visitors."

Visitors? I doubled over and crouched down. Knox found me. It had to be him.

I had to hide.

I had to leave.

Jacob closed the door and came right to me, squatting down to look me in the eyes. "I need you to stay right here. Don't move. Got it?" He kissed me on the forehead. "Don't worry, honey. I promise you're safe. I won't let anything happen to you."

I couldn't breathe, but I nodded—for him, but inside, I was dying all over again. All the fear raged back to life, reminding me that I would never be free of Knox.

Jacob left and pulled his clothes on, strapping his gun into its holder over his shoulder.

Staying close to the floor and walls, I made my way to my room. Pulling out clothes, I hurriedly put them on. In the closet were a few pairs of shoes I assumed were for me, so I slipped on a pair of boots and rushed to the window, careful not to be seen.

A couple of black vehicles I hadn't seen before were out front. The men that came out wore all black clothing, and everyone had a gun. I searched the faces but didn't see Knox.

My heart raced. I knew Jacob's men had guns too, and they carried them as they greeted the men, but it didn't help my fear.

Jacob stood out front, his arms folded. He held such a strong, prominent presence. Everything about him demanded respect.

Doc wasn't far behind him, holding a rifle. I worried about the old man. Having just found him, I wasn't ready to lose him.

A man not holding a gun, although I could see the handle of one under his jacket, stepped out of the vehicle. He was tall, though he didn't reach Jacob's height. He wasn't as broad as Jacob and was a bit older, with gray streaks staining his dark hair and beard, but he was handsome in his own way. And even without being near him, I knew my father when I saw him. He looked a bit older than I remembered, but it was him.

Jacob shook hands with Garcia.

My heart raced, and my stomach rolled. I wasn't sure I was ready to see him. Mixed emotions rumbled through my brain. He was my dad, but he was the reason my mother was dead. He may not have done the beating, but he sent us away with Knox, which was the same thing. It was hard, but I moved from the window and tiptoed to the bathroom to brush my hair.

Jacob wouldn't leave me alone if I were in danger. Would he?

The front door opened, and I could hear voices filling the downstairs area. I tensed. Jacob was letting them in the house?

"I don't care, Jacob. I deserve to see her!" the voice bellowed, echoing up to me. It was the same barking voice I remembered from my youth. Many times, he yelled for me and even at me.

Jacob countered a remark, but it was muffled, and I couldn't make it out. The voices, both Jacob's and Garcia's, were angry and grew louder.

Fight or flight was kicking in, and I knew I needed to move. I needed to hide. I wasn't ready to face my father.

I slipped into the closet in Jacob's room and huddled in the corner. I covered my ears and closed my eyes, needing to block out the yelling.

"Lily?" Jacob's concerned voice filled the room behind the door. "Lily?" He called for me louder, and a slight panic laced my name.

The door to the closet opened, and I froze. Jacob's large frame filled the exit, making any escape impossible. "Lily," he said, breathing a sigh of relief. "You scared me. I couldn't find you."

He crawled inside with me. "What are you doing in here, honey?"

"I don't know. The yelling scared me, and I just had to hide. I'm sorry." I wanted to cry. Earlier, I had a fleeting moment of happiness and thought all my fear was gone, but now I knew better. I wondered if I would always be afraid. If it was now a part of who I was.

"I told you; you don't have to be sorry, and you don't have to be afraid." He held his arms open for me, and I went to him, finding the comfort and protection I desperately needed. "I need you to come downstairs. There's someone here who wants to see you."

"Jacob, I'm sorry if I did something wrong. Please don't send me away."

"Fuck, Lily, is that what you think?" He kissed the top of my head. "No, honey. You aren't going anywhere. I told you, you're mine. You are here with me for as long as you want me." He leaned back and tipped my chin up, forcing me to look at him. "Lily, last night, that was me saying forever. Do you understand?"

My heart skipped a beat. I didn't fully understand anything right now. I was so confused, but what I felt for Jacob was unlike any other love I'd ever experienced. But there was no doubt that was what was happening. Not that I would tell him that I was falling in love with him.

"Damn it, I wish I could erase your past, so all you could see was our future." He stood and pulled me up with him.

I swayed, even with his strong arms holding me. "Why do I have to go downstairs? I'm not sure I'm ready." Being tossed to the wolves was a more accurate description of how I felt.

"Because your dad is downstairs and wants to see you." He guided me out of the closet. "But I won't leave your side. Not unless you want me to, but even then, I'm not sure I could leave you."

"I can't. Jacob, please don't make me." Knowing Garcia was downstairs had my stomach pushing up to my throat. "I'm scared."

"I know, honey. But I won't let anything happen to you. I will kill anyone who tries to hurt you. You trust me, right?"

I nodded. I trusted him, but I didn't trust Garcia. He had already gotten rid of me once. What would keep him from finishing the job himself?

Holding Jacob's hand, I walked down the hall to the stairs. "Jacob, don't leave me."

He stopped at the head of the stairs, pulling me to him. "Never." Leaning down, strong and steady, his lips found mine. It was quick, but everything he didn't say was in that kiss.

As long as I had him, I could do this. I could do anything. With a little more confidence, I held my head higher as I walked down the stairs. It was time for me to be the adult I was and stop hiding. Stop running. Stop being scared. And there was no better way to start than to face my father.

Passing the kitchen, Carter was there, watching me. His smile and nod were encouraging and helped me remember that I had more than just Jacob here for me. I had a family now. I wasn't alone.

Jacob gave my hand a slight squeeze outside the office before opening the door. Walking through the threshold, I searched for Knox and relaxed when I couldn't see him.

But the man I did see stared at me with a rage that had me scooting closer to Jacob. The death grip I had on his hand should be enough for him to know I was scared, but he took another step toward Garcia.

Head held high and tried not to let him see my fear. I was with Jacob, Doc was there, and Carter was somewhere behind me. I could do this. I wasn't going to be afraid.

The anger my father held in his eyes softened as he stared at me, tears welling with an emotion I could only assume was guilt. "Lily."

# Chapter 22

## *Jacob*

The way Lily held my hand had me feeling more protective. I gave her a gentle squeeze, reassuring her that I was there. The poor woman had dealt with so much in her life that this meeting couldn't be easy on her.

In a way, I was glad Garcia showed up. It saved me a phone call. But apparently, Knox had called him, saying that I found Lily and was holding her hostage, and that had him ready to gun down my entire ranch.

I had no choice but to have her come down and meet him. Even though their reunion should have been under my arrangements so Lily could have had time to warm up to the idea.

Garcia stared at Lily. His usually stony expression held a glow only a father could give. Watching a man I hated soften like a house cat was almost amusing. But it also confused the hell out of me, wondering why a man who loved his daughter would give her to a man like Knox. Unless this was all a ruse for the sake of looking like a concerned father. "You look so much like your mother, aside from your eyes. Where is she?" He looked over my shoulder with a hopeful, searching gaze.

Lily looked up at me, and I smiled at her. I didn't care whose eyes she had. To me, they were just hers, a window to her soul that I wanted to spend forever looking through.

"She's dead." Lily's voice was soft but steady. I was so proud of her for masking most of her fear in front of all these men.

"What?" Garcia's nostrils flared, and he took a step toward me. "What the hell did you do to my wife?"

"The real question is, what the fuck did *you* do to your wife? What about your daughter? I had nothing to do with your wife's death. You can thank Knox for that. But I did save your daughter." I pulled Lily closer to my side, acutely aware of every gun in the room. Every movement had me alert and ready to fight.

Behind me, I could also feel the shift of vigilance from my men. Warning signs prepared me to protect Lily at all costs. I wouldn't trust Garcia not to kill his daughter.

Garcia's hard-set stare penetrated the room between us, softening only when he looked at his daughter. "I'm sorry. I didn't know she was dead." He reached out to touch her shoulder. To her credit, she didn't flinch, but I tensed for her, not liking how close he was. Father or not, if he hurt her, he wouldn't make it out of my house alive.

She smiled, but it wasn't a genuine smile that I had gotten to see over the past few days. "Thank you."

Garcia straightened, and his hard face returned as he dropped his arm. "Jacob, I need to thank you. You saved her. You know I don't like being in debt to anyone."

That feeling was mutual. I'd rather chew off my left arm than owe someone. Especially Garcia. I felt there was more to this than just owing me a debt.

Having him owe me was thought-provoking, but Lily was worth more than a debt. I didn't save her for him. "Nothing is owed. She isn't alive for your benefit."

I pulled my hand from her grasp to wrap my arm around her shoulders, keeping her close. "I guess you should know that Lily is mine. And you know that there isn't anything I won't do to protect my own." It was a bold statement to make at that moment, but if I was going to get him to leave without trying to take Lily and be on board helping us kill Knox, he needed to know.

Garcia's eyes widened. "You son of a bitch! If I find out you forced yourself on her, you will die, Cardosa."

I chuckled. "Calm down, old man. No one here would force themselves on any woman. We aren't like the fucking animals you employ." Except for Smokey and Nash, but we took

107

care of them. "Speaking of, where is Knox? I have a few things I'd like to *talk* to him about."

"Fuck you, Cardosa. If anyone talks to that cocksucker, it'll be me." He gestured to one of his men. "Take my daughter to the trucks. We're leaving."

I didn't have to say anything. The lever of Doc and Flapjack's guns were cocked and ready to fire, aimed at the man Garcia ordered to take Lily. Bear and Diesel, who had been guarding the study doors, were there, their Glocks drawn.

I stood calmly with Lily still close to me. No way in hell was I letting her get any farther from me with them here. "No one will touch her. I told you, she's my woman."

"Like hell she's yours," Garcia sneered.

He reached out to grab Lily's arm, but I was faster, pushing her behind me. My fist made contact with his nose. Blood poured out instantly. "Get this son of a bitch out of here before he gets blood all over my floor."

Lily stood tall behind me, and I was relieved she hadn't run. Violence wasn't something that would be easy for her.

"Shit! You motherfucker, you broke my nose!" Garcia held his face as blood sprayed out between his fingers.

"I told you no one will touch her."

Garcia's men pulled their guns, and I shook my head. "You think you'll live long enough if you fire a shot? Don't be stupid."

"Cardosa, you'll pay for this." Garcia let his hands fall away, blood running down his face. "Lily, you're my blood. You're a Ramirez. You belong with your family, not this piece of shit."

Lily took a step forward, and my heart sank, thinking she would leave. "Garcia, I may have your blood, but my family is here. And I belong with Jacob."

Holy shit, I loved that woman.

My stomach flipped. Loved? That wasn't something I had thought much of, but damn, it had to be. My mother's words came flooding back to me about how people fall in love and don't even realize it.

"My granddaughter isn't going anywhere," Doc spoke up, his gun still aimed at a man.

Garcia scoffed. "Too bad you couldn't protect your daughter as well as your granddaughter. Rachael would still be here."

Doc dove at Garcia, landing another punch to his already broken nose. "You son of a bitch, you're the reason Knox took her. She's not here because of you."

"Fuck you!" Garcia swung a fist, connecting with Doc's face.

I knew Doc had years of pent-up anger to let out, and I wasn't about to stop him from pummeling Garcia, but when he drew his gun, I stepped forward.

"Doc, not in front of Lily." Using her name was the only way to stop him. "Besides, it might be best if we work together to find the man actually at fault for all of this."

Garcia spat blood into a tissue from his pocket. "Why in the hell would I work with you?"

"Because I'm guessing after hearing about your wife, we both want the same thing. And if we don't work together, we'll wonder if the other has a lead we need. Those moments could cost us precious time, and you know it." The result would be the same, except it would be my bullet to kill Knox.

"All I want is my daughter. Then we can make a deal." He spat again. "Cardosa, when you have a woman you love taken from you only to find out she's dead, you can act like an asshole. Right now, I just want to bring my daughter home."

There was no way I would allow this man to take Lily from me. "Except, if you take her, wouldn't that be what you're doing? I'm sorry Rachael's dead, but I refuse to have the woman I love snatched from me. I don't care if you're her father. Besides, I have a feeling you're behind their kidnapping. If you loved her so damn much, why'd you sell her to the lowest bidder?"

"You love me?" Lily's question was quiet, meant for just me, but I wasn't about to let her go unanswered.

"Lily, you're like the air I breathe. I couldn't live in a world without you. I know it's sudden and possibly too fast, but screw the world and its bullshit time frames. I love you."

Her face lit up, and a soft smile lifted her lips. "I love you too. It was weird because I thought it was just me, but I can't deny what I feel."

Holy shit, she loved me back. As soon as Garcia left, I would take this woman, *my woman*, back upstairs and show her how much I loved her.

"Enough," Garcia scoffed. "For fuck's sake, Cardosa. Your old man would be rolling in his grave if he knew you loved my daughter."

I chuckled. "I thought you were friends. I'd think he would be pleased to have Ramirez blood in our family."

"Hell no. Your father was a pain in my ass. He was always trying to tell me how to run my business." He continued to hold his bleeding nose with a kerchief. "Hell, I guess I should have listened to some of what he said. Maybe Rachael would still be alive."

Well, that was news. My father always told me they were friends. "My father didn't have a lot of good advice; not sure you could have saved yourself any grief."

"Fuck." He wiped his nose and glared at me. "If I would have listened to him, I wouldn't have made a deal with Angel. In the end, I couldn't come through on my end of the bargain, and he wanted my wife and daughter in return. You see? I had to fucking hide them."

I stepped forward, my arms flinging out. "So you gave them over to Knox? You let them be held like prisoners for years, enduring abuse, all while your wife was being used as a sex slave. That was better than dealing with Angel?"

His eyes widened. "What? No!" He looked at Lily, his body shaking. "I didn't. I couldn't. You have to believe me. You were supposed to be far away from here, in some nice hotel or some shit. Knox was supposed to be taking care of you. I paid him every month, more than enough for you to live like queens. I just told him I didn't want to know where you were, so Angel couldn't get through me to find you." Sweat broke out over his forehead. "I swear. Lily, I didn't. I'm so sorry."

I glared at him. "Yeah, well, your promises don't mean much. You sold your family to a monster to hide them from a beast. Either way, you're a fucking coward. The first rule of the family is you never sell them out. You protect the family at all costs."

The hatred Garcia had for Knox raged like fire in his eyes. "I thought I was protecting them!"

"So, all those times Knox left, it was to get money from you?" Lily questioned.

"What do you mean when he left?" I asked, intrigued.

Lily shrugged. "Well, he would leave for a day or two, then come back. He said he was doing a job for you, but we know that was a lie. It had to be when he met with my dad."

I faced Garcia. "How did you two meet every month?"

Garcia folded his arms and glared at me. "He would call me about once a month, letting me know where to meet, and then hang up. He stopped about six months ago. Haven't heard a thing until Knox called me last night to tell me you had Lily."

"So, he had to have enough reception to call you. There wasn't any, at least not around the cabin he'd been hiding in." I just had to think. He obviously wouldn't want to get close enough to me. Nash and Smokey knew about the codes for the inside security as well as the outside security, helping him sneak on and off the property. Still, after Lily was brought here, I had them changed, and only Diesel and I knew the new codes. That meant Knox had to still be here. "Shit. He's here."

I pulled the map of the Cardosa property down from the wall and laid it on the desk, frame and all. "Diesel, help me mark all the places where reception is the best."

He uncocked his gun but kept it in his hand. Using the barrel, he tapped on the glass. "Echo Mountain is pretty good, but you have to be on the third peak. And right here, if you're on the high ridge, here and here." He studied the map with me.

I grabbed a marker from the drawer and began marking all the places for us to check. Looking at the map, I couldn't resist looking at the spot where the cabin was. It was the only place that wasn't fully surveyed on the map. Damn it. I couldn't help but think my father had a reason for having the cabin built. I hated thinking he could have used it to smuggle other women.

"Up there, towards Flank, might be a good spot. Jax has gotten a few calls up through there. And here." He pointed east of the cabin, about a day's walk from there.

"Alright, come take a picture, and we can saddle some horses and get out there. Garcia, you and your men can start here at Echo Mountain and work your way up there to Flank. We'll start here and work our way to you."

Garcia stared at the map. "We can take a truck up here and walk the rest of the way. I ain't riding some damn horse."

Diesel chuckled. "There aren't any roads, and the terrain is thick with trees. It's best if you ride. A truck will just get stuck, and then we'll have to rescue your ass."

Garcia grumbled about not being a cowboy. "Fine. Get me a damn horse, so I can kill this motherfucker."

Flapjack still held his gun, ready to fire. "I'll stay with Lily."

"Like hell," Garcia spit out. "We don't know where this son of a bitch is. I'm not leaving her to just one guard. Max, Kennan, you two will stay too. Nothing happens to her."

Well, at least we finally agreed on one thing. "Nothing will happen because she's coming with me."

"Cardosa, you can't be serious. Don't you think she's been through enough?" Garcia cursed and wiped at his face.

"Yes, which is why I promised to protect her." I sure as hell wasn't going to leave her with raping mongrels as her security detail. I could protect her better if she were with me.

"I would go crazy waiting here. Carter can come with us. If it gets too bad, he can stay with me." Lily had her own plea in her words, and for whatever reason, she and Flapjack had become good friends. I didn't for one-second doubt that he wouldn't die for her.

"It's settled. Lily goes." I wasn't going to debate this with Garcia. She was with me and what we chose to do had nothing to do with him. "Bear, go tell the boys to get saddled. Leave the second crew here to watch the place, but you, Jax, Diesel, Doc, and Flapjack can come with me."

"Alright, boss. Give us fifteen minutes. We'll have to grab some horses from the lower field for Ramirez's men." Bear headed out, leaving us to wrap up the details.

Lily grabbed my hand. "Thank you for letting me come."

I pulled her in, wrapped my arms around her, and kissed the top of her head. "I told you I won't leave you."

Garcia watched with disdain as I held his daughter. Well, he was going to have to get over it because I wasn't ever letting her go.

# Chapter 23

## *Lily*

The hillside was going from sagebrush to juniper trees, and each horse fell in a long line of cowboys as they followed us up. Sitting in front of Jacob on his horse was rousing. The way he held me as we rode kept me pressed up against him.

He leaned forward to whisper in my ear. "If we were alone, I'd be stripping off all your clothes right now. The way your ass is rubbing against me has me so hard for you."

I could feel my cheeks warm as they turned bright red. It was amazing how his words could build such a fire inside me.

"The next time we're alone, I'm going to finish what we started this morning."

My entire body reacted to his promise, and I pushed back to be closer to him.

"Honey, you do that, and I'm gonna have to take you right here on the horse." He pulled back on the reins, slowing down to hang in the back of the group. No one seemed to notice as we trailed behind them.

"Jacob, what are you doing?" I squeaked as he unbuttoned my jeans and pulled the zipper down. "The guys are right there." They were way ahead of us, but someone was bound to notice we weren't with them.

His voice deepened as he kissed my neck. "I already told Diesel to keep them moving if we fall behind."

"So they'll know we're doing something." I could feel the blush creeping back up my face.

"Honey, I don't care who knows. I want you. Right here." He slipped his hand down my jeans, and his finger slid farther, rubbing the sensitive part lightly. His groan mixed with mine. "You are so wet."

In one motion, he picked me up and turned me around, so I straddled him. I winced slightly, my stomach was still sore, but I quickly forgot any sense of pain as I felt his manhood growing harder under his jeans.

The horse kept walking as Jacob's hands left the reins to entangle them in my hair, pulling me down for a kiss. Sage and leather mixed with his fresh scent in a euphoric blend.

My heartbeat pounded wildly in my ears, drowning out everything but Jacob's breathing and slight groans. His tongue darted into my mouth. The sweet taste of peppermint cooled my lips as he ran his tongue over them slowly.

I wrapped my arms around his neck and gently pulled myself closer, rubbing over his manhood in the process. His moan had me squirming to do it again. Bravely, I ran my hands down his chest, loving how his muscles moved with the sway of the horse. He was so in tune that his body held pace with the animal.

I found the button of his jeans and popped it open, tugging the zipper down. I remembered how he felt in my hands before and needed to feel him again.

I looked over my shoulder to ensure the others were still ahead of us and froze when I didn't see any of them. Jacob turned my head to face him. "All that matters is us. Don't worry. Lady is mated with the stallion Doc is riding. She will follow him anywhere."

"Kind of like how I'd follow you anywhere." I slipped my hand into his jeans and found him hard. He leaned back, allowing me to pull him out of his jeans. I slid my hand up and down his dick. It amazed me how silky it was and how tiny drops spilled out of him as I squeezed just a little while I ran down his length.

I wanted to do it until he spilled out like the first time we touched. My body ached to do that to him. The more I wanted it, the faster I went. He groaned and lifted his hips slightly toward me.

"Don't stop."

I didn't. I couldn't. I wanted to make him feel like he made me feel. I needed him to know I was a woman capable of giving him pleasure.

His length pulsed, and he spilled out. "Fuck," he moaned. My hand was covered in his cum, but I didn't care. I had made him feel good.

Being the one to do that had my panties soaked in excitement.

He picked me up and turned me back around, pressing me to his still throbbing manhood. His hand went down my jeans and began stroking me.

"You're so fucking wet. Lily, cum for me."

Low in my belly, I could feel the need to explode grow, ready to erupt in passion. His finger caressed me one last time, and I cried out. There was nothing that mattered at that moment except for Jacob. Not even air was necessary. I couldn't breathe anyway.

Pulling out a rag from his saddlebag, he handed it to me to clean up.

The horse was still ambling along and didn't seem to mind that her riders were utterly lost in ecstasy. Jacob zipped up his jeans, so I did the same before he grabbed the reins. He wrapped his arm around me, kicking the horse to a canter, weaving our way through the trees. It didn't take long before we caught up to the others.

It was hard not to blush when we again rode to the front of the line. No one looked at me differently, but it was embarrassing.

"Jacob, they know," I whispered.

"Honey, all they're thinking is what a lucky son of a bitch I am." He took his hat and plopped it on my head. "Here, now they can't see you. Besides, if anyone ever says something disrespectful to you, they have to deal with me." He playfully groaned. "Except, seeing you in my hat makes me want to do it again."

I laughed. "Jacob, stop teasing me."

"I'm not teasing. You're sexy as hell in that thing."

Diesel rode up, saving me from Jacob's teasing. "Boss, I saw a few tracks I want to check out."

Jacob held me tighter, and his playful attitude vanished. "You head up. We'll tail you."

Diesel took off, and Jacob twisted in the saddle. "You know the routine. We'll stay close behind him and wait for his signal. Stay sharp, men."

My mouth went dry, fearing the worst. "Jacob, what happens if we find Knox? I mean, what's the plan? I don't know the routine."

"If we find him, you'll ride with Flapjack until you're a safe distance away. He'll protect you until I can get to you." He kissed the back of my head.

"What if…" I couldn't bring myself to say the words. I hated how Knox brought out this kind of fear. "What if… What if you don't find me?" It wasn't what I meant, but I wasn't going to say what I really wanted. Just saying the words aloud seemed to give them power, and I wasn't about to let that happen.

"Honey, I promise that I will find you, always."

Tears filled my eyes, so I blinked them back, sucking in the fresh air. "One of these days, you might have to break a promise."

He nestled into my neck. "When that day comes, I'll let you know beforehand. But today isn't that day."

Up ahead, Diesel was coming back to us in a run. My heart dropped. This was it. Knox was here.

# Chapter 24

## *Jacob*

Damn it. Seeing Diesel riding hard, I braced myself to fling Lily over to Flapjack and start shooting.

Diesel rode up to us, handing over a piece of paper. "He was here, boss. And he left this for you."

Taking the paper, I didn't want Lily to read it, but there wasn't any way around her seeing Knox's scrawled writing.

*Cardosa,*

*By now you know you have Garcia's daughter, and I assume Garcia knows. It also means he knows about his wife. So let's play a game. You have twenty-four hours to kill Garcia. If you fail, I'll kill the girl. But not before I fuck her while she screams for you to save her. I bet she's tighter than her whoring mother. I can't wait. The clock is ticking.*

*-K*

Lily gasped and turned her head away from the note. I crumpled it tightly in my fist. "That son of a bitch!"

Well, I had news for Knox. I didn't play games. Especially when it came to Lily.

Diesel nodded over my shoulder. "His tracks lead back to the main houses. I'm gonna follow him."

I nodded. "Just watch your back, and make sure you shoot first."

"Hell yeah. I ain't about to die by some pussy assed cocksucker." He glanced at Lily. "Sorry, I shouldn't talk like that in front of you. I can have a mouth worse than a fucking sailor. Shit. See?"

Lily laughed. "You're right, though. Knox is a pussy assed cocksucker, and I hope you kill him."

Diesel and I both laughed, and I held her a little closer. "Don't worry, honey. He's gonna die soon."

"Damn straight." Diesel tipped his hat to Lily and spurred his horse into a run.

Now I had to make a decision, one that I wasn't happy about. I turned Lady to face the others. "Alright, we'll head to Flank and meet up with Garcia."

"Are you going to kill Garcia?" Lily asked softly.

"No. Not today." We started heading west toward Garcia. Flank wasn't really a place. It was just a watering hole we used when moving cattle, but he should be there about midnight, so we had to get moving.

Lily's head hung as Lady's gait lulled her to sleep. She shivered, and I wrapped my arm around her tighter. The sun had gone down about two hours ago, and the fall night air crept up faster on the mountainside than in the valley.

I put the reins in my other hand and reached behind me to pull out the small blanket tied to my saddle, wrapping it around her shoulders. She leaned back, resting her head against my shoulder.

She was so fragile in my arms. How I'd come to love her in such a short time still amazed me, but I wasn't going to question fate.

Scanning the darkness, I searched for anything unusual. Occasionally, a coyote yipped, and a rabbit would scurry away from us, but nothing I didn't expect. With Knox still out there, I needed to stay vigilant. I couldn't let myself become careless. Lily depended on me to protect her.

Lady tensed and sidestepped, alerting me to potential danger. She and I had ridden together long enough to read each other. Something out there spooked her. Or someone.

I stopped her and held my hand up for the others. After ten years, we were a well-oiled machine, knowing how each other would move and react. Without a doubt, I knew Bear would be behind me, Doc flanking him, and Jax would hang back, guarding the rear of our group. Diesel would typically take off to investigate ahead, letting us know what we were heading into, but he wasn't here.

Flapjack crept up to Lady. "I can slip ahead and scout."

Lily stirred and looked around but said nothing. I wasn't sure if instinct or fear held her tongue, but until I knew what was out there, I was glad.

I pondered Flapjack's request, debating if I should be the one to scout or not. We were close enough to the watering hole, it could just be Garcia, but I wasn't willing to take the chance. Especially with Knox's threat to harm Lily still crumpled on a paper in my jacket pocket.

"Jacob, it hasn't been that long since we worked a hunt together. I can do more than cook, and you know it."

Hell, I did know. For years he was a part of our tight posse. "Alright."

He wasted no time turning away, fading into the darkness. I strained to see him but couldn't even make out his outline under the moonlight. Damn, he really was good at this.

"Will Carter be okay?" Lily whispered.

It was strange hearing his given name. Still keeping an eye out, I leaned in to speak softly in her ear. "Yeah, don't worry, honey. We've done this before."

"How many times?"

"I've lost count." I couldn't even try to give her an answer. The only difference was this time, it was on my own property, and the girl I was saving was mine.

Lady pawed at the ground and inhaled quickly, only to blow out a puff of breath, letting me know she was getting anxious to move, either toward danger or away from it. I reached over Lily and rubbed Lady's neck. "Shhh, girl. Almost." I knew she wouldn't budge until I told her to. A man couldn't ask for a better horse.

A slight movement flittered in my peripheral. I snapped my attention to search the dark ground. Flapjack was nearly next to me before I saw him. "It's just Garcia and his men."

That was a relief. "Did you tell them we were coming?"

He chuckled. "Hell nah, they didn't even see me."

I smiled, knowing how close Flapjack could get to someone without being seen. "Well, let's go let him know we're here."

Together we all rode toward Garcia.

A small fire flickered, and Garcia and his men looked out of place, sitting around it with their black suits. I was actually surprised any of them could start a fire.

A small trickle of water babbled as it fed the pool of water. The moon reflected on its still surface.

"Who's there?" Garcia stood from his perch atop a cut log, drawing his gun.

"Just me. Put your gun away before you hurt someone." I drew Lady up short, waiting for him to lower his Glock. No way was I going to get Lily closer with a live weapon being waved around.

"Cardosa, what the hell?"

I dismounted and reached up to help Lily down. Garcia watched me with his daughter and grimaced.

Keeping my hand on the small of her back, needing to touch her, I led her to the fire so she could stay warm. I pulled out the note from Knox and held it out for Garcia. "We found this. I think you should read it."

Garcia took the crumpled paper and smoothed it out to read, only to return it to its former state before tossing it in the fire. "That son of a bitch! He has the nerve to not only threaten my daughter but me?"

The next thing I had to do killed me, but I couldn't think of any other way. I had a whole afternoon trying to devise a different plan, but nothing where I thought Lily would be safe enough. "Garcia, I need you to keep Lily."

"What!" Lily whirled around. Her eyes widened but not in fear. The wild rage burned in her beautiful blue irises.

Garcia sneered. "I knew you couldn't protect her."

I spun to face him, grabbing his shirt and pulling my Glock up under his chin, digging into his flesh before he could gasp for air. "Don't you ever fucking underestimate me. *This* is me protecting her. Don't forget, you're alive right now because I'm allowing you to live."

The click of guns echoed around me, but I wasn't afraid. I knew his men wouldn't have the draw on mine, and the sound I heard was Bear and Doc covering my back.

Garcia glared over his crooked nose. "Fuck you."

Lenny, one of Garcia's men, moved to grab me, but the barrel of Doc's gun found his temple before he could touch me. Doc grinned. "You're pretty stupid."

"You made your point, Cardosa. What the fuck do you want from me?"

I let him go and holstered my gun. "You will take Lily back with you while I hunt Knox down. We can't take her with us."

Lily touched my arm, the blanket falling from her shoulders. "Jacob, just let him go after Knox. I don't want to leave you. I can't go with him."

Looking down into her eyes, I searched for understanding. Couldn't she see this killed me? I wanted to be the one with her. I didn't want to send her with Garcia for protection. There just wasn't another way to keep her safe and make sure Knox died. "Honey, this is what I do. Your father's men are no match to mine. As soon as Knox is dead, you can come home. I promise. I'll be there to get you before you even know I'm gone." I pushed a tuft of hair back behind her ear. "And nothing will happen to you." I glared at Garcia. Every threat possible flashed through my eyes. "Isn't that right."

Garcia glowered. "Don't fucking patronize me. She's my daughter. Nothing will happen to her."

I thrust a finger to his chest. "That's right, or I will hunt *you* next."

# Chapter 25

## *Lily*

I couldn't believe Jacob was going to leave me with Garcia. Maybe I could get him to change his mind before we got back to the house. He had promised I wouldn't have to go with him, but now he was determined that this was the only way for him to go after Knox. I was scared that without me, something would happen to Jacob. Or what if Garcia did something to keep Jacob from returning to me.

We rode harder than earlier, and my legs and stomach ached badly. I wasn't used to riding a horse, and my body hated me for it. I wasn't sure I'd be able to walk when we finally got to dismount.

The house loomed ahead. I hated seeing it because that meant I would soon be cast off to Garcia.

Jacob slowed, letting the others go on ahead. Except for Garcia, who held back with us. Jacob nodded toward the house. "They'll sweep the area before I bring Lily in."

"I think we should stay here. Why can't he just stay at the ranch with me?" Maybe I could get him to let me at least stay here. If I were at least in his house, I would feel closer to him.

"No, I don't want you anywhere close to here without me knowing where Knox is. It will be better if you go with Garcia. His place is heavily guarded." Jacob's arm tightened around me, and he leaned in close to whisper. "I don't want to be away from you any longer than I need. Trust me when I say I will be hurrying back to you."

I nodded but said nothing. There wasn't anything I could say that would change his mind.

He reined the horse to a stop and jumped down before reaching up to help me.

"We'll get her packed so you can get her out of here." Jacob led me to the house, and I wanted to cry.

I followed him blindly as tears blurred my vision. My legs could barely get me up the stairs, but I didn't care. I'd take the pain of riding that damn horse all over again if it meant I could stay with Jacob. I'd stab myself all over again if it would change anything.

I went to my room while Jacob left to grab a bag for my things. He lifted it up for me to see before unzipping it on the bed. "You can use mine. I won't need it this time. I won't be gone long enough." He tried to give me a smile but faltered. "I don't like this any more than you, Lily, but I promised to keep you safe."

Reaching out, I touched his shoulder. "I know. I hate it and wish I could talk you out of it, but I think I understand. Besides, Knox probably won't think I went back with Garcia."

He wrapped an arm around me and pulled me to him, lowering his forehead to mine. "I don't know how my heart fell for you so quickly, but damn it, I love you. I couldn't live with myself if something happened to you. I need you to go with Garcia to know you're safe while I'm gone."

Being that close to him was intoxicating. I clutched his shirt tightly and held on to him for all that moment was worth. "I'll go."

He held me closer, his heat radiating through my layers of clothes. "I love you. But when I get back, if you realize this was some infatuation with me, that you really don't want me, I'll understand. I'll hate it, but I'll leave you alone and let you live your life. As long as you're happy and safe, that's all I want."

My heart dropped to my stomach and rolled over. How could he even say that? "Jacob, no, you have to come back. I love you. I know it's too soon and probably under the wrong circumstances how we met, but it doesn't change the way I feel about you. Please don't leave me."

I looked up as his lips crashed down on mine, claiming my soul. He wasn't just kissing me. He was declaring his love, letting every single cell in my body know I was his. He was demanding and pleading, pressing himself against me. His lips urged mine to open, letting his tongue slip past to dance with mine. Faster, his lips seemed to crave more, pressing harder, crushing down on me.

His hand wound its way through my hair, holding the back of my head while he held me close with the other.

I held on, fearing I would fall with my already shaky legs that no longer wanted to support me. His touch left me weak and dizzy.

All too soon, he pulled back, his eyes closed. His heavy breathing was rapid and matched pace with mine.

"I'm expecting a kiss like that when you return," I whispered with a slight rasp, still unable to use my full voice. He had a way of stealing things like my voice. Not that I would complain. And not that I didn't give it freely.

"I'm gonna do a lot more than kiss you when I return," he said, his voice deeper. The way his voice turned rough when we kissed made the fire in me burn harder.

I blushed and playfully pushed off him. "I'm going to hold you to that, Mr. Cardosa."

I turned toward the dresser, needing to find space between us, before I ripped off his clothes. Pulling out undergarments, I packed them in the bag while Jacob took clothes from the closet and placed them in the bag. We worked silently until everything was packed.

He picked up the bag and slung the strap over his shoulder. "Let's get this over with. The sooner I kill Knox, the sooner I can get you back here. There isn't a room in this house I don't want to utilize."

I giggled. I could only imagine the ways he wanted to *utilize* them.

Downstairs, Garcia and two of his men waited for us. "We're loaded and ready to go."

Carter stood by the door, fidgeting, clenching and unclenching his fist. He stepped forward and stopped Jacob, leaning in to speak quietly. "Boss, maybe I should go with them. Help watch over Lily?"

Jacob placed a hand on Carter's shoulder. "I appreciate you wanting to protect her, but we need you."

Carter looked at me and nodded. There was no way he would argue with Jacob. That was one of the first things I learned about the men under Jacob.

I was so fond of Carter and the friendship we had started. It was humbling to know he wanted to go with me. "Carter, I'll be okay. When I get back, we can cook that rabbit. Don't think I've forgotten. You're not off the hook."

He laughed. "I don't think you know what you're in for."

Jacob led me outside to the black vehicles. Doc was there beside the back door like a guard. He opened the door for me, but I hesitated. I'd gone from imprisoned to near death to here in less than a month. My uncertainty begged me to evaluate every move I made. But I was *here*. And I was *alive*.

In a heartbeat, I understood more about living than I had my entire life, and I wasn't about to give up. Jacob's hand at the small of my back reaffirmed my confidence. I turned to him and stretched up on my toes, kissing him before ducking into the backseat.

Garcia slid in beside me. The door shut with Jacob's gaze never wavering from me outside the tinted windows. He couldn't see me anymore, but his eyes never strayed from mine until the car pulled away.

"Lily," Garcia said, tugging at his black suit jacket. It was covered in dirt from last night's ride on horseback. "I'm glad you're here. I've missed you so much. And your mother," he choked but recovered quickly. "Your mother meant the world to me. I promise we'll avenge her death."

I snapped my head to stare at him. "Avenge her? You had us kidnapped and hidden for five years. You shouldn't have to avenge her because she'd still be here if it wasn't for you."

Garcia's face turned hard, and he glowered. "Don't you think I hated what I did? It was what I thought was best. I lost both of you five years ago. Hell yes, she should be here with us right now, but she's not. All I have left of her is you, and damn straight, I'm gonna do everything in my power to keep you safe.

And nothing will stop me from avenging her death." He turned to glare out the window.

I didn't care if he was mad at me or the situation. "Let me ask you one thing."

His glare softened as he turned back to me. "Anything."

"Was that deal you made with Angel worth it?" I'd hate to discover that the deal that went south wasn't worth sacrificing family for.

He cast his gaze to the side. "If you had asked me then, I would have said yes. But after paying the consequences, I can assure you, no deal was worth losing you or your mother." Garcia reached out for my hand, and I didn't pull away. "I am truly sorry." A bitter snicker replaced the small tear in the corner of his eye. "In the end, I ended right back up in the same spot, but without my wife. When Angel finds out you're alive, he will come for you."

"Well, we'll cross that bridge when we get to it. I'm sure Jacob can help."

Garcia chuckled. "I'm just not sure what could help anymore. I'm a broken old man."

I could understand. If Jacob never returned for me, I'd spend forever broken too. I studied the man on the seat next to me, wondering how much of him I had gotten.

My mousy brown hair was definitely his, and his nose was almost a perfect match to mine. Still, more than that, I think his rancorous attitude was genetic. Where my mother was only strong when it came to protecting me, she had been weakened by the years of abuse, and this man let the years harden his heart, making him stronger. I felt that, and while I had a moment of weakness when I tried to kill myself, it actually empowered me. I felt like I had a say over what happened to me.

I stared out the window. Suddenly, I knew where I wanted to go. "Garcia, how far is Lovers Creek from here?"

A slight grin lifted his eyes. "How do you know about that place?"

"Mom used to tell me about it. She said it was her favorite place, and I'd like to see it sometime."

"That was our place. She named it Lovers Creek, but it's just a small piece of Lamoille Creek we used to sneak off to." He sat up straighter and smiled. "I'm pretty sure that's where you were conceived."

I grimaced. "I didn't need to know that."

He chuckled. "Cardosa's ranch is a bit farther north. But, when we get home, I'll have to take you. We don't live very far from there."

I hated how he said *we*. I wasn't moving back in with him. His house was not mine anymore. Jacob would be coming back for me.

The road wound through a canyon past a lake, then twisted left and right as we climbed a summit. It was hard to focus on something long enough to not get dizzy. The tall trees had long ago faded into sagebrush and dirt. But there was a rugged beauty about it.

Garcia's men rode in the trucks in front and behind us, guarding us even on the road. It was strange remembering what kind of world I was born into, but I was beginning to think it wasn't as normal as it seemed when I was a child. No one we passed seemed to have an escort of armed men protecting them.

I leaned against the glass, wondering how Jacob was doing. With me gone, I questioned if he realized he didn't love me and would just leave me with Garcia. There was no reason for a man like him to love some broken woman like me. It made no sense. My heart pinged at the thought, cracking as though the idea of Jacob never coming back would literally cause it to shatter.

The sway of the truck mixed with the lull of the tires on the road had my eyes closing. But I welcomed sleep. I could be with Jacob in my dreams.

# Chapter 26

## *Jacob*

Watching Lily drive away with Garcia was like having a piece of my heart ripped out of my chest. There was no time to waste wallowing in my selfish desire to be with her. I hated that I had to go back on my word that she wouldn't have to go with him. It killed me to do it, but Knox would come after me to get to her, so she had to leave. It was the only way I saw it until Knox was dead.

Diesel waited for me on the porch, following me inside. "He was here, boss."

Stopping at the bottom of the stairs, I turned to face him. "What the hell do you mean?"

Knowing Knox was here, close to my house, the place I needed to be safe for Lily, had my blood boiling.

"His tracks led right to the house, but I haven't seen him. I can't find another trail either."

Damn it. "Keep looking." Taking the steps two at a time, I rushed upstairs.

Passing Lily's room grew the emptiness in my heart. She was gone. But she was safe.

I snatched my cell phone off the nightstand beside my bed, shoving it in my pocket. Pulling out a small bag from the closet, I grabbed a few essentials. My passport leered at me from the bottom drawer, so I thrust it into the zippered lining of the bag just in case.

I had no idea where this asshole was, but I was willing to scour the entire earth to find him.

Now I just needed a lead to know where to start looking.

"Boss! Get down here!" Diesel hollered.

Flinging the bag over my shoulder, I made my way down the stairs to everyone running toward my office. "What the hell is going on?"

Doc came out before I could enter, his face white, and he looked right through me. I pushed past him and froze at the entrance.

Lenny, one of Garcia's right-hand men, was strapped to my chair. His face was bloated and bloodied. It was obvious he died a slow death. But it was the note pinned to his chest that enraged me.

*You're too late. Time is up.*

"Mother fucker!" I ripped the paper off him. Seeing red, I gripped it tight in my fist, rereading the words over and over.

"Boss," Diesel said, but he couldn't be talking to me. I wasn't there. I was in hell. "Jacob!"

He took the paper from me and flung it to Jax. "Get everyone ready. No one stays home this time."

For the first time, I had no idea what I would do. I had saved hundreds of girls, but none of them were mine.

"Boss," Diesel tried again, snapping his fingers. This time, it worked.

"He's got her." I clenched my jaw, and my body tensed. The fucking bastard had Lily.

I couldn't wrap my brain around it. I had sent her off with Garcia. I was there. I put her in the car. How did this happen?

"Jacob, you know how precious time is right now. We'll find her, but you need to pull yourself together."

He was right. I wasn't some pussy who clammed up at the first sign of danger. It was like a nerve snapped, and every tentative thought disappeared. I wasn't going to let that bastard have Lily. Screw him. "If he fucking touches her, I will kill him slowly."

Diesel had a wicked grin. "She must be something special."

I gave a terse nod. "She is."

We strode out to the waiting trucks and jumped in. Doc was in the back seat of my vehicle, and Flapjack drove. The other truck had Diesel, Jax, and Bear. The remaining men would follow us in the last truck.

Flapjack flew down the dirt road, flinging rocks yards behind us. Dust billowed in a thick cloud as the tires sped over the long stretch leading away from the ranch.

I shifted so I could pull out the cell phone and dialed Rodriguez. There weren't enough bars to connect. Damn it. I tapped the phone on my knee.

"She's gonna be fine, Jacob. She has to be. I can't do this again." Doc's face was still ashen, but an angry scowl replaced the faraway disconnected look he had earlier.

"She'll be fine." Even as I said the words, I didn't know if I believed myself. But there was no way I could listen to that because I would go crazy if something happened to her. And I needed to remain levelheaded to protect her.

"I should've gone with her." Flapjack hit the steering wheel. "Damn it."

"You listened to an order. You are here because I told you to stay. Now you have a chance to help me save her."

"Yeah, but if I were there, maybe…" he trailed, not saying what we all were thinking.

"Shut the fuck up. Don't go there." I was already kicking myself in the ass for putting her in that truck. I didn't need Flapjack rubbing salt in my wound.

I refreshed the phone screen, again and again, waiting for the bars to return. Damn remote Nevada wilderness.

Finally, three bars resurfaced. Enough for a call, I hoped. I redialed Rodriguez, and this time it connected.

He picked up. "I'm in the middle of something, this better be a life-or-death call."

I clenched the phone tighter as each word spilled out of my mouth. "It is. That mother fucker Knox has Lily."

"Oh shit, Jacob, I'm sorry. What can I do?"

Well, at least I finally had his attention. "You're closer. I need some men to head up to Garcia's. That's where she was headed. I think he's waiting for her there if he doesn't already have her. I'm on my way."

"I got a guy I can send, but he isn't blue. What do you want?"

"Fuck the blue right now. This bastard is gonna die. I don't care who you send. Just don't send blue." Sending a cop right now would make things harder on my end. I didn't mind paying them off, but I didn't want to deal with that shit right now.

"I'll call when he gets there."

I hung up. It would be two hours before we got to Garcia's, even at this speed. What if the note was right and I was too late? I hit the dash. "We need to go faster."

"My foot can't go any farther unless it goes through the floor, boss."

Damn it. *Lily, I'm so sorry.* I only wished she could hear me. But I'll be there soon. *Just hang on, honey. I'm coming.*

# Chapter 27

## Lily

My childhood home was a lot bigger than Jacob's ranch house. It wasn't hidden in the trees but had a fantastic view of the rugged mountains overlooking the valley. Security gates armed the entrance like a fortress.

The driver leaned forward and buzzed us through. "Where the hell is Hoover and Dean? They're supposed to be out front."

"Is everything okay?" I asked, my always-present anxiety leaking through.

"Yes, we have a couple of men who obviously need to be *talked* to."

I didn't think he actually meant talk. I'm sure there was something worse than being yelled at for missing their guard duty, but I let it go. Even as a child, my father never divulged much regarding his business.

The two other trucks pulled around back while ours parked out front. Garcia got out and waited for me to join him. "Where the hell is Lenny? Tell him I need to speak with him."

Our driver nodded and took off to park the truck. Garcia gestured for me to go ahead of him up the stairs. The front door was actually two doors with frosted glass windows. The whitewashed brick home was massive and loomed over me like a castle. When I was little, I used to think I was a princess. Now I knew better.

I pushed open the door and stepped inside. Cameras dotted the corners, and little red lights blinked as they recorded our entrance. That was new. I didn't remember those as a kid. It was a little creepy, but I supposed my father needed them. I still wasn't sure what he did, but I had the feeling it was definitely illegal.

Garcia closed the door. "I've waited a long time to bring you home."

I tried to smile, but it didn't feel like home anymore. Jacob's house felt like home.

"And I've waited a long time for you both to come home."

I froze. I knew that voice. Bile rose, burning my throat.

Garcia drew his gun, but Knox already squeezed the trigger on his pistol, his bullet hitting Garcia in the chest. "Dad!" I screamed, more out of gut reaction than fear.

I turned to open the door and run, but Knox grabbed me around the waist and wrapped a hand over my mouth. "I don't think so. You're coming with me." He yanked me away from the entrance just as two men rushed in, their guns drawn. They didn't see me being pulled away, but they saw Garcia and started yelling for help.

I screamed into Knox's palm and then bit down, drawing blood. I used my feet to stomp on his and scratched at his face behind me, anything I could to get away.

"You bitch!" He hit me over the back of the head with the butt of his gun.

It's funny. As the world went black, I smiled, thinking about how Jacob would react if Knox killed me. The last thing I saw was Garcia shakily raising his gun and pulling the trigger.

# Chapter 28

## *Jacob*

Flapjack drove the truck like a rally car, maneuvering around the dirt corners leading to Garcia Ramirez's house without letting up on the accelerator. I hung on to the oh shit handle, letting him peel down the road without complaint.

All I could do was hope Lily was okay. I wasn't there to protect her, and now I had no idea if she was even alive. The note we found on Lenny's dead body was meant to rile me, but it did more than that. Lily was mine, and Knox took her. He made a mistake and would pay gravely, and if she's harmed in any way, I will take my time ending his life, quickly would be too easy for a bastard like that.

The entrance to Garcia's property was gated, but it was wide open, awaiting our arrival. Medical units and police cars were parked just outside the house, with their lights blindingly revolving between blue and red.

I didn't wait for the truck to stop entirely as Flapjack slammed on the brakes. "Lily!" I ran for the house, my heart slamming against my chest, preparing for the worst.

"You can't go in there." An officer placed his arm out, trying to stop me from entering the house.

"Like hell, I can't." I pushed past him, not waiting to explain why or how I was above him. "Lily!"

Just inside the entrance, paramedics were loading Garcia onto a gurney. His face was white, his body limp, but he was alive.

"Cardosa," he whispered gruffly. "Stop moving me, you damn heathens. Let me talk." He barked at the EMTs.

135

He was belted to the gurney, and they lifted him up, ignoring his demands. I made my way to him, disregarding the medical crew's complaints. They could go to hell. All I cared about was Lily. "Where's Lily?"

"The fucker shot me and took her. You go get my daughter and kill him." There was a mutual understanding between his intent stare and mine. It was confirmed. Knox had Lily.

The paramedics pushed me out of the way and took Garcia from the house. Rage I would use later on Knox, built like an inferno.

Rodriguez stepped through the entrance. His slender frame didn't do much to intimidate me. Hell, I doubted he could scare a mouse, but his badge was all I needed. I owned that badge as far as I was concerned. "What the hell happened? I told you to send some men!"

"I did," he replied calmly. "One of them is following Knox right now." He handed me a burner phone and walked away.

Only two numbers were programmed into the cell. Rodriguez's and another I didn't know. I hit call next to the number and waited before the other end picked up.

"Who the hell is this?" I demanded, walking around the foyer, looking for clues. The marble floor and vaulted ceilings were not out of the ordinary for men like Garcia. Even the cameras at every corner were expected.

"The man you're paying to keep tails on this woman of yours." He was confident, yet he lacked the maturity that usually came with this job. I hoped Rodriguez knew what he was doing when he sent a fucking boy to do a man's job.

"If I'm paying you, then you answer me. Who the hell are you?"

Bear and Diesel found me by the stairs. Diesel crouched down and pointed at a few drops of blood. My stomach rolled. I had no way of knowing if that was Lily's or not. My breath caught in my chest.

"Fox."

"Fox? Your name is Fox?" Fuck. I didn't have time for these games.

"You asked. Now you're gonna get all effed up over my name?"

"Effed up? For fuck's sake, kid, how old are you?" Damn it. I probably had some hormonal, barely old enough to drive boy running tail on the woman I loved.

"I'm nineteen, not that it matters to you. You want me to continue to follow them or not?"

"Yes!" I rubbed my face, trying to block out the entire situation with him being so young and focusing on what mattered. "Where are you? Do you know where he's taking her?"

"We're headed south. Looks like Vegas, my man."

Vegas. I could do Vegas. I had many friends there, and all I had to do was get there before Knox to intercept. "Okay, you keep tailing them. I'm gonna fly down there. Keep me informed with every move. If he changes course, you let me know."

"Yeah, yeah, I got it. Chill, brah, I know how to tail someone."

"For your sake, I hope so." I couldn't deal with this right now. I hung up and slipped the burner into my back pocket.

"Boss," Bear started, crouching next to Diesel, staring at the blood.

"Yeah, I know." I couldn't pretend that the blood didn't bother me because inside, I was franticly wondering if Lily was okay. Was it hers? Was it somehow Knox's? "I've got to call ahead and get the plane ready. It looks like he's taking her to Vegas."

Diesel frowned. "Jacob, the ring is down there."

"I know. Damn it!" I hit the wall with my fist and then braced myself against it, looking for support. "I know," I said a hell of a lot quieter. The words were for me, not them. Because I did know. I knew more than them.

The ring was notorious for having its meetings in Las Vegas. It was easy for them to get in and out without too many people noticing them or giving a shit if they were there. Too many girls had been sold to a ring member and carried out of Vegas. The idea of Knox trying to sell Lily to anyone in the sex trafficking world had me boiling.

Having the Cardosa name had its privileges, but having money attached to that name meant I had a lot more than just my name could give me. Owning a private jet on standby was a perk I was extremely thankful for today.

It didn't take more than one phone call to have the entire crew prepare the plane for takeoff. Garcia lived forty minutes from the small airport where my aircraft was parked.

Flapjack, Diesel, Bear, and Jax rode with me to the airport. I sent everyone back to the ranch, including Doc. Lately, I didn't have Flapjack with me, but I felt I would need his cunning abilities to sneak up on a man. He never hesitated when I told him he'd be going. His friendship with Lily had him brandishing his own sword of hate for Knox and willing to do whatever it took to get her back as well.

Doc didn't want to go home, but I told him it was best if Lily found a way home for one of us to be there. Not that either of us believed Knox would let her out of his sights for her to escape a second time.

Exiting Garcia's house, the ambulance was just leaving, the lights and siren blaring through the air. Rodriguez stood beside a patrol car talking animatedly.

"Rodriguez!" I said, jogging down the stairs to meet up with him.

"Now is not a good time, Cardosa." He turned back to the officer who had tried to stop me from entering the house earlier. "Listen, you don't get paid enough to open your trap about a case that's not yours. This is mine."

"What about him?" The officer gestured to me.

I almost laughed—almost. He had to be new to the force because no one else dared question me or my presence.

"Who's the newbie?" Irritated that my time was being wasted.

Rodriguez shifted his weight. His usually clean boots that hardly seen the outside of his office now had a layer of dirt on them. "Cardosa, this is Sammy Price. He just started last week, and I haven't been able to talk to him about you yet."

I didn't really give a shit who the officer was. I stared Rodriguez down, reminding him of who the boss was here. "Well, I suggest you get that talk over with because the woman I love has been kidnapped right out from under your fucking hands. That man you sent after her is nothing but a damn kid! What the hell, Rodriguez?"

Rodriguez stood taller, trying to keep his clout with the young officer. "Look, you said no blues. I only have a few guys in town I could call. London is actually pretty good at this."

I scoffed. "London? Hell, the kid told me his name was Fox. And how am I supposed to trust someone who hasn't even had their balls drop yet? It's like you have a fucking death wish."

"His name is London Fox. He's been in the system more than most juveniles, so I know what he's capable of, and utilizing his talents with a job like this is right up his alley. It's better than him wasting his abilities on some dumbass outside a bar."

I pushed a finger to his chest. "You better hope he doesn't lose her." My threat wasn't negotiable.

Flapjack drove the truck over to me, and I jumped in, leaving Rodriguez to explain how things were ran to his new man in blue.

Diesel clamped a hand down on my shoulder from the backseat. "Don't worry, boss. We'll find her."

I couldn't believe anything less. And once we found her, I was never letting her stray from my arms again.

# Chapter 29

## *Lily*

If Jacob didn't kill Knox, I would. The son of a bitch had me locked in the trunk of a car. The mix of gasoline and something rancid clung to the interior carpet, making my head split worse than when he hit me over the head with his gun.

The horrible thought that Jacob wouldn't come for me tried to sneak into my head, but I dismissed it immediately, not wanting to let myself drive down that depressive road. He promised me that he'd always find me. I had to cling to that hope.

A tight rope bound my wrists behind my back, and my shoulders ached in protest. The dirty gag in my mouth had me choking back vomit. I tried not to focus on the smell of the cloth, but the sour sweaty stench refused to give my senses a reprieve.

The back of my head had bled enough to leave streaks of blood down my neck and shirt. I couldn't touch it with my hands roped together, but I was sure there was a large lump. It hurt to lay back on it, leaving me to keep on my sides. Not that there was much room to move around in the trunk.

We sped down the road for what seemed like forever. The taillights came on, giving the small space a red glow. I had long ago tried to kick them out to draw attention to passing cars, but I couldn't get them to budge. I needed more momentum.

I couldn't kick them out, but maybe I could short the light itself out? I kicked the light again, harder and harder. After a few attempts, it flickered and went out. A small victory, but now I had to wiggle around to change position to get the other light. Moving was hard and painful. It took longer than I wanted, but finally, I faced the opposite light.

The car rolled to a stop, and I could hear a door slam shut. The trunk popped open, and I squinted under the brightness of an orange streetlight.

"What the hell do you think you're doing?" Knox asked, pulling me up by my hair.

The gag muffled my screams. Damn, that hurt!

"Apparently, I need to tie your legs too." He dropped me and began wrestling my legs.

I kicked at him and tried to jump out of the car, but without my arms, I just fell before I could leave the trunk.

He got me back down and began wrapping the new rope around my ankles. "You have more fight than your mom, that's for sure. I can't wait to have these legs wrapped around me. I should have fucked you when I had the chance. But now it will be better because I'll be taking Cardosa's woman." He chuckled as he slammed the trunk shut again.

I screamed again to no avail. No one could hear me. But it felt good to release something, anything. Damn, I really hated that man.

The car started rolling again. I could hear cars zoom by us, but no one knew I was locked in here. What an invisible world I lived in.

I wondered where Knox was taking me, but more importantly, I wondered how Jacob would find me. It wasn't like Diesel could track me like in the mountains.

Bound and gagged, I couldn't do much to escape, and I wasn't sure there would be a rescue mission, so I had to think of how I would survive. Without knowing if Jacob was even coming for me, I needed to rely on myself to get away from Knox. I've done it before. I could do it again.

My stomach ached, reminding me of how my last escape went. But I refused to go down that path unless there was no other way. I had something to live for with Jacob, and while it only lasted a short while, I wanted a lifetime with him. Just keeping my mind on him helped keep my sanity.

The dark space closed in, pressing around me through the hours. I nodded on and off, trying to stay awake, but found it easier to just sleep.

The car lurched forward and stopped, and the door slammed shut again, but Knox never returned for me. Did he leave me to die in the car? No way, I was sure he had other plans for me.

I screamed again and wiggled the best I could to try to break free of the rope, but it dug into my skin more.

"Hey," a man said quietly outside the trunk.

Yes! Someone heard me. I screamed again, the muffled sound probably wasn't as loud as I wanted, but I had nothing else.

"Shhh, listen, my name is Fox. Cardosa's on his way. It's gonna be okay. Crap, I gotta go, don't worry, I'm watching."

What the hell? He left me? I screamed and squirmed around again. Damn bindings. I rubbed my face up and down the carpet, rolling the gag out of my mouth. "Wait! Come back, please! Help!"

My throat hurt as I yelled for the man.

Footsteps echoed outside the car, and I froze. Was it the Fox guy or Knox? The trunk popped open, and I screamed for help again.

"Shut the hell up!" Knox grabbed the gag and tied it securely back around my mouth.

I looked around for the man who told me Jacob was coming, but all I saw were cement walls and ceilings and lots of cars. Red lights steadily remained lit over the vehicles, and green ones were over the empty spaces. We had to be in some kind of parking garage.

Knox looked around before cutting the rope at my ankles. "Get out and don't even think about running."

He pulled me by the upper arm and roughly tugged me out of the trunk. It was hard for me to stand. My legs were nearly asleep, and I couldn't feel them. I wasn't sure how many hours I was stuffed in the back of the car, but it was too long.

My head throbbed, and my vision threatened to leave as blackness faded in and out. Where was that guy? I tried to survey the area, but Knox yanked me toward him. Maybe I had made Fox up, hoping Jacob was coming.

I stumbled but found my footing before face-planting it on the cement. The air here was heavier and much warmer than back home.

I let Knox lead me away from the car and into an elevator. Wherever he was taking me, I needed to be alert and ready.

His arm held onto mine tightly, and his fingers dug into my flesh, bruising the tender skin. "I should have done this years ago."

I glared at him and tried to spit the nasty rag out of my mouth.

He laughed. "You are a lot feistier than I gave you credit for. Whatever Cardosa did to you was worth it." He forcefully squeezed my chin to hold my face close to his. "Maybe I'll get a piece of you before I'm done here. I'm ready for a good fuck."

I held my head high, wishing I could will him to die. There was no way I'd let him touch me. The only man I would ever give myself to was Jacob.

The elevator dinged, breaking the intense stare between us. Two men in dark suits stood outside on the elaborate carpet. "Follow us. We have a room waiting for you."

Knox gave me a wicked grin. "It's payday."

## Chapter 30

*Jacob*

I paced the bottom floor of the suite. It was the same room I used every time I came to Vegas. It had two floors, with an adjoining room attached to the lower floor for a couple of my men. This time, they all stayed with me. With any luck, it would be a short trip.

The burner phone Rodriguez gave me buzzed, and I answered it immediately. "Where is she?"

"Knox grabbed her from the trunk and took her to the top floor. I'm at the end of the hall, and security is everywhere. But they haven't left the room."

Knowing Lily had been shoved into a trunk for the entire trip to Vegas had me pissed. But at least she was alive. I breathed a sigh of relief. "Just stay there and watch. I'm on my way."

Fox gave a quiet laugh. "Yeah, I told her that."

"You what?" When did he have time to talk to her?

"Well, when Knox left for a minute, I ran to the car and told her you were on the way. I figured it would help her sanity, ya know?"

"But you didn't help her escape?" What the fuck! This little boy was seriously pissing me off.

"Heck no. There is no way I'm good enough to do that yet. I wasn't going to risk her life or mine. I'm good at staying in shadows and following people, not breaking them out of trunks."

Well, I guess he wasn't all bad. Knowing what he was capable of and not risking Lily's life earned him bonus points. "Alright, just watch her. I'm on my way."

He gave me the casino and room number before hanging up. They weren't far away, just down the strip. "Come on, boys! She's here."

With the traffic, especially at this time of night, there was no way I would waste my time. Flapjack would have to grab the truck and meet us there.

I ran out the front doors and down the packed sidewalk. Shoving through people and weaving my way around groups and cars. I made it in record time down the strip. Past the dancing fountains and lights, I pushed myself to go faster.

*Hold on, honey, I'm almost there.*

The cell rang. I could barely hear it over the casino ambiance as I ran inside. I dug it out and answered, following the signs to find the tower I needed.

"They're moving her."

"Fuck." I stopped and waited where I was. "Where is she?"

"Headed back toward the parking garage."

"Don't lose her!" I turned around and headed toward the elevators. "I'm on my way." Hitting the hang-up button, I kept the phone in my hand, waiting for him to call back.

Diesel was behind me and followed on my heels while Jax and Bear ran to the opposite elevators to cover more ground. My heart wouldn't stop racing. I was losing time. So help the person who stopped this elevator. I'd kill them.

The doors finally opened, and I called Fox. He picked up immediately. "What level is she on?"

"Three, but you better hurry. He's already got her back in the trunk."

"Son of a bitch!" I didn't have time to wait for the damn elevator again. I ran to the stairs and jumped down the flights. "Stay with her, Fox!" I said, leaping over the rails to the last flight.

"I gotta go, or I'm gonna lose her, sorry."

The squeal of tires had me running faster. I drew my gun and watched for the car. Where was it?

Taillights vanished quickly around the corner, and I ran back up the stairs, trying to beat them to the exit. Level 2... Level 1. Headlights filled the exit, and I ran toward them, but it was only Flapjack. He slowed down enough for me to jump into the passenger side and sped off. Diesel, Bear, and Jax were already in the back.

"I saw him but couldn't get a clear shot," Bear reported, his pistol still gripped in his hand.

I called Fox again. "Where are they headed?"

"Looks like the Henderson airport. Look, brah, if they get on a plane, I don't know how to follow them."

I hit the dash. "Damn it!" Rage consumed me. "We need to get back to the airport." At least I had one thing going for me, and that was the same airport we landed in. It was premier for a private jet. But that scared me too because there were a lot of people I knew who had access to a private plane.

Flapjack punched the gas and weaved through the traffic, using the sidewalk when available. He knew how precious time was and didn't waste it.

"They just pulled in. Heck, I don't know what to do. Wait, they stopped. He's getting her out of the trunk."

I tossed the phone back to Diesel. "Keep talking to him." I pulled out my personal cell and dialed the airport. "It's Jacob Cardosa." Another perk of my name was I didn't have to deal with anyone I didn't want to, even at the airport. They immediately transferred me to the head of security. "There's a plane getting ready to take off. I need you to stop it."

The man hesitated. "Mr. Cardosa, you know I can't do that."

"Like hell, you can't! They have my woman and are taking her somewhere. If you can't stop it, then tell me where the fuck they're going."

Diesel leaned forward. "They're getting on the plane. Numbers are C-two-four-eighty-nine."

"Listen, you piece of shit, the numbers on the jet are C-two-four-eighty-nine. Now tell me where they're going." I gestured to Jax. "Call and get the plane ready to fly. We'll be there in five."

"Alright." The security guard gave in and looked into the plane's flight schedule. "Looks like Mexico."

I turned to Diesel. "Tell Fox to get his ass on my plane."

We pulled in, tires screeching onto the tarmac as we stopped just outside the security gates. I opened the door and watched as a small jet took off over me. It climbed higher and higher, and I couldn't breathe.

I was losing her.

# Chapter 31

## *Lily*

I'd never flown before and could honestly say I didn't like the weightless feeling it offered. Mixed with fear, it didn't sit well on my stomach, and I dry heaved with nearly every bump from turbulence.

But what scared me more than anything was I knew there was no way Jacob would be able to find me now.

The two men who guarded my room back at the hotel were with us but said nothing. They were like silent bodyguards.

At least Knox had taken the gag off while we were in the air. It wasn't like screaming would help me now.

"Where are we going?" I asked, my voice raspy from lack of water and screaming. "How'd you get a plane?"

Knox sat beside me. He still didn't let me get far, even thousands of feet in the air. He chuckled. "The plane is a friend of a friend's. After I drop you off and get paid, I'll owe him, but it'll be worth it."

His malicious grin made my stomach roll again. "Why me?"

Knox leered at me. "Because Cardosa fucked everything up for me. I had something over Garcia, and now they both will pay *with you*."

"I ran away. Jacob didn't help me escape. He had nothing to do with it."

He laughed. "Except now you're not a fucking virgin. Do you know the price a man can get for a girl who hasn't been fucked yet? Damn, why the hell else would I have waited to screw you like I did your mother? Jacob definitely had something to do with that. He got in between your legs and ruined everything, and you let him!"

Years of pent-up anger burned under my skin. My hands might have been tied still, but my mouth was free. I lashed out toward him, catching his cheek and biting as hard as I could. The metallic taste of blood filled my mouth, but I didn't let up.

He yelled and pushed me, but I held on tighter until a small chunk came off in my mouth, and I flung backward, hitting the floor on my side, spitting his flesh out at him. I glared back at him with a cocky smile.

He held both hands to his face, covering his cheek. "Cocksucking, motherfucker! You bit a damn piece of my cheek off! Fuck you, bitch." He kicked me in the stomach, and there was nothing I could do to block out that pain.

I cried out, and tears poured from my eyes relentlessly. Stabbing myself hadn't hurt that much. But he had managed to get me in the same spot. My vision wanted to go black, but I focused on breathing, willing myself to stay conscious.

"Aw, does that hurt?" He kicked me again. "Fuck you."

He left me on the floor alone. One of the guards lifted me up, helping me back to my seat. "I like a girl with that much fire." He leaned forward and whispered in my ear. "I'd like to show you how a real man feels inside you." He leaned back and buckled me in so I couldn't move, a wicked grin lifting the corners of his mouth.

I glared at him. "Go to hell."

He laughed and returned to his seat. Soon both men were laughing and watching me intently. I could feel Knox's blood drying on my chin, and I worked my head to wipe off as much as I could on my shoulder.

I couldn't believe I had done that. I knew my need to fight back was growing, but even that surprised me.

The pain near my healing wound killed me. It was so intense I was sure I'd throw up, but only stomach acid rose to my throat, reminding me that I'd had nothing to eat or drink since the night before.

My arms ached to be released from their position behind me, but all I could do was cry. Silently, I let the tears fall. It wasn't just the pain but also the fear that I'd never see Jacob again. And if these guys got their way, I wouldn't be just Jacob's woman anymore, and he wouldn't want me. I could never face him if that happened.

No. I wasn't some small child anymore. I could fight back. To hell with these men because the first chance I got, I was running.

Knox came back with a first-aid kit and patched up his cheek. He didn't say anything, but he didn't need to.

I turned away from him and looked out the small window into the black abyss. An insistent urge to go to the bathroom continued to press on my bladder. I was surprised I needed to go at all being so dehydrated. "I need to use the toilet."

Knox chuckled. "And what the fuck do you want me to do about it? You bit me."

"Can you please untie me so I can go?" I smirked. "Unless you want me to go right here all over the seat of your friend's plane."

He sneered. "One of you guys take her to the restroom. But don't underestimate her. She might bite you too."

The guy who helped me to the seat earlier grinned and came over to unbuckle me, pulling me to my feet.

I winced. Everything hurt.

He marched me to the back of the tiny plane, where the toilet was inside a room smaller than my closet at Jacob's house. He flicked out his pocketknife and roughly turned me around to cut the rope.

He leaned in close to me. "Leave the door open. I want to watch."

The moment my arms were loose, they dropped to my sides in agony. I wasn't sure I could pull my jeans down. The small space made it even harder to move. I went to shut the door, but the guy slammed it open, holding it against the wall.

"I told you to leave it open."

I was nearly ready to mess my jeans and didn't have time for his twisted game. "You're sick if you get off watching someone pee."

"Seeing you will be well worth it." He challenged me with a wicked smile while his eyes roamed over my body.

I shuddered in disgust, but I couldn't wait any longer. I yanked my jeans down and found the seat just in time. But woe to him, I'd had years of going to the bathroom in front of Knox and his buddies. I was well trained in how to hide myself from peering eyes. And his crestfallen face let me know I had doused his dreams of seeing what he wanted.

I would take any victory, no matter how small.

Lifting my jeans, my shoulders protested the movement. Before he could tie me back up, I held my hands out, crossing them in front of me. Hopefully, he wouldn't think about it and tie me up this way instead of behind my back. I didn't think I could handle another minute of that position.

He reached for the cut piece of rope and frowned. "Knox, you got more rope?"

"No, why? What the hell did you do?"

"I cut it off her." He held it up to make a point.

Knox rose from his seat and tossed his arms in the air as the plane hit another air pocket. "Shit. Now what are we gonna do?"

I remained quiet, not wanting to ruin any good luck that might be coming my way.

"She can sit with Brad and me. We'll make sure she doesn't escape or bite you." He said the last part with a bit of a chuckle.

"Fuck you, Jude." Knox sat back down. "Do whatever you want, just don't lose her. She's worth a lot."

It was like a piece of luck had befallen me after all. No gag, no bindings. Maybe once we landed, I could find a way to escape after all.

# Chapter 32

## *Jacob*

The four-hour flight to the city just east of the capital was the longest hours of my life. Knowing Lily was only thirty minutes ahead of me kept my adrenaline rushing.

The kid sent to follow her sat across from me, staring out the window. He might have been young, but he wasn't some scrawny kid, either. His silence was welcomed, as I wasn't sure I had the patience to deal with him yet. Fox had a background, but I also knew there was more to him than just getting into fights. I didn't get to be who I was without following my instincts.

I watched out the window as the city spread under us like a blanket of crammed houses and buildings. The outskirts of the town where we were headed were run down with a high poverty rate, but the perfect location to make a transfer. I'd been here many times. On some missions, I got lucky, and others would haunt me forever. I prayed I wouldn't find Lily like I'd found some girls.

I shuddered. No. Those girls had been there a lot longer than Lily.

The plane landed, and my phone dinged, alerting me to a missed call. I didn't recognize the number, but it was a Nevada number, so I called it back.

"Cardosa," the man on the other end answered.

"Who the hell is this?" I stood up as the plane taxied to its assigned station. Parked next to us was the jet that carried Lily. I couldn't get off fast enough.

"It's Jose. I have some information for you." His Spanish accent was thick.

The only Jose I knew was Jose Cortez, the right-hand coyote for Angel Martin. "I'm listening."

"There was a meeting last night. Some pendejo named Knox brought in a woman he claimed was yours trying to sell her."

I clenched my jaw. "What do you know?"

"Once Angel and a few others found out she was yours, they backed out. They figured it would give them a pass for the next week, yeah?"

"You want me to look the other way while you smuggle a few women, is that it?" Fuck. Lily was worth every single woman to me, but my conscience fought me. However, I'd have to fight with it later. Her life was at stake.

Jose laughed. "We wished. But we figured you wouldn't be so kind to us holding your woman over you like that. Just a free pass for a few kilos."

Shit, that was it? Hell, I didn't ever get into their drug business. Why would they use that as their bargaining tool with me? It didn't make sense. "I don't fucking care how many drugs you pass through. You could send the entire fucking stash for all I care. Tell me what you know."

"Agh, la chingada, you're not understanding. You have the cops working for you. They have to turn a blind eye too, amigo."

Aw, there it was. It wasn't me. It was the police Angel wanted off his back. Shit, I didn't care if I had to pay off the entire country to turn a blind eye. I'd do it. "Deal. Now tell me what I need to know."

"There was a cabrón who made a deal. He isn't worried about pissing you off. I think it was a challenge for him. You are old friends, yeah? I think you know him."

"Who the fuck is it, Jose? I don't have time to play games."

"Red."

My world flipped, and I couldn't see. Of all the people Knox could have sold her to, Red was one of the worst. We went way back, and none of our meetings ever ended on friendly terms. The last time I had killed a handful of his men, saving a young girl. But I could never get close enough to kill him.

Not only did I cost him loyal men, but also an income the girl brought in. But it wasn't the first time. I'd rescued more than half the girls I was hired to find under his control. Our hatred for each other ran deep.

And knowing Lily was mine would bring out a side to Red that I'd never wanted to see. He would use Lily in ways I couldn't imagine just to get to me. My stomach rolled, and all I could think was my sweet innocent Lily being tortured.

"I'll let Angel know we have a deal. One week, my amigo."

I shoved the phone into my pocket and unlocked the cabin door. I didn't care that we were still moving. I needed to get the fuck off this plane.

"Wait, sir," Amy, my private attendant, cautioned.

"I don't have time to wait." I pushed the door open as Amy began yelling for Jay, one of the pilots, to stop the plane.

The plane lurched as Jay hit the brakes. With the stairs pushed out, I jumped down them to the tarmac, running for the other plane. It wasn't likely Lily was still there, but I couldn't not see for myself.

I could hear the others running behind me. After years of hunting together, we were like one.

The stairs on the jet were still lowered. I climbed them in one leap and pushed through the short entrance to an empty cabin. "Damn it!"

I held my face and rubbed down my chin. A couple pieces of cut rope lay on the floor near the back, and a few drops of blood splattered the rear left seat.

Everywhere I chased after Lily, there was blood. It wasn't the best sign, but at least I knew she was still alive. And the price Knox was probably getting for her wasn't an amount he'd be willing to lose with a dead woman. Red probably had never paid so much for a woman, either.

"I'm sorry. I should have helped her when I had the chance." Fox stood at the top of the stairs. His gaze locked onto the blood.

"Hell, kid, I wish you could have too, but like you said, you aren't good enough, and you're right, you could have gotten her killed." It might have been a dick move, but I sure as hell wasn't going to make him feel better.

He winced and stepped back down the stairs as I pushed forward.

Diesel stood near the steps with his bag and mine hanging over his shoulders. "I got an idea."

Fox stood beside him and let me off the steps. "I'm all ears."

"Well, I think we should send a motherfuckin' fox down a hole." He grinned and looked from me to Fox and back to me.

"What? You want to send *him* to get information? They'll sniff him out, and he'd be dead in less than an hour."

Fox raised his hands in protest. "Heck no. I can't do that. If she dies because of me, brah, I don't think I can handle it."

My patience snapped. Lily was slipping farther away from me with every second. "First of all, I'm not your brah. Second, Diesel might be right. They don't know you, and you aren't exactly what they'd be looking for. You don't act like one of us."

"Just because I don't cuss at everyone and everything doesn't mean I'm not a man."

Bear laughed. "It has nothing to do with being a man. But you'll get there. You're still a young pup. You probably don't even know what you got yourself mixed up in."

Fox tensed, and his entire attitude shifted like a secret about to burst out from him. "I know what you guys are. I'm not stupid. I asked to be here."

Diesel groaned. "Why the fuck would you do that?"

Fox glared at Diesel, almost challenging him silently. "Look, are we gonna send me in or not?"

I reached out for Diesel to hand me my bag and slung it over my shoulder. "Alright, stop your pissin' match. Fox, you think you can go in and find her?"

His face was still stern, but he nodded. "I'll find her."

The kid was growing on me. His confidence would go far in this business. I strode to the gates to find a truck. "Let's go hunting, boys."

# Chapter 33

## *Lily*

The van that waited for us when we landed clunked down the rough road. I had no idea where we were, but the fact that they were driving me away from the city didn't evade me. The countryside was gray and dusty, with run-down brick and clay homes dotting the sides of the roads.

Dark tinted glass filtered the scenery, shielding me from anyone we passed.

Not that they could help me. The men that picked us up carried guns and ammo as a part of their attire. I knew Knox had at least one too, as well as the other two guards.

It sure was a lot of security for just restraining me. But if Jacob found me, they'd need it. I almost smiled at the thought.

Almost.

But the bigger fear that Jacob could get hurt because of me twisted my heart. Maybe he should just forget about me.

We stopped outside a gate to a stone wall surrounding a small house where the driver honked the horn. I wasn't sure I could even call it a house. The cabin where I was held the last few years looked safer.

Another man armed heavily with guns opened the gate for us to come in and then shut it behind us. Escaping would not be easy.

As soon as we stopped, the side door to the van opened, filling the bright sunlight into the interior. I blinked, trying to let my eyes focus in the brightness.

Knox grabbed my upper arm and yanked me up before shoving me out the door.

I couldn't find my footing fast enough and fell to the hard dirt. It didn't take me long to stand up, despite the aches of my body. I wasn't about to be careless and unaware of everything around me. I needed to keep my guard open and be ready for the slightest chance to run.

Callous laughter erupted as my ever-present guards, Jude and Brad, grabbed my arms, holding me close to them.

"Lily Ramirez." The man's voice held a smooth lilt. "What a treat to have you here."

The well-dressed man walked toward me, flanked by heavily armed men. His white attire looked out of place among the dirt and ruins. He stepped up to me. His crooked smile revealed gold teeth as he grabbed my chin, staring into my eyes. His breath was rancid, making me gag. "So, you are Jacob Cardosa's woman." He let go of me roughly and laughed. "Not anymore."

With the two men still holding my arms, I did the only thing I could and spit on him. It wasn't much. Being dehydrated, I barely managed to spew out any moisture, but the gesture was enough to make my point.

The man glared at me and swung his hand, backhanding me across the face. Instantly, my ears rang, and black dots spotted my vision. "Gag her. And somebody tie this bitch up before she tries anything else."

Men from all over encircled me, making it impossible to move or breathe as they did as the man said. I bucked and squirmed as much as I could, but it was useless. The gag was tighter than the last one, and while my hands were tied in the front, the thin wire cut into my skin, drawing blood.

Knox walked by me slowly, heading back to the van. "I'd like to stay and take the pleasure of fucking Cardosa's woman, but I have a paycheck to cash."

"Fuck you!" I tried to scream at him, but the words were so muffled all he did was laugh at me. I'm sure he got my meaning.

I kicked out at him, barely missing his leg, but was caught by Brad. "I guess we'll have to tie these pretty things to the bed, so she doesn't try to use them against us." He snickered and picked up my other leg while my torso was carried by Jude. I continued to resist, bucking and fighting them, but their grip was tight.

They carried me into the rubble of a home and tossed me to the dirt floor. I scrambled to get up but was kicked back down by one of the guys now encircling me.

Each time I tried to recover and stand, I was pushed back down, followed by laughter, until the man in white intervened. "Enough."

The way the men listened to him scared me. It was the way Jacob's men listened to him. The authority behind his tone made my hair stand on end.

He crouched down beside me as I attempted to stand again. "It always amazes me how much spirit a woman has until I break her." He grinned. "But breaking her is my favorite part, and knowing I'll be breaking Cardosa's bitch excites me even more."

He stood and dusted off his pants. "Strip her and tie her to the wall."

I screamed and thrashed when strong hands grabbed me and began ripping my clothes off me.

They dragged me completely naked to the wall where hooks were mounted into the stone. Raising my arms above my head, they tied them to a hook. Forcefully, they spread each leg out and pinned them separately near the floor.

Being so vulnerable and open to these men made me sick. My heart had never beat so fast as I watched in horror, wondering what would happen next.

The boss slowly took me in his sight and gazed over every part of my body. "I don't usually do it like this. I like to fuck my women, but you're special. I'm going to fuck you over and over and then let my men use you until there is nothing left of you. I won't sell you," he came close enough to whisper next to my cheek, his body close enough to brush against my bare skin, "I'm going to kill you."

## Chapter 34

### *Jacob*

"Let me out," Fox said, nearing the outskirts of the airport.

I looked over my shoulder at him. "We need to get into the city. We have to get closer to Red before we split up."

Fox shook his head. "Naw, you see these people?" He gestured out to the crowded corner mart. "They saw something. They had to. It was within the last hour. Let me go see what I can find."

I wanted to protest. I couldn't waste any more time than what we already had. The longer we stopped, the farther Lily got from me.

I'd tracked women to Red's many compounds before. They were always in the city. He liked the women he bought and controlled to be easily accessible for his clients.

"Please, Jacob. I'm actually pretty good at this. It's how I found you."

I wasn't sure what that was supposed to mean, but the confident look in his eyes wasn't about to be overlooked. I released a deep breath that came out more of a growl. I'd never forgive myself if there was a lead here and I missed it, but then again, I'd never forgive myself if I waited too long and missed my chance to find Lily. "Fine. You have two minutes."

Fox opened the door and bolted out before I finished speaking. He was hard to follow as he blended in with the locals and mingled with a few old men. I watched intently, my hand resting on the handle of my pistol. Fox left the men and laughed with a couple small boys with bikes. In the two minutes I gave him, he seemed to talk with everyone at the mart and rushed back to the truck, slamming the door.

"Drive east."

"But that's heading away from the city." Flapjack looked at me. "What do you want to do, boss?"

I grimaced. "How do you know to go east?"

"The boys saw a white van about forty-five minutes ago that usually holds girls going that way," he said, pointing to the east past the airport landing strip.

"Shit," I said, hitting the dash with my palm. I didn't know what to do. Usually, I had a plan and confidently carried it out. I knew what to do and had plans A, B, and C. I had never been afraid of failing before. But then again, I'd never had something of my own hanging on the line. I hated second-guessing myself. "Drive east."

Flapjack hit the gas, and we sped off down the old roads. We didn't have any other direction but east. How in the hell would I find her now?

The tiny homes were like blobs of color as we passed by. I couldn't understand why I was here and not headed toward the city. This was not a place Red would go. He wasn't a manly man who liked to get dirty. I doubted he ever left the confines of the city and the lavishness his private housing offered.

I'd never been close enough to his personal residence, as all of the girls were located far away from him, but I knew how to find it.

Up ahead, a woman pushed a pram with bare feet. A small dog followed dutifully beside her. Flapjack slowed and lowered his window, asking the woman if she'd seen a white van.

She tensed, and her eyes widened. Flapjack reassured her we weren't there to hurt her but needed to know to help a young woman. Obviously, she was scared, but I wasn't sure if it was from us or if it was the fear of what Red would do to her if she spoke. Finally, she gestured down another road but took off with her stroller full of water without saying anything.

Flapjack took the next left and traveled past more dilapidated homes. The poverty level on this side was hard to witness. I had so much to give, but it wouldn't fix anything. I could give money all day long, but it wouldn't change their world.

The farther we drove into the slum housing, the more I was certain Red wouldn't be here. We all watched out the windows looking for any sign of a white van.

"There's nothing here, boss," Bear said solemnly from the truck's back seat.

A black dot moved in my peripheral vision. I focused on the SUV, watching it leave a gated home. It stood out among the old, run-down, barely moving cars on the side of the roads. The shiny wheels probably cost more than these people made in a year.

I pointed to the car. "There, go there."

Flapjack swerved and took the next right, flinging the truck around the corner. Our tires kicked up rocks and debris off the half-paved, half-dirt road. A plume of dust trailed behind us. Usually, we were stealthy and quiet, sneaking up on our enemies, but today I wanted them to know I was coming.

The SUV picked up speed and tried to lose us, but Flapjack wasn't about to be shaken. He stayed on the vehicle's tail and got close enough to touch the bumper, pushing the SUV slightly.

A man from the other vehicle slid out of the window, sitting on the edge, and began shooting at us. Flapjack swerved, and the bullets hit the side of my door and down the bed.

Diesel was already out his window, blasting a clip of ammo into their back windshield. "You mother fuckers! You don't fucking shoot at me, fuckers!" He was in his element, letting his rage loose. I was glad he was on my side. I'd hate to be on the receiving end of his anger, yet he was as gentle as a baby lamb with the women.

I pulled my gun from the shoulder holster and aimed through the broken glass for the driver. A headshot was the only way to hit him but fuck them. If they had Lily or knew about her, I didn't care who I had to kill. I squeezed the trigger, and the SUV jerked to the left, running off the road, smashing into a clay wall.

Like fire ants, men climbed out of the wreckage firing their weapons at us. Flapjack turned the wheel and slammed on the brakes, so the truck stopped with its side toward them. He jumped out, used the hood as a shield, and began firing back. Ducking, I found my way over the middle console without being shot and found my place behind the truck's cab with Diesel, Jax, and Bear, using the bed as a guard.

Fox jumped out and hid behind the driver's side door. I tossed him an extra pistol I had tucked in my jeans. "Use it!" It was an order. If he was here, he worked.

He swallowed hard, and with wide eyes, he nodded, turning around by Flapjack and began firing.

The other car seized fire, and one of them began to laugh.

I held my hand up to stop my men.

"I told Red you'd find him." I knew that voice. It was one of Red's personal guards.

"Where is she?" I didn't give a fuck about Red. I'd find him later.

"I think you're too late." More laughter. "Yeah, last time I saw her, she was naked and ready for Red to fuck her."

My blood boiled so high all I saw was red. Fuck him, fuck Red, fuck them all! I jumped up into the bed of the truck, then over the other side, and started firing into the SUV. I didn't care about my safety. All I cared about was Lily. I heard my men backing me up as I made my way to the vehicle.

Two men lay on the ground dead, and the driver was obviously gone, but Jude sat on the ground, squeezing the trigger of his empty Glock, as I descended on him

He had been shot in the shoulder, but I wouldn't let him live much longer. I grabbed him by the collar and pulled him up. "Where the fuck is she?"

He spat out blood and coughed. "Fuck you."

"No, fuck you." I pressed the barrel of my gun to his cock and squeezed the trigger. His screams filled me with the need for more. He had seen Lily naked. I couldn't think of him touching her. "Where is she?" I yelled, but it was useless. He'd passed out.

I dropped him to the ground and let him bleed out. He didn't deserve anything better.

Diesel slid around the corner of the SUV, his gun drawn and ready to fire. His eyes darted to Jude. "Holy fuck, boss."

I leaned over Jude to peer into the vehicle. Red wasn't in there. Damn it. "It's a decoy."

"Come on, we'll find her." Diesel ran over to the truck and jumped in the back of the bed. He thumped on the roof. "Flapjack, go back to where that piece of shit came from."

Bullet holes decorated the side of the truck like mesh netting. I slid into the passenger seat and watched the wreckage and bodies disappear in a cloud of dust as we took off. I didn't feel an ounce of guilt for leaving Jude to die like that. He deserved more in my book.

Flapjack slowed and stopped the truck about a block away from the house we saw the SUV pull away from. I wanted to go in guns blazing, but I had no way of knowing if Lily was in there, and I wasn't about to endanger her more.

Just like a natural routine, we found our places and didn't talk as we made our way to the gate. I led the party, crouching low in the overgrown vegetation to watch for the guard. If Lily was here, there would be at least one at the gate. If Red was here, there might be even two more.

Finally, one guard stopped next to the gate and lit a cigarillo. He puffed on the small cigar and let the smoke roll off his tongue. The rich scent rolled through the air.

I held up one finger and shifted closer to the wall. Jax snuck up next to me, slipping a large knife out of its sheath on his back. He gave a curt nod before creeping around the wall to the corner, where he scaled it quickly, dropping down on the other side behind a shed. Not a sound came from his stealthy movements.

I watched and waited as he came up behind the guard and slit his throat. He caught the man's body as he fell and lowered him to the ground to search his pockets for the key to unlock the bolt on the gate. He quietly cursed when he came up empty-handed and dragged the man to the shed, hiding him from immediate view.

With the gate locked, I couldn't wait and scaled the wall with everyone following behind me. I landed on the other side just as quietly as Jax.

Crude laughter echoed from the house. I couldn't make out what they said, but I knew there was more than one man inside.

Inching my way closer, I stayed close to the wall. Bear took the other side, following my movements like a shadow. I didn't have to look to know Diesel was behind me and Jax would tail Bear. Flapjack would go between us, keeping our backs. I just hoped Fox stayed out of the way. I didn't have time to worry about the kid.

Red's voice carried through the small courtyard, and I stiffened. That son of a bitch was here. That meant Lily had to be here too.

Bear made it to the house before me, peeking into the one room. He held up four fingers, and I nodded. We could take four. Hell, the way I felt I could take on four hundred.

He continued to survey and tensed. His face fell, and my heart stopped. He looked at me and nodded. But I didn't heed him after that. My world raged. My life and only purpose for living was behind that door.

I pulled out both guns and strode through the door like I was bulletproof. I aimed at the first man I saw and fired. Bear came through the door next, pressing the barrel of his gun to a man's head. Diesel and Jax followed through. Jax pinned a man up to the wall, his knife held firmly to the guy's throat.

I saw a blur of white and spun to see Red with a gun to Lily's head.

My beautiful Lily was gagged and stripped naked, hanging from the wall for everyone to see. But the gun pressed to her temple had me begging and pleading for divine intervention. I wasn't a church-going man, but I'd sell my soul to save her if I could.

Her eyes locked with mine. I wanted to tell her everything would be okay, but I couldn't lie. I didn't know if I could keep that promise.

"Cardosa, what a surprise." Red grinned and pressed the gun harder to her head. "If you think she's going to make it out alive, you're fucking stupid. It's better this way, though. You can watch while I blow her fucking brains out."

My stomach twisted, and I couldn't breathe. Fuck. What could I do?

I looked back to Lily. I hoped she couldn't see my fear.

"Red," one of his men tried saying before Bear snapped his neck.

It all happened so fast. I didn't understand what was happening until I saw Fox's frame sneaking through the back window and slide up behind Red. He lifted the gun I gave him earlier to Red's head. "No, you're the one who's not making it out alive." Fox pulled the trigger and jerked back with the recoil.

I ran to Lily and unhooked her from the wall. Her limp body crumpled against me, and I held her tight. "I'm here, honey. I'm here." I couldn't believe I had finally found her. She was here, in my arms. I kissed her head and sucked back the massive tears I wanted to cry.

I yanked the gag off her and kissed her mouth. "I'm so sorry."

"Jacob," she said weakly.

I wiped at her face, moving her hair to look into her striking blue eyes. I never wanted to stop searching them to see inside her soul. I looked over my shoulder at Bear. "Fucking kill them all." I shed my shirt to place it over Lily while holding her in one arm. "I'm so sorry, honey."

Her body trembled, and tears flowed freely down her cheeks. "Jacob."

"Shhh, it's okay. I'm here." I pulled her close to my chest, letting her bury her head in the crook of my neck.

I turned to Fox. He stared at Red's body. It was apparent shock was taking over. "Hey, kid. I'm damn proud of you. Thank you." He would be one hell of a man someday.

He looked up at me, and reality snapped back into his eyes. "Is she okay?"

I nodded. "I think so." Hell, she was alive. That's all that mattered to me.

# Chapter 35

## *Lily*

Jacob was here. His strong arms held me tightly to his bare chest while his shirt covered me. I clung to him, afraid he would disappear and let him carry me away from the awful house.

Outside, the sun was setting, casting shadows all around us, but I kept my face buried in his neck, not wanting to see anyone. I hated that they saw me like that.

"I'm gonna get you out of here, honey," Jacob cooed against my ear.

I was too weak, tired, and emotionally drained to answer. I knew as long as Jacob was here, then I was safe.

"Somebody break this damn lock." Jacob's voice was deep and strained, but it sounded beautiful as it resonated through his chest.

I jumped as a gunshot rang out, and the bullet ricocheted off metal.

"Shhh, it's okay. It's just Flapjack shooting the lock on the gate. I promise you're safe." Jacob kept trying to reassure me, but I didn't think I'd ever relax again.

The way those men tried touching me had my stomach rolling, and against my will, I began dry heaving. I couldn't look at Jacob again. He'd never want me again after seeing me tied up naked in front of other guys. Tears sprang to my eyes, afraid of being rejected by the man I loved.

Jacob lowered me to the ground in the courtyard and held me as I gagged. I hated those men and what they wanted. The tears fell harder with each heave. They were so close to raping me. I didn't want anyone to ever touch me like that but Jacob.

One of the men even had his pants down, rubbing his manhood against my leg when the boss wasn't looking. More dry heaves. How could Jacob even stand to be around me now?

When Jude told the boss that Jacob had been spotted at the airport, the boss sent them as a decoy, sending Jacob off the trail. Knowing Jacob was close gave me the courage to stand there without crying as the boss touched me. His fingers never found the one spot that remained Jacob's, but I couldn't shake how his touch revolted me.

Jacob's hand softly ran down my head through my tangled hair. "It's okay, honey."

I shook my head and sobbed. "No."

"Is she okay?" I recognized the voice from inside the trunk. Tipping my head slightly, I saw a young man about my age watching me with wide, scared eyes. He was the one who killed the boss.

"Not yet." Jacob's sincere remark had me crying harder. "Honey, let's put this shirt on you and get you out of here." He picked up his shirt and held it to shield me from the others as I slipped my arms through the sleeves. He buttoned the oversized shirt, letting it hang almost to my knees.

My heart still cried, but I had used all my reserve energy to cry the last tear.

Jacob stood and scooped me back into his arms. He carried me to a truck with bullet holes peppered along the side. He climbed into the front passenger seat and cradled me in his lap, keeping me safely pressed against him.

Carter jumped into the driver's seat while everyone else filled the back seat. I was embarrassed that they saw me so vulnerable, but they were like family, and I was secretly glad they were all there. And no one had yet acted as if they saw anything. They were like real brothers.

"Airport?" Carter asked.

Jacob took in a long breath. "I refuse to let Lily out of my sights right now, but Knox needs to be found and dealt with."

Bear leaned forward. "Just say the word, boss."

No. My heart raced. I don't think I could handle being separated from Jacob again. Besides, no one hated Knox more than me. "I want to kill him."

Jacob rubbed the small of my back. "Honey, it's not safe for you here."

"It's not safe anywhere without you." My voice cracked and hurt my throat. "I don't want to leave you."

Jacob closed his eyes and kissed the top of my head. "I won't ask you to."

Diesel leaned up and rested his elbows on the back of the front seats. "Boss, she's safer with us than anyone else in the world. We could hunt the bastard with her. She deserves to have some fucking closure too. Besides, there ain't a single one of us who wouldn't die for her."

Jacob growled. "I'm not risking her life again. Knox has already put her through hell and back."

Diesel nodded his dispute. "Which is why she should be there. We can all keep an eye on her. Nobody is gonna hurt her again. Fuck that."

"Please, Jacob," I whispered, looking up at his cringing face.

"Lily, I can't fight you, but I *will* protect you."

The guys broke out in whoops of excitement. "Let's hunt the mother fucker!" Diesel cried out, clearly excited.

Jacob lowered his head so only I could hear him. "But I swear, Lily, if Knox gets you and there isn't another way, I will kill you myself. I won't let him have you again."

I'd rather Jacob kill me than at the hands of Knox. The vile things those men wanted to do had me wishing for death. "Promise?"

"I can't lose you again." He rested his forehead on mine. "I have to know, did they… Did they…"

He didn't have to finish. I knew what he asked. "No. They touched and hurt me, but you came before they could do more."

His jaw clenched, and his entire body tensed. "I'm so sorry, Lily. I should have been here sooner. I shouldn't have sent you with Garcia. I should have been with you." He pulled me in tight. "I'll never forgive myself."

The heat of his body and the roar of the truck made my eyes heavy, and I couldn't resist the need to close them. I was safe enough to sleep for the first time in days. I was with Jacob, and I knew he'd watch over me.

When I opened my eyes, it was dark out, and we were deep in a city. Tall buildings and bright lights lit the sky.

I was still cradled in Jacob's arms as we pulled into a circular driveway to one of the tallest buildings. Carter put the truck in park and got out. I wasn't sure what was going on and watched curiously as he disappeared behind the glass doors. It didn't take long before he returned and drove the truck under the building to park.

It was a little daunting to be in such a strange underground area. The last time I was in a parking space close to this, I was trapped in a trunk. I shuddered and closed my eyes to shut out the memory.

After the truck was parked, Jacob got out and carried me through the garage to an elevator. Carter wasn't far behind us, and I was glad he was here. Besides Jacob, he was my only real friend.

I almost smiled at the badassery that followed us to the elevator. Bear, Diesel, and Jax looked menacing and dangerous with their guns and ammo strapped to their bodies. They walked with confidence and purpose, and I caught how their eyes watched everything and everyone around us.

The new guy was a bit standoffish, but I felt he deserved more credit. He saved me too. He just didn't have that seasoned, intimidating aura yet.

And I'm sure Jacob and I would draw just as much attention with his perfectly muscular, bare chest, carrying a naked woman wearing only his shirt.

We went up higher than I ever had been and got out together.

"We got the room across from yours," Carter said, holding a card out to Jacob. "I figured you'd need the privacy."

"I appreciate that," Jacob nodded and slid the card through a black box at the door, unlocking it.

The door shut behind us with a loud click. He carried me to the gray sofa across the room and set me down. Expansive windows and double glass doors led to a balcony overlooking the city.

Jacob left me to go to the kitchenette, where he grabbed a bottle of water and brought it back to me. He was silent, probably lost in his own thoughts.

But his silence scared me. What if he had time to think about not wanting me now that those men had seen me? Touched me? All I wanted was for him to take those memories away.

I needed him to touch me, to tell me he loved me. He could reclaim those places and make me his all over again. I wasn't sure I could live if he turned me away.

I sipped on the water and watched him, wishing I knew what he was thinking. The water felt heavenly on my throat, and I gulped it down. "Can I get more?"

He nodded and grabbed another bottle, handing it to me before turning away and walking to the windows. My heart sank. He couldn't even look at me.

Bravely, I stood and went to him, placing my hands on his rock-hard chest. The fire he created before came back to life low in my stomach. Looking up, I saw the silent tears well in his eyes as he stared at me.

"Jacob," I said, breaking the silence. "Please tell me what you're thinking."

He swallowed hard. "I almost lost you." He lifted my hands to kiss them and winced, kissing my palms down to my raw wrists. "They hurt you. They touched you." The words he spat like venom.

"You can take it all away, the pain, the memories." *Please.* "Unless you don't want me anymore."

His mouth crashed down on mine instantly, it wasn't gentle, but it was what we both needed. He was reclaiming me. His hand was in my hair, holding my head close, while his other hand gripped his shirt at my back, pulling me close.

I needed this more than him. I needed to feel him. His tongue darted in and out of my mouth, tasting every inch of me. Reaching up, I wound my arms around his neck, holding myself as close to him as I could.

His thick manhood pressed hard against my stomach, making the fire rage even hotter. He pulled back, breathless. His forehead resting against mine. "Wait, honey, I can't. We shouldn't."

"Please." It was all I could say. If he turned me away, I would die.

# Chapter 36

## *Jacob*

I shouldn't want Lily right now. She needed to heal, physically and emotionally. I was a selfish bastard to even think about making love to her right now.

But fuck it all, those men had touched my woman. *My woman.* Seeing her tied, naked, and spread out on the wall had me seeing red. They were going to fuck her and then discard her like a piece of trash.

My blood boiled just thinking about it. I needed to hold her, touch her, and make her mine. Every part of me had a natural, carnal instinct to reclaim her. She was mine, and nobody would touch her and live to talk about it.

Tears filled her eyes as she stepped back, reaffirming my judgment to not go further. She'd been through hell, and having sex would be the farthest thing from her mind. "Honey, I'm so sorry."

She looked away and wiped at her cheeks. "I understand."

"But I don't think you do." I turned her face to look at me. "Lily, I won't hurt you. I can't."

She held my stare, and her blue eyes faded with sadness. "This. *This* is hurting me."

"I don't understand." My soul ached, knowing I was somehow causing her pain.

"I need you, Jacob. I meant what I said. You can take it all away. I *need* you to take it away. Please don't reject me." Her tears fell in streams down her cheeks.

"Fuck, is that what you think? Honey, I'll never turn you away. I love you. It's killing me not to be with you right now."

She stood on her tiptoes and kissed me. She was going to break me, and I was letting her. I couldn't deny her. I didn't want to hurt her, but we both needed this.

I picked her up and carried her to the bed. "Are you sure?" I asked, my voice betraying me with a deep whisper. I wasn't sure how to stop, but I would find a way if that's what she needed.

She nodded. Her eyes pooled with desire, making my dick grow harder, pressing against my jeans. "Please. Jacob, I need you. I need you to take it all away, so I only remember you. I need to know you still want me."

Oh fuck. There was no turning back now. I lifted my shirt from her and tossed it aside, taking her all in as she lay back on the mattress. Every inch of her was beautiful, even the fresh scar on her stomach where she stabbed herself, and I had to burn her to save her. I went to my knees and kissed there first. It was our spot, the one that brought us together.

My lips trailed lower to her thighs. The one place that belonged only to me, beckoning me to taste her. "I will always want you, Lily. You are *mine*," I told her before licking between the soft folds of her womanhood, the tip of my tongue finding her sweet nub.

She moaned and raised her hips to meet my mouth. The motion and sound had my cock pulsating, begging to be buried inside her, but it wasn't time. I wasn't going to rush through this. I would make her cum over and over until every memory of any other man was erased from her mind until all that was left was me. She would know she belonged to only me once this night was over.

Damn, she tasted so sweet. My Lily. I licked short flicks over the bud, then longer and slower as I moved lower. My tongue dove in, tasting her, my mouth filling with her wetness.

I gripped her ass and pulled her closer, wanting to taste her deeper. Her legs spread wider, giving me more access. My innocent girl was quickly becoming my confident woman, filling me with a stronger desire.

She trusted me. Only me.

I felt like a caveman. In my mind, all I could think was *mine*. Mine. Fuck. Mine! The word repeated over with each beat of my racing heart.

She reached down and twisted her fingers in my hair. "Jacob." She was breathless and raspy.

"Cum, honey. Let me taste you." Fuck. The thought of her coming in my mouth had me wet. If I wasn't careful, I'd spill out in my jeans.

I licked her again, diving back into her heat. She cried out and gripped the bedspread as she came. Her wetness filled my mouth, and I sucked, not wanting to waste any part of her.

She thrashed and shouted my name. Hell yes, it was my name. She was mine.

I licked her one last time and rocked back to my heels to stand. She lay in a ruffled mess of sheets where she had grabbed them in ecstasy. I smiled and climbed over her, placing one knee on each side of her. Leaning down, I claimed her lips and drank of her drunken state of pleasure. I sat up and licked my lips, still tasting her wetness.

She reached up for me, but I stood up. "I have so much more I'm gonna do with you tonight, but first, you need to eat. You're gonna need the energy."

She blushed and turned her head.

I leaned over and tipped her chin, so she had to look at me. "Don't hide from me."

The heat in her cheeks warmed my insides, knowing I had caused the flush of desire. I wanted to bury myself inside of her so deep.

She flipped the button of my jeans open, and I held my breath. Her gaze never left mine as she reached down and felt my hardness.

I got up and tugged my jeans off. My dick stood rigid and tall. She sat up and scooted to the edge of the bed. "I want to do the same thing."

Her mouth found me with soft kisses trailing down my full length. She explored me slowly. She leaned back just enough to look up at me. "What can I do for you?"

I traced the side of her breast. "Hell, honey, you don't have to do anything."

"I know but tell me. Teach me. Please." Her eyes pleaded with me. I couldn't resist her. This part of her was all mine.

"You can use your hands and move like this," I said, wrapping my hand over hers, moving it up and down my cock. "Or you can use your mouth."

She grinned wider. "How do I do that?"

Her hands continued moving slowly over me, gripping me tight enough to make me groan. "Put me in your mouth and suck while moving back and forth like your hand."

"Will that be like what you just did for me?" Her hand tightened around the tip and slid off.

I nodded as I watched her innocently take me into her mouth. The need to have her escalated as she opened her mouth wider to accept more of me.

Natural instincts took over as she began to suck my cock. I pushed my hips forward, thrusting deeper, but careful not to scare her. Fitting my length wouldn't be easy, but she eagerly opened up for me.

This was not what I planned to do tonight, wanting to wait until she was more comfortable with sex before showing her all the ways of lovemaking.

The heat of her mouth and the wetness combined pushed me deep into rapture. She sucked and pulled, coming back for more, her tongue swirling around the tip as if she'd done this a million times. I thrust again, groaning as words evaded me. My body couldn't get enough of her, needing more. Harder, I plunged deeper into her throat.

She backed up quickly, and I worried I'd gone too far. I stilled and pulled away, even with the insistent urge to bury myself deep inside her pulsed and throbbed. "We should stop." If I continued, I didn't know how I'd be able to stop.

She looked up at me sweetly, her eyes glossed over in desire, and shook her head. "No. I want to make you feel good."

"Honey, you always make me feel good. But you don't have to do this."

Her small shoulders raised in a shrug. "But I want to. I want to be there when you cum, as you did for me. I need this, Jacob."

She slowly grabbed my dick with her hand and pulled me to her. Hell, just her touch about sent me over the edge. "Lily, you remember that first night with us?"

She eyed me curiously and nodded. A new blush warmed her cheeks.

I brushed the side of my hand down her face to her neck. "Remember how I spilled out?"

"Yeah," she said, lowering her eyes. "It was amazing, but I thought I did something wrong."

Just remembering her that first night had the tip of my cock dripping in pre-cum. I groaned as her hand moved slightly. "I'm just reminding you because if you keep doing this, I'm gonna do that again, and I can't stop it."

"Then don't stop. Let me do this. Unless it's wrong?" Her hand stilled. "Maybe I'm just broken and shouldn't want this right now."

I placed my hand over hers and moved it up and down. "No, nothing about what you've done is wrong. Everything is right. *You* are right."

She smiled and leaned in to take me back into her mouth. I kept my movements slow and steady, teaching her how to move.

She sucked as I thrust in a rhythm that only we could have. Just as she was made for me, I was hers.

I couldn't hold off any longer and knew I was done. Diving in one last time, I spilled out in bursts of euphoria. "Lily," I tried to speak, but my body shook, still not ready to communicate.

Holy fuck. She sucked everything in, swallowing as I spilled inside her mouth. I didn't expect that. Still erect and pulsating, I slowly pulled out.

She nibbled on her bottom lip. Her lazy smile was filled with new heat. "That was amazing."

I dropped to my knees and wrapped my fingers through her hair, pulling her to me. "You have no fucking idea how amazing. I love you." My mouth crashed down on hers. Her tongue slipped past my lips, searching for mine. I demanded more, pressing harder. The kiss was deep and rough. I was already hungry for more. Hell, I would never be sated when it came to her.

She pulled back first, emitting a small giggle. "You said something about food."

I laughed. As hungry as we were for each other, it was easy to forget about real food. "I'll have food brought up. But we aren't leaving because I'm not done with you yet."

Lightly, she grazed her lips over mine. "Promise?"

Damn, I was the luckiest man alive. And for tonight, I was going to pretend that tomorrow wouldn't come and that yesterday never happened.

# Chapter 37

## *Lily*

I slipped Jacob's shirt back on and curled up on the sofa next to him as we waited for our food to arrive. Apparently, I had to try some local cuisine, never having anything remotely close to Mexican food before.

I was so exhausted that my body screamed to sleep, but I couldn't. I didn't want to waste a single second with Jacob. I knew how precious these moments were and how quickly they could be taken from me again.

Heat rose to my cheeks as I remembered him licking me until I screamed his name. And then, he let me kiss and taste him until he spilled out inside my mouth. Just thinking about what I did made my body tingle with the need to do it again. I never thought doing something like that could bring so much pleasure.

Someone knocked on our door, and Jacob picked up his gun from the table and then looked out the peephole before opening it. He lowered his weapon and smiled as Carter walked in, thumping him on the back.

Carter carried two plastic bags, setting them on the counter. "Best in the city. Unless I were to cook it." He winked at me.

I smiled. "That's just because you haven't tasted my rabbit yet."

His laugh filled the room. "Oh, I'm still planning on it. We have a bet, don't expect me to go easy on you." He stared at me, and his expression softened. "I'm glad you're okay."

I lowered my gaze, not ready for this talk. I'd rather everyone forget about it and never speak of it again. That's what I wanted to do myself. Pretend it never happened.

"So," Carter started again, clearly getting my hint that I wasn't ready to talk. "About that other thing you asked me to pick up. It will be here in the morning."

Jacob nodded and thanked him.

"See ya later, Rabbit." Carter waved at me before closing the door behind him, leaving Jacob and me alone.

Blissfully alone.

Jacob chuckled. "Rabbit?"

I shrugged. "Could be worse. You call him Flapjack."

Jacob's laugh was deep and hearty. "You're right." He picked up the bags and brought them to the table in front of the couch. "Now we feast. There is nothing like traditional home-cooked food."

"Home-cooked?" I watched as he pulled out bowls of food from the bags.

"Yeah, there's a lady here who takes care of us when we come through." He slowed and took in a long breath.

"Was she, I mean, did you and her..." I wasn't sure if I wanted to know if there was another woman in his life.

He grinned sadly and shook his head. "No. Her daughter was taken by a sex trafficker. I tried to find her, but it was too late. So now, when I'm here, she feeds us."

"Wow. It's strange. We've lived the opposite end of this life." I lowered my gaze, suddenly embarrassed. He'd seen so much and I so little.

"Well, now you're part of my life." He held food out for me. "Try this. Her tortillas are to die for."

Taking the flat piece of bread, I bit into it. It was still warm and soft. "That's really good."

He chuckled. "Wait until you put the meat with it."

Together we shared food and talked like the last few days had never happened. It was just him and me. We stayed away from touchy topics but dove farther into who we were, our likes and dislikes, our wants and hopes. My list was pretty short, but

181

his wasn't long either. Somehow, I hoped I could be there with him when he was able to do everything he wanted.

Jacob placed the leftover food in the refrigerator and then sat back on the couch, letting me curl up next to his side. "Your mother had so little in the way of choices but gave you so much. I'm impressed by her savviness."

I smiled sadly. Thinking of her was hard. "You would have liked her. I miss her."

He kissed the top of my head. "Well, I love her daughter."

It was strange how safe Jacob made me feel, even hours after being tied to a wall. It was almost like a bad dream, not reality.

I sat up, hating to leave the warmth his body offered. "I think I'm gonna take a shower." Water could wash away the worst moments in life. And I finally felt calm enough to do such a feat.

Jacob's eyes glazed over, making the pit of my stomach burn with need. I knew he was the only one who could put out the fire. I blushed, ducking slightly under his intense gaze, knowing what he was thinking. Hell, I was thinking it too.

He laughed. "Go on, I'll be in soon."

Getting up, I left him on the couch to find the shower. The hot water sprayed with pulsating power. I slipped out of Jacob's shirt and held it up to smell his clean scent, still clinging to the fabric.

Was it so wrong that I wanted him again so soon and after everything that happened? Hell, I didn't care. Who said what was right or wrong until they were the ones who lived through it.

I placed the shirt on the counter and stepped into the shower. Tipping my head back, I let the water fall over my face and drench my hair. Tiny bottles of shampoo and conditioner sat on the shelf. I dumped almost half the bottle onto my palm. It smelled like flowers.

It felt so good to scrub my head. Removing all the dirt, grime, and memory of any other man but Jacob was refreshing.

A gentle touch at the small of my back startled me, but I knew those fingers and opened my eyes to see Jacob standing naked in front of me. Water sprayed his body with droplets cascading down to where his manhood grew larger.

It excited me to watch him, knowing that it was me who made it happen. He pulled me close and turned me to face the wall, moving my hair to kiss along the back and sides of my neck. I braced myself with my hands against the slick tile.

His stiff dick pressed against me, and my body cried out, wanting to feel him inside me again. Even though the last time was painful, he told me it would get easier each time, and I believed him. It didn't matter. The feeling he gave me was worth all the pain in the world, every time if needed.

His hands reached around and grasped my breasts. I let out a small whimper as his thumbs rolled over my nipples. Between my legs quivered and sent waves of pleasure through me.

I was already weak, but my legs threatened to give out completely. I turned to face him, and the water rolled down my chest between us.

He lowered his face to take a nipple in his mouth. I wobbled and reached out to grab something... anything, to help hold me up. Jacob's arm went around me and held me firmly.

Picking me up, he pushed me against the wall. His manhood throbbed near my center, and I silently begged him to enter me.

"Lily," he breathed, his voice husky. It was a silent plea that I was more than ready to fulfill.

"Please." It was the only word I could get out.

He lowered me for a moment, reaching out of the shower to the counter where he had a condom waiting. He ripped the package open with his teeth and slipped it on his thick dick before lifting me back up against the wall.

His dick slipped inside of me, and I held my breath waiting for the intense pain from last time, but it didn't happen. It was tight and sore, but nothing sharp. I relaxed as he began to move inside me.

His mouth found mine and softly grazed over my lips. It wasn't the desperate need we both had earlier. This was gentle and slow. This was his soul talking to mine.

Feeling him deep inside of me felt so good. I wanted him to stay there forever, never wanting this moment to end. His body pressed against mine, his hands holding me up, his lips caressing my skin. I wanted it all.

I craved more. But what *more* was, I didn't know. I could only trust that Jacob would know how to give me the *more* I hungered for. He was the only one who could quench the inferno escalating inside me, building in my soul.

He groaned as he thrust. My name rolled off his lips in a raspy whisper.

I couldn't fight the mounting pleasure as it peaked, erupting, sending my soul to fly into a million pieces. "Jacob," I cried out. His name was the only word my mind would register.

He thrust one more time, letting out a moan so deep I knew he had reached that peak too.

Deliriously spent and ready to collapse, I held onto him. I rested my head on his chest, letting the water roll down my face.

Nothing else mattered anymore but Jacob. He was everything to me, and no one would take him away from me again.

# Chapter 38

## *Jacob*

Lily's bare legs intertwined with mine as she slept. Her head snuggled into the crook of my shoulder while her arm draped over my stomach.

I used my free arm to move the hair from her face. Watching her sleep was the most peaceful feeling. She was here, safely tucked into my arms. I couldn't ask for more.

A light tap at the door had me reluctantly scooting out from under her warm body. I wrapped the hotel robe around me before grabbing my pistol. I didn't trust anyone. And with Lily, I would never fail to protect her again.

In the peephole, I could see Flapjack. I unlocked the door and opened it enough to see him. I didn't see anyone else, so I opened it fully to let him in.

He held out a couple shopping bags from retailers. "I assume Rabbit will be needing these?"

I chuckled at the use of his nickname for Lily. As odd as it was, it kind of fit. "Well, around you guys, yes." I took the bags and looked inside. Everything that I asked for seemed to be there.

Flapjack laughed. "We'll meet you guys downstairs in an hour, yes?"

"You have everything else ready?" I walked to the fridge and pulled out a tortilla from last night.

He nodded. "I'm glad she's here, but are you sure you're okay with doing this? I mean, this world is not an easy one to live in."

I swallowed the last piece of tortilla and looked toward the bedroom. "I've thought a lot about it." I returned my stare to my friend. "I'm the selfish bastard who can't live without her, but I can't see myself stopping either."

He nodded and clamped a hand down on my shoulder before leaving. "Alright. One hour," he said over his shoulder.

I locked the door behind him. His words stabbed me in the heart. What if I couldn't protect Lily in my world?

Lily's arms wrapped around me, startling me. I hadn't even heard her leave the bed, let alone sneak up on me. "You and Flapjack must be related."

She giggled. "Why's that?"

"You both know how to sneak up on me." I turned to wrap my arms around her, finding her still naked and glowing with last night's whole night of lovemaking.

I groaned and felt myself growing, wanting her again. I backed up and handed her the bags. "You better put these on before we're late getting downstairs."

She blushed. "What's this?"

"Clothes. I can't have you walking around in my shirt, or everyone in Mexico will want you." I brushed my hand over her neck to her shoulder. She shivered. "*I'll* want you."

She grinned bashfully and pulled the bags open. "Jacob, how do you do this? These are perfect. Thank you." She stood on her tiptoes and kissed me quickly before jetting off to the bedroom.

Following her would only make it harder for me to resist dragging her back to the bed. I resolved to stay and eat another tortilla.

Lily came out dressed in jeans that hugged her curves and a long-sleeved, dark blue shirt with embroidered neckline, sleeve cuffs, and hemline. The v-cut dipped lower on her chest, flaring under the supple mound of her breasts.

In her hand was a brush, and she worked her long tresses. "You seriously thought of everything. There was even a hair tie in those bags!"

I laughed. If it weren't for Rosa and her connections down here, I'm not sure those bags would have held anything other than lacy panties. I'd have to get Rosa a gift to say thank you. Even back home, she had a way to come through for me. "I'm glad you're happy."

Getting down from the small stool near the kitchenette, I decided I had better get dressed too.

In the last bag, Lily took out a box with boots inside. She touched the leather gently and looked up at me. "Thank you, Jacob."

I smiled at her. I loved seeing her so cheerful. I'd do anything to keep her happy. "There isn't anything I wouldn't do for you. All you have to do is ask."

Her mouth twisted into a tight smile. "I might not know everything I want."

I finished pulling my boots on and walked over to her. "Then it's my job to show you."

She waved me off. "Stop. You're making my stomach flutter again."

I chuckled, glad to know I had that effect on her. "Mine hasn't quit since meeting you."

She rolled her eyes. "I was dying when you met me."

I shrugged teasingly, liking the new playful side of her. "Didn't take away from your beauty."

She eyed me with a mischievous smile. "Okay, what are the plans today? How do we find Knox?"

I clutched my chest. "Ouch, shot down."

She laughed. The sound was better than any music in the world. "You're the one who said we had to be ready in an hour. I assumed it was to go after Knox."

Shaking my head, I reached for my gun, placing it in the shoulder holster. "Not today. I have eyes and ears open all over this city, and when we find him, we can go."

"Then what's today?" She sat on the edge of the bed and slipped her boots on.

I checked the magazine for the other Glock and clicked it into place before shoving it into its spot at my side. I knelt down before her, giving her my full attention. "Lily, you're already in my life, and I realized I can't live without you, so today, you become a part of my world."

# CHAPTER 39

## *LILY*

Jacob wouldn't elaborate on what we were doing, but knowing he was bringing me into his world had my heart racing.

In the truck, I sat in the middle in the front, between Jacob and Carter, with the other guys in the backseat. Everyone was full of smiles, but not one of them said anything about what we were doing. Aside from Carter dropping us off to grab a new vehicle, I knew nothing about today's plans.

We drove outside the city facing the mountains. The sight of them made me homesick, and I couldn't wait to leave this desert to go home to Jacob's ranch.

Carter turned the truck down another dirt road that led to a dusty canyon. An adobe house rested in the clearing with multiple outbuildings. A tall clay wall surrounded the home with a large, well-manicured courtyard. We pulled up to the gate, and an old man greeted us.

He wore an old tattered white cowboy hat and a red and black flannel shirt, paired with worn jeans and dusty boots. He reminded me of Doc, but with darker skin and no braid.

Carter turned the truck off, and the other guys jumped out. Diesel talked with the man like an old friend.

Jax looked back at the vehicle and began talking animatedly. The man turned solemn and nodded. Bear walked to the truck. Jacob lowered his window.

"Alright, boss. Lupe has everything ready." He thumped the truck excitedly and went back to the small group.

Carter got out first, leaving Jacob and me alone. "Who is that?" I asked, watching all the guys, who were becoming my family, joke and laugh with the old man.

"Lupe is the husband of the woman I told you about last night. After his daughter was taken, he became set on revenge, helping in any way he could. Now he is one of the best informants with more guns and ammo than the Mexican government." Jacob chuckled and opened the door. "And he's excited to meet you."

I grabbed his arm. "Wait. Jacob, is he dangerous?"

"Not for you." He slid out of the seat and waited for me to join him outside.

I scooted out and took Jacob's outstretched hand. If he was letting me enter his world, I needed to stop being so scared.

Jacob's hand went to the small of my back as he led me to Lupe. It was probably my favorite feeling. That alone made me feel protected. Which was strange because it was just the slightest touch.

"Ah, mi amigo!" He pulled Jacob in for a big hug. "It's been a long time. And now you bring me a beautiful senorita as a gift?"

Both men laughed, and Jacob stepped to the side, replacing his hand on my back. "Lupe, I'd like you to meet Lily."

Lupe smiled, but his eyes teared up slightly. He reached out and enveloped me in a hug.

"Okay, Lupe, she's my woman, not yours. You can let go now." Jacob teased.

The entire group laughed, and I felt my body relax.

"Yeah, yeah." Lupe shook his finger at me. "But if Jacob hurts you, you come to me."

I laughed. I couldn't imagine Jacob hurting me. "Thank you, Lupe, but I think I'm in good hands."

Jacob stood a bit taller, clearly happy with my response. "Alright. We have lots to show Lily today. We better get going."

"I'll be back," Carter said, heading to the truck. "Hey, Rabbit, try not to kill anyone while I'm gone. I'd hate to miss seeing Diesel get his ass shot off." He laughed as he ducked into the cab, and the engine roared to life.

Diesel threw a rock at the truck, missing by a few feet. "Damn cook. He should be in the fucking kitchen with the women." He looked at me. "Except for you. You don't have to be in the kitchen. Shit. Jacob, help me out."

Jacob chuckled. "I think you're on your own."

Lupe laughed. "I missed this. You need to come back more." He started walking to an outbuilding. "Come on."

We followed him to a shed where he disappeared inside. I watched each man go in after him, single file, and then disappear. It was a tiny building, and I wasn't sure how so many bodies could fit in such a space.

"After you," Jacob said, leaning down to whisper in my ear.

I hesitated before entering the dark space but quickly realized there was so much more to the shed. The floorboards were slated together and held up by a piece of rope, revealing cement stairs. I looked over my shoulder at Jacob, who gestured for me to keep going.

Reaching the bottom, I was met with another door. I opened it, and light flooded the stairwell. Inside was filled wall to wall with all kinds of guns. Crates stacked two high with AMMO written in black crammed into the corner. The room had to be the same size as his entire courtyard and buildings above ground.

The men turned into boys as they picked up weapons and checked them out, tossing them back and forth, showing off their finds to each other.

Lupe pulled out a drawer and took out a gun just a bit smaller than the one Jacob carried on his chest. He held it in his palm and felt the weight before handing it to me. "This would have been the one I picked for my daughter."

I took it carefully. It wasn't as heavy as I thought it would be. Its sleek black slide and barrel were only about the size of my hand from palm to fingertips. Jacob showed me how to slide the top back to lock it. It slid easily, gliding like butter.

The handle was the perfect size for me to hold. I didn't know much about guns, but this one *felt* right.

Lupe handed Jacob a box of ammo. "I think it's time to shoot."

We all found our way back above ground, the guys each carrying a new gun to shoot. Lupe just shook his head and chuckled at them.

I followed Lupe out to the courtyard and down the canyon a bit. Over the small hill was a large area set up with targets.

"Here," Jacob said, handing me a pair of orange foam pieces. "Earplugs. You'll thank me when we're eighty, and you can still hear."

I pushed them into my ears just as Diesel took a shot at one of the targets, letting out a whoop when he hit the center.

Jacob showed me how to load the magazine and insert it into the gun, then proceeded to go over every safety aspect he could think of.

"So, take it off safety, aim, and pull the trigger," I said, holding the gun straight out from my body so I could look down the barrel.

"No, never pull, always squeeze." He smiled and wrapped his arms around me, his hands finding mine, helping me aim. His breath was hot on my cheek, sending a hot shiver down my back. "Aim, take a breath, then squeeze."

Easy for him to say. I didn't know how to breathe when he was that close, let alone focus on a target. All I could think of was how perfectly we fit together in every possible way.

The target lined up with the sight. I did my best to breathe slowly, exhaling and letting go of everything. I squeezed the trigger and jerked back with a slight recoil, but Jacob held me steady.

His smile said everything. Whatever I had done pleased him immensely. "Woo! Look at that, boys! Looks like you might have some competition."

Bear grabbed the paper target and trotted back up to us. "Pretty close. Damn, she got skills. Are you sure this is your first time shooting?"

I blushed, unsure about the praise. "It was probably just a lucky shot."

Jacob kissed my forehead. "Honey, every shot is lucky. You just have to direct your own luck." He took the target from Bear and grinned at it, whistling. "I think Lupe is right. I think that gun is perfect for you."

Lupe thumped Jacob on the back. "I'm not an old fool. Of course, I'm right."

Jax and Fox laughed.

Diesel picked me up and twirled me around. "Fuck yeah, you're gonna be a badass like us in no time."

I giggled as he sat me down. "It was just one shot. You all might be celebrating a bit early." I shrugged playfully. "But then again… maybe it's just natural for me." It felt so good just to be me with them. Teasing flowed naturally between us like they truly were my brothers. My nerves were no longer captured in a state of fear. I was beginning to experience a feeling of confidence I never had before.

Jacob joined in the laughter. "Bear, set up another one. I think we've just been challenged." He grabbed me around the waist, still careful of my tender spot, and hugged me. "How did it feel? Did it kick too much? How's the grip?"

I shrugged. "Good, I guess. I don't have anything to compare it to, so I'm not sure."

Diesel held out his massive gun for me. "You can compare it to this. Then we'll see who's a natural." He chuckled.

Jax placed a hand on Diesel's gun and lowered it, pushing it away from me. "Shit, Diesel, we aren't trying to kill her the first time out." He turned to me, holding out his weapon of choice. "Try mine."

His wasn't as large but had a stocky build with a wide butt. I shook my head, feeling more confident with my smaller handgun each minute.

Lupe chuckled. "Shit, you both want to see her knocked on her ass."

With new targets set up, we all lined up. I was between Diesel and Jacob. I shot my gun, and each time I squeezed the trigger, I got better and felt more comfortable. Soon, my clip was empty, and Bear was grabbing our targets.

Lupe and Jacob chatted behind me. I pulled out my earplugs, grateful Jacob had given me some. I could only imagine how loud it would have been without them.

"What are you doing with this young woman, amigo? This is no life for her." Despite his low voice, it was hard not to listen to what Lupe said.

"I thought I'd lost her once. I can't do it again. This is the only way I know to protect her." Jacob paused. "I can't live without her." He might not show it, but I could hear the fear in his voice.

I took my paper from Bear and turned to smile at Jacob, pretending not to hear anything they said. "It looks like I might be a natural after all."

"*That* is the woman I love." Jacob accepted the target I offered him and looked it over, whistling. "Shit, you might have Diesel beat."

Diesel cursed and flipped Jacob off. I laughed.

"Who beat Diesel?" Carter asked, coming up over the hill.

"Lily, she's a natural with a gun," Jacob said proudly.

"Rabbit? Let me see that target." He held his hand out for the paper, inspecting the bullet holes. "Dang. Not too shabby for the first time. It does look like a bit of a tighter grouping than Diesel's normal targets."

Diesel slapped Carter on the back with a big grin. "You're so fucking funny. I haven't seen you shoot a gun since your balls dropped."

Carter handed me my target back and stole Diesel's massive gun. Checking to ensure it was loaded and ready, he fired the automatic weapon into the face of another target. He then handed it back to fetch his paper. He jogged back with a shit-eating grin plastered to his face. He thrust the paper onto Diesel's chest. "Suck on this."

Diesel pulled the paper out to inspect it and started laughing. In tight formation, the bullet holes spelled out the words FUCK YOU.

I couldn't contain the laughter as I handed Lupe my gun. "Thanks for letting me use it."

He placed it back onto my palm and closed my fingers around it. "No, Mija, this is yours."

"Thank you," I whispered, trying not to tear up. He was such a sweet old man.

Jacob's hand found my lower back once again, and I melted. His touch was like lava. "It looks like we have a new truck and a lead for Knox."

Lupe nodded, tipping his worn hat to me. "Good luck, Miss Lily." He gestured over his shoulder. "Don't forget to grab a box of ammo for that gun."

Jacob reached out to shake Lupe's hand. "I'll make sure you're compensated. And tell Maria thank you for the food."

Lupe chuckled. "You know that woman makes more food for you than me. It makes her happy."

My heart ached for Lupe and his wife. They had been through so much. Jacob's world still held many secrets and a lot of pain, but one thing I knew, I wanted to be a part of it more than ever.

# Chapter 40

## *Jacob*

It was hard to contain how proud I was of Lily. For her first time shooting, she indeed did have a natural talent.

The guys crammed into the backseat of the truck together, laughing and joking with her. She sat next to me in the front. Her hand found mine, and I gave her a gentle squeeze. I could tell she and the guys had begun forming a good friendship. They accepted her as part of our family, and my heart thumped wildly in my chest.

It was good for her to be able to let go, relax, and not worry about anything while around them. I knew they would respect her and die protecting her, but I was still trying to figure out how to keep that part from happening. We had a job to do, and I couldn't have Lily stay back because I would not be focused on the tasks at hand, and it might cost us or someone else valuable time or the entire mission.

Having her with us eliminated my worry about her but created new fears. What if she was injured or killed? I would never forgive myself. So then, my new concern was how would I protect her and still keep my head on the mission?

It was Diesel's idea to teach her to shoot. He had some of the same concerns and relayed to me his plan to teach her to be one of us. If she could protect herself, then none of us would worry so much.

Except, I didn't think I'd ever stop worrying.

Fox leaned up behind me. "So, um, I hate to be the one to ruin all this fun, but what are we gonna do about Knox?"

"We kill him." It was an easy answer. After what he did to Lily, I wasn't about to grant him a white flag.

"Okay, I get that, but how do we find him?"

It was easy to forget Fox was still new to this world. His inexperience didn't bother me. We all had to learn at one point. Only most of us had to learn at a much younger age. Some of us were born into this world. Even Lily was born to it, just the other side of it.

"I have made a lot of *friends* over the years. My family has ties all around the world. While I run the family business much differently than my father did, I have kept many truces and built enough alliances to keep my back covered at all times." I gave Lily's hand a slight squeeze. "There are eyes all over, watching everything. We just have to find the right person who's seen Knox in the last twenty-four hours. It's a game, a puzzle, if you will."

Fox shrugged. "That explains why Knox kept Lily on your property this whole time. He was invisible there. No eyes to watch him because they were focused everywhere else."

I growled. That was still a very sore subject for me. Knowing Lily had been held captive only miles from me, on my ranch, ate at my soul. "Yeah."

Flapjack drove us deep into the heart of the city. Mixed among the mass of people and buildings, a small park produced a vivid color palate next to the road. Tall trees cast shadows as the afternoon sun beat down on the earth.

"Let us out here," I said, grabbing the door handle.

Yanking the door open, I jumped out and looked around before helping Lily out. I wasn't about to be caught off guard again.

"I'll park and meet up with you." Flapjack slammed the gear stick into drive, waiting for everyone to get out.

It had been a while since Flapjack had been on a mission with us, but it was like he'd never left.

Fox huddled close to the guys with the borrowed gun tucked into the waist of his jeans. I watched how his eyes darted to everyone around us, observing everything. He was definitely growing on me, and while I wasn't sure about training another kid, I'd hate to see him get mixed up with someone else.

Jax had a toothpick sticking out of his mouth, chewing on the wood while donning his shades. He dumped his Stetson on his head and gave me a nod. It was his telltale sign that he was amped up and on the hunt. His focus was on the mission and nothing else.

Diesel got out of the truck and cracked his neck. He spun his ball cap around, positioning it, so the curved brim covered the back of his head, while Bear tapped the side of the truck to let Flapjack know they were ready.

Lily stood close to me with her gun nestled close to her hip in its holster.

"You have to be on guard always. Notice everything about everyone. The way they move, their patterns, their ticks. A seemingly innocent passerby could be the one who takes you out." It was the same thing my father told me when I was only six. Before he killed my mother. Before I killed him.

But it was a valuable lesson, and now it was my turn to teach Lily.

She nodded, and her eyes widened as she strained to catch all the movement around her. "It's a lot harder when I'm not sure what I'm looking for."

I chuckled. "That's fair." I pointed out a few people, and we watched them walk by, finding comparable distinctions and analyzing them. The way they walked, their clothes, and the direction of their gaze.

Then, the hair on my neck rose, alerting me with a natural instinct that *we* were being watched. "Walk with me," I whispered.

Bear had already picked up on my cues and nodded at Diesel and Jax. They split, Bear taking Fox with him. In seconds, they had disappeared from my sight, but I knew they still had me in their view. I didn't have to see them to know where they were. Jax would be on my back right, Diesel straight back, and Bear would be back left. Flapjack would find us and see the formation and have my forward.

I placed my hand on the small of Lily's back and guided her through the park, trying to reach the other side. My hand placement was more for me than her. I needed to touch her, to know she was safe. As long as I could feel her, I knew she was okay.

A shadow crossed our path, and I yanked Lily behind me just as a man stepped out from behind a tree. He was thin, and his hair hung in oily strands past his face. He was closer to looking like a homeless man than a cartel member, but his gaze locked on me, and I knew he wasn't here randomly. Pulling my Glock, I aimed it at his head before he could blink. "What the fuck do you want?"

He laughed. "We haven't met. I'm Fonsie."

He took a step forward, and I shook the gun slightly. "I don't give a fuck who you are. This isn't a toy. I will use it. Don't fucking move."

He held his hands up and laughed, sobering as his eyes fell on Lily. "You're Garcia's daughter. So, you're the one everyone is talking about." He grinned. "You have the ability to start wars in this world with just your presence. No wonder Cardosa helped hide you." He looked at me, his grin wider like he was about to reveal a huge secret. "I'm not the only one out looking for her. She's an asset, and everyone wants her. She's the key to power."

"Fuck you." Lily spit, missing him by a foot. "I'm no one's key."

"What makes her so valuable that you'd gamble your life to get her?" Something wasn't right. I needed to stall him for time. I could feel more bodies pressing in on us than just this one scraggly man. I couldn't see the others, but I knew they were there. Fonsie's eyes shifted, looking away from us, giving me a head's up on his friends. I pulled Lily closer to me, still holding my gun toward him. "Who's looking for us?"

He twitched and laughed again, lost in a reality far from the real one. His manic cackling died down as he began to cough. I noticed his eyes were rimmed in red as he wiped his leathery, pockmarked face with the back of his filthy hand.

"Everyone is looking for you, pendejo. You should have left while you had the chance."

Shadows weaved in and out of my peripheral. From both sides, men appeared with guns raised. Instinctively, I pushed Lily down and fired, hitting one of them as the others darted behind trees for protection. Lily was quick to get low on her feet and pull her own weapon, drawing it on Fonsie and firing before I could. She hit him, but it wasn't fatal, and he limped off into the panic-driven crowd.

Bullets whizzed past me with the unmistakable sound as they ricocheted off the buildings.

Glass shattered as stray bullets reached the storefronts behind me. Diesel was obviously in the action too.

Fonsie's disturbing laughter echoed with the gunshots. Women and children screamed around us as they rushed for cover. To my left and right, shots rang out. My men were good, even outnumbered. I wasn't worried. Yet.

Lily crouched beside me, her gun still out as we made our way to the edge of the park, looking for better cover. I tried to shield her the best I could, but we were surrounded.

Shit. How did they get such an upper hand on me?

I spotted an empty car and led Lily to it, letting her get in before me. Bullets pelted the side of the vehicle but never made it through. We stayed low. She crouched on the floor on the passenger side, and I splayed over the middle console. She looked at me with such confidence, and I was scared I would let her down.

"Don't hit the girl!" Fonsie's wildly high-pitched voice screamed over the gunfire.

Fuck. I needed a plan to get her out of there. Peeking over the dash, I saw Diesel watching the car we were in and nodded for us to follow him. He pointed to the left and right with his hand, telling me Jax and Bear still had my back. They would cover us as we ran to safety.

"When I say, I want you to get out and run to the building right there. Diesel is waiting for us. Don't look back, and don't stop." I stared at her like it was the last time I'd see her beautiful blue eyes. "Do you understand?"

"She cringed. "What about you? I won't leave you."

"I'll be right behind you." I leaned closer and kissed her forehead. "Go. Now!"

Getting out of the car, the bullets began to pelt down on us more, more specifically, on me. I slowed, letting her get ahead of me, away from the shots. They wanted to kill me, not her.

She slowed and looked over her shoulder for me. "Jacob!"

Damn it, I told her not to turn around. "Run, Lily! Fucking get her out of here!" I yelled at Diesel, who grabbed her, getting her out of the street just as a searing pain ripped through my shoulder.

Diesel slipped behind the building with her kicking and screaming to get back to me, but he held on, and soon they were both out of my sight. At least she was safe.

Gunshots echoed around me, but they faltered with my eyesight. I fired the gun at everything that moved, not ready to give up yet. Fonsie came into view as I dropped to my knees. I blinked and tried to focus on shooting him, but the magazine was empty, and someone kicked the gun out of my hand.

Fuck.

Even though I knew I would die, I just hoped Diesel got Lily far enough away to not see it happen.

# Chapter 41

## *Lily*

Kicking and screaming, I tried to wriggle out of Diesel's arms to get to Jacob. I saw the man behind him with a gun and had to help him. "Put me down, you motherfucking son of a bitch!" I used every curse word I could think of, feeling each one roll off my tongue like my emotions were attached to them, spitting fire with each syllable, hoping to burn Diesel to the ground.

"My job is to get you the fuck out of here." Diesel didn't turn to help Jacob, and I swore I'd never forgive him if something happened to him.

Carter came around the corner in the truck, the backend swinging as the tires squealed to keep up with the tight maneuvers. He didn't fully stop but opened his door, and Diesel threw me over Carter's lap.

"Let me go! Jacob needs me!" But Carter's grip on me was just as tight as Diesel's. He slammed down on the gas, and we ripped out of the area, away from the park and Jacob.

Carter pulled me into the truck all the way, and I crawled across to the passenger side, glaring at him. "Why are we leaving Jacob?"

"We all made a pact. You come first, Rabbit. And before you open your mouth, it was Jacob's idea. No matter how badly I want to stay and help him, he's still my boss, and I respect him too much. I'm not about to piss him off by getting you killed, too."

"Too?" I spun in my seat and watched out the back window. I couldn't breathe. "You mean, is Jacob... Oh, Carter, he can't be dead."

"Not yet. As soon as you're safe, we can figure out a plan. We are talking about Jacob. He's not going down easily." The engine roared as if agreeing with Carter.

I turned back around and doubled over, holding my stomach. It would have been better if they had just taken me. Then he'd be here, safe, unharmed, alive.

I shook my head. No, I couldn't think of him as dead. I sat up straighter. Anger replaced my fear. Jacob wouldn't let someone tell him no if he was looking for me, and I wouldn't either.

"Stop the truck," I said calmly.

Carter shook his head. "Hell no, we aren't far enough away yet. They could be tailing us." He looked in the mirrors, watching our rear.

I grabbed the handle of the door. "Fucking stop the truck, or I'm jumping out."

Carter reached out to grab my arm, but this time I was faster, and I drew my gun up and pointed it at him. "You're my friend. You're like a brother. But Jacob is my life. Stop the truck."

"Damn it, Rabbit. I can't. You're gonna have to shoot me because I won't betray Jacob like that. You're his life too, and you come first. I'm sorry."

I lowered the gun, shoving it back in the holster. "Me too."

He snapped his head to look at me, his foot hitting the brakes when he realized what I was doing. The handle lifted easily as I opened the door. Closing my eyes, I jumped out before Carter could stop me. The hard ground came up fast. Damn, that hurt a lot more than I anticipated. I crossed my arms as I rolled to a stop. Damn. I was going to feel that for days. It took a second for me to sit up.

The truck slammed to a stop, and Carter shot out of the driver's seat, rushing toward me. I got up and ran back the way we came.

Left, right, another right. I no longer heard the sound of Carter's footsteps behind me. I thought I had lost him until I heard the truck roar behind me. "Lily, get in the fucking truck!" Carter yelled, hanging half out the window.

I ran faster, dodging between buildings and people. I wasn't willingly getting back in that truck without Jacob.

Around the corner, Carter swerved the truck to block me. He jumped out and grabbed me before I could get away. I squirmed in his arms, trying to get free. "Lily, if you want to help Jacob, you need to get in the truck. You're wasting valuable time we could use to save him."

I stilled at his words. "You mean we aren't leaving him here?"

"Hell no. We all go home, or none of us do. I just have to have you safe first. Now get in the damn truck." He pushed me into the truck's passenger seat and slammed the door.

In the driver's seat, he fumed. "You are stubborn. Damn, Rabbit. You really do have a death wish, don't you?" He hit the steering wheel with his palm. "What was your plan? To go in and just start shooting?"

"Maybe." It wasn't the worst plan I'd ever had.

"And then when Jacob watches you get shot, then what? That's not going to help any of us." He spun the tires around another corner. "We've been doing this a hell of a long time. Some of us have been doing this our whole lives. We have a plan. We *always* have one."

I sat on the edge of the seat, grabbing the oh shit handle as he weaved his way through the city. "Okay, so what's the plan?"

He honked the horn and yelled out the window at slow pedestrians. "First, to get you to safety. Jax and Diesel will follow Jacob. He won't get far from their sight. I promise."

I nodded and pursed my lips together, wetting them with my tongue. "What about Bear and Fox?"

He yelled out the window again. "That's where we're headed if I can get these fucking people to move." He laid on the horn for the fifth time. "We'll rendezvous with them and then go after Jax and Diesel together." After a few obscenities from both Carter and the crowd, they moved, and Carter hit the gas.

I tried not to watch outside the truck, the motion quickly making me dizzy. "Then why'd we separate? We should have stayed together."

He shook his head. "No, we shouldn't. We'd all die if we stayed together. They can't follow all of us. And you're what they were after this time, so we're most likely the ones being followed. Bear and Fox will be behind us, watching for whoever it is, and take care of them, so we don't lead them to our rendezvous or back to Jacob."

"Oh," was all I could say. They had planned all this out so much more than I thought. "Will they kill Jacob?"

"No." He glanced at me, the serious expression scaring me. "Don't get me wrong, they will try, but not yet. They'll use him like a bargaining chip to get you."

"Then what are we waiting for? Hand me over, save him!" I had already been through so much. What was a little more to save the man I loved? I could handle it. I think.

"Hell no." Carter shook his head vigorously. "There is no way in hell I'm handing you over to them."

"But you just said they were using him to get me."

He interrupted me before I could plead with him more, driving more erratically. "Rabbit, they don't get their way. We decide how this goes, not them. The first time you let them lead, you die."

While Carter clearly had a plan, I mentally began forming my own. Jacob had saved me more than once. It was my turn to save him.

# Chapter 42

## *Jacob*

The air-conditioned room I was in smelled vaguely of spicy cologne and alcohol. I wasn't sure where I'd been taken. Many compounds in the area came to mind, but I wasn't sure I knew who was behind this. I had my suspicions, and Angel Martin was the first name to come to mind. If it was him, this wasn't going to be quick. He was known for drawing out his torment on many men—and women. He was also the man who had Garcia sending his daughter and wife away. He must have learned of Lily's return. It made sense for it to be him.

The eerie quiet of the room was torture by itself. The only sound I could hear was the rapidly increasing heartbeat in my ears. The thick black hood over my head didn't let in enough light for me to know if it was still daytime or not. Hell, it barely let in enough air for me to breathe. I was in a chair with my hands tied in front of me, but the rope was also used around my ankles, preventing me from reaching up high enough to rip the damn hood off.

Between the pain and the utter darkness, I drifted off to Lily. My mind caressed every inch of her body. Her soft voice begged me to hold on. If I concentrated hard enough, I could feel her cool fingers graze my feverish skin. She was my saving grace as a searing pain ripped through my body. Being shot wasn't something I had experienced before, and I'd be damned if I ever did again.

It was hard to think of what the plan was if one of us were caught. Shit, I never planned for it to be me. I would have done whatever it took to save one of my guys. They were my fucking family, and I'd protect them at all costs.

But now, they had to think of Lily. The thought that they might not be able to get to me in time was real. There was no doubt they knew where I was. Bear and Fox would have followed me. Per protocol, they were relaying back to the others. Securing Lily's safety would be Diesel's foremost job, and it might take him longer than I had to ensure her protection. As long as she lived, I could die.

But I wasn't going down easily. I would fight until my last breath to see Lily one more time. To hold her. To kiss her.

And if I got out of this mess, I would make sure no one ever came this close to hurting her again. Once I was free, there wasn't a fucking man I would leave alive.

Each second that ticked by weighed on me like an hour. Time bore down like a heavy sentence, foreboding of what was to come. I wasn't sure what my captors were planning, but if the tables were turned, I knew what I would do to find Lily. If they thought I was their bargaining chip, they would quickly find out they had a losing hand. I would die keeping her safe from them.

A thundering clomp of footsteps entered the room, and someone ripped the hood off my head. I blinked rapidly, trying to see under the intense light hanging over us.

"What the fuck! I told you to grab the girl. Does this fucking look like a girl to you?"

I squinted, still attempting to focus my sight. A slim man in a purple suit stood poised with a gun in his hand, the tip of the barrel pressed against Fonsie's forehead. At least I knew that shithead survived. I would have fun killing him. A bloodied rag wrapped around his leg where Lily had shot him, and I grinned.

I watched the man in the suit. I hadn't seen him before. Which was either a very good sign or terrifying. If it was the latter, he must be well hidden and heavily guarded. I was good at my job. Hell, I wasn't just good, but I was the fucking best. So if we haven't crossed paths before, this told me this man had to be in unreachable circles. Ones I hadn't even begun to hunt in yet.

"I know, boss," Fonsie stuttered. His scared wide-eyed stare flicked to me out of the corner of his eye. "But he's all I could get. The girl got away. I thought maybe we could use him to get her. You know?"

"What the hell am I going to do with him?" The man said, pushing the gun harder.

"Boss, do you know who that is? I'm sure you could use him to get her." Fonsie stumbled through his words. If I wasn't the one tied up, I would have laughed at his lack of confidence.

"Of course, I know who that fucking is! Shit, it's like you want to die, Fonsie. You brought me fucking Cardosa!"

Well, at least one of us knew who the other was. But that left me at a disadvantage.

Fonsie swallowed hard, going cross-eyed, staring at the gun barrel between his eyes. "She's his girl. You see, boss. We can use him to get to her."

Yeah, like that was going to happen. I bit my tongue to keep from retorting and continued to watch the men in front of me. I could learn a lot if I stayed quiet.

A man standing behind me grunted. "Leman, it might not take much to get something outa him. He's already injured."

Leman. I tried to recall his name, but nothing came to mind. Who in the hell was he?

Leman chortled. "Oh sure, so we can all die? I don't think so. Just let me think."

Smart man. Too bad he had to die.

Leman pulled his gun away from Fonsie and swung it around the room, conveniently stopping at each man and letting me count along the way. Five. There were five men in the room. "This was supposed to be an easy job, boys. You let me down."

Fonsie sputtered and winced as he dropped to his knees. "Please, boss. We can fix this. I'll fix it."

Leman dropped his gaze to the groveling man. "No one let me down more than you." He lined the gun to Fonsie's head and squeezed the trigger.

Fonsie dropped to the wood floor while Leman tucked his gun into a holster under his suit jacket. "Somebody clean this mess up." He made eye contact with me. "So, Lily is what to you?"

Just hearing her name roll off his lips revolted me. He didn't deserve to speak of her. I remained stoic. To hell, if I would cooperate with him.

He held my stare. "Strong silent type, huh? I heard that about you. Do us both a favor and tell me what I need to know. You tell me where she is, and you get to go. It's not like she's really yours, right? I mean, a bitch might spread her legs for you, but that doesn't mean you have to keep her."

The deep anger I had pent up boiled into a rage. "Don't you fucking talk about her like that."

He smiled. "So, there is something between you two. Good to know. Maybe I can use you after all."

Damn it. He had been baiting me, and I fell for it.

Leman nodded at a man behind me. "Clean him up. He's useless to me if he's dead."

He buttoned his jacket and left the room. One man followed, dragging Fonsie's body out with him. That meant three were still here with me.

"Shit. Now we're nursemaids."

"Fonsie fucked up, and now Leman's gonna get us all killed."

They whispered, but I could still hear them. I wanted to laugh at how scared they were of me. And for good reasons. They were about to die.

"This is gonna hurt," were the only words I heard before a wet rag pressed against my shoulder.

"Son of a bitch!" Damn, that hurt. Stars dotted the room as my vision threatened to give away.

The man continued to wipe the dried blood away. "At least the bullet went straight through. We don't have to dig it outa ya."

I winced and clenched my teeth. "Gee, I guess that means we're friends then."

"Hell, Cardosa, I'm just hoping I live to see tomorrow." He laughed nervously.

These men didn't act like normal sex traffickers. "Where you guys from?"

"Not here. Hell, I just want to get back to Vegas, where things are normal."

Vegas. So that's how they heard of me. "What do you guys do in Vegas?" They answered the other question. I might as well keep trying.

"Not this shit. I'd never kidnapped anyone before. My stomach is all in knots. Man, I don't want to hurt your girl. I swear."

I twisted the best I could to see him better. He had a full beard and a bandana wrapped around his forehead, keeping his stringy brown hair off his face. "What's your name?"

"They call me Boulder."

I'd seen his expression before. He didn't want to be here. "Why are you here?"

Boulder tossed the rag down and cursed. "'Cause I needed the money. I didn't know the job would entail this. It was a don't ask before kinda deal."

"Must have needed money pretty bad to follow this jackass to the equator to kidnap a girl." I needed to push him, to get him to tell me more.

"Shit, Boulder. This man will kill you. Don't tell him anything." This man looked nothing like Boulder with his scrawny arms and addict twitches.

There was no way these men were dealing in human trafficking. They were users. Leman was probably a dealer or some shit. But Boulder confused me. He didn't fit either category.

Boulder glared at the other man. "Hell, Cravitts, I didn't want to be here in the first place. If I'm gonna die, then I'm gonna die with a clear conscience."

The third man, who I still couldn't see, piped up. "Cardosa is tied up. He can't fucking kill you. Grow some balls, would ya."

"Fuck you," Boulder retorted. He grabbed a clean rag and wrapped my shoulder.

I grimaced but quickly replaced it with a cross stare at Boulder. "You didn't answer me."

"My niece needs a procedure, but my brother died, and his wife can't afford to make ends meet, let alone get the help her daughter needs. I would do anything for them." He met my stare, but what his eyes said tore at my soul. This man clearly was put into the wrong spot at the wrong time and offered the wrong job.

I leaned the best I could before my ropes prevented me from going closer. "You help me, and your niece's procedure will be paid for in full," I said low enough just for him. No need for the druggies to think I was handing out dough.

Boulder's hands never faltered as he finished tying the makeshift bandage and gave me a nod. A glimmer of hope showed in his eyes. But my heart hammered with the same feeling. I had an ally.

# Chapter 43

## *Lily*

The farther from Jacob I got, the harder it was to breathe. It felt like I left him behind... like I was somehow betraying him and leaving him to die at the hands of the enemy.

I leaned my head against the cool glass of the window as Carter drove us across the city limits toward Lupe and Maria's. The old man must have known we were coming because he met us outside the gate, motioning for Carter to drive the truck inside. He looked around. His wide, high-alert stare peered into the dusk shadows that followed us.

It had already been five hours since we left Jacob. The original plan to meet at the hotel was squashed by more men waiting for us. It was like the entire country knew who I was, and everyone wanted me. But I would gladly give myself over to save Jacob if that's what it took. He wouldn't let me, and neither would any of the guys, so I either had to convince them to use me as bait or find a way to do it alone. Neither option was smart, but I'd spent the last few years of my life playing it safe to just survive. I was done playing it safe.

Carter parked the truck but didn't get out. Instead, he locked the doors and turned to me. "I see that look in your eyes, Rabbit. Stop thinking about it. It ain't gonna happen. Do you think Jacob would let us live if we let you get anywhere close to where he is?"

Defiantly, I pulled the lock up and gave him my best go-to-hell glare. "Do you think I care what happens to me if Jacob dies? To hell with you and everyone else who thinks I'm some fragile flower that can't help. I've lived through a hell of a lot more, and I will not be told to stay put. Not when the man I love is in danger."

"Damn it, don't you see? If we let you go with us, then we'll be placing you in danger, and what do you think Jacob would do when he found out we carelessly just let his woman come with us?"

I opened the door. "I don't care." I jumped out. "I'm going. With or without you. Take your pick." I slammed the door shut and turned away to nearly bump into Lupe.

He gave a sad smile. "Ah, Mija, I'm sorry about Jacob."

"Rabbit!" Carter slammed his door and hit the hood as he rounded the truck. "Damn it." He nodded at Lupe. "Tell her. Tell her this ain't no damn place for a woman." He turned to me, but it wasn't anger I saw in his eyes. It was worry. He was scared. "Rabbit, we save women from these assholes all the time. I know what they would do to you. You know how Red treated you?"

I nodded. The memory was seared into my mind forever. I will never forget how Red and his men stripped me and made me feel filthy with only a look.

Carter calmed, and his voice lowered, trying to soothe us both. "You had it easy. It gets worse. Much worse."

Lupe placed a hand on my shoulder. "He's right, Mija. These kinds of men are merciless." He turned and motioned me to follow. "Which is why you will need more than just that pistol to go after Jacob."

I smiled and darted to catch up with him.

Carter groaned. "Lupe, you're not helping!" He sputtered and cursed as he caught up to us.

Lupe led us back down to his armory. Flipping the switch, the lights flickered overhead until they held a steady hum. It was a bit chillier than I remembered, and I rubbed my arms.

Lupe began grabbing rifles and other semi-automatic weapons off the wall and handing them to Carter. He pulled out a drawer full of knives and grabbed a few, setting them on the makeshift table.

Carter placed the guns next to the knives. "Lupe, she's not going with us. She needs to stay here. You know what Jacob would do if he found out you told her to go after him?"

Lupe grunted and braced himself against the table. The menacing look he gave Carter sent chills down my back. "Do you think she'll stay here?"

Carter rubbed his face. "I don't know. She could if you made her."

They talked as if I wasn't even in the room. But I was too hung up on the possibility of Lupe's help to interrupt.

"Make her? Gah, you know nothing about women." Lupe scowled at him. "I can't blame her for going. Jacob would move mountains to save her if it were the other way around."

My heart picked up its pace. I really liked Lupe. He was saying what I felt. It was like he understood me. "Exactly. Carter, there isn't life without him. I can't stay here."

"I say she goes." Diesel's voice filled the room, and I spun to see him. I hadn't even heard him come down the stairs. I wondered when he would meet up with us. After the hotel, we split ways again. It seemed we were always leaving someone behind.

"Diesel, shit. You know she can't go." Carter slammed the table, and the knives clanked together.

"Bullshit. My job is to keep her safe. I can't do that and go after Jacob. If she goes, I can keep her safe. With Jacob gone, it's me who is in charge, and I say she goes."

I flung myself into his arms and hugged him tightly. "Thank you!"

He wrapped his arms around me and squeezed. It wasn't like hugging Jacob but my brother. He leaned in to whisper against my cheek. "So help me, if those assholes get you, I will kill you myself. I won't think twice about putting a fucking bullet in your head. I won't let them have you. Do you understand? I know Jacob would do the same thing."

I closed my eyes and nodded against his neck. Jacob had already made me the same promise. But this felt different. His concern echoed in each word. He would honor Jacob and his word to protect me at all costs, even if that meant he had to kill me. "I understand."

He pulled away and smiled. "Lupe, toss me a gun. We need to get this lady ready for a hunt."

Carter hung his head and groaned. "Shit. We're gonna die."

Lupe laughed and picked up a large gun, tossing it to Diesel, who caught it with one hand. I stared at the weapon and inwardly wondered if I'd be able to carry such a heavy beast, let alone shoot it. Diesel winked at me. "Don't worry, this one is mine."

Lupe and Diesel began shuffling through the arsenal, picking out a mass of weapons. Carter strapped a belt to me that held a knife I was sure could skin a man alive and shoved magazines full of ammo into the bands. How many men would I be shooting at?

My mind flashed back to when we were attacked at the park and the sight of Jacob falling behind me. "Put a few more in there. I don't want to leave anyone alive."

Diesel chuckled. "Shit. Now she's talking like one of us. Jacob would be proud."

I checked my gun and made sure it was loaded before slamming the magazine back in place. I eyed Diesel. "I'm just fucking pissed."

Lupe handed me a second handgun, practically identical to mine. "Use it. Use it to save Jacob."

I took the gun and shoved it into the chest holster he gave me. "I intend to."

---

The truck was silent, with only the sound of the engine and tires to lull me into an eerie calm. I felt my head bob as I tried to remain awake, but it was a battle I couldn't fight.

Even as my eyes closed, I thought of Jacob. I could hear his husky whisper telling me he loved me on repeat in my mind.

The back of his knuckles grazed over my cheek as he looked deeply into my eyes. His crooked smile slightly lifted the corners of his mouth before he claimed mine.

His lips felt so real I couldn't decipher between reality and dream anymore. I reached up, wound my arms around his neck, and held him close. I would never let go again. If I let go, he would disappear.

It wasn't hard to reimagine the last night we spent together. My mind quickly went back to the hotel and the shower, then the bed. Every inch of Jacob filled my mind. Tears welled behind my closed eyes as my heart ached, thinking I might never see Jacob again.

"Lily." I heard my name, but it was distant, and it wasn't Jacob. If it wasn't him, I didn't want to answer. Couldn't they just let me hide away in my mind where Jacob was alive and well?

"Lily," they tried again.

The dream of Jacob faded as my eyes fluttered open, and I was instantly mad that someone had taken that from me.

Carter touched my arm. "Lily."

I glared at him but sat up straighter when I noticed the truck was stopped. "What's going on?"

"We're here." He took his hand from my arm. "Are you sure you want to do this?"

It was sweet that he wanted to protect me for Jacob, but hell itself couldn't keep me from Jacob. "I'm going."

Diesel leaned forward from the back. "Jax, Bear, and Fox are waiting for us in the house across the street." He gestured to a house that looked too ruined to be inhabited, but after the place where Red had taken me, I wasn't so sure no one lived there. "We'll go there first." He pulled out a single handgun and pulled back the slide. "Remember what I said, Lily?"

I nodded and looked at the gun. "I know." I reached back and touched his shoulder. "Just don't miss."

Diesel clenched his jaw, but the look in his eyes held me in a sad stare down. "I never miss."

"What the hell are you two talking about?" Carter drilled.

I pulled myself back and made sure my own gun was ready. "Nothing."

Carter wouldn't let it go. "Like hell, it's nothing. Diesel, what are you talking about? What did you say to her?"

Diesel shrugged. "It's between Lily and me. Don't fucking worry about it."

Carter fumed from the driver's seat. "This isn't how we work, Diesel, and you know it. Tell me what the hell is going on. We need to be on the same page. We can't have secrets. Secrets get people killed."

I glanced at Diesel out of the corner of my eye. "Some more than others."

Carter watched the silent communication between Diesel and me. I could see the gears turning in his mind as he began to put two and two together. Quicker than I thought possible, Carter had his gun out, spun in his seat, and had the barrel pointed at Diesel. "You and I are friends, family even, but if you even think of fucking killing Lily, you will die."

I gasped and pushed myself back against the door watching the two men. "Carter," I breathed.

He looked at me, his eyes wide and livid. "You aren't dying. I promised Jacob."

"So did I." It didn't faze Diesel that Carter had a gun pulled on him. He sat in the back, watching me calmly.

I nodded at him with my lips pressed together. "Carter," I tried again, taking my eyes off Diesel.

Carter shook his head. "Lily, don't."

"Listen to him, Carter. Please." I didn't think he'd actually shoot Diesel, but I was worried that if something did happen to me, he would hold through on his threat to kill Diesel.

"Flapjack, you know me. I ain't about to kill no fucking woman, let alone Jacob's. It would kill me to hurt her. But there is no way in hell I'm gonna let them get their filthy fucking hands on her. Jacob would rather her die than be put through what they'd do to her, and you know it. So, this is me keeping my promise to him." He looked at me solemnly. "And to her."

Carter lowered the gun and turned to slump back in his seat. I couldn't mistake his defeated scowl as he refused to look at me. "I don't like it. And I hold to my promise. If you kill her," he couldn't finish.

Diesel placed a hand on his friend's shoulder. "I know. But I'm the only one who could do it. I wouldn't put that on anyone else, and if you don't kill me, I might just do it myself." He said the last part so quietly I almost didn't hear it. It wasn't meant for me. Hell, I don't think it was even meant for Carter.

"Diesel, no," I said, but it was too late. He was out of the truck. I jumped out and ran around to him. "I don't care what happens. You can't die." I grabbed his arms. "Promise me. Please. You have to help Jacob."

He clenched his jaw. "I'll help him. But…"

There were no words that could be said. I knew he wouldn't promise anything right then. Damn it. Why did it feel like I was now trying to save two men?

# Chapter 44

## *Jacob*

It was hard to think it was only yesterday that I'd been shot and watched Lily escape. Boulder's attempts to keep my wound from infection seemed to pay off as I could now raise my arm slightly without wanting to pass out. It still hurt pretty damn bad, but at least I wasn't going to die from it. Being tied to a chair didn't help me keep my muscles moving much, though, and they clenched in pain from the restriction.

Boulder came in to check the wound. Under his scruffy beard, I could see the frown. "I wish I could do more. I'm sorry."

"Nah," I said, mentally waving him off. "It's not like you shot me." I winced as he pressed the warm rag to my skin.

"I shouldn't be here. Damn it, I just, I don't know." He continued to wash the wound.

My shoulder begged for him to stop, but I couldn't afford an infection, so I ignored the searing pain. "You did what you needed to do for your family. I get it. I'd do anything for my family, too." Every word was through clenched teeth, but I had no malice for the man caring for me. He was a good man.

He nodded and finished his work on my shoulder. "I know. That's why you're here. Lily... she must be something special for you to follow her to the equator."

I caught his stare and held it. "I'd follow her anywhere. There isn't a place on earth I wouldn't go to find her. If it was in my ability, I'd move heaven and hell for that woman."

Boulder gave a sad grin. "I believe it."

I gestured to the door. "Who is this Leman guy? I haven't seen him around before. Does he work for Angel?"

"I don't know who Angel is, but Leman was working with a guy named Knox."

Just the sound of that man's name had my rage boiling. "Knox, huh. Is he here?"

Boulder chuckled. "No, that's the funny part. He took off when he found out we had you and not Lily. Now Leman doesn't know what to do."

So, Knox was running scared. Interesting. But he also knew Lily was out there without my protection. Shit. I had to get out of here. "Boulder, I already told you I'd help you with your niece, but I need out of here to do that."

He grinned. "Don't worry about that. I am way ahead of you. I just talked with one of your men across the street. We have a plan to get you out tonight."

One of my men? "Who did you talk to?" Instantly, my mind was taken to Lily. Was she there? Of course not. It wasn't safe to be this close to me.

"His name was Jax. He said he was waiting on others before they come get you."

Others? Hell, that better not mean they were bringing Lily. "Boulder, I can offer you a job. It's yours if you want it. But I need you to untie me. Now." Just thinking they had Lily this close had my adrenaline rushing to an all-time high.

"Sure thing, boss." He quickly began loosening the ropes until my legs were free.

"What the hell are you doing?" Leman walked in with his small entourage of only two men trailing close behind him.

"He needs to get up and walk," Boulder quickly lied. "You're the one who told me to keep him alive."

Leman eyed him, his warning gaze telling us both we were dead should he find out otherwise. "I suppose I did say that."

Boulder jerked on the rope. It was painful, but I knew he could have done it much worse. "Get up. You need to move."

His voice was rough and demanding. It was a ruse, but Leman seemed to have bought it.

I played along, hoping to buy us enough time for Jax to make it before this crazy drug dealer shot me again. Standing felt good, and I longed to stretch my full height but refrained.

A commotion downstairs alerted me that my rescue party was here.

"What the fuck is going on down there?" Leman waved at one of his men. "Go check it out!"

Boulder grabbed a bowie knife hidden in a sheath at his side and slid the blade up through the rope, cutting me free. He yanked me to the side just as Leman fired a shot. We both fell to the floor.

I rolled off him and got up to my feet as quickly as I could before Leman raised his gun again. A ping ricocheted off his weapon, and he dropped it, cursing as he held his hand.

Jax came in the room, his gun trained on Leman while he searched the room for me. I nodded at him but not before the other two men began shooting. Bullets zinged around the room. I ducked, having no weapon of my own to use.

But my heart nearly leaped out of my chest when Lily bound in, Diesel and the others close behind her. She raised her gun and aimed at the men firing at us. Her shots rang true, and both men dropped to the ground. They weren't dead yet, but they would be soon enough.

Fuck. Watching her, I couldn't believe that woman belonged to me. Her eyes sought mine in wild fury and panic. She ran to me as if we were two halves of a magnet, and I wrapped my good arm around her.

Lily. She was here. I was torn between being pissed that she was here and proud of her. Damn. It didn't matter. She was here.

"Jacob," she repeated.

"Shh, honey, it's okay." I held her tight, afraid to let her go. She had better get used to it because I wasn't going to stop touching her anytime soon. I needed her more than life itself.

Jax held Leman at gunpoint. "You need to learn how to reinforce a house. This was entirely too easy."

Leman's face paled. "What are you gonna do to me." The man who once had complete confidence strutting around in his purple suit now quivered and dropped to his knees.

Boulder grabbed my ankle. I had almost forgotten about him. "Jacob," he moaned.

Shit. I hadn't realized he had taken a bullet for me when he pulled me down. Lily and I both began assessing him. Blood poured from his stomach, spilling out onto the floor. Fox came over with Diesel.

Boulder gripped my hand. "My niece," he started.

"I know. She'll be taken care of. I promise." Damn it. He was going to die because he helped me, saved me. I owed him so much more than paying a damn medical bill.

He sputtered her name and where to find her. Lily nodded at me, letting me know she was mentally taking notes. Blood stopped pooling, and I knew he was gone. I closed his eyes. "Thank you," I whispered.

Lily touched my hand, still covering his eyes. "Jacob."

I looked into her eyes. "He saved me. That bullet was meant for me."

She gazed down at Boulder. "Thank you for saving him."

"Hey, boss. You okay?" It was Diesel who asked. His close proximity to Lily bothered me. He had been like her shadow ever since they entered the room. Not that I thought Diesel would betray me with Lily, but there was something between them that I would have to figure out later.

I smiled for Lily. "Just a small bullet. I think it missed the important things."

"What do you want me to do with this piece of shit?" Jax asked, still holding Leman at gunpoint.

Leman was now visibly shaking. I almost laughed at him. He wasn't so haughty now that the tables had turned.

Lily huddled next to me like we couldn't get close enough after being apart. Keeping my arm around her, we made our way over to Jax. Leman looked up. His gaze darted between

Jax and me. "I didn't kill you. I could have, but I didn't. You owe me." His voice shook in desperation.

"Owe you?" Lily challenged. "What do we fucking owe you? You almost killed him!"

Leman's skin dripped with sweat as he stared at her. "But he's not dead. That's got to count for something. Right?" He nodded over to Boulder. "I killed him instead."

"He was one of my men," I spoke up before anyone else could ruin the surprise.

Leman jerked and leaned back farther on his knees. "What are you talking about?"

"Yeah, I have men everywhere. Didn't you know that? I thought a man of your stature would have known that. Makes you wonder who to trust anymore, doesn't it." I liked playing with him. Make him think I had the upper hand the whole time when in fact, if my men hadn't shown up when they did, I might not have made it through this.

"Listen, I was hired to find her, not you. Fonsie messed that up, and he paid the price. You were here. You saw that."

Yeah, I saw, but it didn't change the fact that Leman was working with Knox. "Tell me. Where's your partner?"

He looked surprised that I knew about Knox. "He left. I don't know where he is."

I grimaced. "Not good enough. If you want to stay alive, you have to pay with more than some bullshit story that you don't know where Knox is." Lily stiffened beside me, and I wanted to reassure her she was safe, and that I wouldn't let Knox have her again, but right now, I needed answers. "Jax is probably getting tired of holding that gun. His fingers could slip at any moment."

Jax grinned and let his steady hand fall just slightly before squeezing the trigger, shooting Leman in the knee. "Oops."

"Fuck!" Leman screamed.

Diesel chuckled. "You're lucky it was him shooting and not me. Damn cocksucker."

Leman fell to his side and grabbed at his knee, holding it tight. "Shit, okay. He was going to report back to Ramirez or somebody. I don't know, okay. Shit. This hurts. I can't believe you shot me!"

Ramirez? I was expecting him to say Angel. "Leman, was he going to find a man named Garcia?"

Lily pressed her lips together as she waited for him to answer. It was hopefully a coincidence. There were a ton of other people named Ramirez, especially in Mexico.

"Hell, I don't know. I just heard Ramirez." Leman groaned again.

"Lily," I turned to her.

"Jacob, it's fine. Let's just find Knox and get this done."

I kissed the top of her head. "Alright." I'd worry about it for both of us. So help me, father or not, if Garcia set her up to be killed, he would die. "Let's go."

Leman yelled. "You can't just leave me here!"

I crouched down and grabbed the collar of his shirt. Everything about him now seemed so ridiculous. I pulled him close so he would get the menace I laced in each word. "You had the intention of hurting my girl. You're lucky I'm leaving you here."

Bear led the way downstairs, holding his point position. After seeing the destruction and bodies lining the walls, most of who were already dead, I was impressed. I had only five men upstairs, but there was at least double that down here.

I pulled Lily closer and wondered how much of this she did if any. Remembering her coming in and shooting Leman's guards, I chuckled and made a mental note to tell her how proud I was of her later.

We made our way out to the trucks. Flapjack took the driver's seat, and Lily hopped in the middle with me beside her in the front seat. The others took their seats in the back. Diesel gave Lily a curt nod as he closed the door and let out a visible breath.

Whatever they had between them shook him hard. I'd never seen him so upset after a hunt.

Lily was careful not to touch my arm but kept her hand on my thigh. I wound her fingers with my other hand and squeezed them. That was the longest forty-eight hours of my life.

## Chapter 45

### Lily

It was still surreal having Jacob next to me. Everything had happened so fast that I was still processing it all. I couldn't stop touching him, afraid he would disappear, and this would all be a dream.

For the most part, things went according to plan, and some almost more so than others. It was hard not to picture Diesel raising his gun to shoot me when a guy snuck up behind me, but Carter took a shot, killing the man holding me before Diesel could hold up his end of the promise.

"I told you, she doesn't die," Carter had said, pushing past Diesel toward the stairs.

Downstairs was secure. It was just me and Diesel left. His body shook. "I'm sorry," was all he could say.

In my mind, there was nothing to be sorry about. We had an agreement. End of story. I was prepared. Maybe not as prepared as I thought I was, but Carter saved us both in a way.

I closed my eyes and let my soul sink into Jacob's. I was so close to losing him. I couldn't do that again. He would have to get used to the fact that I wasn't going anywhere without him. He gently squeezed my hand as if knowing what I was thinking and silently agreeing.

His thumb rubbed small circles over my palm, and I cried. I hated being so overwhelmed that I looked weak. He let go of my hand to wipe the tear off my cheek. "Don't cry, honey. Everything's gonna be okay. You're safe."

I half laughed at his words. He was always telling me I was safe. And when he said it, I believed him. I couldn't think of any person who would protect me more. I turned to look at Diesel and Carter. It was true. I was safer than the damn president. I wasn't sure I should tell Jacob what happened or what deal Diesel and I had. Carter was already pissed enough at us. I could only imagine what Jacob would do or say. But then again, he had promised the same thing at one point.

The moon overhead reminded me of the night I escaped Knox. Its silvery glow illuminated the road ahead as we headed to Lupe's. The old man was growing on me like family, and I was eager to see him again. I was secretly excited to tell him how well I did. But I'd leave out the part when I got caught.

Headlights came toward us fast, the other vehicle not slowing down or giving berth down the road. It had to be Angel coming for us. We were only a half mile from Lupe's, and I wondered if we could make it to his small fortress in time.

Carter cursed and hit the brakes as he turned the wheel. Both vehicles came to a rest. Dirt billowed like clouds in the headlights.

A door slammed, and I jumped, unable to see who it was. Jacob reached into the glovebox and pulled out a smaller Glock before opening the door. Everyone was already out, their guns drawn and aimed at the SUV.

"Lily!"

I knew that voice and climbed out of the truck. Jacob grabbed my arm and pulled me behind him, keeping me between him and the vehicle.

The dirt settled, and Garcia came around the vehicle. "Lily! Jacob, tell me you have her. Damn it, Lily!"

"Dad?" I whispered as I saw him in full view. Jacob was still tense, but I walked around him and went to Garcia. "You're okay? I didn't know if you were alive after Knox shot you. I was so worried."

"Shit. It takes more than a bullet to put me down." He held me out, grasping my upper arms. "I thought you hated me."

I had many reasons to hate him. And if Leman told us the truth, I might have more, but right now, I had to worry about Jacob. "I do, but you're still my dad. I'm glad you're alive."

He scoffed. "It's a good thing I don't have a heart, or so I've been told. Or I wouldn't be here. Barely missed it."

"Lily?" Doc's voice echoed behind me.

I hadn't realized how much I missed him until he was there. I ran to him and hugged him. "Grandfather."

He held me back just as tightly. "Oh, Lily. I was so worried. When Garcia said he was coming, I couldn't stay back there. I had to come."

I pulled back. "I'm glad you did. Jacob needs you."

Doc's brows furrowed together. "Jacob's hurt?"

I nodded. "Yeah, he was shot two days ago."

"It's nothing." Jacob tried to blow it off, but I could see the pain etched on his handsome face. I hated seeing him hurt so much. He leaned against the truck and held his arm out for me. I couldn't refuse him and rushed to him. His touch was a soothing balm to my emotional soul. It was hard to admit how much I needed this man.

Doc gestured to the truck. "Let's get to Lupe's and fix you up."

"So that's how Garcia knew how to find us," Jacob smirked at Doc. "I think he let you come for his own selfish reasons."

He climbed in the backseat while Bear jumped in the bed. "Hell, I don't care why he let me come. I'm just glad he did."

Lupe was out by the gate, a rifle raised as we pulled up. He eyed the other truck with Garcia. Carter explained who it was, but Lupe was unconvinced to let him in. Jacob winced and leaned against the glass. "Lupe, I promise he'll sleep in his truck. Just let us in."

I nearly snorted in laughter. Jacob wasn't ready to trust Garcia either, which made me feel better about my doubts.

Lupe let our truck in but told Garcia and his men to stay outside the gate. I could only imagine the amount of uproar that ensued. I was glad I wouldn't have to deal with Garcia right now. I wasn't ready.

The men decided to take turns doing a protection lookout through the night. I wasn't included, but I was okay with that. That meant I could stay with Jacob. No one trusted Garcia, and no one knew where Angel was, so everyone was on high alert, and no one would really sleep anyway.

Maria rushed to the door and ushered Jacob to a small room with a bed. For a tiny woman, she was demanding, and no one went against what she said. Even Lupe stood back and let her direct the men. Then she came to me and touched my face. "I fix food. You go to him."

I wasn't about to argue with her. Food sounded lovely but being with Jacob sounded even better. Doc already had Jacob's shirt stripped and was examining the wound. "It's not infected, but it's still oozing blood. I'm gonna have to stitch you up."

Jacob winced but nodded.

I grinned and sat down beside him on the edge of the bed. "It could be worse." I leaned in close to whisper. "He could burn it."

It was meant to be in jest, but Jacob grimaced. "Lily, I'd have done anything else for you. You know I didn't want to hurt you. And hell, you could burn me right here, and I wouldn't think twice about you doing it. I deserve it."

I took his hand. "Jacob, I was teasing."

He leaned back against the stone wall. "How are you doing? This can't be easy on you. You're still healing too."

I shrugged. "I'm sore, but it's not bothering me much anymore."

Doc came back with rags, needles, and thread. "Lily, you can go out there if you want."

"No," Jacob and I said together.

I smiled at Jacob but spoke to my grandfather. "I'm not leaving."

Doc kept getting ready, unfazed by my unwillingness to leave. "Okay, then you just hold his hand. This will hurt. I have front and back to close up."

Jacob didn't take his eyes off mine as Doc began. He tensed, and his muscles jerked, but he held my stare. I could see the pain rip through him, but he never uttered a word. I wanted so much to take it all away. I touched his face as Doc finished wrapping his shoulder. A few days of growth covered his jaw in a rough attractive shadow. "I love you."

He moved so he could kiss my hand. "I love you, too."

"Okay, you two lovebirds. I'll be right outside if you need me." Doc winked at me before leaving.

Finally, I was alone with the man I loved. The man I actually killed for. But I wasn't going to think about that right now. Maybe not ever. I was getting good at blocking things out.

"Come here, honey." Jacob held his arm out, beckoning me to curl up next to him. "I need to feel you next to me."

My heart sputtered and stalled. He still had a way of making me blush. I climbed up on the bed and tucked myself under his arm, resting my head on his chest. Hearing his heartbeat was the best thing in the world. It meant he was alive.

More tears pelted my face and pooled on his bare chest.

"Honey, don't cry."

I didn't want to cry. I couldn't contain all the pent-up emotions over the last few days. "They're happy tears," I half lied. I was happy, but I was also exhausted.

He kissed the top of my head. "Lily, look at me."

I turned my head up to stare into his gorgeous amber eyes. It was like staring into a pool of caramelized honey. I could stare into those eyes forever.

He raised his hand to gently graze my cheek. He winced slightly.

I pulled back. "Jacob, don't. It hurts you."

His good arm held me tight, not letting me pull away farther. "It will hurt more if I don't touch you."

My heart sped up as his lips neared mine. I wondered if he could feel how much he affected me.

His mouth hovered over mine. The tantalizing heat from his breath warmed my lips. "I'd spend my last breath kissing you."

Our mouths weren't even touching, and my body melted against his. It was torture the way he was savoring the moment... if torture was pleasurable.

When his lips touched mine, it was like the world left, and only we remained. He pressed harder, crushing my mouth with a need I matched. He wasn't just kissing me but was rebranding me as his.

Everything in me agreed and accepted him as the only man to sear my heart with his name. Lost in the moment, I captured each second in my mind to relive later. My hands gently grazed his chest and lower along the band of his jeans. He groaned, and my heart skipped a beat. I loved hearing that but knew he wasn't near ready for more. He'd just been shot, for hell's sake.

And, the fact that we were in Lupe and Maria's bed didn't evade me. It just wasn't time, no matter how much I wanted it to be.

I hated what I was about to do but pulling back was the only way to save him from my building desire. I sucked on my bottom lip and could still taste him as I lay back on his chest.

His chest shook as he slowed his breathing. "It's a good thing you stopped. I'm not sure I would have."

"I know," I whispered against his skin, loving the connection we still had. It wasn't without difficulty. I wanted to rip off my clothes and feel his body next to mine. I needed to feel him inside of me. Saving him was killing me.

## Chapter 46
### *Jacob*

Last night was possibly one of the longest nights in my life. Having Lily so close after being ripped apart but unable to take her and show her how much I needed her tore at my soul. Everything in me, especially the primal, predatory, protector part, craved her. I couldn't contain the silent growl in my head as my body pleaded with me to satiate the building desire.

Lily's head fit perfectly in the crook of my shoulder. The steady rise and fall of her chest was calming. I slowly pulled my arm out, trying not to wake her, but her eyes fluttered open. "Shh, honey, go back to sleep."

"Where are you going?" She tried to sit up, but I pressed her gently to the pillow.

"I smell coffee. You just sleep. I'll be here when you get up. Promise."

She yawned and snuggled into the mattress. "You better."

I moved the hair off her face and smiled. I still couldn't believe I was lucky enough to have her as mine. Standing, I stretched the best I could and tried to lift my left arm. I was surprised at how much farther I could move it compared to yesterday. It hurt but was tolerable. The makeshift sling Doc made me was on the small dresser across the room. I picked it up and fit my arm gently in it, shifting it until it sat comfortably around my neck. No shirt. I would have to go out and grab my bag from the truck for a new one.

It was early, but Doc and Bear were still out patrolling, and everyone else but Fox sat around a round table. Lupe and

Maria had a more modern home for the area, with most of their rooms under the same roof. Lupe had built it and every square inch of what sat under it.

Fox had his feet kicked out and crossed with a woven blanket tossed over his torso. Sleeping on the hard floor would have killed my back, but he was still young. I envied Fox's ability to drown out the world and just sleep.

"Hey, boss. You look like you're doing better." Jax handed me a cup full of Maria's strong brew.

I took in a deep breath and accepted the cup. "Thanks. Yeah. It won't be long, and I'll be good as new."

"How's Lily?" Diesel asked, his face set hard. He glanced toward the door where she slept but quickly averted back to me.

What the hell was going on? "She's good. I told her to get a bit more sleep. She's been through a lot."

Diesel nodded, and Flapjack scoffed. "I think I'll go out and take watch for Bear." He downed the last of his coffee and kissed Maria on the cheek as he set his cup down. "Thank you, it was just what I needed."

Maria blushed and slapped him with her apron. "You get out of here before I trade you for my husband."

Lupe laughed and grabbed his wife from behind. "Mi Amor, you couldn't trade me. Who else would know where you like to be kissed?" He kissed her neck quickly before jumping back to miss the swing of the wooden spoon in her hand.

I smiled. It was good to see them act so normal, so in love. I glanced at the door where Lily slept. It gave me hope for us. This world could be hard, but if these two could still love through it all, I knew Lily and I could make it.

Flapjack left to relieve Bear, and I grabbed his seat. The legs scraped against the wood floor. I took a sip of coffee and nearly choked. It was some of the strongest I'd ever tasted. I was sure I could stand a spoon up in it, like tar. It would definitely wake a man up in the morning. I set the cup down. "So, what do we know?" I went right into our normal morning hunting routine.

Bear tossed his thumb over his shoulder as he closed the door behind him. "Who pissed off Flapjack?"

"He's just pissed he can't cook like Maria," Jax playfully flirted with Maria. It was the way they were. Lupe knew that not one of my men would ever disrespect his wife. And nothing but pride showed in Lupe's eyes as he watched his wife receive the compliments.

Diesel chuckled and swallowed the rest of his coffee with a wince. He covered the top when she went to pour more. "No thanks, I want to sleep sometime in the future."

Lupe held his cup up for more. "You can fill mine up, Mi Amor."

She sloshed the hot liquid over into his cup and grinned at him. Yes, those two definitely gave me hope.

"Alright, back to business. What do we know?" I hated being the one to sober up our mood, but the fact remained that someone was still out there watching for us. Angel was desperate to find Lily, and it was my job to protect her.

Maria somberly walked to Lupe and placed a hand on his shoulder. He reached up and clasped her hand, holding it tight. These kinds of talks were hard for them, but they never shied away from them. The more women they could help, the closer they felt to their daughter. I still hated that I couldn't bring her home for them, but they never blamed me or hated me. In reality, it brought us closer. They truly were family to me, and I would do whatever I could to protect them as well.

Jax reached for a warm biscuit on the table. "We know Angel is still out there. We know he wasn't the one behind your attack. And we know that Knox is still after Lily."

I nodded. "What else?"

"We know we're being watched," Bear grumbled, taking his own biscuit and shoving half of it in his mouth. He raised the other half up for Maria and grinned. "And it's true, Flapjack is not near as good a cook as you. Damn, woman. You should leave your old man and come cook for me."

Maria rolled her eyes and rolled a mix of Spanish words off her tongue. But her smile said everything. She lost her daughter but gained a whole house of sons.

"We know we can't trust Garcia," Lily said, walking up behind me.

I hadn't even seen her sneak out of the room. She really did have the same talent as Flapjack, I mused. Her arm went around my neck as she leaned down and kissed my cheek. I pulled her around to sit on my lap. Shit, she was gorgeous. My heart thumped wildly in my chest, thinking every man here could see her looking so damn good in her morning glow. I was the luckiest man in the world.

"She's right." I looked around at everyone. "We can't trust Garcia. We don't know who Knox was working with, but it stands to reason it was Garcia Ramirez. They'd been working together for so long. I don't see how it could be anyone else."

Lily dipped her head, her gaze not even meeting mine. It had to be hard knowing your father wanted you dead. Hell, I killed my father, so I could understand a bit more, if not differently.

I lifted her chin to look into her incredibly blue eyes. "Honey, don't do that. You have nothing to hide or be ashamed of. We are your family now, and there isn't a man," I looked at Maria and winked, "or woman, who wouldn't protect you. Don't let that man devalue your worth. Cardosas don't fucking hide."

I knew I'd used my name as hers, but damn, she was mine. She might as well be a Cardosa.

Her mouth parted softly as if to respond or argue, but a radiant blush flushed her cheeks, and she pursed her lips together in a shy smile.

"Jacob's right. Don't let Garcia make you feel like you're fucking less than him. You don't owe that cocksucker anything." Diesel pushed himself away from the table and rubbed his jaw. "Jacob, I have to tell you something."

Lily tensed. "Diesel." It was a warning, but he couldn't heed it. He'd already started, and now he had my rapt attention.

"When you were being held, you had me protect Lily."

I nodded. My arm wound its way around Lily's waist, both for my comfort of having her close and so she couldn't bolt.

"I treated that order as if I were protecting my own. Like you said, she's family now." He held my stare. Only his was filled with remorse, while mine was the opposite.

I tried to remain calm, but my nerves flared, thinking Diesel could have touched Lily... or worse. What the fuck did he mean he treated her as if she was his?

"Jacob, I told her she could come with us to get you. It was under my orders she came. It was my fault." He looked at Lily, but his face hardened, and he turned away.

"What the hell are you talking about, Diesel? What happened?" I gripped Lily's waist tighter.

Diesel flicked his tongue against his teeth, grabbed the chair's back for support, and leaned over. "I almost killed her." He stood up, and there was no mistaking the grief pouring from his soul. "You need to know because if something happens, I'm not entirely sure I'd change my mind. You know, if you place her in my charge again. With what we're talking about doing, going after Knox or Angel, hell, even Garcia. If something happens...."

"Diesel, we agreed. This wasn't just you." Lily stood up and looked right at me. "He did it because I wanted him to."

"Somebody better fucking tell me what the hell is going on because I don't take someone *almost* killing you as a good thing." I grabbed her hand before she could get any farther away and pulled her back to me.

"Before we came to get you, Diesel told me that if something happened... if I was taken... then he would kill me before they could do anything to me. He said he refused to let me live through whatever they would do to me. I agreed. I don't think I'd survive going through more than what Red did, and I saw what Knox did to my mom. I just couldn't think about living through that, Jacob. I just can't. So, I agreed." Lily gazed at Diesel, and I understood there wasn't anything happening between them. They both had a connection impressed upon them by a promise. It was hard not to feel relieved.

"What happened?" I asked, much softer this time.

"We were downstairs, and one of Leman's men grabbed me. At the angle I was at, and with the gun he had to my head, Diesel couldn't do much. He didn't want to but wasn't going to break his promise." Lily sucked in a long breath, closing her eyes, probably seeing the event over in her mind.

"I aimed my fucking gun at her, Jacob. I almost killed her. I wasn't going to let those sons o'bitches have her." He winced as he spoke, as if poison laced his words.

Lily opened her tear-filled eyes and sought my steady gaze. "But Carter came back down the stairs and saw what was happening. He shot the man holding me."

Holy shit. I couldn't believe I was that close to losing Lily. Just down the stairs from where I was. Fuck. And Diesel, how much that would have killed him to do something like that. I could now see why he was so moody. Hell, he had every right to be. And now, Flapjack's annoyance made sense. "You guys should have told me sooner."

"I know, boss. I'm sorry. Really. I just can't stop replaying it in my mind. You know?" Diesel turned to leave but gave Lily one more look. "I've replayed it a thousand times, and each time I am sure I would have done it."

"Diesel," I growled, getting his attention. "I would have done the same. I'm truly thankful you would protect her even to the end." I touched Lily's face. "If it comes down to it, I'd rather kill you myself than let them have you. Diesel was right to give you that promise. I promised it too, remember?"

Diesel nodded and opened the door, needing a moment. While I would do the same, I couldn't imagine living with the fact that he'd actually raised his gun to her and nearly pulled the trigger. It would shake me to the very core too.

"Well, I guess that explains the moody shit." Bear reached for another biscuit. "Hell, she's alive. That's all that matters."

Fox stirred. "What are you guys doing up so early?"

We all laughed. It seemed he was exactly what we needed. I wasn't sure how he slept through all that, but he was up now. "Get enough beauty sleep?"

"Shut up," quipped Fox, stretching as he stood. He snatched the blanket from the floor and placed it over a chair. "So, what's the plans today? Are we headed back home?"

"No," I shook my head. "I won't be hunted, and I sure as hell won't let Lily be hunted, so it's time to turn the tables. We're going after Angel and Knox for sure."

Bear grunted with a nod. "Maybe I should go get Flapjack and Doc. They should be here for this."

It didn't take long before they returned and sat around the table. Everyone had their own opinion over where we should go or what we should do. But it came down to what I said.

I went with what we knew. Knowing Knox was still here had me reluctant to leave too soon. He would be the first one to find. I was done with his bullshit, and it was time he paid for everything he'd done to Lily.

So far, there hadn't been any real reason to believe Angel was even in Mexico, but I wasn't letting my guard down. Maybe while we hunt Knox, we could find out more about Angel. Somebody was bound to know something. They always did. And in many cases, money talked. I wasn't opposed to paying for information on any man threatening my woman. I wasn't opposed to killing for that information, either.

With that settled, I stood to grab mine and Lily's bags to get ready. It was going to be a long day, and we needed to get going.

Outside was fresh, but the heat that radiated held a heavy humid mix to it. Damn equator. I snatched both bags effortlessly with one arm from the bed and started for the house.

"Cardosa!" Garcia called from the gate.

I groaned. I had hoped not to deal with him yet. It was inevitable, and I might as well get it over with.

"Cardosa, what the hell? I came all this way, and you left me outside all night, only to ignore me now? What the fuck is going on?" Garcia's withered brown eyes looked older today, tired and droopy. Lily definitely didn't inherit her father's eyes. Just one more thing to be grateful for.

"You weren't invited," I pointed out, lowering the bags to the ground.

Garcia's eyes bulged. "I don't give a fuck if I was invited or not. Let me in to see my daughter."

I picked the bags back up and hefted them over my good shoulder. "We'll be out soon. We're getting ready to leave."

"Leave? What about that son of a bitch Angel? You have to find him first. I'll take Lily home while you stay and look for him."

I snapped. With everything going on, the thought of leaving Lily riled me. I dropped the bags and reached through the gate, grabbing Garcia by the collar. I yanked him close. "Fuck you. Lily's safer with me. She goes where I go, and I sure as hell ain't going with you."

Garcia stumbled, showing he still wasn't up to his usual strength. "Watch it, Cardosa. You don't know what you're really getting into. Just because you're fucking my daughter doesn't mean she's yours."

Garcia was lucky there was a gate between us. Still holding on to him, I rammed him into the iron as hard as I could. He tried to drop, but I wouldn't let go. I kept him close, pulling him tightly against the gate, and leaned in. "You don't ever get to fucking talk about her again. She is mine. And I will send any man to hell who thinks otherwise. Including you."

# Chapter 47

## *Lily*

I wasn't sure what happened outside with my dad, but Jacob barely let him follow us to town. I knew what Leman said, but it was still hard to understand. True, Garcia told everyone I was dead and had me kidnapped, but he didn't want me dead. Did he? He was my father. I had to give him the benefit of the doubt.

In the truck, I waited with Jacob and Carter for the others to come back, hopefully with news about Knox or Angel. Knox had been making the rounds leaving breadcrumb trails for us to follow, but there was nothing on Angel. I knew that bothered Jacob, but I wasn't worried. I knew he'd find him.

My stomach growled, rumbling loudly between both men. For the first time in two days, Carter actually smiled at me before chuckling. He looked around me at Jacob. "It sounds like we need to feed this woman."

Jacob laughed. "I think you're right."

"The others should be back any time. We can look for a place on the way to the hotel." Carter leaned back in his seat and tapped on the steering wheel to a rhythm I couldn't hear.

"You remember that little corner place with the lady who wanted to marry you?" Jacob asked. His body shook with laughter.

Carter groaned. "Ugh, how could I forget."

"Well, they had pretty amazing food. I think you should grab us dinner from there." Jacob winked at me.

Carter scowled. "You get your own damn dinner. I ain't going anywhere near that woman. She damn near did everything but hog-tie me and hold me prisoner."

I decided to join in. A little playful teasing might help. "Carter, are you saying you'd let me starve?" I jokingly placed my hand over my chest and feigned being hurt.

"Aw, hell, not you too! You guys are gonna be the death of me." He opened the door and jumped out. "Fine. But if I come back dragging some woman at my ankles, *you* better shoot *me*." He flashed me a smile, and I knew we were okay again.

Jacob shifted, so his back was against the door. His mouth lifted into a half-cocked smile as he watched me.

"What?" I could already feel the deep crimson blush warming my cheeks. He always had a way of doing that to me.

"You are so beautiful," he whispered, lifting his hand to my face. He slid his fingers to the back of my head and pulled me in.

I braced myself with a hand on the headrest and scooted closer, unable to deny him. Our lips were so close I wasn't sure a sheet of paper could fit between us. Gently, his mouth covered mine. My free hand found his chest and inched my way up to his neck and back down.

His hand at the back of my head held me firmly from escaping. Not that I had any intentions of moving from that spot. His lips caressed mine urgently, pressing deeper. Between us, his hand in the sling rubbed my stomach, releasing a new swarm of butterflies.

It was like a natural instinct for me to get closer, climbing into his lap and straddling his legs while he turned to sit forward. His hand found its way down my back and grabbed my hip, pulling me down harder with a slight groan dripping off his tongue. I could feel his dick growing under me, pulsating tight in his jeans. My lips crashed back down on his, and I pressed myself harder against him.

The driver's side door opened completely, breaking the spell over the moment. "Ah, hell, you two need a room." Carter jumped in the seat and set a bag of food next to him.

I leaned forward and tried to hide in the crook of Jacob's neck.

Jacob laughed, but a hint of the husky rumble still lingered. "Flapjack, you sure are a killjoy."

"Well, I was the only one with enough guts to interrupt." Carter turned the key, revving the engine to life.

"What do you mean?" I asked, lifting my head to peer outside.

Diesel, Doc, Jax, Fox, and Bear were all there, waiting with shit-eating grins plastered on their faces. I was mortified. I slunk back into my seat and leaned over to bury my face in Jacob's chest, careful of his shoulder.

Doors opened, and I could hear Doc, Jax, and Fox getting in. That must mean Bear and Diesel were in the back of the bed. I couldn't look at them. The heat in my cheeks burned, and I was sure I was a brighter shade of red than a cherry.

Jax laughed and patted my shoulder. "Don't worry. We weren't watching."

Like that made me feel better. If anything, that made it worse. They *knew* what we were doing and just stood guard so we could make out like teenagers.

"How about we get to the hotel," Carter teased. He paused. "You know, so we can eat dinner and *sleep.*"

Shit. It really was like having a bunch of brothers. I was never going to live this down.

The hotel wasn't as fancy as the other one, but it wasn't a dump either. Whatever Carter got us for dinner teased me more than the guys did about Jacob and me kissing. My stomach rumbled again. It smelled amazing.

Like last time, Carter went in and checked us in, coming back with room keys for everyone. Three rooms. Jacob and I had our own. Jax, Diesel, and Fox had one, and Doc, Bear, and Carter had the other. We opted to eat dinner together before separating for the night.

Jacob had let Garcia know where we were, saying it was better to keep an eye on him than to have him out there doing shit we didn't know about. A keep your enemies closer thing. He would be there soon, checking into a room next to ours.

Dinner wasn't as good as Maria's cooking, but it was pretty close. I devoured every bite.

"Rabbit?" Carter got up and walked to the door. "Can I talk to you for a minute?"

I looked at Jacob. He shrugged, clearly just as curious as I was. Out in the hall, Carter made sure we were alone.

"I want to say I'm sorry. I was being an ass to you, and it wasn't fair. I just couldn't fathom the thought of you dead. You've really become like a sister to me, and I just couldn't understand. But I do now."

I wrapped my arms around his neck and hugged him. "You don't have to be sorry. Thank you for saving me."

He pulled back. "Well, it's not like I was gonna let you out of our little bet that easy."

"Haha. You just wait."

He opened the door and gestured for me to go before him. "I'll see ya tomorrow, Rabbit." He chuckled. "At least *try* to get some sleep."

"Hey!" I twisted to smack him, but he was already darting away.

"Goodnight, Rabbit," he sang as his door closed.

Jacob came up behind me and placed a hand at my waist. "Everything okay?"

I smirked. "Yeah." Damn brothers. Deep inside, I was happier than I'd ever been, even with them teasing me.

Everyone else decided it was also their time to go, one by one, they slipped out the door. Jacob locked the door and leaned back on it. "I didn't think I'd ever get you alone."

And just like that, my body responded with building desire, wanting him to touch me. He must have understood my silent plea because he was at the door one second, and the next, his hand was in my hair, pulling me to him.

He was slow and gentle, pressing his forehead against mine. Time stilled around us, and my heart slowed, beating only for him. His fingers trailed from my hair, grazing the side of my face down to my mouth, where he traced my lips. The feather-light touch ignited a fire across my skin, tingling in pleasurable pain, a new ache begging to be quenched.

"Jacob." Just saying his name kindled the flame.

His hand left my lips, making a path down my neck. The tips of his fingers circled the hollow of my throat before dipping lower, drawing his hand through the valley between my breasts. Even with a shirt on, I could feel the blazing trail his fingers left along my skin.

Grasping the hem of my shirt, he pulled it up. My arms were raised like an obedient student. The thin material was no longer between us. I pressed myself closer, hating that his shirt was now the only thing keeping me from feeling his skin against mine. I slid my hands up and began slowly unbuttoning each button, wanting to create a burn in him like he'd done to me.

Careful of his shoulder, I peeled the shirt off, revealing the most beautiful chest. No other man in this world could compete with him. And he was mine. Jacob Cardosa was mine. The slow burn moved lower, burrowing between my legs. Already I was wet, soaking my clothes.

Jacob found my hand and began walking away, pulling me with him. He stood at the foot of the bed. I stared into his eyes, getting drunk off their whiskey coloring, growing darker with desire. My fingers worked smoothly, unbuttoning his jeans and lowering them until I was on my knees before him. He stepped out, and I tossed the jeans away, reaching for the last part of clothing, keeping me from seeing all of him.

"Lily," he groaned, touching my hand at the waistband, but didn't stop me as I slowly pulled them off. His dick bound free and stood tall and erect. Nothing could compare to this man who stood before me. He was everything to me.

Softly, I trailed kisses across his thighs as I made my way up. I wanted to touch, kiss, and take him in any way I could. Under my lips, his dick pulsed. I caressed every inch of him, loving how velvety he felt and knowing I was the reason a low moan escaped his lips.

My tongue licked the tip as I found my way along his length. Just the taste of him about sent me over the edge. I groaned in pleasurable excitement as I tasted him again and couldn't resist the urge to take him in my mouth. This was different than last time. The last time I did this, he was teaching me. This time, I was letting my desire lead me. After everything we'd been through, this was more than just taking back what was ours.

Jacob leaned his head back and growled, "Lily." His hand found my head and gripped his fingers in my hair. His hips pushed forward, giving me better access to his full length.

I took him in my mouth, every inch I could fit, but I wanted more. I needed more. I wanted to consume him, to be a part of him and let him inside of me, melding into one.

"Honey, wait." His eyes glossed over as he looked down at me. "I want more of you." He flipped the sling off and let it drop to the floor before pulling me to stand.

I touched his bandaged shoulder gently and felt tears well in my eyes. He tipped my chin up. "Don't cry."

"I came so close to losing you," I breathed.

His mouth crashed down on mine, claiming my heart and soul. "You'll never lose me," he purred between breaths. His hand inched its way up to my bra, unclasping the hooks and allowing the lacey material to slip off my shoulders. "I'm gonna need help with your pants," he drawled in a husky whisper.

Stepping back, I watched him watch me as I slowly unbuttoned my jeans, pushing them over my hips and letting them fall to the floor. The way he looked at me made me feel so beautiful.

I stepped toward him, but he held his arm out, stopping me. "You're not finished." His chest rose and fell raggedly as he eyed the matching red pair of panties I still wore.

Heat filled my stomach as I slipped my fingers under the thin strap at my hip and pushed them down, letting them fall around my ankles.

"You're killing me." His deep voice rumbled through to my soul. "You're so beautiful." He went to his bag and pulled out a box of condoms.

I chewed on my lip and watched. My eyes couldn't tear themselves away as I watched him expertly slide the thin barrier over his fully erect length. Watching him handle himself had me close to coming.

Stepping to him like a magnet, he wasted no time claiming my mouth again. He twirled me around to the bed before finding his way to the mattress. "Come here," he said, lying back on the pillow. "You're gonna have to be on top."

I hesitated; not sure I could do what was needed. I wasn't experienced enough to give him what he gave me.

"Lily, I need you." He held his hand out for me. "Trust me."

My body reacted without further thought and went to him, crawling onto the bed. My heart sped up at what was about to happen.

He reached up and held the back of my head, pulling me down to him. His breath quickened. "Straddle me. Ride me like a horse."

I blushed, thinking about the last time we were on a horse. I slipped a leg on each side of him and felt his manhood throb between my legs. Just having him that close made me wetter.

"Lean closer," he whispered.

As soon as I was close enough, his mouth captured my breast. His tongue teased my nipple while his hand kneaded and cupped the mound. Sounds of rapture slipped past my lips that I couldn't contain.

"Let me in," he groaned against the erect bud, licking the tip.

Slowly, I arched my back. Widening my hips, I lowered myself onto him, fully accepting him into me. *Jacob*. His name was the only word I could think of as he filled me.

"Fuck me, Lily. You're so wet." Jacob growled and thrust his hips up. His hand grabbed my waist and pushed me down fully onto him.

I whimpered and moved with him.

He stilled. "Are you okay?"

I leaned over and kissed him with as much passion as I felt. My tongue swept his, and I pressed deeper. "Mmhm." How could he expect me to use actual words right now? My hips shifted to let his entire dick slide back up inside of me. I cried out again. The intense desire built inside me, pushing me closer to the edge.

He moved with me, lifting his hips and running his hand over my body. Harder, faster, he couldn't get deep enough to sate my mounting desire. Rocking up and down on his dick, feeling him inside me, I arched to meet him, giving him all of me. No holding back.

I ground my hips against his craving more as the rapture pushed past the edge and dove right for my soul. "Jacob," I cried as my insides exploded in a fury of pleasure.

Jacob groaned so loudly I thought I'd hurt him, and I stopped moving, but both his hands found my hips and began moving me up and down. I watched as his eyes closed and his jaw clenched tight. Rough growls rumbled from his chest, and he breathed my name. He thrust once more, and I could feel him pulsating inside me.

"I love you," he whispered breathlessly. "You're incredible. *That* was incredible."

"I love you, too." I went to move off him, but he held me there.

"Not yet." He winced as he moved his left arm back to his waist. "I want to feel you. Fuck, you feel so good. Even with the damn condom, I can feel your wetness soak me. You don't know what that does to me."

Leaning over, I kissed his cheek and made my way to his ear. "I think I know." I giggled and carefully rolled off him.

I practically danced to the bathroom, still reeling in euphoria. I cleaned up just as Jacob's naked frame filled the doorway. I could feel the blush creep up my face, and I ducked to hide from his view.

"I thought I told you no hiding from me."

I shrugged. "I can't help it. You are forever making me blush."

He wrapped his arm around me and kissed the top of my head. "I'll forever be doing whatever I can to make you blush." He pulled back and playfully smacked my butt. "Besides, it's sexy as hell how you get so heated."

I tossed him my best smile and tried to keep the blush from spreading anywhere else. "If you weren't so sexy, it probably wouldn't affect me so much."

He winked at me, sending my heart into a flurry of sputtering. "You better get out of here and put some clothes on, or you'll be looking at round two."

He didn't budge when I left the room, making me feel all of him along my body. Every inch. Every part. The familiar warmth pooled in my belly. Holy shit, that man had a way of creating a need inside of me that no one else would ever be able to do.

Clothes. I needed to find clothes. My bag was next to his. The box of condoms still rested on top of the opened bag, and I blushed. Gah, I needed to stop doing that.

Finding clean underclothes, I returned to the bathroom and turned on the shower while he was still cleaning up. I smirked at him as I stepped into the shower and closed the curtain. It didn't matter how many times we made love, it would always be my favorite time, but this time was special. I had made him cum. He gave me the power to move and lead.

I let the water cascade down my back, allowing the memory to flood me, needing to replay the event as the echoes of ecstasy filled my chest. A new feeling of strength took over, and I felt older. I felt like I could be the woman Jacob deserved.

This life wasn't exactly new to me, but I still had a lot to learn, and I knew if I was beside Jacob, he would teach me. I could do this.

I was sad when I got out, and Jacob wasn't there. I had half expected him to be waiting for me. Quickly, I slipped on the new garments and towel-dried my hair before leaving the bathroom. I padded my way over to Jacob on the bed.

He opened one eye to watch me cautiously. "You sleep in just those, and you're likely to get raped."

I laughed. "Well, I'm not going to bed in jeans. Besides," I lifted the blanket he was under, "it's not like you're wearing anything more." And he wasn't. His briefs were the only thing he wore.

He gestured to the other side of the bed, holding up the blanket on his good side. "Come here, woman."

I darted around the bed and climbed in next to him. My hair was still wet, but he didn't seem to mind as he wrapped his arm around me, holding me close. "Try to sleep. I have a feeling we won't be getting much after tonight."

"Not if you sleep in just those," I teased, trying to stifle a yawn.

He chuckled and kissed my head. "Goodnight, Lily."

Morning came too quickly. Leaving a bed with Jacob in it was possibly one of the worst things I'd ever had to do. But too many pressing issues needed to be taken care of for me to be selfish.

Donning my clothes, I grabbed my holster and tightened it, so it fit snugly around my waist. I held the gun that Lupe gave me and studied it. This gun helped me save the man I loved. It was quickly becoming a safety blanket for me, and I had no intentions of going anywhere without it again.

I would no longer be some stupid chess piece for men to play with. I was a stronger woman than I was yesterday, and tomorrow I will be even stronger. I placed the gun at my side and took the brush out of my bag.

Sleeping with wet hair was a pain in the ass, and I was awarded with a glorious mess of tangles. Once finished, the silky strands fell over my shoulders. It was long enough now that it almost touched my bra strap.

"I love your hair."

I jumped at the sound of his voice, not realizing he was awake, let alone watching me. "Well, it's a mess right now."

"Mmm," he breathed. "I can think of a way to mess it up even more." He winked at me.

My heart skipped a beat, and I was ready to undress myself just for him to prove his theory, but a knock on the door had me keeping my clothes on. I went to answer the door.

"Wait," Jacob said, my ever-present protector. He left the bed and went to the door. He grumbled. "Hang on," he called through the door.

I questioned him with my eyes.

"Garcia." He turned, grabbed his clothes from his bag, and pulled his jeans on. He held up the shirt and, with one look, pleaded with me for help. I giggled and took the shirt from him and helped him into it.

The sling was still on the floor from the night before, along with our discarded clothes. I swept the room, grabbing everything up. I tossed him the sling and my panties from yesterday went with it.

He held them out with two fingers and grinned wickedly. "If your father wasn't waiting outside that door, you wouldn't be picking up clothes. You'd be taking them off." He flung them back to me. "Hell, I'm not so sure I care who is outside the door."

"I can hear you, Cardosa," Garcia yelled from the hall.

I dropped the clothes on top of the bags. "I suppose we should let him in now."

Jacob growled and opened the door. "Garica."

My father entered the room, and the first place he looked was the bed. "I'm not sure I'll ever get used to the fact that my daughter is with a Cardosa."

I slipped my arm around Jacob. "Well, you better get used to it because it's not changing."

He let out a harrumph and turned his attention to us. "I think this is a waste of time. We could return to Nevada, where you'll be safe."

I shook my head. "This is the only way I'll be safe."

Garcia frowned. "Look at you, wearing a gun, holding onto Cardosa. I'm afraid you're not thinking straight. Like he's gotten inside your head."

Everything he said bristled against my nerves. "Jacob saved me. He has done more than you ever have for my safety. If you haven't forgotten, you're the reason this started in the first place!"

# Chapter 48

## *Jacob*

Not only did I not trust him, but my hatred for Garcia roared its head fully. It was no secret our families had never gotten along. Not even when my father was head of the family. But listening to him talk to Lily this way made a new ugly side of rage boil in my blood. I had already warned him back at Lupe's, but obviously, he needed something more.

I'd never felt as protective over anyone the way I did for Lily. Not even for my mother. It was embedded in my soul, like an imprint of a duty given to me before I came to this earth.

Maybe I should take Lily far away from this world and find a way to keep her safe elsewhere. I couldn't bear the thought of something happening to her. I couldn't see how I could ever go on a hunt again, knowing I might have to leave her behind. I couldn't. Wouldn't.

Garcia glared at me, but I just smirked and held onto Lily. He was sadly mistaken if he thought I would back down from anything, especially when it came to the woman I loved. "This isn't fucking right. I raised you. I protected you our whole fucking life! Everything I did was for you. And now, you spread your legs for one man, and you think he'll protect you?"

White flashes streaked through my vision. Adrenaline pulsed through my body, and my fist hurled toward Garcia's face. I connected with his jaw, and he flew backward into the door. Again, I swung. The need to pummel him raged through me. "I'll fucking kill you!"

"Jacob!" Lily cried for me. Her voice was the only thing to soothe me, calm me just enough to come back.

Shit. I'd never lost it like that before.

She touched my arm, and I leaned into her. She wrapped her arms around me from behind and kissed my shoulder. "Jacob, he's not worth it."

Garcia clutched his chest with one hand while his other hand covered his jaw. Pure malice dripped off his expression as he glared at me. "You made a fucking mistake, Cardosa."

"I don't think so. Get out." I opened the door. "Get out before I kill you."

He glanced at Lily and scoffed. "You're just like your mother."

I went for him again, but Lily grabbed my arm. "Jacob."

Garcia snickered, backing out into the hall.

"Next time we meet, I won't stop," I promised.

Lily closed the door and leaned against it, releasing a long breath. "Holy shit." She looked up at the ceiling. "Is it wrong that I wanted you to kill him?"

I chuckled and grabbed her waist pulling myself to her, resting my forehead on hers. My shoulder protested in anger over my altercation with Garcia. "Then why'd you stop me?"

"Because a small part of me wants to remember him as a dad. Growing up, he wasn't very invested as a father, but he's blood." She clenched her jaw, and I could see her fighting back the tears. "But everything I've been through. It's because of him. I hate him. I *really* hate him."

"I'll go kill him right now. All you have to do is say the words." I knew she wouldn't, but I also meant it. I would kill her father just like I killed mine and not think twice about it. If that's what she needed, I will do it.

I'd do anything for her.

She licked her lips and raised on her tiptoes to kiss me. "Not yet."

I released a shaky breath.

Her hand came to my chest and pushed me back slightly. "How come I feel you're mad for more than what he said?"

It amazed me how she could already see right through me. "I've been thinking that my world isn't for you. That I can't protect you from all the scumbags out there while I'm constantly hunting them down. And when Garcia said what he said, I just kinda lost it." I picked up her hand and brought it to my mouth, kissing her fingertips. "But I promise, I will protect you. Always."

Her smile warmed my aching heart. "I know you will." She paused. "But this world, it's mine now too. I need to help other women. I *need* to be with you. I need to be here, a part of all this."

I pressed her hand against my chest over my heart. "Lily, if you do this, it's all in. I can't do anything halfway with you. And I'll not go easy on training you because to hell if I let you come with me unprepared. You might even have to kill. Do you understand? And my promise still stands, if something happens to you, I'll kill you first, then myself. I won't live without you."

"I know what I'm doing. I know what your world entails. And you better not go easy on me. I want to be able to kick some ass. Besides, I've already killed, which means I've already been inducted. You can't get rid of me now." She leaned forward and placed her face against my chest. "And I hope you never have to kill me, but I wouldn't want anyone else to do it."

I hoped the same thing. I choked back my emotions, lodging them in my throat. This was raw. It hurt to even talk about. "Together."

"Together. From now on, we do everything together."

"Even death," I jested, but it really wasn't a joke. This woman was mine; if she died, there was no reason to live.

Another knock on the door had me on edge. Lily's eyes went wide and moved so I could look through the peephole. I relaxed. "It's just Jax."

Her petite frame visibly let go of tension.

Opening the door, I looked out and down the hall, half expecting Garcia to still be out there. Jax's stare followed mine. "What are we looking for, boss?"

"Garcia. If you see him, let me know." I sure as hell wasn't giving that man another chance.

Jax raised a brow.

"Come in. I'll explain later." I held the door open for him.

Lily walked over to the bags, shoving all the clothes into them and zipping them up.

Jax let the door close behind him but didn't move further into the room. He eyed Lily cautiously before leaning toward me, speaking low. "We got a lead on Knox this morning."

"Shit." I carved a hand through my hair. "Where is he?"

"He's a couple towns over, holding up in some bar in Iguala. Apparently, he's been a little loose with his tongue. Spreading stories about how he had Cardosa's woman, and well, I don't have to paint you a picture of what else."

"That son of a bitch!" Was this how it would always be? Someone spreading lies about Lily just because she was mine? Just the thought of hearing those lies roll off his filthy tongue had my stomach rolling. She wasn't some piece of ass that just gets passed around. She was mine. Always mine. Never his, never Red's, and never Angel's. Mine.

Lily drew up to my side, wrapping her arm around my waist. She gave Jax a sad smile. "It sounds like you guys have been busy this morning."

He clicked his tongue and nodded. "Bear and Flapjack are already on their way, scouting ahead of us."

"Good. Get the others. We'll leave in five minutes. It's a good three hours or more to get to Iguala." Damn. "What the hell is he doing all the way down there?"

"We're ready whenever you are, boss." Jax walked over and picked up our bags. "I'll take these out and meet you at the truck."

I knew he wasn't trying to be disrespectful, but just because I was shot didn't mean I was useless. "Nah, I got em'. Just tell everyone we're coming."

Jax shrugged and set the bags down. "Whatever you say, boss." He gave Lily a quick nod. "We'll be at the truck."

With Jax gone, a small part of me knew I was being an ass and should have let him help with the damn bags, but I refused to let Lily see me as any less of a man just because I got hurt. Hell, I was much better than a few days ago. I could move my arm now.

Lily sat on the edge of the bed to slip on her boots. Her tight jeans and snug shirt hugged all the right places. Just watching her had my cock growing. But there wasn't time for that now.

I followed her lead and sat next to her while I put my boots on as well. It was a bit harder one-handed, but nothing I couldn't handle. Once done, Lily held up my shoulder holster. "I'm not sure this is a good idea."

I chuckled. "No, probably not."

She faked a pout. "But you look so incredibly sexy in it."

I grasped her hip and pulled her close to look up at her. "Maybe I'll wear just that to bed tonight."

The crimson blush swept across her cheeks. "Maybe you should."

"You are gonna kill me, woman." I pulled her down to kiss her head and then nodded at the bags. "There's a spare holster for my waist in there."

I stood as she found the holster that fit on my belt and came back to me. Staring right into my eyes, she unbuckled my belt and slipped part of it out from the loops. Fuck, it was sexy as hell. She placed the holster on the leather strap and then slid the belt back around my waist. Her fingers slowed as she came to the buckle, letting the tips slide between the jeans and my skin.

I stood still, letting her tease me. Damn near ready to toss her on the bed and show her what she was doing to me, but no, I stood there and let her fingers graze my lower abdomen while she buckled the belt.

I wasn't sure who started breathing again first, but the spell broke when she pushed herself back to admire her work. "Perfectly in place."

Her fingers were dang close to being in the perfect place. "Woman, you are a minx."

She giggled and grabbed her bag, slinging it over her shoulder. I quickly took it from her. "I got it."

To hell, if I let her carry her own bag, especially after telling Jax no.

Iguala was much further south in Mexico than I wanted to go. I hated it. It wasn't just hot and humid, but it was crammed with even more people. That could be good and bad, depending on what I needed.

Jax pulled the truck up to a rundown building. Hell, everything here looked dilapidated. Everywhere was crowded and congested. Old cars and trucks lined the streets, making it nearly impassable. The entire city had an old western cantina vibe lacking the modern improvements of other places worldwide. It was all too easy to take the comforts easily indulged in at home for granted.

"Looks like Bear and Flapjack over there." Jax opened the door.

I checked to make sure Lily had her gun. "Shoot if you need. Don't hesitate."

Her calm face held an expression I hadn't seen on her before. The confidence she radiated had me bursting with pride. This woman, who had already killed to save me, was the only woman for me.

Diesel and Doc followed us outside. Diesel still felt he had something to make up to her or a promise to uphold. Keeping his guard over her, he didn't stray far. At least I knew she had a backup bodyguard if something happened to me.

Bear nodded at me as we walked up. He and Flapjack were at an outside table, both with drinks in their hands and sunglasses donning their faces. It was all part of their stakeout. Bear looked menacing with his bald head, tattoos, glasses, and a beer pressed to his lips. Shit, if I saw him on the streets of Mexico, I wouldn't want to dance with him.

"Knox is holed up across the street in that little cantina with the orange roof." It was hard to see where Flapjack's gaze landed behind his glasses. He lifted the brown glass bottle slowly, meticulously to his mouth, and took a swallow. "Behind us, we have a couple of watchdogs, not sure of their names, haven't seen them before, but not too worried."

Bear finished his drink with a long swig and set the bottle on the table. Leaning back in his seat, his stance wide and apparently comfortable, he nodded at me. His ruse to throw the men watching us off track had him playing a part I knew well. He was really good at acting calm and collected. After all these years, I could see things others couldn't, like how his right hand hung off the back of the chair, showing me three prominent fingers telling me there were three men. Or like how his head cocked back and to the right told me where they were at. If his leg bounced, it would tell me they were moving faster and closer... or slow and steady meant they were moving position.

I gave them both a polite nod and placed my hand on Lily's back to lead her away, knowing they wouldn't be far behind.

"So, he's in there, right?" Lily lifted her chin to the orange roof.

"Yup." I pressed her to move closer to me, not liking how many men were already drunk and watching her as we passed.

She turned, moving from my grasp, and headed toward the bar. "Lily." I tried to get her to turn back, but she just kept going. I hastened my pace to keep up with her, not letting her out of my sight for one second.

Behind me, Bear, Flapjack, and Diesel flanked me. Doc and Jax had the outside to watch while we went in.

I expected her to stay in the shadows and leer through the crowd to find Knox, but not my girl. She walked in like she owned the fucking place. I couldn't keep the damn smile off my face as I watched her. A calm came over me, and I realized she was right. This was her world, too, and damn did she look good in it.

Knox was in the back corner. His boisterous voice carried through the crowd. The slur of words he said made no sense, and hardly any of them I could hear until he said her name. My heart leaped and stuttered. I reached out to touch the small of her back, letting her know I was there, but also to calm my nerves.

Lily didn't stop, she just kept walking, but I wasn't about to stop her. Curiosity got the better of me, and I was excited to see what my little minx had planned. Whatever it was, she knew I had her back. I would follow through whatever she wanted.

# Chapter 49

## *Lily*

My mind went blank but was actively spinning with every damn memory at the same time. My stomach churned, and bile rose in my throat. Jacob's hand on my back was the only thing tying me to the present.

I just kept walking toward Knox as if my legs held their own vendetta and refused to not seek revenge. The closer I got, the worse I felt. The vile memories that would haunt me forever consumed my mind. The things he'd done in front of me and to me, I would never be able to forgive him for.

He'd kidnapped me. Raped my mother. Abused us. Killed her. Kidnapped me again. Shoved me in a trunk and sold me to the highest bidder.

His cheek was still raw from where I bit him a week ago. I smirked as he looked up to see me standing there. I wish I had bitten more off.

My heart thundered loudly in my ears, drowning out the music and drunk men. I wasn't worried, not in the least. Jacob was there. He would make sure I was safe while I dealt with my demon.

Knox's eyes shifted from me to Jacob, then back to me quickly before trying to look calm. Except I knew him. He was anything but calm. The sweat on his brow glistened, and his lips quivered. "I'm a bit surprised to see you here, Cardosa. Alive anyway."

Fuck him.

All I could see was red flashing in my eyes. Call it instinct. Call it rage. I didn't fucking care what it was, but I knew it felt right as I reached for my gun.

The handle slipped perfectly into my hand, and my finger naturally took its place at the trigger. I wouldn't miss. Knox's eyes widened as he saw what was about to happen, but it was too late. I squeezed the trigger and felt the power of the gun shoot through my arm as the bullet found its way to my mark.

The bar patrons whizzed by me, pouring out the door and escaping the scene.

Jacob didn't even flinch. Everything that led to that moment flashed before me. A million times, someone could ask if I regret killing him, and the answer will always be no.

"Aw, shit, that's our girl," Bear bragged as he squatted down to examine my handy work. "Well, she sure as hell didn't miss."

My hand remained steady as I replaced my gun back at my side and looked for Jacob. His smile widened, and he winked. "Cardosas don't miss."

Carter whistled. "It looks like Diesel is gonna have to brush up if he's gonna compete against our girl. Damn, Rabbit, you got him right between the eyes." He slapped his knees as he stood. "It looks like you met your match in every way, boss."

Jacob chuckled. "That I did."

While they talked wildly over Knox's dead body, I was still reeling. I was numb, void of the excitement they brandished. I thought I would feel sick or shocked. Even wrong. But I didn't. I felt stronger.

Blood stopped pooling around Knox's body, and I stepped over him.

"Lily, you okay?" Jacob asked. He tilted his head and held me in an intense gaze, seeking the answer from my soul.

That was a loaded question. I looked down at Knox and smiled easily. I closed my eyes and leaned back, taking a full breath. A wave of peace rolled through me. "Yes." I left Knox's body, determined not to look back. "I'm better than okay. I feel free."

The bartender, unafraid of our group, stalked up to Jacob. He was a short man with round beady eyes. Everything he said was in Spanish, and I could pick out only one or two words, neither of which were good.

Jacob pulled out his wallet and handed the man a few bills saying something back to him in the man's language. I didn't know Jacob could speak Spanish and watched in awe. The man stopped complaining and opened his arms out for the whole building, shaking his head yes and smiling.

"He said we could shoot anyone here for that kind of money," Jacob laughed. He wrapped his good arm around my shoulders and leaned in. "Are you sure you're okay?"

I nodded. "Yeah. It kinda feels like I took my life back. It's hard to explain, but I just had to do it myself."

He kissed the top of my head. "How'd I get so damn lucky?"

Diesel held his fist out for me to bump. "Damn, woman, you got some skills."

Jacob held his head high. "Hell yes, she does."

My heart skipped at his praises. Knowing he was just as proud of me for overcoming Knox as I was of myself had me falling a little more in love with this man. I gave him a smug grin. "I told you I was meant to be with you."

"Boys, leave that bastard to rot. I have a need to take this woman home." Jacob took my hand and pulled me with him.

Outside, Doc found us first. "I assume he's dead?"

Jacob nodded. "Lily took care of him."

My grandfather eyed me with a crooked smile. "Well, damn if I didn't see that coming. As it should have been. He deserved it, honey, don't think back on it and twist it. You understand?"

I didn't, but I nodded anyway. Why in the world would I twist it? Maybe it was something he'd experienced before and didn't want the same for me? Either way, I wasn't about to let Knox steal any more of my life. He was dead. I killed him. And damn, it felt good.

# Chapter 50

## *Jacob*

Holy shit. I still couldn't believe Lily just walked right in with no fear and shot Knox. Not that I blamed her. Fuck, I wanted to kill the man too. For everything he'd done to Lily, he deserved nothing less than death. Although, my way would have been longer, dragging it out, making him pay minute for minute for all the things he'd done to her. But there was no way in hell I would refuse her a chance to heal. If shooting him helped her, then I was all for it. Hell, I was sure she had more reasons than I did to want that bastard dead.

I clasped Lily's hand tightly in mine as we boarded the plane. It was late by the time we made it back to Toluca, but there hadn't been any sign of Angel in Mexico. The last place anyone had heard of him being was in Vegas, so I decided to head back home. No reason to hide out in a foreign country when I could be at home with my own security, sharing my bed with the woman I loved.

One day everything I had, including my bed, would be hers, legally. I didn't want to go through this life without her as my wife. I wanted to share everything with her. My house, my bed, my name. Just thinking about it had my insides raging with a need to consume her body.

She leaned her head to rest on my shoulder and sighed contently. "Home."

"Home," I repeated. "Now try to sleep. It's been a long day."

She yawned and scoffed at the same time. "It's been a long few years."

I squeezed her hand and watched as her eyes closed. It wasn't long before everyone else was asleep aside from Doc and me. He shifted in his seat across from me and gazed at his granddaughter. "It's easy to see how much you two love each other. You've already gone to the ends of the earth for each other. But I want you to be careful, Jacob. Take care of her."

That was the easiest promise I'd ever have to keep. "Doc, that is one promise I'll never break."

He chuckled. "I don't reckon you would."

The flight back to Vegas went through the night, but we made it back mid-morning. Lily slept through the whole flight. It was good for her. She still had so much healing to do, physically and emotionally.

The hotel already had my suite ready for us when we got there, along with two other rooms for the men. I wasn't sharing my room this time. It was more of a need than a want to be alone with Lily.

It was best to come straight to the hotel. I didn't want Angel to know we were in town yet, or that I had Lily with me.

"Boss, if it's okay with you, I'm gonna sleep for a week." Fox's shoulders slumped as we all trudged to the elevators.

I kept my arm around Lily, not letting go. I couldn't. I wasn't sure when I would be able to do so without fear or panic setting in over losing her. But she clung to my shirt just as tightly as we walked.

Everyone but her and I got off two floors below my suite. I had never taken her here yet, so she had no idea where we were going. Her surprised look said it all as she walked into the room. "Jacob, this is huge. Surely we don't need so much room."

I growled and briskly walked to her. "I'm gonna christen every inch of this room with you." I claimed her mouth with mine, fulfilling the desire to do that since last night.

Her lips moved quickly under mine, thrusting her tongue to search for mine. Wildly, my hands were everywhere. Both hands. Pain be damned, I was going to love my woman.

Rubbing down her back, along her neck, tangled in her hair, at her waist, I couldn't pick a place I wanted to stay. I needed to feel all of her. No. She deserved more than a two-minute fling on the floor. Which is where this was headed.

I pulled back and tried to slow my breathing. "I want to do this, really, but I need to love you more." I reached out for her hand. "Come with me, Lily."

Her eyes, already clouded with desire, watched me as she followed me up the stairs to our bed. Beside the bed on the nightstand were two glasses and a bottle of white wine chilling on ice. I didn't drink wine often, but the ice was working in my favor. I grinned.

Taking the sling off, I didn't even grimace when I moved my arm. I didn't want her to worry or think anything about my wound. Today was about her.

I pulled her shirt up, untucking it from her jeans before lifting it all the way off. Her hair fell down, cascading across her chest. I gently moved one side over her shoulder and followed her bra strap to the back. Expertly, I pinched the fabric unhooking the clasps. Taking one strap at a time, I stared into her eyes as I slipped it off.

The throbbing intensified in my dick as it grew, held back only by the restriction of my jeans. I wasn't sure how I was moving so slowly when everything in me screamed to bury myself in her.

Without touching her skin, I unbuttoned her jeans and pushed them down around her ankles, where she stepped out. She didn't move away but stood there, letting me take her all in. Damn, she was beautiful. Only one more article of clothing had to go, but I was losing myself in the sight of her. I gripped the thin fabric of her panties and ripped them off in one swoop.

Her chest rose with heavy breaths, beckoning me to taste her. Stepping forward, I found her neck and left a trail of kisses down her collarbone. "Lay on the bed," I damn near demanded.

She turned to the bed and crawled to the middle. Fuck. She was doing that on purpose. "Lay there and close your eyes."

With her on her back, everything was spread out for me to see in all her beauty. I picked up a piece of ice and relaxed on the bed beside her. Gently, I let the ice touch the hollow of her throat. She tensed for only a second before arching slightly in a silent plea that my body understood. Slowly, I moved the ice down, cresting her full mounds to the tight peak of her nipple, letting the ice drip as it melted. I captured the cold bud in my mouth and groaned as she writhed in delight.

I sucked the water off her and pushed the ice lower. She gasped as I slid it down between her legs. The ice was almost gone now. Only a tiny piece remained between my fingers as I settled it over her small nub. I took her nipple between my teeth and teased before letting go. There was more water to lick off her.

My lips feathered her skin, taking the time to softly kiss around her wound that looked more like a distant scar from the past now. I loved it, though. It was what brought her to me. But I vowed that she would never again have a reason to attempt to kill herself.

The ice was gone, but I let my fingers remain there, touching her ever so slightly. My tongue found her wet nub and licked with enough pressure to have her squirm. Her legs widened, and she moaned my name. Fuck me. My cock pulsed in response and begged to answer her.

Damn, she tasted so sweet. It took everything I had to not devour her entirely and have her cum in my mouth. Hell, I wanted that. I dove my tongue deeper, slipping inside of her, and groaned. She was so wet.

Lily whimpered and arched her back. "Jacob," she said breathlessly. Her hands reached for me, framing my head.

"Cum for me, honey. Cum, and I promise I will do anything you want." I leaned on my good arm and trailed my other hand to her wetness. I licked her again, filling my mouth of her. Slipping a finger inside her, she tightened, and I damn near came in my jeans.

"Please," she begged. "Jacob."

"I know, honey. Just let go." I pulled out and thrust in three fingers. I was being fucking greedy, needing her to all over me. To feel her tighten around me.

I held my breath, trying to stop my cock from beating me to what was coming.

She tightened around my fingers and cried out. Her hips bucked up, trying to get more. I moved my hand, replacing it with my mouth, sucking her wetness until she stopped coming.

"Jacob," her words came out in broken, raspy whispers, "you said... you'd do... anything."

I nodded and sucked my fingers, tasting her all over again. "Anything, honey."

"I need you. Please." She writhed on the bed, her motions erotic.

"Fuck. You are amazing." I stood and shed my clothes. I stood beside her, fully erect, pre-cum dripping off my tip.

She reached for me and grabbed my dick. Her hand tightly ran up and down the entire length. "Please," she begged again. "You said you'd never deny me."

Kneeling over her, I braced myself with my good arm. No way in hell was I going to keep a fucking gunshot wound from making love to my woman. Her legs were still spread, waiting for me. I climbed between them, and the tip of my dick barely touched her as I waited for a moment.

Shit. I needed a condom. I got back out of bed, found exactly what I needed, and rolled it on in record time. I reclaimed my place between her legs and pressed gently at her opening.

Lowering myself to my elbow, I found her mouth, and my tongue darted in and out as I slipped inside her. A deep growl resonated in my chest. Fuck. She fit me perfectly. Her hips lifted to meet mine and take me inside her even more.

I would never get enough of his woman. She was mine. I thrust harder, needing to bury myself deep inside her. I couldn't tell where she began, and I ended. Her body wrapped around me in every way.

The heat from her flared my desire, and I couldn't stop my hips from rocking faster. I needed her. "Lily," I cried out, wanting her to know she was the only woman for me. Forever, it would only be her.

Mounting pleasure erupted, and pure bliss drenched my soul as momentary blindness took over. My cock pulsed as I came inside of her. Damn fucking condoms. I hoped she wouldn't be against birth control soon because I couldn't do this without feeling her too many more times. It was the last barrier between us. Something about the thought of my cum spilling out into her had me throbbing again. I thrust one last time, wanting to keep us connected, and she writhed underneath me. The hottest wetness soaked around my length, and I knew she came for a second time.

I collapsed beside Lily with my dick still buried inside of her.

"Jacob," she breathed heavily.

I lifted to gaze into her eyes only to drown in their deep pools of heated desire. Sex looked amazing on her, lying sated and well fed.

"That was amazing." She blushed but didn't hide it from me.

I took her hand and brought it to my face. Her palm was warm against my cheek. Pulling it down, I kissed her fingers. "Everything with you is amazing." I kept kissing her hand, working my way to her palm.

"At first, I was afraid I wouldn't be enough for you. That my inexperience would turn you off." Her cheeks grew brighter. "But, I don't think anyone else could ever feel what I just felt."

I grinned. Damn, if my insides didn't tremble knowing I had given her so much pleasure. Knowing it was me who filled her with rapture and a reason to thrash on the bed in agonizing ecstasy. "Lily, what I feel is much more. I love you, but it's even more than that. You're my breath, my life, my soul."

"Cardosa, you took the words from my heart."

"You've taken so much of me. I don't even belong to myself anymore." And nothing in the world would make me want it any other way.

# Chapter 51

## *Lily*

Being in Vegas wasn't my ideal vacation but having Jacob with me this time almost made the memories go away. I stretched and got up. I was a little sore from last night, but definitely in a good way. I lost count of how many times he made me cum. And his stamina throughout the night was impressive. I was still new to everything we did, but I knew enough from sex ed and high school that most men couldn't do *it* that many times in a row. But then again, Jacob wasn't most men.

I stood at the window, completely naked and unashamed. No one would see me this high up anyway. The only eyes on me were Jacob's. Down below, the street was nearly empty. Morning was like Vegas's midnight. Everyone was sleeping.

I crossed my arms over my chest and shuddered. As much as I wanted killing Knox to fix everything, I knew Angel was out there. It didn't matter how fearless or courageous I had been. It was still a bit scary wondering if we'd find him before he found me.

"I'll have breakfast brought up. It shouldn't be long before everyone starts knocking on our door anyway," he laughed and rolled out of bed.

It was hard not to watch his perfectly sculpted backside as he slipped into the bathroom.

It didn't take long before breakfast arrived, along with all my newly acquired brothers and a grandfather. It was a good thing I had dressed and run a brush through my hair first.

Jacob ordered enough food to feed an army, but after the men grabbed what they wanted, I was lucky there was anything left. I shook my head and smirked. They really were brothers. I grabbed a bunch of grapes and a bagel and then curled up on the sofa. Jacob joined me, and I tossed my legs over his as I finished my breakfast. He sipped on a cup of coffee and something that looked like a cream-filled donut.

"Well, word on the street is that Angel *is* here," Fox said, his mouth full of toast.

Diesel took a swig of orange juice. "Yeah, but like usual, no one has seen him to confirm anything."

I picked at the bagel. "So we need to draw him out."

Jacob raised a brow at me. "No, *we* aren't doing anything."

Diesel nodded. "Yeah, it's too dangerous for you to show yourself around here." He looked at me knowingly. "I refuse to follow through on any promise right now."

I rolled my eyes. "For the love, do you guys hear yourselves? I am not a fucking puppet. I'm not a doll. I refuse to spend the rest of my life living this way. Either I'm with you," I glanced at Jacob, "or I'm not." I tossed the bagel to the plate. "Look, yes, I'm a woman, but if I'm going to be doing this right alongside you, then you better stop treating me like I'm a china doll." I sat up straight, leaving Jacob's comfort. "Jacob and I already agreed that we do this together. I'm part of this world, in more ways than any woman should ever have to be, but I'm not leaving. So, what do you say?"

Carter whistled and plopped down beside me. "Rabbit, I wouldn't want to do this without ya. But remember, if you break, it isn't just Jacob who has your back."

Bear and Jax nodded. Diesel just stared at me, our silent bond speaking for us. Fox shrugged, "Heck, I'm still new here, so I'm not sure I get much say in this, but I've seen you with a gun. I'd like to have you on our side."

Doc grunted. "Being family doesn't depend on time spent with us. You saved Lily with Red. That makes you family, and you get a say in it."

"Agreed." Jacob took another sip of coffee. "Lily's right. She's a part of our family now. And while my order still stands that nothing happens to her, as she will be my first priority always, we have to let her live too."

I mouthed a thank you to him. He winked at me, and my insides heated.

"Fine," Jax settled in a chair and chowed down on scrambled eggs. "So, what do you want to do?"

"I think we draw him out. Let him see me. We need to flip it, so we have the upper hand." I saw the pride in Jacob's eyes as I kept telling them my plan. "So, that's why I think Jacob and I should go out. Just the two of us, like a date," I giggled.

Jacob had eyes only for me. "Oh, honey, if a date is what you want, then a date you shall have."

"Seriously, didn't you guys get enough time last night?" Fox's sarcasm had everyone laughing, but I blushed.

"Okay, so you two go out, we follow." Bear nodded. "Sounds easy enough. And there's enough of us to protect you should something happen."

I wanted to say something about not needing protection but remembered that they always protected each other. They hunted together, like a pack, a family. I nodded. "Yes. If Angel shows his face, then you'll know it."

The day went by so slowly. I was finally getting to go out on a date with Jacob Cardosa. We were way past dating, but it still excited me.

Jacob went downstairs to grab something and came back up with two boxes. He handed it to me and left the bedroom part of the suite to let me open it alone. Curiously, I lifted the lid and gasped. A royal blue dress filled the box. I pulled it out and held it up. It had an asymmetrical hem and a belted waist. The round neckline scooped over like a halter leaving it completely sleeveless.

I set the dress down and picked up the second box, finding black strappy heels. I grinned so wide my cheeks hurt. It really was a date. I squealed and clutched my new outfit to my chest, darting to the bathroom. Donning the dress, I sighed in contentment. It fit me like the seamstress made it just for me. I stared at myself in the mirror and couldn't believe the woman staring back was me. When did I get those curves? And my hair... I touched the soft tresses and smiled. Somehow, during all of this, I had grown up. I was a woman. I was Jacob's woman. Holy shit. I couldn't wait until he saw me in this.

Leaving the bathroom, I didn't have to wait long as he stood at the window, dressed in tight-pressed jeans that he filled out entirely and a white button-down shirt with his sleeves rolled a quarter of the way up. My breath caught in my throat.

Even from across the room, I could see him stop breathing. "Lily." It was so quiet I barely heard him. He was across the room in three swift strides and had me in his arms. His mouth crashed down on mine. I smiled, breaking the kiss.

He took my hands and pushed me out to twirl me. Admiring me. All of me. If ever I felt like a woman, it was then.

"You are so damn gorgeous. Honey, there ain't a guy in this city who won't think I'm the luckiest bastard in the world." He twirled me again for good measure.

I batted my lashes. "Why, Cardosa, if I didn't know better, I'd say you were trying to undress me with your eyes."

He growled and twirled me to him. I crashed into his chest, where I was met with hard muscle. "If you don't stop teasing me, I'll undress you with more than just my eyes."

A knock on the door broke our fun little banter. It was probably a good thing because I was ready to let him keep me here and have his way with me.

"Your limo is here, sir," the doorman said before accepting a tip from Jacob.

"Limo?" I asked, descending the stairs to the lower level of the suite.

He grinned shyly. "Well, my girl wanted a date." He held his arm out for me. "Ready?"

## Gracin Sawyer

I was never more ready for anything.

# Chapter 52

## *Jacob*

I couldn't stop staring at the woman across the table from me. Hell, I still couldn't believe that woman was mine. The way she smiled. Her laugh. Damn, even her voice. Everything about her had me enthralled. I loved hearing her stories of when she was younger before Knox took her. We stayed away from those years. Tonight, while not the perfect date, was about us. I couldn't wait to take her out on a date and not to be bait.

The waiter came by and asked about dessert. Lily shook her head, but I ordered a decadent chocolate dessert. Seeing her eyes twinkle after taking the first bite was worth a million dollars. "Mmm, this is so good."

I chuckled and wiped my mouth on the napkin. "I think I'd like a taste." She grabbed her fork, but I held her hand down and came around the table. I leaned over, capturing her mouth with mine, and sucked gently before letting my tongue taste hers.

"Jacob," she whispered against my lips. "People are watching."

I stood up and walked back to my seat. "Good. Then they know you're mine and you are well loved."

I loved the blush that crept up her face. I couldn't get enough of her. Unfortunately, the kiss wasn't just to taste my dessert. I needed to move to confirm my gut feeling. I knew we were being followed, but I wanted to see who it was and by how many.

I held my hand up for the check so Bear could see the three fingers. I'm sure he already saw them, but I needed to tell them we were indeed being followed.

I smiled at the waiter and gave him my card to pay for dinner. Lily stood, and I wrapped my arm around her. My shoulder was starting to kill me. I would have to slow down with it and let it heal a bit more before I used it too much.

The waiter brought my card back, and I signed the receipt. Leaving the restaurant, the night air hit me like a brick. Being this warm at night was not something I liked. The mountains of home cooled every night, even in the summer, giving me a break from the heat of the day.

"Let's walk," Lily said, ignoring the limo.

The lights of the strip were quite mesmerizing, and it was her date. I shrugged and told the driver we were done for the night.

"I love the energy. It feels so alive." She held my hand and pulled me along the strip. Fountains called to her, and she stopped to watch the show, but all I wanted to watch was her. She had no idea she was more beautiful and intriguing than anything this world could show her.

"Hey," I pulled out my cell phone. "There is something we are missing." I wanted to capture this moment and hold it forever.

"Oh yeah, what?"

"A picture. A selfie more accurately. Everyone does it." I stood next to her, so our backs were toward the water fountains spraying high, and held the phone up, capturing our picture on the screen.

She snagged the phone and curled her lip. "Ugh, seriously? We can do better."

I laughed. She held the phone out, and just as she snapped the picture, she turned to kiss me on the cheek. "There, now that is better," she said, handing me the phone back.

"Come on," I held my hand out for her. The hotel wasn't far, and we made it without the three men striking.

Inside, I spotted Jax in the corner. His arm was around a pretty lady, and they laughed. He gave me a slight nod, and I knew his scouting had gone well. He cocked his head, letting me know where to look. It was amazing how well-oiled our routines were. He knew how to blend in. That part was certain. No one would think he was spying. Hell, no one but me knew he probably paid the woman to stand there and act like they were happy.

We walked through the casino on our way to the elevators. The way Lily looked, she was lucky we were being followed, or I'd find a place to hide and hike that dress up and bury myself in her. I could imagine how she'd look on a table, her dress still on, with me pushing her panties just off to the side to thrust into her. How wet she would be. How incredibly sexy.

I hit the elevator button and tried not to think about it. If I kept it up, I'd be hitting the stop button and holding her up against the glass walls, cameras be damned.

We were the only ones in a usually crowded lift. The doors almost shut when a hand stopped them from closing. I pushed Lily behind me. The three men entered the elevator and closed the doors.

Angel sure picked his bodyguards to look the part. The black suits and dark glasses were a dead giveaway. Especially when they wore them indoors. "Angel wants to meet with you."

"I'm sure he does," I drawled.

To Lily's credit, she didn't look surprised. Actually, her face held a completely stoic expression, not showing any kind of emotion. I smirked inwardly. I'd have to teach her how to play poker one day. The boys would love that.

I kept Lily's hand tightly and followed the men to one floor under ours. We kept pace quickly enough, and I wondered if they knew they were also being followed. I had no doubts that my men had eyes everywhere we were right then.

They opened a door and held it open for us. Once Lily and I were inside, they closed the door and waited outside. Well, whatever Angel wanted to talk about, he didn't want an audience. Interesting.

His room wasn't as lavish or large as my suite, but it wasn't the worst room in the building. Reds and blacks orchestrated a variety of shapes and colors around the room. It wasn't soothing or calm, but quite the opposite. And exactly what I pictured for a man like Angel. Not that I'd ever met him in person. Hell, not many had. He was elusive and kept to himself, using his guards to do his work for him.

"Come on in," Angel said, swirling a glass of what looked like bourbon or whiskey. He stood to greet us from his oversized chair, setting the drink down on the table.

Lily clenched my hand, and I gave her a gentle squeeze back, hoping to let her know everything would be okay. I wouldn't let anything happen to her.

"Angel," I presumed, stopping about five feet short of his outstretched hand.

He was a tall man but not scrawny. He had a neatly trimmed goatee and vividly blue eyes. Eyes as blue as... Oh fuck.

"Jacob Cardosa." Angel smiled and assessed me, then slowly let his gaze roll over Lily, his smile fading. "Lily."

"What the fuck do you want, Angel?" I held my stance and watched for any signs of danger, just in case.

Angel glanced back at me. "I'm glad you found her. When I had Jose call and warn you about your woman, I didn't know it was Lily. If I'd had known that she never would have left here. I would have kept her safe."

I scoffed. "You? Keep her safe? I'm confused."

Angel sat back down and gestured to the sofa. "Sit. I promise neither of you is in danger here."

Lily took the first step forward, which brought a grin to Angel. I kept her glued to my side and placed myself between her and our host.

He picked his drink up and took a sip. "I'm sorry. How rude. Would you like a drink?"

"No, thank you," Lily answered for both of us.

"So, like I said," Angel cleared his throat, "when Knox had some girl he claimed was Cardosa's, I didn't know it was Lily. But I decided to use that as leverage. And I thank you, by the way. It was a very uneventful week." He swirled the liquid and took the last swig. "After I found out the girl was, in fact, Lily, and she had been sold to Red, the only thing I could do was wait and hope you found her in time." He glared down his nose at me. "You *did* find her in time, yes?"

What the hell did it matter to him? I glared back. I was not one to be intimidated. "Angel, why are we here?"

"You know, I had men ready in case you failed. I wasn't about to head to Mexico myself just yet, but I had a backup for her safety."

Angel was pissing me off. I was in no mood for a bedtime story.

He continued. "I have a question for you, Cardosa. It will help you solve this little riddle. Who did Red work for?"

What game was he playing? I needed to figure it out. Too many things bounced in my head, and each one fought for a way to keep Lily safe. "Red didn't work for anyone."

"Wrong!" Angel stood up and paced. "Everyone works for someone. Even you, Cardosa. You work for the people. You do your saving the women shit. So, tell me," he slowed down to enunciate each word, "*who* did Red work for? There is always someone higher up."

Shit. Angel was fishing for information, but why? For what? There was something I was missing.

"How about another one." Angel picked up his glass, walked to the bar with a crystal carafe filled with amber liquid, and poured himself another drink. "Why do you think Garcia faked his *daughter's* death?" The way he spat out Garcia's name was nothing but poison. There really was a deep rift between them.

I listened, looking for the right clues, but came up empty.

Angel downed the entire drink in one swallow and slammed the glass down. "It was never about a deal." He looked right at Lily. "It was about the truth."

# Chapter 53

## *Lily*

The way Angel stared at me sent shivers down my spine, but not in a good way. The truth? What truth? I should have been afraid of the man who wanted me so badly that my own father faked my death, but I wasn't. As long as Jacob was with me, I wasn't afraid.

Everything this man said was confusing, like he spoke in riddles, wanting me to figure shit out on my own. Another game, I concluded. I was so sick of games. Fine. I'll try to play along. But only for a minute.

The truth. Everything was over the truth. Did Garcia lie to him? Was Garcia covering up the truth? Or was Garcia blackmailing Angel over knowing the truth about something? Ugh. I gave up. I wasn't playing anymore. "What did Garcia lie about that was so bad he was willing to have his wife and daughter kidnapped? Why did he have to fake my death?"

Angel smiled sadly. "Good questions. The answer? Because you aren't his daughter."

What? There is no way I heard him correctly. "Could you repeat that?"

"He could kill you off because you aren't his." Angel poured another drink and held it out for me. "Are you sure you don't want a drink?"

Hell, I wasn't sure about anything. I took the glass and sniffed it. It smelled horribly strong. I handed it back. "No thanks."

He took the glass and drank it like a shot, all in one gulp. It had to burn. I cringed for him. "I don't understand. If I'm not his daughter, then who's my father?"

Angel sat back down and leaned forward, placing his head in his hands and wiping his face. I wasn't sure he was going to tell me anything, but his voice cracked. "Rachael and I were in love a long time ago." He smiled fondly when he said her name. My heart fluttered, scared at what I was about to hear. "I loved that woman more than life itself. There wasn't anything I wouldn't have done for her." His wistful gaze left us, and his mind was somewhere else. "I knew about you, about the pregnancy, before I left. I had a *business* trip."

Angel shook his head and looked at me. His eyes, his very blue eyes. I gulped. "Garcia always wanted her. She was gorgeous. She was exactly the right kind of trophy wife. So while I was gone, he manipulated her. He told her I was dead. Told her that was the price she paid for loving me and not him. She grieved and told him he was lying, but he was very *persuasive*." His jaw clenched, and his fists tightened. "He told her he would kill you. He would kill the baby she carried. The last thing she would have of mine if she didn't marry him."

"Angel," I whispered, hating his words but needing to hear them just the same. My heart squeezed in agony for him.

"When I returned, they were already married. At first, I was furious. I thought she had betrayed me. I'm sure you could imagine how I felt," he asked Jacob.

Jacob nodded and squeezed my hand. "There are no words."

"Mmhm. He's right. Nothing can describe what I felt. By the time I learned what happened, Garcia wouldn't let me get close enough to tell her I was alive... to come for you. So I waited. And finally, about five years ago, fate intervened for me." He chuckled. "I keep to myself, so I can get closer without anyone knowing who I really am. And it worked. I was in the same room as Garcia. I wanted to kill him. I wanted to put my hands around his neck and take his last breath, but I couldn't because he held you and your mother over me. I had to make sure you were safe first."

He stood and carved his hands through his nearly black hair. "I told him I would go public, reveal everything. I've spent your entire lifetime collecting dirt on him. Every breadcrumb trail he left, I found. I have more proof than I need to convict and put him away for thirty lifetimes. He thought he had everything covered up, but he didn't. I paid a hell of a lot more to the same people. I wasn't as stingy with my money. So I had it set. I would reveal everything, and Rachael could finally be free. I could have my family."

He choked back a sob and slammed his fist on the bar, shaking the glass. "But then he pulled that fucking stunt and told me he killed you. He even had a death certificate drawn up. My heart couldn't take it. I thought I had killed you. And if I didn't play along, he would kill Rachael too." He leaned forward, bracing himself on the bar. "I thought I killed you," he repeated.

I shook. My nerves were shot. I didn't know whether I should believe him or not. His story was so convincing, and it was no secret my mother hated my father. But... Why was he doing this?

Angel straightened and wiped at his face. "News travels fast in this world. So, when I heard about you, I came back to Nevada as fast as I could, but I was too late. Again. Knox had you on a plane. By the time I found out it was you, I was inconsolable. I had Jose call Jacob. I didn't know what else to do. I deal with drugs, but I'm not in the same circle for trafficking. I didn't know who else to call. My only hope was that he would find you. Like I said, my men were ready to go to Mexico, but we wouldn't have made it in time. But it didn't mean I would have stopped looking for you. Or hire someone who could find you."

I felt like screaming. It had to be all lies. "I don't believe you."

"Lily, please." He looked desperate. A spark lit his eyes. "Her dad. Before I left, I had asked for her hand in marriage. I don't know if he knew about the pregnancy then, but he would remember me. Hell, Rachael practically left him overnight with no explanation to marry Garcia. He had to have known something was wrong. He knew how much I loved her." Red rimmed his eyes. "I loved her so fucking much. I still do. If only she had trusted me enough to know I wasn't dead. I was coming for her. My men would have told her about me, not fucking Garcia!"

Seeing him break down was hard, but I wasn't ready to console anyone. I turned to Jacob, seeking my own comfort. Words evaded me. I didn't know what to believe. I just knew Jacob was there and everything would be okay. Tears welled in my eyes, flowing over onto my cheeks. "Jacob," I whispered, unsure what to say.

He pulled me in for a hug, but I could feel him shaking. "So," he was talking to Angel, not me, "Red worked for Garcia."

He'd figured it out, and I wanted to throw up. He continued, "Garcia had Red take her and do those things to her all because he didn't want the fucking world to know who she was." He wasn't asking anymore. He was spewing the truth like venom.

Angel's tears faded, and his face clenched into a fierce glare. "What did Red do to you? He will pay. I promise he will pay."

Jacob held me closer as I freely let the tears fall. He sneered at Angel. "He already has."

I sobbed into Jacob's shoulder. "It doesn't matter now." I sniffed back the tears and sat up straight.

"Cardosa, your family has been in the circle for longer than most. Tell Lily. Tell her how Garcia would never have been the one to tell Rachael I was dead." He pleaded with Jacob as if this held all the truth keys in one fact.

"She already knows." Jacob lifted my chin to peer deeply into my soul. "But just in case. Lily, if anything ever happens to me, it would *only* ever be one of my men who tells you. You don't believe *anyone* else. Ever. Do you understand?"

I nodded, wiping my eyes dry, and watched Angel. Could this man be my actual father? "I want to believe you. It's just so much to take in right now."

Angel leaned forward, resting his elbows on his knees and clasping his hands together. "Why do you think Garcia came so fast to Mexico? Why didn't he come back with you?"

"At first, he was hell-bent on taking Lily back with him, but when he found out that she wasn't going anywhere without me, he got pissed." I knew Jacob was thinking back to the things Garcia said about me. I could feel his anger seep through his fingers, but I held on, knowing we both needed to touch.

"I left the bastard a trail. Making him think I was down there." He gestured to Jacob's arm. "Sorry about that, by the way. Like I said, I had men ready to help as a backup. They found you in the park, but it was too late. You were surrounded by Leman's men. I heard you were hit in the crossfire. My men were sent to help if you needed it, but your men," he let out a whistle. "Your men are fucking good. They never left even a slight chance for anyone to get close to Lily."

I held my head higher, completely proud of my *brothers*. They really did take good care of me while Jacob was held hostage.

Angel chuckled and smiled at me. "I also heard you are not one to mess with if you have a gun, my dear."

Okay, so I was a little smug at that compliment. So far, my gun has saved Jacob and killed Knox.

"Anyway, I knew you would bring her back here, so I waited." He shook his head and grimaced. "You didn't have to take her out to bait me, though. I knew you were here when you landed. But I waited because she deserved a night out on the town after everything she's been through."

"So what do you want?" Jacob asked, a little more relaxed.

"I'm afraid it might be too late to have a relationship with my daughter. I want Garcia to pay. He took everything from me. It's only fair to return his kindness."

I gasped. "You want him dead?"

"Of course, I want him dead. He killed your mother. He took you away. Kidnapped you. Sold you! He would have killed you or worse too!" Angel released a long breath. "But I won't. For you."

"Fuck that," Jacob shook in anger. "If he truly isn't her father, and I find out you're telling the truth, there won't be anything left of that man." He stood and began to pace.

I went to him. "Jacob. We don't know anything yet."

He touched my cheek softly. "Lily, we know enough."

# Chapter 54

## *Jacob*

I knew I should have killed Garcia a long time ago. My heart clenched watching Lily. I wanted nothing more than to take it all away for her. This was some fucked up shit that she didn't deserve.

I walked to the bar and poured a drink. It wasn't often I drank, but right now, I'd say it was justified. I barely let the amber liquid breathe before tipping it back. It burned going down, soothing the fury building in my chest.

"Take another one. I find it helps." Angel gestured to the carafe.

Lily took the glass from me and poured a swallow. She pressed the glass to her lips and took a sip. Her eyes closed as she enjoyed the burn. Her head tipped back slightly, giving me the perfect view of her slender neck. Fuck me. Even furious, she had a way of turning me on. But we were with Angel, in his room, and it would have been angry sex. Hard, deep, heated sex.

I took the glass from her, unable to watch her drink more. I tossed the liquid back, coating my throat. Now I needed it to quench not only my rage but the possessive desire to claim her.

Angel stood, walking to us. "Now you know the truth."

"Yeah," I snapped. I knew enough to kill Garcia.

Angel started to reach out to touch Lily but drew his hand back. Good thing because the mood I was in, I would break his arm if he touched her without her wanting him to. "Maybe some rest will help. We can talk again tomorrow." He dipped his head, so Lily could see him clearly. "You look like your mother. I miss her so much. I missed you."

Lily faked a smile. "I don't have her eyes, though."

Angel shook his head. "No, my darling. You have mine." The corner of his mouth twisted up as he looked at her. "Now go get some sleep. We have lots of time to decide how the rest of this will go."

I knew how it was gonna go. Garcia would die.

She reached out and touched his arm. "This is hard for me. I've been through a lot. Like *a lot*. Give me some time, okay?"

He patted her hand. "You can have all the time you need, my dear. I'm not going anywhere."

I touched her lower back and held my other hand out for Angel. "Let me just make it clear, Lily is the most important thing. Whatever this might be between you and her, this will all be on her terms. Okay?"

He shook my hand. "Agreed."

Diesel met us at the elevator. "I didn't like leaving you there alone."

I chuckled, leading Lily into the lift. "I didn't think you would."

"So? We good? Is Angel taken care of?" Diesel pressed the button for my floor.

"Hardly," Lily drawled. "I'm still trying to wrap my brain around everything he said, but I don't think he will kill me."

Diesel looked right at me. "What the fuck happened in there?"

"A lot." I found Lily's hand and squeezed it. "Get everyone together. We have a lot to discuss."

A ding echoed in the tiny space, and the doors opened. Diesel let Lily out first. "They're all in your room. I'm the only one out here."

I nodded and used the card key to open the door to the suite. I almost laughed at the men. I'd never seen a bunch of worried suckers. Flapjack's shoulders relaxed, and Jax released a breath.

"Boss, that was a long time. We were ready to storm the room. I can't believe you took Lily in there." Flapjack crossed the room and enveloped her in a big hug. "Shit. You guys can't do that to us."

Lily laughed, and then Bear took Flapjack's place. Her squeals of laughter filled the room and made my heart feel lighter.

It didn't matter how much Lily wanted them to treat her like one of the guys. She would never be equal. She was so much more. I knew it, and they knew it. Damn, I felt sorry for anyone who actually hurt her from here on out. Looking at my family, I knew she was well protected. Good luck getting through this group of menacing men.

I smirked. "Alright, guys, let her breathe."

"One more," Doc blubbered, coming up for his hug, and I wondered if what Angel said was true, and if so, why didn't Doc say anything?

I shook my head and grinned at Jax, waiting in line. These men were impossible. And they thought I was whipped. It was good for her, though. Every woman needed brothers like this.

"I'm fine, you guys. Really. You think Jacob would let anything happen to me?" She playfully pushed Jax away.

"They better not," I said, clamping a hand on Diesel's shoulder as I passed him to take a seat in one of the oversized chairs.

Fox sat on the edge of the sofa and bounced his knee.

"You okay, kid?" I watched his knee stop, and his fingers tapped the side of his leg.

He nodded. "Yeah, the whole thing has me wound up. Ya know? I mean, knowing Lily could be... I just didn't like it."

There was something more to his nerves. "You know, we haven't really talked about you. Things have been a bit crazy around here." I leaned forward and laced my fingers together. "What makes a kid like you want to be with a group of men like us?"

He stilled and sat up straighter. "I'm not a kid. I told you, I'm nineteen."

Lily came, and I moved back so she could sit on my lap. I loved how easily she curled up with me.

"Okay," I started, "but you realize you're the kid of this family, right?"

He smirked, "Yeah, I guess so. I am kinda young for this job, but I won't fail you if that's what you're asking."

"No. I know you won't." I thought back to when he killed Red, helping me save Lily. "Rodriguez said you'd been in the system. Troubled teen shit. That true?"

He nodded. "Look, I'll tell you everything, but don't think I'm a bad person 'cause I'm not."

We all laughed, even Diesel. "Hell, Fox. There ain't a fucking man in this room who could judge you."

"I was in foster care after my mom sold my sister for drugs. I was in the system because I went after the man who bought her." He held his breath and watched me expectantly.

Holy shit. This kid had way more to him than I expected. "Fox, did you find him?"

He nodded, and I didn't need to know what happened after that. If it were my sister, he'd be dead. "What about your sister?"

His head dropped with his shoulders. "No. I don't know where she is."

Shit. "Well, I know why you took the job. You want help."

His head snapped up, his eyes wide and hopeful. "Will you help me?"

"Fox, you're family now. We already talked about this. This is more than a job. If your sister is out there, we'll find her." Damn. Fox had earned my respect and a place with me after he killed Red. I would do what I could to find his sister, although, after that many years, I wasn't expecting much. But maybe I could help him find closure.

"Thank you," he breathed. He got up and held his hand out for me. "Thank you, Jacob."

I took his hand but shook my head. "Family protects family. It's what we do."

He gazed at Lily. "I can see that."

"Speaking of protecting family," Diesel pressed, taking a seat on the arm of the sofa. "What the hell happened with Angel?"

Lily sighed, and a slight groan murmured in her throat.

Diesel chuckled. "That good, huh?"

I gently rubbed a hand up and down Lily's back. "Well, it isn't what we thought." I looked over my shoulder at Doc. "Actually, I think you can help us make sense of some of it."

Doc cocked his head and rubbed the back of his neck. "I'm not sure how I can help. I wasn't there."

Lily sat up straighter, and her eyes followed him. "Do you know Angel?"

He jerked and stopped to look at her. "What do you mean? How would I know him?"

"He told me you knew him." She stood up and took a step toward him. I waited to see what she would do, not wanting to stop her from dealing with this how she needed. Besides, right now, it was literally a family issue. "He said you would remember him."

Doc kept looking from her to me. "Lily, I'm not sure what you're talking about."

She took one more step, closing the distance between them. Her fists clenched at her sides. "I'm talking about the fact that you knew he and my mother were in love. I'm talking about how *he's* my biological father!"

Doc's face went ashen, completely drained of color. That was all I needed to see for proof. He knew more than he let us all know. I decided to take over for her. This was now more than her. I was up and behind her in one swoop, rubbing her arms. But my glare was set hard on him. "Doc, you lied to me."

His hands went up. "Wait a minute, Jacob. I haven't lied to you." He stared wide-eyed at Lily. "Or you."

"You have five minutes to tell me what the fuck you know before Fox learns what happens to traitors in this family."

Doc was one of my oldest friends, but I wouldn't deal with lying. Betrayal has not nor would be tolerated on any level.

"I don't understand," Doc stammered. "Please, Lily. I don't understand."

She thrust a finger to his chest. "He said you would remember because he asked your permission to marry my mom."

He shook his head. "No. It's not possible." Blinking slowly, he looked around the room at each of us. "He was dead."

"Do you know him?" Lily repeated.

Doc nodded. He shuffled past us and sat down. His blank stare fixated past what was in the room, watching an old memory. "If it's who you are saying, Angel didn't go by Angel back then. His name is Robby. He and Rachael were high school sweethearts. They were so in love. Robby, I guess Angel, came to me, asking me if he could marry her. Of course, I said yes. We laughed and had a drink at the house to celebrate." He scoffed. "That was the last time I saw him. Rachael came to me two days later, heartbroken. Even the life had left her eyes. She told me he was dead." He snapped back to the present and looked for Lily. "But she never told me about you then. She left two days later to be with Garcia. I thought it was her way of grieving, moving on, finding a way to deal with everything."

"So, could it be true then? Is he my father?"

"I think so. I always thought it was too soon when she told me she was pregnant. The dates didn't add up." He choked up. "Lily, I'm so sorry. I didn't know. He was dead."

"How did you not know he was alive? How come you didn't tell mom?" Lily dropped to her knees and pleaded up at him. "Why are there so many secrets!"

I pulled Lily up and wrapped my arms around her. She was shaking with her face buried in my shoulder. "I can't look at him right now."

"Shh, honey, you don't have to." I rubbed her back and let her hide from the world.

Doc panicked. "I didn't know, just like everyone else didn't know. Angel doesn't show his face to anyone. Hell, Jacob, you know that. I didn't know he was Robby."

I did know that, but it didn't make anything better admitting it. "Doc, I think you should come with us tomorrow. We're going back to talk with Angel in the morning."

"You couldn't stop me," he mumbled.

I scoffed. The thin edge Doc was riding on may have gotten a bit wider, but he wasn't clear yet. I needed to make sure all the secrets were out, and nothing more could hurt Lily.

Flapjack blew out a long breath. "That's a lot to take in. I think it's best if we give you guys some space. Let Lily rest."

Everyone agreed and made their way to the door, including a grief-stricken Doc. The door clicked shut, and Lily picked her head up. "I really think we need a do-over for our date night." She tried to jest, but I could see the strain streaking her face.

I lifted my hand and brushed her hair away. "I wish I could make everything better for you." I took her hand and pulled her to the stairs. "Come on, let's get some sleep. I don't think tomorrow is going to be any easier."

She slipped her heels off as she walked, flinging them to the floor. Her bare feet padded across the lush carpet. Upstairs she untied her dress and pulled it over her head, revealing a matching white bra and panties.

I gulped back the raw emotion I experienced every time I looked at her and closed my eyes. "You better be sleeping in something else, or we aren't getting any sleep tonight."

She giggled. I loved the sound and knew she was blushing without even looking. "Mr. Cardosa, are you saying you can't keep your hands to yourself?"

"Not when my woman looks like that." I opened my eyes and groaned as I watched her crawl across the bed and slip under the covers wearing just her bra and panties.

I pulled my clothes off, leaving just my underwear on, knowing damn well I didn't have the same effect on her, but needing to feel her skin against mine. I climbed under the covers and pulled her to me. "Sleep, you little minx. Tonight, you sleep."

"What about you?" her voice was already drifting off.

"I'm gonna be awake all night thinking of what I'm going to do to you tomorrow with you pressed against me like this." She smiled, and I kissed her cheek. "Goodnight, Lily."

She snuggled closer to me and intertwined her legs with mine. "Goodnight, Jacob."

Fuck. It was going to be a long night.

Loud banging had me shooting up out of bed and darting to my bag for my gun. Disorientated, I looked around to get my bearings. Lily was sitting on the bed, watching me with wide eyes.

"What was that?" she asked, pulling the blanket over her chest.

"Just stay right there." What the hell were gunshots doing in a hotel? I slipped on my jeans and darted down the stairs just as my men burst through the door. Next time I wasn't sure I would give Bear a key.

"Boss," Diesel scanned the room wildly. "Where's Lily?" He was frantic but released a long sigh when she padded down the stairs.

She wore jeans and a t-shirt but was still barefoot, just like me. She pulled her hair back and tied it up in a ponytail. "What's going on?"

"It's Angel. His room is just down from ours. We heard the gunshots and ran out. He's dead. So are his men." Jax leaned over and braced himself on his knees. "We ran up here as fast as we could."

"Shit." Bear's nostrils flared. "Boss, we got to end this."

Lily clung to my side. "Angel's dead?"

Jax nodded. "I'm sorry, Lily."

"Fucking Garcia!" I roared. "He had to have known we talked to Angel. When the fuck did he get back from Mexico?"

Flapjack was already on the phone digging for information. He hung up the cell and shot me a furiously glowering stare. "He got back right after us. The bastard has been tailing us, and we didn't even know it!"

Damn it! I was not one to be hunted. If Garcia thought he would win this, he was sadly mistaken. He threatened my woman, killed her parents, and seriously pissed me off by coming after my family. It was time to turn things back around. I would never be prey for some asshole.

"We need to get Lily out of here," I said the words as I left her standing with the men, grabbing my cell phone. "Flapjack, call the airport. Get the plane fucking ready."

"Already on it, boss," he said, pulling the phone up to his ear.

I dialed Rodriguez. He answered but was not groggy as I half expected, seeing as it was only three in the morning.

"Cardosa, when did you get back? Have you turned on the news? Angel Martin was shot."

"I know. I'm a couple floors above him. We're getting ready to leave Vegas to head back home. I want every man you have watching for Garcia Ramirez. And don't even think about sending any blues." I started shoving everything back into our bags.

"Shit, do you think it was Garcia who shot Angel? Fuck, Jacob, what's going on?"

Lily's gun sat on top of her clothes, but I wanted her to keep it with her, so I pulled it out before zipping her bag. "Yeah, it was Garcia. He's after Lily. So help me, when I see him, he's dead. I don't care what kind of fucking mess this is for you to clean up. He *will* die."

Rodriguez cursed. "Cardosa, you never let me have anything easy, do you. Shit. Okay, let me make some calls. You want me to send them to your place?"

I ran a hand down my face. My shoulder ached in protest, but I didn't care. I used the pain as a reason to keep moving. "Yeah, but send some to his house too. If they see him, they call me."

I hung the call up before he could say anything. I was done talking to him. The less he knew, the better. It was easier for him to clean up for me.

Ugh. I was going to owe him huge over this. The damn man was a bit greedy, but he was the best at his job. Well, the best man for me. Maybe not for the state.

Lily found me upstairs, and I tried my best at a smile for her. I handed her the gun. "I want you to keep this with you. Don't go anywhere without it."

She nodded and accepted it, placing it at her waist. "Jacob," she breathed.

"Honey, you're safe. Don't go thinking about things that aren't." I took her in my arms and inhaled deeply.

A knock at the door had me pushing away from her and practically jumping down the stairs. "Stay there," I ordered.

Diesel was already there, his gun in hand as he looked through the peephole. Slowly, he opened the door to a scrawny guy. He couldn't be much older than Fox. He looked around nervously. "Cardosa?"

I stepped forward. "Who are you?"

He held out a cardboard box. It had a lid and looked like it came right from an office. "I've been holding these for Angel. He said if anything ever happened to him, make sure you got them immediately."

"What is it?" I asked, taking the box.

"I don't know. I didn't ask, and I know better than to look. Shit, I did my job. I'm outa here." He darted back down the hall toward the stairs.

I set the box down and opened it, half worried there would be something other than paperwork inside. I picked up paper after paper and started to laugh.

"What is it, boss?" Bear came over and took a few papers from me. His laugh was deep and bellowed through the room. "Holy shit. Is this what I think?"

It was. It was every single paper trail, every breadcrumb, every single piece of fucking proof of everything Garcia has ever done. Damn. Angel wasn't lying. He really had tracked down enough to put Garcia away for thirty lifetimes. There were things in the box that even I was surprised about.

I slipped the lid on. "We need to get out of here." Not only did Garcia know Lily was here, but I was sure he knew I now had a box containing every miserable thing he'd ever done. I smiled. The prey just became the predator.

# Chapter 55

## *Lily*

I wasn't sure if I should feel pissed, sad, or tired. My whole life had been a lie. I didn't even know who I was. Jacob held my hand in the truck, but my thoughts were everywhere, and I couldn't keep up. The radio kept talking about Angel's death on repeat. It made me sick that he hadn't even been dead for an hour before the world started talking about him like he was some monster that deserved to die.

My stomach rolled. Okay, yes, he sold drugs. Yeah, he probably killed a man or two. But damn, it didn't mean he deserved to die. Jacob had killed many men, but he wasn't a monster. Shit, I'd killed a few men. Did that mean I was no better than Angel? I wanted to wring the radio announcer's neck. Blah, blah, blah. Ugh. It was sickening. They didn't even know him.

My heart sank. *I* didn't even know him. And now I never would. The pain started in my fingertips and ran up my arms to my heart. Grief had a funny way of sneaking up. I may not have known the man, but he was my father. It was confusing, but damn it, it didn't make it any less truthful.

The hatred I felt for Garcia mounted. He hid behind the title of father my whole life, and then when my real father called him out, he had me kidnapped. And my mother... My stomach twisted. Garcia had now killed both of my parents. And he wanted me to be next.

The dude on the radio kept talking about Angel, and I flipped it off. *Asshole.* Just hearing his voice made my skin crawl.

The airport treated Jacob as if he were the president of the United States. They might as well have rolled out a red carpet for us to walk onto the tarmac. It seemed like they were doing some serious ass-kissing. I guess dropping the ball on letting him know Garcia flew in right behind us would scare them into such a service.

I sure wouldn't have wanted to be the one Jacob was pissed at. I knew him as a lover, but the world knew him as something different. They knew him as someone to be afraid of. I smirked as I watched him settle in his seat on the plane. It wasn't that long ago I was scared of him too. But now, I trusted him with my life. Hell, he was my life.

It wasn't a long flight, and even if it was, I don't think I could have slept. Adrenaline was a better drug than any kind of caffeine. We landed, and two trucks were waiting for us on the tarmac. I recognized one of the drivers as Rosa's husband, Gunner.

Jacob and I rode in the backseat this time, with me in the middle. His hand slid in between my thighs and held onto my leg. He was silent, but I knew he was more aware of everything around him than I was. He had gone into full bodyguard mode.

The sun was breaking over the mountains as we pulled in. I hadn't realized how much I missed this place until we arrived. A part of me would forever be on this mountain. But even a bigger part of me belonged here at Jacob's house. It was home.

Men were swarming around everywhere. So many more than I remembered. "Who are all these guys?" I asked, stretching on the porch.

Jacob glanced around. "Security," he chuckled and touched my chin. "I told you. You're safe." He was trying so hard to make everything seem normal and fine. I loved him even more for it.

"Well, I didn't doubt that. Just you alone is more than enough for me." I walked into the house before him. Taking a deep breath, I let the peaceful calm envelop me. It was funny how just being in a particular place could do that.

"I'm glad you have so much faith in me, but I'm not taking any chances." Jacob dropped the bags by the front door. I worried about his shoulder and knew it must be killing him.

"Well, we're here at your house. Now what?" I implored, closing the front door.

His brow rose. "Well, the first thing is for you to call it like it is." He touched the tip of my nose. "This is your house too, which means *we're home.*"

Ugh, I hated how easily the heat filled my cheeks. He called it my house too. Knowing he was offering me so much made my heart skip. "Well, Mr. Cardosa, now that *we're home*, what will we do?"

His laugh echoed through the downstairs. "The guys went to grab a few zees before we meet later."

"What if I said I wasn't tired?" I was, but I wanted something more. Truth be told, I *needed* something more.

His eyes darkened with desire. "Lily."

I held a finger up to his lips. "Don't. I need you, Jacob. I need you to take the world away."

The deep groan quivered in his throat. He picked me up in one arm and carried me to the stairs. I laughed but hung on around his neck. He set me down at the foot of his bed. He pointed to the king-sized mattress. "*Our* bed."

He was really pulling out all the ammo. Didn't he know he didn't have to say anything? I didn't care whose bed it was. I would lie with him in the gravel. I pulled my clothes off before he could take the time to do it himself and was met with another throaty moan.

I wasn't waiting this time. I unhooked my bra and slipped my panties off. I needed him now.

He freed himself of all his clothing, and I couldn't help but stare at his dick. How that thing ever fit inside of me was a miracle. A blissful miracle. Between my legs warmed, and I could feel the wetness seep down my thigh.

"Turn around," he breathed, raspy and deep.

I had no idea what he was thinking, but I obeyed. I trusted him, and at this point, I didn't care what he did as long as he was inside of me.

I braced myself over the bed, and he came up behind me, grabbing my hips. It was strange but so sexy. I felt his manhood throb near my ass. His fingers went up between my legs and found that sweet spot. I cried out as a shock of bliss erupted.

His other hand reached around and kneaded my breast. Holy shit. I pushed back, searching for him. I couldn't tell who was moaning, but I heard my voice in my ears loud and calling his name. Everything mixed together.

He removed his hand, and his thick pulsating dick thrust inside me. I arched back and pressed against him. "Jacob," I cried for him. Why did something so animalistic feel so fucking good?

He thrust harder. It ached in painful ecstasy. I met each thrust, opening up to allow him to ram himself as deep as he could. I could feel him in me, so deep, so far up. I bucked back, and my head lifted as I arched, trying to find a way to fit more of him.

He was so deep I couldn't tell our souls apart. We were truly one. He pushed faster, slamming into me hard. It felt so good I didn't want it to ever stop. His dick was so big I felt the shudders as I clenched around him.

"Fuck, Lily," he groaned in pleasure. He pulled out, and I flipped around to watch him grab his dick and slide his hand up and down.

I reached out and took over. My wetness covered him, and my hand slid easily up and down. His fingers found my opening and began to stroke me while I gripped him harder. He cried out as he spilled out over my hand, but his fingers kept stroking me. Hearing him and seeing him cum pushed me over the edge, and I called out for him. My body exploded, and I knew I needed him to save me.

Opening my eyes, the room spun. Jacob leaned over and breathlessly pressed his lips to mine. "I love you."

I couldn't breathe, let alone speak. "I love you," I murmured, falling back on the bed.

He chuckled and went to the bathroom for a washrag.

Wow. Why in the hell hasn't he done this with me before? That was a lot different than the other times.

"Jacob," I sighed, still living in the pleasure he created. "That was incredible."

"Sex is only as good as the trust and love between two people." He winked from the doorway. "I want nothing more than to make sweet, slow love with you every time, but sometimes, we need a release. Sometimes, we just need... *that*."

"Well, *that* was incredible." I sat up. "Wait a minute. Why'd you leave? It was so amazing. It felt better than before."

He laughed. "Yes, it did. Fuck, Lily, that was the best feeling in the world. I wasn't wearing a condom. I felt you. And damn, was it good. I'd never experienced anything like that before."

"So, I was your first, um, first time with *nothing*?" The thought that I was his first something had the fire raging again.

He took a rag and walked back. His hand swiftly wiped me clean. I could have done it, but there was something so intimate about how he did it. "Yes, that was the first time I'd ever gone without a condom." He grinned at me. "That's also why I pulled out. We have to be careful."

I fell back again. I didn't want kids, but I didn't want to be careful. He just gave me a taste of something he couldn't take back. And I wanted more. I wanted to feel him cum inside of me. I wanted to feel his cum fill me. Just the thought had me moaning in anticipation.

"If you are okay with it, we can get you on birth control. I don't think I could go very long without feeling you like that again." His raspy voice slowed.

I would do whatever it would take to never have to use a condom again. I nodded and chewed on my lip. "Jacob, could we, you know, do it that way again sometime?"

"I'm hoping to never do it any other way again."

I rolled my eyes. "No, I meant, with you behind me. It was really hot. Like, a natural instinct took over."

He laughed and tossed the rag on the floor before coming to rest next to me. He touched my face with the back of his hand and stared into my eyes. "You amaze me." He swallowed hard. "I want to know you in every way, Lily. I want to make love to you in every way there is. I have no barriers. Everything I own is yours, even my body."

If my heart wasn't already lost to him, it would have been right then. "Why. Mr. Cardosa, I do believe I love you."

He pulled me, so I was snuggled next to him, my back against his chest. "You better."

The smell of bacon and coffee wafted up to the room, rousing me from a deep sleep. Jacob was already up, showered, and dressed. He winked at me when I sat up, still completely naked. "Flapjack is downstairs cooking breakfast. Head on down when you're ready."

"What time is it?" I yawned.

"About a quarter past ten." He kissed my forehead before leaving the room.

A shower would do wonders for me. I rummaged through my bag for the last of my clean clothes and headed to the bathroom. I let the water get as hot as possible before melting off my skin and letting it roll down me.

My life had become such a whirlwind I needed time to think. I pondered over things that happened in the last month. I escaped Knox, nearly killed myself, found and fell in love with Jacob Cardosa, was kidnapped again, then flown to another country because I was sold to Red, Jacob saved me, I killed Knox, only to find out Angel Martin was my father, then Angel died, and now Garcia wanted me dead. Yeah, it was no wonder I was exhausted.

I got out and slipped into my clothes only to find the contents of my bag gone. My heart stopped but picked back up when I saw my gun on the nightstand beside Jacob's. I grinned. It was as if they were meant to be together, just like him and me.

I grabbed the gun and attached it to my hip. I already missed Lupe and Maria and wondered if I'd ever see them again. Downstairs the men were talking, and I could hear Jacob's laughter a few times.

My stomach growled, and I let it lead me down the stairs to the food. I gave Jacob a quick peck on the cheek as I passed him to sit at the counter. Plates piled with food lined the island. Carter smiled at me as he flung a hand towel over his shoulder, filled a plate of food, and then set it down for me. "I wasn't sure you'd ever wake up."

I picked up a piece of bacon that I swore melted in my mouth. "I wasn't sure I wanted to."

They had Angel's box on the oversized dining table, and the contents spread all around. They were going through everything. One colorful paper caught my attention. I slipped off the barstool and picked it up from the table. It was my birth certificate.

I'd never seen it before. And now I knew why. I couldn't stop staring at the father's name: Robby Angel Martin. He really was my father.

Another certificate was on the table, but it had a few papers stapled to it. Curiously, I snatched it up as well. It was another birth certificate for me, but it was much newer, and Angel's name was gone, replaced with Garcia's. I scowled. Lifting the paper up, I inspected the papers attached to it and found that they were application papers to have a birth certificate changed. I wanted to let out a crazed laugh but held it in. Garcia really was a piece of shit.

I had more than enough proof now to know the truth. Doc looked at me with concerned eyes. "Lily, I really didn't know."

I nodded. "I know. It's fine." I sucked in a long, deep breath and tossed the papers back to the table. "The sooner we find him, the sooner this can all be over."

# Chapter 56

## *Jacob*

It had been a long week. I had exhausted myself going over every single paper in the box Angel left for me. But it didn't matter in the end because I was going to kill Garcia. I would then hand over the entire box of paperwork to Rodriguez, tying Garcia to more unsolved and some wrongly solved events around the world.

Garcia didn't know how to clean up his trails very well. And Angel had been very good at following him. Too bad Angel wasn't around to see the man who stole everything from him go down. If someone tried to take Lily from me, they would burn in hell for their mistake.

I could sense Lily before I saw her. Her hips swayed just enough when she walked that I was mesmerized. Her hair was pulled up as usual, and she wore tight jeans. Damn those jeans, hugging places that belonged only to me. It was sad that I was jealous of the material. Her gun sat ready at her side, and I made a mental note that I really needed to thank Lupe. I'm sure I funded almost his entire arsenal but seeing her so confident made me think he deserved more.

The way her smile lifted to her eyes had my heart thumping wildly. I don't think she had any idea how beautiful she was.

She made her way around the desk. I pushed myself away from the desk, letting the wheels on the chair glide me to her. She sat down on my lap and wrapped an arm around my neck. "Jax and Diesel should be back from patrol soon. We should go after them."

I chuckled. She'd been trying to get me to take her out on patrol all week. She didn't understand that her safety, her being alive, was everything to me. I knew I'd have to come to terms with it sooner or later. The first time we would go out on a job together would be hell. But I promised her *together*.

"Alright, fine, you win. Tell them to get our horses ready." I winked at her for good measure, knowing a fresh crimson blush would sweep over her cheeks. "Besides, it's been too long since we rode a horse together. Last time was very satisfying."

"Cardosa, you're impossible," she squealed.

It's not likely I would ever forget our first time on a horse. After everything with Knox was taken care of, a repeat of history might be in order.

"Boss!" Bear slammed his way through the house.

I grabbed my gun and was up out of the chair, holding Lily behind me before Bear made it to the study.

He stopped at the door, and his focused look fell on me. "Someone's coming. The first alarm tripped not a minute ago. They're coming up the road."

This was it. I could feel it. "I'm coming."

Bear took off, leaving Lily and me behind. I turned to her, but she was already shaking her head. "I'm not staying here. I'm not hiding. I'm with you, and you said *together*, remember?"

Damn it. I didn't have time to argue with her about what a bad idea this was. I grabbed her hand and pulled her with me. "Stay close. Do *not* leave my side."

A lone SUV screamed up the drive just as we reached the porch. It was Garcia's. But the vehicle didn't stop and barreled into the side of the barn, crashing through the wood and metal.

I ran with Lily beside me, both of our guns raised and ready. Smoke and dust filtered the air. Bear was there first, closely followed by Fox. Doc came out of his house, his rifle cocked and ready, aimed at the SUV. Flapjack was near Lily, a weapon in his hand pointed at the same place.

A few of the men Rodriguez sent gathered cautiously around, sidestepping to the wreck. Bear closed in first. Fox took his flank and guarded him as he opened the driver's door.

"The driver's dead. Shot in the head." Bear peered around the man in the seat and then backed away, looking around him. "It's empty. Garcia's gone. Damn it. They tied a rope to the steering wheel and had his foot pressed against the gas pedal."

"Shit," I growled, searching around us. It was a setup. Garcia was drawing us out.

Static blared from the radio Fox carried. "Need... help... fuck... get... ass...." Diesel's voice broke through the connection. Then clearly, "he's fucking here. Get up here now!"

Fox clicked the radio, trying to reconnect with Diesel, but it was too late. "Diesel, crap, Diesel." Fox looked at me and shook his head. "Sorry, boss." The radio wouldn't work any longer. Diesel had warned us, and that was all he could do.

Fuck. Everyone ran everywhere. Lily. Where was Lily? I turned to see her leading our horses. She mounted the smaller one and dropped the reigns to Lady for me. I was up in the saddle and kicking Lady to run before Bear would even notice we were gone.

Lily kept up, her determination equal to mine. Hearing Diesel had to have upset her. They had a stronger connection than the others, except for maybe with Flapjack. This was personal for both of us, and we both had too much at stake to lose.

We slowed as the trees wouldn't allow us to move as quickly through them.

"Jacob," Lily shook. "If something happens to him. Just know that I promised him, too."

I figured as much. "You won't have to keep that promise today." I wasn't entirely sure that was true, but she didn't need to think about that right now. I would do it for her if the need arose. No way in hell would I make her live with that.

Lady traipsed up the mountain, heading toward the cabin. It was the only logical place Garcia would have gone.

Fuck. When this was over, I would burn that place to the ground.

Gunshots rang out, and I stopped Lady, holding my hand up for Lily to follow suit. Silently, we dismounted and crouched low, using our horses as shields, not knowing where the bullets were hitting.

The small cabin was just a few more yards away. Behind us, more horses could be heard gaining on us. Doc led the new party, jumping from the back of his gelding. The rest all dismounted in sync with the shots being fired.

All their eyes were on me, waiting for orders. Using my hands, I reverted back to our own silent language, one I would have to teach Lily. I watched her proudly as she tried to follow along and grasp what I said without actually knowing for sure. She never cowered as bullets zinged past us. She stayed close to my side as I left Doc and Flapjack with the horses. Bear and Fox took the right, and we went left. Everything moved fluidly. We were once again a well-oiled machine working toward the same goal.

A flicker of movement caught my attention, and I saw Jax hiding behind a small shed. He was loading his gun with what looked like the last of his ammo. Keeping to the tree trunks and shadows, Lily and I made our way to him.

His grin was filled with relief when he saw us. "About time. You almost missed all the fun."

Lily crouched low and double-checked her gun, making sure it was fully loaded and ready. I knew she didn't need to, but I was glad she was preparing herself. "Where's Diesel?" she asked, her voice hardly quivering, considering how worried she was.

Jax gestured with his head to the other side of the cabin. "He's holed up in that ditch over there. Fucking Garcia started shooting before we knew he was here." He looked at me. "Hell, boss, the alarms didn't even go off. He didn't trip a damn one."

I clamped a hand down on Jax's shoulder. "It's okay. But I gotta go get Diesel out of there. He's a sitting duck with nowhere to go."

"I know. I've been trying to give him enough cover, but I haven't seen him move."

I pushed back the sick feeling in my stomach and left Jax, knowing he'd give us as much cover as he could. Sticking to the shadows, Lily crept close beside me as we made our way to Diesel.

"Shit," Lily slid down the bank of the ditch to Diesel.

He was unconscious and bleeding from his head. But he was alive. I tensed. That meant Garcia knew he was out cold, and we would come for him. It was another trap.

Lily ripped her shirt and wrapped it around Diesel's head. He was only hit with something hard, not shot. I stepped low and crouched down close enough to Lily to touch her. Garcia was somewhere close, but I couldn't see him.

Jax started shooting again, and I knew he saw something. A few grunts and moans not far off told me he had hit his target, but the man who fell not five feet away from me was not Garcia.

Lily jerked and looked behind me toward Jax. She pulled her gun and aimed steadily. A shadow crossed my vision, and my heart stopped as it lunged for Lily. I didn't have time to think. I dove for Lily and threw my body on top of hers, shielding her from the man, but not before her gun went off. I had no idea where the bullet went.

The man grabbed me, and I couldn't contain the grunt as his fingers dug into my still tender shoulder. I pushed him off and flung him to the ground, then we rolled, and I was on my back. It was then I noticed his gun and fought him for it. Not having full strength in my left arm put me at a disadvantage.

Out of the corner of my eye, I could see Diesel stirring. His eyes shot open, and he was up, pouncing on the man, flinging him off me. He reached the man and pulled the gun from his hand like it was no more than a toy. He was like a wakened bear, and he was pissed.

I scrambled to my feet and turned to see Garcia holding a gun to Lily's head. My heart stopped. I was crazed with fear and anger. I had to do something. Fuck. He had Lily. He had my woman. My life.

I held my gun tightly aimed at Garcia, but he moved, so all I had a shot at was Lily. I played through each scenario, hoping to find one where I could save her. Garcia laughed. "Come on, you little bitch. It's time for your lover here to see what I'm gonna do to you."

Sick fucker. I didn't know what he had planned, but I knew it wasn't something I thought lily could live through. I was losing her.

I held my gun trained on her and felt the hot tears roll down my cheeks. She gave me a sad smile and mouthed, "I love you."

Fuck. Fuck! No. I couldn't do it. I didn't know how to pull the trigger. There had to be another way. Time pressed down on me, and I knew what had to be done. I refused to let this bastard hurt her. I choked back my natural instinct to protect her and told myself this was me protecting her.

She looked past me with no fear in her eyes. Her attention was no longer on me. I didn't see Diesel raise his hand or the gun he now held. All I saw was Lily as he fired. His promise to protect her blared through my soul. My heart shattered, and I cried out for her. "Lily!" No! I lunged for her, not caring if I died. If she was gone, then I would die too.

But it wasn't her who fell. Garcia dropped, and his lifeless body collapsed to the ground. One shot through his head.

Lily ran to me, her arms clinging tightly around my neck. "Jacob," she cried.

With her in my arms, I dropped to the ground, kissing her face, lips, and anything I could touch. Shit. "Lily," I breathed.

I pulled her close and breathed her in. Diesel grinned, watching us with blood running down his face. He knelt down and touched Lily's shoulder. "You are the bravest woman I know. You were gonna let me shoot you!" He sniffed back his own tears. "You didn't think I'd miss, did ya?" He wiped at his eyes. "I never miss."

She tilted her head to see him. "I trusted you." Then she looked up at me. "I trusted you both."

Still holding her to me, I stood up and carried her to the horses. I sure as hell wasn't letting her go to ride her own horse. In the saddle, I kept my arm around her and kissed her head. I kicked Lady and left Garcia's body for the birds. Rodriguez could come up here and get what was left of him.

The others mounted their horses, and we all began the journey home. Diesel grunted and pressed a hand to his head, but thankfully he would be okay. Nothing a few doses of aspirin wouldn't fix.

"Jacob," she whispered. "Thank you. You just keep saving me."

I squeezed her tighter. "Lily, you are worth saving. I love you so damn much it hurts."

Her body curled up next to mine, fitting perfectly in my arms like she was made for me. She was mine. And I would always protect what was mine.

# Epilogue

## Jacob

Deep breath. I wasn't sure how I was supposed to breathe. After six months of planning, I couldn't believe today was finally here. The warm summer breeze wafted in through the open windows of our bedroom. I smiled and looked around. Last night had been wild, and I was sure Rosa would be finding articles of clothing all over for days.

But tonight. Tonight would be different. Tonight I wanted to please Lily in every way I could imagine and then some. I stared at the perfectly cut diamond, and my heart began racing.

The smell of cooked rabbit found its way up the stairs and brought me back to the present. I closed the little black box and tucked it into the pocket of my jeans. Who knew rabbit could smell so good? I found my way down to the counter and took a front-row seat.

It only took this long for Flapjack and Lily to decide on a date to do their little cook-off, and I had to laugh because they were having so much fun. Flapjack tried to taste her meat but got a slap to the hand. Lily giggled and continued to bait him with sarcastic remarks about how his rabbit looked.

Oh, how I loved that sound. I would do anything to hear her laugh every day. I straightened in my seat and looked at the clock. Time was passing too slowly, and yet, it was rapidly approaching. Tomorrow we were leaving on Lily's first job with us to look for Fox's sister. But I had another promise to keep on our way. Boulder's request still weighed heavy on my mind, and

I knew I couldn't just send his sister money, but I knew I needed to give it to her in person.

"Jacob," Lily met me at the counter with a sweet kiss. "Mmm, you taste good."

I laughed. "Not as good as you."

She climbed up in my lap and leaned her head against mine. "That's because I just tasted my rabbit. It is *so* good."

"Alright, Rabbit, no bribing the judges!" Flapjack warned. "It's already not fair that you're sleeping with one of them. I'm pretty sure that's favoritism. Biased votes shouldn't count."

Lily splayed a hand across her chest. "Are you saying I'm only sleeping with Jacob for the votes?"

Diesel and the others walked in. "Is it time to eat yet? I'm starving, and you all are in here teasing us with these smells."

Lily jumped up and grabbed her dish, making sure to get hers to the table before Flapjacks. "We're just waiting on Carter."

I laughed and joined her at the head of the table. "Before we start, I'd like to make a toast."

Diesel grinned knowingly, as did the others. Hell, they all knew. I dropped to my knee and pulled out the box, lifting the lid for her to see. "Lily, you are my heart. My life. I will spend forever protecting you if you let me. Will you marry me?" My heart raced as I said the practiced words aloud.

She dropped to her knees and grabbed me around the neck. "Yes!"

I pulled back to take the ring from the box and slipped it onto her hand, branding her as mine. Forever it would be us. Jacob and Lily Cardosa, together, always.

Thank you for stepping into the world of **Men of Cardosa Ranch**. These stories aren't always easy—they're dark, raw, and full of broken men who would burn the world down to save the women they love. But at their core, they're about **survival, redemption, and the kind of love that refuses to be tamed.**

### 📖 A Quick Note on Escapism 📖

This is fiction—an escape into a world where mercenary men deliver justice, love heals even the deepest wounds, and danger is met with unwavering devotion. These stories are not meant to reflect reality but to provide a safe space to explore intense themes in a way that always leads to a satisfying ending.

If this book kept you up at night, made your heart race, or had you gripping your Kindle, I'd love to hear what you thought. **Leaving a review—even just a few words—helps other readers find these stories and supports indie authors like me.**

💜 Tell me what you loved by leaving a review here:
https://www.amazon.com/dp/B07ZZLNVGY

Your support means everything, and I can't wait to share more of this world with you.

Until next time,

*Gracin*

# CHAPTER 1

## *DIESEL*

The dingy countertop held years of memories, marked by the rings of the thousands of drinks served to lonely patrons. I liked to pick the old rundown establishments over the modern ones. There was history and camaraderie from each of us drowning our lives at the bottom of the barrels. The dim lighting captured the heaviness of the day. I tapped the rustic wooden bar for another round. The bartender flipped a stained rag over his shoulder and poured the caramel liquid into my long, thin glass, letting it slosh over the rim.

It had been a long day with no new leads. I felt bad for the kid, but eventually, Fox would have to learn that not everyone gets a happy ending in this world. Fuck, I knew that more than anyone did. The kid had gusto, and one day, he would make one hell of a man. He was like a brother now, a part of the family. After he helped save Lily, Jacob's fiancé, he cemented a spot in the family.

Eve, Fox's sister, has been missing for years. Jacob has followed every lead he could find, but as the days lagged on, we all knew the probability of us finding her was zip to zero. Yet, none of us was ready to tell Fox it was time to give up. I don't think any of us knew what giving up meant. I knew if it were me, I would never stop looking. Hell, it was me, once, a long time ago.

So now, we were back in Mexico, drinking to wash away the reality of the situation. I nodded to the bartender. "My brother needs a drink too."

Fox shook his head. "Nah, bruh, I ain't old enough yet."

"Fuck that shit. You've killed a man. You're old enough." I gestured to the man behind the bar again. "Just leave it." Twenty was old enough for a damn drink, and there wasn't a man who could change my mind. Twenty seemed like a hundred years ago for me, but to him, it had just begun. Thirty was pounding on my door, but I was no closer to hanging up my hat.

I gripped the neck of the bottle and poured Fox a glass. Raising mine, I waited for him to pick his up before tipping mine, so our rims clinked. "To finding Eve."

Fox nodded and took a sip. His eyes watered, and his cheeks puffed out as he tried to contain a cough. Laughing, I slapped him on the back. I took another sip, letting it sit on my tongue, savoring the rich vanilla taste as it melted perfectly with the deep oak flavor of the tequila.

"How do people shoot this stuff?" Fox sputtered and picked his glass up, studying the contents before attempting another taste.

I let out another deep chuckle. "Because they're fucking stupid. Real tequila isn't meant to be chugged like some damn beer. It's meant to be savored, like a woman. You appreciate it."

Another sip touched my lips, and my heart stopped. The doorway filled with the slender hourglass figure of the perfect woman. Tied in a high ponytail, her long hair flowed down her back in waves, but its coloring reminded me of a glass of champagne. She peered into the dark room, scanning the regulars until her gaze locked with mine.

The way her mouth curved into a full smile captivated me, holding me hostage on the hard barstool. Fuck. I'd kill to see that smile again. The world, the bar, everyone around, everything but her disappeared.

Confidently, she sashayed toward me. Her hips moved rhythmically in tune with my heart, keeping me entranced. She was only a step away when her scent engulfed me. The sweet smell of heaven clung to her.

The gun snug tightly under the waistband of her jeans, and the knife strapped to her thigh did little to curb the desire filling my jeans. I lowered my glass to the bar and watched her.

For as confident as she acted, there was something off. I turned to face her fully. I had my gun strapped to my hip tonight, and it was only fair she knew she wasn't the only one carrying.

Her eyes drifted down, catching sight of my weapon, then returned to meet my stare. A disturbance outside echoed in the bar, and she jumped. Her smile, albeit this time looking fake, returned as she threw her arms around my neck, clinging to me as if her life depended on it.

She giggled and leaned closer to whisper in my ear. "Please play along. I need help."

Fuck. I knew something was off. Whatever guard I had let down was instantly back up. Every patron accounted for, each exit located, how much ammo I had on me, everything came to me like a war plan perfectly executed in my mind, preparing myself for an attack. While my mind whipped out different scenarios, I remained calm and confident, dropping my hands to her waist.

"You came to the right man." I gripped her hips and thrust her up to settle her on my lap. She fit perfectly nestled against me. Pulling her to me, I nuzzled her neck to get a clear view of whoever was behind her. Damn, she smelled good.

Fox raised a brow at me and used his hands to gesture to the woman on my lap. "Women just come to you?"

I frowned at him and was about to reply when two men entered the bar. The taller one scrutinized each face as he looked for someone. Both guys had a gun hanging loosely from shoulder holsters, but neither looked like they would do much good in a fight. Lanky frames with baggy clothes hung off them. They definitely didn't intimidate me, but clearly, they were here for the woman pressing her body to mine.

Shit. Why did she have to smell so good? I nearly groaned aloud when her lips grazed my neck as she whispered again. "Did they find me?"

My fingers gripped her tighter, pulling her higher up. Not a good move. The way she rubbed against me wasn't doing anything to stop the pulsing happening in my jeans. "Not yet."

My voice came out huskier than I intended, giving away my body's craving for her.

She leaned back slightly. It was the first time I was able to clearly see her green eyes. They were like staring at the ocean with a hint of blue hidden in the seafoam green. I would wage a bet that wars have been raised over staring into eyes like hers.

Keeping my stare, she slowly raised her hands to slip off the tie holding my hair back, then ran her fingers through the shoulder-length locks. I knew it was all an act, but damn, it was doing so much more to me. Holding her in my arms, feeling her pressed against me, with her boldly acting like a lover, had me wishing this wasn't a rouse. I wished she wasn't in danger, needing help. Shit. I was fantasizing about what if, and she was only here for help. I clearly needed to focus.

As she sat on me, staring intensely into my eyes, my hands begged to travel from her hips and explore. This was the most exquisite form of pain I've ever had. Her fingers dropped from my hair to follow my jawline back up to my lips, tracing them lightly. I let her do whatever she wanted. Happy to be the one she chose to find an escape with. And damn, I would do whatever in my power to help her. She didn't know who I was or what I could do.

Her eyes pleaded with me for something, but no words sounded between us. The shorter man took another step closer, showing off a slight limp. His scruffy beard hid half his face, but the malice in his eyes gave away his intentions.

The taller one had a more polished gait as he tread deeper into the establishment. Tufts of his inky black hair curled out around the straw fedora on his head. "I'm looking for a woman," the toothpick he chewed on clipped his smooth voice.

"We don't have those women here, Romeo." The bartender braced himself against the counter.

The woman stiffened, knowing the bartender had unknowingly called attention to our little place at the bar.

"Trust me," I whispered, not taking my eyes off her.

Her lips quivered as I reached up and placed a hand at the back of her head, pulling her down to me. My lips captured hers softly. We needed to look natural, oblivious to the world, lost in our own. We needed to be just two lovers in a bar.

Electricity built between us, and I couldn't just sit there. My fingers wound their way through her hair and pressed closer to her, deepening the kiss.

I breathed her in and filled my lungs with her. The tequila mixed with her sweetness as I slipped my tongue past her lips, tasting her. A small whimper came from her, and she froze.

Her body shivered, and I pulled back, almost forgetting why she was there kissing me in the first place. Shit, what was wrong with me? She was here for help, not a fucking kiss. I couldn't lose sight of the enemy.

I was protective by nature, but these men had me wanting to kill them for just scaring her. I didn't even know what they had done to her.

I winked at her, letting her know I was still playing along, even though that kiss felt like anything but an act. She was motionless, her eyes not leaving me. I wasn't sure if I had scared her or if it was the men.

I caressed the side of her face and gave her a subtle nod. "Baby, I'm ready to go home." I gestured with my eyes to the restrooms in the back, hoping she would understand. "Why don't you freshen up, and we'll get out of here."

She wound her arms around my neck once again. "Thank you." Her sultry voice rolled through me like a wave.

She hopped off my lap and bound over to the restrooms, keeping her face turned away from the men. I picked up my glass and watched the guys from the mirror behind the bar.

"What was that?" Fox asked, slowly taking another sip of his drink, ogling the restroom where the woman had just escaped.

I licked my lips, still tasting her on me. "See those two guys?" I took a swallow of my drink and frowned before taking the last swig. I wasn't about to let it go to waste. And after that kiss, I was going to need a whole lot more than that.

"Yeah," Fox said, turning back to face the bar.

"Not sure what's going on, but she's running from them."

"So you kiss her?"

I almost laughed. "Yeah. It seemed like a good idea at the time."

The tall one nodded to the other one and walked toward the restroom. My heart hammered as if they were hunting something that was mine. Ridiculous. I had no claim on the woman, but hell, she came to me for help. That kind of made her mine to protect.

I pulled my gun from the holster and stood up. I gestured to Fox to follow. He was still learning the ropes, but right now, he was the only wingman I had. Besides, he'd already proved he wasn't scared of killing another man.

Analyzing the woman's stalkers, ease enveloped me. This was where I felt the calmest. In my element, so to speak. For the last twelve years, hunting bad guys has been my life.

Both men had their guns drawn and were ready to go inside the restroom after the woman, but neither of them noticed me. It was almost laughable at how oblivious to their surroundings they were. I wasn't sure who they worked for, but they were dispensable. They should have been paying attention.

It was too easy to sneak up behind them. "I said she was coming home with me, not you." Using the butt of my pistol, I whacked the shorter one on the back of his head, knocking him out. The taller one turned to me. His eyes widened, taking in what had happened. He raised his gun but wasn't as fast as me. I squeezed the trigger of my gun before he could aim.

The door flung open, and the woman came out, her own gun held steadily in her hands. Her eyes landed on me first, then the men on the ground. Her shoulders visibly relaxed, but she still gripped her gun. She aimed it toward the men and kicked the one I shot. Satisfied he was dead, she uncocked her weapon and placed it back under the waistband of her jeans.

"Thank you," she said, stepping over the unconscious man. "Really, thank you, but I gotta go."

Reaching out, I grasped her arm, preventing her from leaving. A part of me was selfish and wanted just one more minute with her, but the other part said she wasn't entirely out of danger. "I think you owe me a name."

"Um," she looked down at the guys, "that's Nico, and that's Jorgie."

Jorgie was the one I had shot. It didn't surprise me that she had no remorse over his death, but I was a bit shocked. This didn't seem to be the first death she'd seen. There was so much hiding behind her eyes, and I wanted to know it all.

I shook my head. "Not them. You. What's your name?"

She looked at Fox, then back to me. "Samantha. Sam, actually."

Sam. Damn, it fit her. It was unnerving how much I liked her name. A name shouldn't affect me like that, but there wasn't a nerve inside me not firing off her name, claiming a piece of her, memorizing everything about her. "Well, Sam, you want to tell me why I killed this man for you?"

# ABOUT THE AUTHOR

Gracin Sawyer pours her heart into every story, crafting dark, intense romances where broken men will burn the world down for the women they love. Writing has always been her passion, and while she's published multiple paranormal and fantasy romances under another name, stepping into this new world of dark romance felt like coming home.

If she had her way, she'd live on a cruise ship, sailing to every corner of the world—but for now, responsibilities keep her anchored on land. Thankfully, she's happily married to a man who'd follow her onto the open sea in a heartbeat.

After raising four kids, they now have one married and two still at home, life is a mix of adventure and transition, but the love for storytelling remains constant. When she's not writing, you'll find her dreaming up new stories, planning her next getaway, or lost in a book that's just as intense as the ones she loves to write.

Made in United States
Troutdale, OR
03/22/2025